In Which Our Dashing Duo of Derring-Do Make Plans to Catch a Train

"The Orient Express." Wellington looked up to the Director. "That madman is on the Orient Express."

"You realise it is a trap." The Director leaned back in his chair and fixed them both with a stern gaze. "Jekyll wants you to rush after him. He wants you on the chase in the hopes that you will make a mistake, giving him a chance to remove you both from service. Permanently."

"We know Jekyll wants us dead, sir," she began, "What is the alternative? We can't let innocent people continue to be his message to us. If we don't take this bait, he'll happily just keep killing."

Sound's eyebrows drew together as he glowered at them. "I should send a team with you—"

Wellington held up his hand, and Eliza's heart sank. "I am sorry sir, but we can't do that either. Jekyll has shown almost superhuman abilities to detect a trap. The only way we can set one for him, is to walk into his."

Other Books from The Ministry of Peculiar Occurrences

Featuring Agents Books & Braun

Phoenix Rising (Book One)

The Janus Affair (Book Two)

Dawn's Early Light (Book Three)

The Diamond Conspiracy (Book Four)

The Ghost Rebellion (Book Five)

Featuring Verity Fizroy & the Ministry Seven

The Curse of the Silver Pharaoh (Book One)

The Mystery of Emerald Flame (Book Two)

Anthologies

Ministry Protocol: Thrilling Tales of the Ministry of Peculiar Occurrences

Operation: Endgame

Book Six
of
The Ministry of Peculiar Occurrences

Pip Ballantine & Tee Morris

Imagine That! Studios, Copyright 2018
All rights reserved.

Cover Design by Designed by Starla
Cover Photography by Go ForWard Photography
Interior Layout by Imagine That! Studios

No part of this publication may be reproduced, stored in or introduced into a retrieval system, or transmitted, in any form, or by any means whatsoever without the prior written permission except in the case of brief quotations embodied in critical articles and reviews.

This book is a work of fiction. Any resemblance to any person, living or dead is purely coincidental. Any actual places, products or events mentioned are used in a purely fictitious manner.

www.ministryofpeculiaroccurrences.com

For Christina, Verena, Peej, and Matt

Voices always omnipresent

and welcomed

in the direction of the Ministry.

Thank you

for being a part

of this amazing adventure.

Acknowledgements

There's a funny story about this cover. It happened by accident.

We were doing test shots in-between covers, and while Michael Ward of Go ForWard Photography was getting the light and the settings, our cover model Verena Vorsatz—being the incredible professional that she is—posed. In that test shot, Verena embodied our Eliza Braun and Michael captured the emotion of what would become *Operation: Endgame*. It wasn't a formal pose. It just happened. Organically.

That encapsulates this journey that we have taken with Wellington and Eliza over the years. We had an idea of where we wanted to go, of the final destination we set for our Ministry agents; but if you were to ask us how it all happened, we would describe the series as organic. Idea spurned other ideas, a word shared between characters would plant the seed for a plot twist, and our adventures which started almost a decade ago would follow a path to this point. The end. The grand finale.

Saying goodbye is always hard, and there is no way to pretend it didn't happen. When Tee finished the final chapter of *Operation: Endgame*, he needed a moment to take a breath, perhaps even pull back a few tears. Over half a million words, two wildly successful Kickstarters, a role playing game, hours upon hours of podcast audio, and awards and accolades from our peers, all leading up to this final instalment. For Wellington and Eliza, the curtain drops on their adventures. We have enjoyed this run with the two of them, but their story is over. We hope you have enjoyed reading this story of an Archivist and a Colonial Pepperpot as much as we had in telling it. Now, we move forward with Wellington and Eliza in our hearts and new adventures to discover. Thank you, everyone, for coming along with us.

Speaking of thanks, we are eternally grateful to out editor K T Bryski in editing with a red pen that seems to have an eternal flow of red ink. You helped us with working through the complications of early drafts and forced us to ask uncomfortable questions that would bring about severe consequences to our cast. Thank you for keeping us honest.

Then we give a nod to our creative team behind the cover. The earlier-mentioned Michael Ward of Go ForWard Photography captured the moments we needed while Starla Huchton of Designed by Starla took these moments to offer readers a glimpse at what lay ahead. Another huge "thank you" to the earlier-mentioned Verena Vorsatz that brought Eliza to life, and continues to do so in Bavaria and other European conventions.

Making sure our cover models looked the part we needed for this cover is due in part to Tamara Barnett of Tennille Makeup Artistry, along with Jared Axelrod, Piper J Drake, Kevin Houghton, and Brute Force Studios for providing fantastic props and costume pieces. Then you have the people that work to keep the artists moving forward through the day. Thank you so much Wendy Ward, Matthew J Drake and Christina Payton for herding cats when needed.

But this book wouldn't exist with you, Gentle Reader. You were the support team that kept us going, that inspired us to explore, and who made amazing things like the *Ministry Protocol* anthology, the *Ministry Initiative* role-playing game, the *Tales from the Archives* podcasts, and the somewhat-ridiculous *Countless Hues of Crimson* all happen.

Yes, you make *Countless Hues of Crimson* happen. You should be ashamed of yourselves.

And now we are here to say goodbye, at least say goodbye to Wellington and Eliza. It's been a great run, but all good things must end. Maybe Operation: Endgame will join the ranks of Captain Picard, Sam Beckett, and Edmund Blackadder under great finales remembered fondly by fans.

Come with us and find out.

CHAPTER ONE

⇢⇌⇠

In Which Agents of Her Majesty's Ministry Become Star-Crossed

It was a very good thing that Wellington Thornhill Books, Esquire, had a stout pair of shoes, and a comfortable jacket. Then again, his tailor catered to the needs of the Ministry of Peculiar Occurrences, and knew his clientele had different needs to the average Saville Row gentleman.

The alterations allowed Wellington to pump his arms in a proper fashion and his footwear, while flattering the cut of his suit, provided more arch support and cushioning for his feet as he raced through the avenues of New York City, with his fellow agent and lover Eliza D Braun at his side. These American streets and alleyways were just as busy as any London ones, but displayed far more technology.

While bastions of tradition such as horse-drawn hansoms and carriages still beat hooves on the roadway, Americans embraced *mechanications* of all manner. This embracing of technology however meant living within a cacophony of metal. The smell of horse manure overpowered the choking plumes of steam and soot from motor vehicles chugging by. Wellington's throat burned from the sharp-scented chemicals release into the air, even as his chest ached with the effort of the chase. As Wellington clamped a hand down on his bowler, lest it slide off his head, a trickle of sweat ran down his cheek. A sign of good effort.

The agents dodged motorcars, *mechanicarriages*, street vendors, and a throng of city residents, all of whom appeared oblivious to the industrial chaos that churned around them. Through it all Wellington and Eliza struggled to maintain their pursuit of the Eastman gang member, identified as one Derbin O'Halloran. The Eastman were the most feared ruffians on the Lower East Side, and 'Derby' was leading them on quite the foot chase—a good enough reason to shoot him. Apart from being unsporting, though, such a shot—even Wellington using his crack talent with firearms—would endanger the locals, draw the attention from the local constabulary, and defeat the notion they were carrying out clandestine operations on foreign soil.

"Bugger me," Eliza spat as Derby leapt over the crowd. "There he goes again."

"Language, darling," Wellington scolded. "We're in public."

The look he got in return put him in his place. "You're worried about my language," Eliza asked, pointing above the pedestrians, "with *that* bouncing through the crowd?"

Derby vaulted skyward a second time, the Jumping Jacks extending and retracting like metallic cricket's legs secured to his own. These novel inventions gave their quarry six foot high leaps as well as three feet of extra distance with every bound. The odd citizen glanced up, but Jumping Jacks were invented in New York, and were all the rage. Since this city seemed obsessed with moving faster, Derby was nothing more than another pedestrian on his way to some destination, taking full advantage of the city's latest trend.

Despite the clear advantage being a bouncing Jack-in-the-box afforded, Derby was having a difficult time of it. Maybe he'd been unable to practice with the devices, or perhaps it was the chaos of pedestrians around him. In any case their perpetrator did not to have full control of them. He slammed into the top of a carriage, nearly toppling when the narrow wedges of the leg extensions made contact with the causeway, but he righted himself and sprung away.

"Bloody hell," Eliza grumbled as they burst through a gaggle of drunken sailors.

"Watch it, ya tart," one of then snapped, grabbing hold of her bicep.

Her free arm moved with superhuman alacrity, punching the man in his gut so hard it was a wonder his lover's hand did not emerge from his back. The sailor's blubber cushioned the *plures ornemtaum*-powered blow—fortunately for him. Eliza loved the device on her arm and had used it on many missions. It was a veritable Swiss Army knife of a creation, packed with powered pistons, blades, and grappling hooks, but hopefully she wouldn't deploy its full arsenal on this sot.

The remaining three sailors took only one step before Eliza produced her pistol with her other hand. "Make an appointment, boys."

A rapid blast from a train horn ripped their gaze back toward the leaping gang member, and Wellington's heart seized for an instant. Derby was bounding towards an incoming train, a small crowd waited along an elevated platform as he and his Jumping Jacks made quick work of the stairs. The agents pounded their way upwards as shrieks and shouts indicated Derby's arrival. Wellington's eyes darted from one end of the platform to the other, searching for their target. Another quick succession of blasts from the train was when he noticed the car did not slow. *It must be an express,* Wellington thought. That would play in their advantage.

Derby however only widened his stance. Wellington and Eliza continued to sprint over the landing, even as the Eastman made another leap—and an impressive one at that. His curved trajectory outlined him against the lights of the city. Then in a blur he was on top of the train, just managing to grab hold of the roof before he could slip off to the crowded streets below.

Eliza darted back to the landing from where they emerged and removed the lid from the trash can. She threw the flat side against the pavement and jammed her booted foot under its handle.

"Time to catch the express, darling," she said, pulling Wellington's arms around her and bringing them close against each other. Any closer, and they would have been at risk of lewd and lascivious behaviour. As always it was a delightful experience being this near to her; yet their bodies pressed against one another reminded him it had been awhile since they had enjoyed such intimacy. *The perils of the chase,* he supposed. Serving the queen as they did in the Ministry of Peculiar Occurrences, those distractions of love and affection were put aside. When Eliza's left leg locked around his own, a blush bloomed up from Wellington's collar, but he knew this was not anything amorous, especially when she bellowed in his ear: *"Hold on!"*

She fired the plures ornemtaum's grappling hook into the back car of the train. When it went taut, powerful winches inside the arm began to retract, dragging Eliza and Wellington on their makeshift sled across the platform. For a moment, they were sliding at incredible speed, closing the distance between them and the express. Wellington would have found this almost as exhilarating as having his love so close to him...

... had it not been for the end of the platform closing on them.

"Eliza..." he said into her ear.

"Not yet."

"Eliza..."

"Almost there."

"Darling, I really think..."

"JUMP!" she screamed, pulling Wellington down into a deep crouch.

They both leapt in unison, their hands outstretched and reaching for the back of the car as the plures ornemtaum continued to yank them closer. Together their hands slapped hard against the cold railing. Wellington tightened his grip and tucked his knees up to his chest as his body slammed into the back of the train. The loud gasp from Eliza said she'd experienced the same rough landing. For a moment, they hung on the back of the car, gathering their breath, before pulling themselves up and begin their climb to the train's roof.

It might have been March, but on clearing the ladder he experienced the full force of the wind. That blast was reminiscent of a British December. *Could be worse,* he thought. *At least I'm not trying this on a moving hypersteam.* Wellington's glasses protected his eyes enough so that he could make out their target ahead, now crouched on the top of the train, waiting for a stop where he could spring away.

A gust blowing past his glasses blinded him for a moment. Oh, how he would love a proper pair of goggles, he thought just as Eliza clambered over the edge of the train carriage.

Adjusting her own protective eyewear, she grinned, the wind whipping strands of hair around her face. "No science-respecting lady's outfit is complete without goggles."

Through streaming eyes, and feeling rather under-prepared, Wellington observed their gang member hunched further down the carriage. His back was to them, and the clatter of the train masked any sound. Eliza jerked her head towards Derby and began to shuffle closer to their prey. Wellington had a sudden pang for the Archives and the uneventful life he had grown comfortable with there, but then again if he hadn't left he would never have experienced a chase across the rooftop of a moving train, nor had to run from an exploding giant automaton. Then there was undoing a grand confidence game against the Crown, and the American inventor Thomas Edison turning lighthouses into death rays. Perhaps life in the Archives was quiet and safe, but this life suited him just as well.

Damn, Wellington thought.

Keeping their bodies bent low as best they could, he followed Eliza forward. This train was not a smooth ride as it rattled and shifted beneath them like the world's most obstinate horse. One glance up ahead revealed clouds gathering on the horizon. If it should rain on them, remaining on the roof would prove impossible. He tapped Eliza on the shoulder and pointed. If they were to catch this man, they had to be quick about it. Against the darkening skyline it was harder to tell what Derby was about; would he make a leap off at any moment or ride to another platform? Either option would mean a swift escape.

A quick nod to one another at the junction, and together they leapt across the gap to the next carriage. Perhaps the gang member hadn't heard them, but the impact of their arrival must have run through his feet. Derby's head, masked and goggled, flicked over his shoulder. He leapt once, then twice, and Wellington knew without question what his next action would be. Eliza must have reached the same conclusion as she brazenly ran across the moving roof—damn safety—even as Derby leapt from the train.

A flash of lightning in the distance silhouetted him against the sky. The winged eagle, a titan straight from the legends of Eliza's own New Zealand, swooped down and snatched Derby from the air. Wellington blinked and locked gazes with his partner, who had come to an abrupt halt. They watched as the eagle turned on one wingtip, circled around, and then banked towards the approaching terminal. The train underneath them began to slow.

"Oye!" someone shouted from the platform ahead. "You know we're supposed to be working in secret, right? Mighty conspicuous doing Hawaiian surf riding up there, Lizzie!"

"Bruce?" As they lurched to a stop Eliza's voice was able to be made out. The Australian with his chiselled jaw and wide smile dressed as if he had just emerged from the West, a leather hat tipped back and wildly patterned boots adorning his feet. Agent Bruce Campbell was an Outback peacock amongst identical Americans. Yet he was being critical of Wellington and Eliza standing out?

"Did you miss me?" Bruce asked with a wink in Eliza's direction.

"With the way you're dressed, that would be impossible," she returned. Wellington was certain another inappropriate word crossed her lips before she said, "Let's get down off this thing before we're forced to ride to the end of the line."

Wellington and Eliza grabbed the side railings of their carriage, swung off the roof, down onto the platform. A few of the locals looked askance at them, but in the way of big cities, no one dared to make a comment. They had places to be, apparently. Eliza glared at Bruce out of the corner of her eye. The adversarial relationship between her and her South Pacific cousin had never gone away. Considering his own experiences with Bruce, Wellington couldn't fault her for that. At all.

Bruce surprised him with a somewhat chummy slap on the back. "Good to see you, mate." He refrained from doing the same to Wellington's partner. Probably a very good choice unless he wanted a punch in the throat. "Been enjoying the Americas?"

"Never a dull moment," Wellington said, rolling his shoulder.

"Especially you pipping us at the post," Eliza hissed. "Are you responsible for that infernal contraption flying about us?"

"Oh yeah, she's a beaut, ain't she?" Bruce said. "Borrowed her from those American agents. She—"

"That was *our* target," Wellington interjected, hoping to cut off Eliza's rage before it hit boiling point. "We were just about to apprehend him when you arrived."

"Looked more like *our* mark was about to give *you* the slip," Bruce replied, tucking his thumbs into his jacket pockets.

Eliza's words were so pointed, commuters boarding the train paused and looked back at her. "*Your* target?"

So much for cutting off her rage.

"Yes, my darlin' Lizzie. The Fat Man assigned us to the task force dedicated to Ragnarök. and you all were assigned on that Jekyll bloke."

"We still are. Derby was our lead to Jekyll."

"That as may be," Bruce said with a sigh, "but not today. We've been watching him for almost a month now. Them Houseboys started building laboratories now."

Houseboys. Agent Campbell's pet name for agents from the House of Usher. Wellington couldn't help raising his eyebrows as realisation washed over him. "Usher is establishing laboratories as part of Ragnarök?"

The Australian shot them both a bemused smile. "What? You didn't think mad science was reserved for Jekyll, did you?"

Eliza replied in a surprisingly even tone, "We had intelligence that Derby was smuggling nadnerczyna."

"Now there's a word straight from Oxford."

"It's an extract from the adrenal glands. Nadnerczyna is a natural stimulant, and one of the key ingredients in Jekyll's serum."

The Australian motioned to Wellington. "You've been around this bloke for too long!"

"We've taught each other a great deal," he replied.

"As I was saying," Eliza said, "Derby was moving copious amounts of this solution."

"Come on then," Bruce said, as he led them down to street level where the ornithopter had landed in a wide alleyway. Its tail section protruded into the sidewalk, and citizens of New York weaved and dodged around it as best they could. A small raggedly dressed boy muttered, *"Who the hell parks an ornithopter on 2nd Street?"* On seeing Bruce rest his hand on the tail, the young lad shot him the filthiest of looks as he took a long detour around it.

"Lesson learned," Wellington said to Eliza. "New Yorkers are patient to an extent—but Heaven forbid impeding their progress on a public thoroughfare."

She looked at the hostile passers-by and nodded. "Duly noted, Agent Books."

The three of them stepped around the giant eagle-like device's tail and into the alley. Currently its talons held Derby O'Halloran. One of his springing legs was absent while the other dangled from his ankle, but the glazed look in his eyes was probably from the forceful nature of his apprehension. With a better chance to see the ornithopter, Wellington could only admire it. A beautiful construction, light and sturdy at the same time, but one would have to be a right nutter to try to fly it.

Then its pilot emerged.

"Wellington, Eliza!" Agent Brandon Hill exclaimed, placing his goggles to the top of his head. Before either could evade the gesture, he pulled them both into a tight, awkward three-way hug. "It's been too long."

"Not long enough between these intimate greetings," Wellington muttered into Eliza's ear. She snorted delightfully.

"So, Derby," Bruce said, walking up to the man in the grasp of the ornithopter's claw, "You've been a busy bee, I've hea—bugger!"

The curse wrenched Wellington's attention from Hill to Bruce and Derby. The street thug had his tongue against the inside of his cheek. Bruce leapt forward and shoved his fingers into Derby's mouth.

"No, push the cheeks!" Wellington called out, struggling free of the awkward embrace. "Otherwise, he'll jus—"

"*ARRGH!*" Bruce rapped Derby against the bridge of his nose—almost hard enough to break it. Pulling his fingers free of the man's mouth, Bruce shook them. "Bastard bit me!"

Wellington grabbed the man underneath his jaw and pinched hard, but under his fingers and thumb Derby worked something between his teeth. His eyes filled with defiance as he bit through the soft flesh inside his cheek. Both of them froze for a moment, then Derby convulsed before him. A foam, tinged with blood, seeped from between his lips as his body jerked once, twice, then sagged into Wellington's arms.

"Dammit!" Bruce swore, bending to one knee to examine the dead man's face. "Bloody poison tooth!"

"I thought only Usher's agents were using those infernal things," Eliza said.

"Yeah, well, that's standard for any Usher associate now, even the hired help." Bruce looked up at the two of them. "You would have known that, had you been working this case like we have, but you didn't, and you spooked him."

Eliza paused. Wellington knew that expression. She was about to explode. "Are you saying this is *our* fault?"

"This was an emergency plan, in case we had a runner." Brandon waved cheerily at them both. Bruce gave an awkward wave back. Wellington admired the man's patience, until he added, "Which thanks to you, we had."

"You've got some nerve, Bruce," Eliza barked back. "We were following up on a lead…"

"That directly intersected with an investigation we'd been carrying out for at least two months! Would it have bothered you to check and see if there were any active operations in the area?"

"You must beg a pardon, Campbell," Wellington offered, his tenor growing less and less patient with each word, "as we were chasing a madman who single-handedly orchestrated the near-destruction of London's East End! Or had you forgotten about that little tussle we had in and around St Paul's Cathedral?"

"Usher is changing their tactics. Seems they are in the business of snatching people right now." Bruce shook his head in disgust at the poison seeping out of Derby's mouth before flicking open the man's jacket to reveal the silver pin of a raven tucked inside. "Not quite sure what they are doing with all of them, but he might have."

The idea of the House spiriting away people was not a comfortable one, but it was yet another example of the change in their ranks. "Usher used to prefer the shadows," Eliza muttered to Wellington.

Bruce adjusted his collar. "You're right there, Lizzie. Bloody hell if it doesn't seem like things are stepping up with them, but thanks to you we won't be getting anything out of Derby now."

"Then let us make this up to you, Campbell, Hill." Wellington motioned to Derby's cooling corpse. "We'll clean this up for you."

Eliza rounded on him. "Welly?"

"No, no, no, we should take responsibility for this cock-up. Eliza and I will take care of the body, proper paperwork and all that. As you said, Bruce," Wellington said, looking over to Eliza and locking his gaze with hers, "you can't get anything additional from the poor sot, so let us take care of this."

Her brow remained scrunched until she understood Wellington's stratagem. "You are talking about a substantial amount of paperwork, Agent Books."

"*No*," Wellington insisted though a tight smile, "*we insist*." He cast a glance to Bruce who was pinching the bridge of his nose, his eyes screwed shut. The man was probably pushing back a headache of some description. Wellington looked back at Eliza. *Play along,* he mouthed.

No, she mouthed back.

Wellington raised an eyebrow. So did Eliza.

"That would be good of you, mate," Bruce admitted. "I'll keep this whole hullabaloo out of my report to the Fat Man."

"Excellent!" Wellington exclaimed, turning back to Bruce with a bright smile. "Then we have an accord."

"Sorry about the bother, Books," Hill said from the ornithopter. Wellington considered it a stroke of luck that the Canadian was more preoccupied with his flying machine than the dead lead. "But as it is your blunder that got us here, it's mighty fine of you."

"Own one's mistakes, I always say," Wellington said with a chuckle and a shrug.

"Good show, Books!" Brandon flipped a few switches on the ornithopter's modest engine. It chugged and churned to life again, but instead of assisting the mechanical bird's great wings to flap, the device started to collapse. Wellington was trying—and failing—not to stare at how the invention was folding upon itself, becoming smaller and smaller in its size. "It stops when it becomes the size of a valise."

"How very clever," Wellington said with a smile.

"A valise that weighs just over four stone."

Wellington's face fell. "Oh... oh dear... most unfortunate."

"On the contrary, good way to get in a bit of exercise," Hill said. Wellington wasn't sure of the agent's conviction in those words.

"Alright then," Bruce said, looking at the steady stream of people passing. "I'd wish you luck on getting this body out of here without notice, but I honestly don't know if anyone in this godforsaken city would even give a toss."

"Something we will use to our advantage," Wellington said.

"I'm sure." The hiss behind them ceased, and a valise roughly the size of a large dog now stood where the ornithopter once did. "Right then, we're off. Try communicating with us next time."

"Of course, Brandon."

"See you back at the hotel, mate," Bruce said to Brandon with a nod. With that, Bruce slipped into the crowd.

Brandon gave Wellington and Eliza a quick smile and then hefted the valise. It rose into the air a few inches, but then slammed back to the pavement with a hard thud.

"Well now," Brandon said, his words a tad winded, "bit heavier than four stone."

With a quick intake of air, Brandon brought the suitcase up once more. This time, he compensated properly, or at least the best he could.

"Cheers, all," Brandon groaned, and waddled off.

Wellington waved to the odd man before turning back to his partner, to find Eliza's expression thunderous.

"I know what you're going to say," Wellington began, holding his hands up.

"No, you don't."

"I have a very good idea..."

"You *know* how I feel about this."

"Damn it, Eliza, this is not about your odd phobias, this is about Jekyll!" Wellington took a step back and turned his gaze to the body at their feet. "That was uncalled for. My apologies."

"This is personal, yes," Eliza admitted. "And we're knackered."

"Indeed." Wellington adjusted his cravat as he bent down to look at Derby. "For the time being, though, we must push on and take advantage of any lead we might have."

"Should we contact Bruce and Brandon if we find out anything to help them?"

"Remember this 'favour' we are doing is completely off-the-books. If we tell Bruce and Brandon, they will be asked questions... questions that could implicate them in what we are about to do."

Eliza nodded. "Fast thinking, Welly."

"I have my moments."

Eliza joined him by Derby, allowing her hand to slip into his. "So... how are we planning to move a body?"

"I confess I am not sure about that part."

She looked at the body from head to toe, then turned back to Wellington. "Well, that's just jolly."

There was only one option. "Perhaps a call to our hostess is in order?"

"Quite," she replied, "but I'll let you do the explaining." Her smile was sharp, but perhaps well-deserved.

CHAPTER TWO

In Which There May be a Ghost of a Chance

Eliza D Braun didn't mind ghosts so long as they knew their place. That, she believed, would be gothic mansions, haunted moors, and the odd theatre along London's West End. She considered herself fortunate, since becoming a full field agent, to have avoided those stragglers from this mortal coil. Generally hauntings were something *juniors* in the Ministry dealt with, on account of their frequent debunking. Regardless of the fraction that proved true, these cases required the same amount of paperwork—and that she had no patience for. So, when it came to ghosts, that was someone else's job.

Only one time, just after she was assigned to the Archives, she and Wellington handled a triple-event at Christmas time. It was a rather *lively* haunting.

After her fair share of time chasing down and containing vengeful spirits, Eliza viewed ghosts as her least-favourite of peculiar occurrences. Very few of these legitimate apparitions had conscious thought. Most just replayed wrongs done to them in life. It was the kind of trapped existence that made Eliza very uncomfortable contemplating. Was it evidence of the afterlife, made so true and convincing that not even the most hardened of sceptics could deny it? Was it an indication of God's cruelty, condemning both innocents and the guilty to a life trapped in a world from which there would be no escape? Or was it a reminder of her own mortality? Whatever it was, ghosts bothered her. Thankfully, not every person turned into a spirit at the moment of death, or the Ministry would be drowning in the damn things.

So with every flash of light, and every muted moan from the other side of the door, Eliza's skin prickled. Then, when the young girl emerged from the room where Derbin O'Halloran's corpse lay, Eliza tried to swallow back her fear. *Why was this poor creature using the bloody door?* she thought. *Surely not for my benefit.*

"Please," the girl spoke, her smile kind. "Have a seat."

Bettina Spinnett looked young and reasonably solid, but there was no getting passed it: she was a ghost. The echo of a life once lived, and from the looks of her, cut tragically short. They all sat around a small table with a modest tea set Eliza had seen Bettina placing there earlier. It should have been adorable that the ghost took such care, but it only added to Eliza's disquiet. Bettina looked tired as she folded her hands on her lap. Another impossible thing for a spirit, but there it was. Still, she had enough strength to pick up the teapot and pour for her living guests.

"I hope I made it to your liking," she said, filling herself a cup as well. Why, Eliza could not fathom. Discussing the interrogation of a dead man of possible hiding spots of nefarious secret laboratories in New York City *with a ghost* Eliza could hardly fathom either. "The last time I attempted to make tea for Mr Books here, it was a bit of a disaster."

"Tosh, Miss Spinnett," Wellington said with a light shake of his head. "It had just steeped too long. I will admit I was a bit jittery but the amount of work I accomplished that day? Unparalleled."

The girl chuckled just before taking a sip of her own tea. Eliza smiled tightly at her before casting a quick glance at the teapot handle. A faint sheen of ectoplasm was just visible against the finish of the teapot's willow pattern. *Don't stare... don't stare... don't stare,* she thought to herself as she took a sip from her own cup.

Her eyebrows raised slightly. My, but she did brew a good cuppa.

"So, the interrogation went as well as one would expect," Bettina said, setting her cup to one side. "Derby did not take too kindly to discovering that he was no longer one of the living."

"As we gathered from the moaning," Wellington agreed.

"Yes. The moaning." Bettina shuddered, and for a moment Eliza saw through her. Literally. "You would think I'd be used to it by now."

"I suppose everyone handles death differently."

Bettina nodded before picking up her cup again and taking a sip. As the interior of the cup came into view, Eliza peered in to see if there were any traces of the ghost's touch on its rim or floating in the brew. A soft clearing of a throat tore her gaze from the setting. Wellington's pained expression was not helping her settle, and Eliza took a slow, deep breath to quell her roiling resentment. This was all very well for him since he'd met this phantasm before.

"Once I managed to calm him down, allow him to gather himself, as it were," Bettina continued, oblivious to the silent exchange between Eliza and Wellington, "I questioned him about his intentions, about his affiliation with Usher and with Hyde."

Eliza blinked. "Hide?"

Bettina paused, then shook her head. "Sorry. Old habits. Hyde. H-Y-D-E. That's OSM's code name for Jekyll." Bettina bit her lip as she looked outside the parlour where they sat. "Mrs Marsh would tan my backsides if she heard me telling you this. Our communications were breached several months after the San Francisco Incident. We believe it to be Usher as the attack coincided with increased activity from them. A new protocol we have put in place is to use codenames for potential hot targets in the field."

Wellington's brow eased as a smile crossed his face. "Jekyll was both Lawson's and the Maestro's physician, hiding in plain sight. Very clever."

"Code names?" Eliza said with a slight roll of her eyes. "You Americans do love the theatrics. I suppose Usher's code name is 'Lenore' on account of the poem?" Eliza gave a little chuckle at the obvious name, but her laugh disappeared on reading Bettina's face. "You're joking."

"So far, so good," Bettina admitted. "So, Derby was working with both Usher and Jekyll. The man was a piece of work, seeing as his loyalties went to whoever greased his gears. Derby did not care what he was getting paid, so long as he got his coin. He served both masters, not bothering to note why they would want similar goods. To him it was just another opportunity, one that served him well."

"Did you manage to find out where Derby was running this little endeavour from?"

Bettina held up a solitary finger and then set aside the tea setting. She rapped a knuckle—and how she did that, Eliza was at a complete loss to explain—against the table and its round centre section flipped over to reveal a map of New York City. From a desk just behind her, she opened a drawer and extracted a clear overlay of what looked like thick blood veins. "I think you will find plenty of tunnels under the street here," she said, positioning the overlay across the map. "I can help you scout ahead, but my abilities with weapons are not... well, they are lacking on account of my ethereal nature."

"Just a moment," Eliza interrupted, "you poured us a cuppa and you're saying you cannot carry a gun?"

"It's a bit complicated. I can handle household objects. I can even operate scientific devices. Weapons of any sort? No."

"That's quite all right, Bettina," Wellington broke in, cleared his throat, and turned his attention to the map. "We've been on the trail of Jekyll for months. It's the specific demands of his serum that serves as his Achilles' Heel. I'm amazed his laboratory is so portable."

"He's been popping up everywhere," Eliza said, giving him the slightest of nods. "Paris, Kansas City, Singapore, and now unfortunately, New York. It's rather astounding."

"Should we inform OSM?" Bettina asked. "Especially after the incident on the commuter express?"

This tiny, covert office of their American counterpart, the Office of the Supernatural and Metaphysical, appeared more a boarding house to passers-by than a base of operations for spies. A sudden uptick of boarders all at one time might be suspicious. They also didn't want their operation to come to the attention of OSM's Director Highfield.

"Bettina, you and Mrs Marsh know that we are not officially operating in New York City. Merely dropping in socially as Miss Braun and I are passing through." Wellington blushed a bit as he continued, "I know I am asking quite a bit from both of you, but no one knows New York City better."

"Jekyll is our problem," Eliza added. "We're not even sure if he has established roots here. This laboratory could just as well belong to some other mad scientist. You'd be surprised how many there are running around these days."

Bettina's eyebrows twitched. "New York is full of them." They stared at each other for a moment, and Eliza found herself the first one to break. It was hard to win that kind of competition with a dead person.

Eliza stood up from the table and walked over to the bay window that looked out over America's grand metropolis, already a match for London. "So many people, so many immigrants, so many poor." She turned and faced the ghost. "Excellent pickings for Jekyll and scientists like him."

Bettina nodded. "The Lower East Side of the city has become the hunting ground for all kinds of dangerous people. If an immigrant or two goes missing every week or so, the police won't bother looking too hard. Even I don't feel safe in certain parts…"

Eliza wasn't sure if the ghost was making a joke, but then she considered the paranormal was not without its hunters either. Cities like New York suited Jekyll's pattern very well. Find a transient community, take his pick of victims, perform whatever experiment he needed to carry out, and then move on before the local constabulary caught up with him. In previous cities, she and Wellington had always arrived frustratingly too late to catch him. This time, however, their information was fresh. Derby had been asking for ingredients that could only serve one purpose: replicating the Super Soldier serum developed by Dr Henry Jekyll and Arthur Books, Wellington's father. Finally, they were a step ahead—maybe two—of the mad doctor.

"So did Derby tell you anything about his dealings with Jekyll?" Eliza asked, returning her gaze to the table map.

"It took some doing, but he informed me of a delivery he was to make," Bettina said, rising from her chair. Goose flesh rippled along her arm as the ghost did so. She stood and did not make a sound. So bloody unsettling. "Tonight."

Wellington already had his satchel slung over one shoulder. It contained more than enough weapons for them both, plus a few specialties from Axelrod and Blackwell. She had her trusty *pounamu* pistols tucked under her jacket, her plures ornemtaum on her arm, so really what more did they need? "Did you get the time?"

"Midnight." Bettina glanced at the clock on the desk behind her and nodded. "Shouldn't take us long to get there."

"Then let's get on with it," she said. "Show us the way."

Though Eliza had to admit working with the supernatural did provide benefits, she found working in public with ghosts a real challenge. As they walked through the crowd, no one gave Bettina a second glance, even if she was nimble enough to step out of people's way. Perhaps being walked through was not a pleasant sensation for one of her kind. Eliza had to concede that Bettina had mastered the appearance of being solid.

Tugging on the elbow of his jacket Eliza whispered into his ear, "I still don't think this is a good idea."

"Still don't think what is a good idea?"

She did love him so, but how could one so incredibly brilliant be as thick as clotted cream? "We really can do this operation without our little friend here."

"What part of *'No one knows New York city better...'* did you fail to grasp?"

"Oh, come on, Welly, the Ministry have their own network of confidential informants and I certainly have my own contacts who are more..."

"What? Qualified? Reliable?"

"Corporeal."

Wellington cleared his throat. "Why Miss Braun, I would never have taken you for a bigot."

Her mouth dropped open. "Welly, what do you..." She stopped and considered her words, her recent thoughts. Wellington was completely misconstruing this. "I just..."

He raised one eyebrow. "Yes, yes, you are, I am afraid, my love. Just because Bettina here is a person of a somewhat deceased nature..."

"You do hear yourself, don't you?"

"... *is a person of a somewhat deceased nature,*" he repeated, «you are making snap judgements about her. Mrs Marsh has spoken quite highly of Miss Spinnett, and she has performed admirably according to all accounts. In fact, her unique condition has proved remarkably useful at times.»

"Her unique condition?" Eliza grumbled, considering how the ability to pass through walls and turning invisible would play to her advantage. It was a talent she herself would hopefully not develop in the immediate future. "I hardly call being dead a condition. Or a skill. It's not like she can shoot weapons, or punch any villains."

"No," he said and reached across to squeeze her hand. "That is what you excel at, darling."

Eliza couldn't help but shake her head. He had a point, but she was not going to say it out loud. Instead, she remained silent as they climbed up to the elevated railway they had grown to know on the previous evening's foot chase. Giant bridges of iron stacked like a layer cake, the one on top the express line. The lower one—the one they wanted—was the local line. This transit was a marvel of Manhattan, and from the looks of his smile, Wellington remained distracted by it.

As they waited for it to arrive, Bettina kept her distance, making sure to stay well away from the rest of the passengers. It would not do to phase through an unsuspecting citizen of New York.

The rattle of the train didn't sound sane, with an odd syncopated rhythm and roar that only two engines could provide. To make matters worse, the tall buildings echoed it back again and again.

She exchanged a glance with Wellington and saw he was—as she would have expected—very excited. Even though they'd ridden on its roof, he hadn't gotten a good look inside. Leaning across, he whispered, "Wondrous way to shift a lot of people, and powered by electricity too."

She nodded in response, knowing a ramble on the marvels of electricity would be coming with the slightest provocation. The train arrived, and this time they got into it, rather than clamber on the top.

Bettina took a seat at the front, perfectly aligned with the window and out of the way of any other passengers. Seeing her like that, Eliza realised how lonely her existence must be. Here was this girl, barred from an unknown fate beyond this world, working to protect those she could never touch again. So very near to all, and yet so completely far away. Did Bettina long for contact? Eliza knew exactly how terrible it would be not to touch Wellington ever again. The mere thought sent a stab of chill through her gut.

A thumb traced the side her finger. Eliza did not know when she had taken Wellington's hand, but she now held it with quite the firm grasp. She pressed her lips together hard. This whole situation was very strange, but she should have been used to peculiar. There was a time when such thoughts rarely distracted her. Even with Harry in Paris, she had been tempted, but thought better of it. True, a part of her regretted taking a more sensible path. Now, looking into Wellington's eyes, there was a deep-seated regret roiling inside her. Why could she have not met him sooner? There had been so much time lost between them…

"Darling, are you alright?" Wellington whispered.

Before she could formulate an answer, the train clattered to a stop. Bettina gave a slight jerk of her head, and Eliza and Wellington followed her off. The shadow of New York's mechanical transit system blanketed the road below, which swarmed with so many people that for a moment Eliza thought she was a salmon battling upstream.

"Welcome to the Bowery district," Bettina said to them, trying to keep the three of them clear of impatient pedestrians. This part of the city reminded Eliza somewhat of the East End of London, though far more crowded. The smells of so many people packed together were the same the world over. The tenements were taller than in London, most at least four floors, with laundry flapping from their small balconies, and women leaning out of windows to shout or gossip at their neighbours. Below the street was littered with people hawking their wares from carts, and children running about splashing in dirty puddles. The accents around her mingled together, but she could pick out Polish, Irish, and German.

So similar was it to the slums of London, it wouldn't have surprised Eliza if the Americans had their own versions of the Ripper or Spring-Heeled Jack kicking about.

"It's a bit of a crush, so stay close," Bettina whispered.

It was early evening, so many people were leaving work, while others headed to their night shift. Not even the ghost was nimble or quick enough to keep entirely out of the commuters' way, and several times she was definitely walked through. It stunned Eliza how no one took any notice of her, but then she noted how New Yorkers barely looked up or made eye contact with even the living.

"Now I see why Jekyll might have chosen this city," Eliza hissed into Wellington's ear. "They all really have places to be."

"I love it," Wellington replied, straightening his waistcoat, and almost getting knocked sideways by a burly pedestrian. "Rather invigorating."

Sometimes, it was impossible to anticipate what would come out of her lover's mouth, and Eliza liked that.

Bettina's pale form led them off the main thoroughfare to a decidedly less salubrious part of the city. The buildings might be taller than those in London town, but the same poverty was all around. A babe's wail, shouts of quarrels, and laughter between mates over a bottle were all around them. As it was closing in on midnight, Eliza knew there would be other sounds in the air. Many of those cries would go unanswered, unnoticed.

"Stay here," Bettina whispered. "This is Eastman territory, so I will scope out ahead."

Eliza curled her lip. "We have a few gangs of our own back in London, they don't..."

Bettina raised one pale hand. "I am sure you do, but the Eastman are best avoided. Give me a minute to go see if this lair is even occupied."

She strode off into the darkness, with not even a glimmer of æther trailing in her wake. Bettina could sometimes look like a regular human being... but that illusion shattered as Eliza watched her slip into a nearby building through a wall.

"All right," Wellington said in an undertone, "I will admit, that is a bit unsettling."

Eliza did not like to hide in the shadows, but this was not her city. She would trust her ghostly colleague for the moment, bide her time for a bit. While she checked her satchel, she shot a look at Wellington. "So what are the chances he's actually here?"

He smoothed his moustache and tilted his head. "The chemicals being sent to this location are ones we found in other abandoned laboratories. Considering how important they are to Jekyll, I think the possibilities are quite high."

Eliza checked her pistols one more time. She wanted to be certain both were loaded to capacity. "I hope so—I am heartily sick of chasing our tails on this."

"Doesn't help that Jekyll's using *electroporter* technology."

"Not a jot, my love. Not a jot."

Just at that moment, Bettina poked her head out of the wall through which she disappeared. Her sudden appearance startled a cat resting on some crumbling boxes to her right; it ran off with a hiss. "Books, Braun," she whispered, waving them over.

Keeping an eye on the windows above them, they approached.

"Go to the back of the alley," Bettina said, poking her hand through the bricks to point to their left. "I've picked the lock for you, but on the other side of the door, there is a guard you'll have to take care of."

Eliza hoisted her pounamu pistols. "So more than just an abandoned laboratory, then?"

"Much more. They seem to be readying a shipment of some kind. Best you hurry." With that, she disappeared back through the wall again.

As they trotted around the rear of the building, Wellington muttered, "A properly modulated *ætherfrequency* might do it, I suppose…"

She knew what he was thinking. "No one will try it, my love. Besides, who on earth would take the risk of getting buried alive in brick in case something goes horribly wrong?"

Wellington's eyes gleamed in the dark as he reached into Eliza's satchel and pulled out a three-piece apparatus and its stock. "I am sure Professor Axelrod might be persuaded."

She kissed him on the cheek. "Don't be vindictive, Welly. Forget about the turtle incident, and focus on that pesky Jekyll fellow, if you please."

He shrugged, snapping the stock into the main body of the Lee-Metford-Tesla X3, and replied over its soft hum, "For now, Eliza. For now."

Through the small receiving room that Bettina had checked, there was no sign of any movement. The second door to the ground floor was ajar. Wellington took up a position on one side and then gave a nod to Eliza. She could feel that want, that need, to kick in the door which given her frustration over their pursuits of Jekyll might have been understandable. Rather, Eliza holstered one of her pounamu pistols, eased the door open with her free hand, and crept in. They slipped silently into a short hallway, a wooden stool at the far end had a book resting on it. Behind it, another door that remained closed. A guard had sat here. Maybe nature had called, or he was summoned away to help with loading? Whatever the case, muffled voices came from the end of the hallway, and feet interrupted the light visible between the bottom of the door and the floor.

Eliza shook her head a little. So often security breaches could be prevented with just a little more staffing.

Reaching the door at the end of the hallway, she listened, but with the muffled, muted voices, it was impossible to narrow down how many were on the other side. Could be five blokes. Could be five blokes, hanging about with ten quiet ones. Hard to say.

When Bettina stuck her head through the wall next to her, Eliza nearly punched the girl... which would have been unfortunate for her fist.

The ghostly secret agent raised her hand to show three fingers and then gestured beyond the door. A glance back to Wellington. He gave Eliza a nod. Apparently they were ready to make a bit of noise.

Eliza smiled. One of her favourite parts of the job.

Her boot connected with the door, shoving it open. She slipped over the threshold, ducked low, and stepped right, her pistols coming up and firing at the first sign of movement. Her target had been enjoying a smoke while a modified Winchester rested across his forearm and stomach. Her bullet punched through his shoulder, and the rifle clattered to the floor as he lurched off-balance.

Wellington stepped to the left, training his rifle on the other two gents that Bettina had hinted about, but his foes had both distance and warning. His two adversaries ducked behind large barrels as they opened fire. The blast from his Lee-Metford-Tesla unleashed a sphere of energy from its bell-shaped barrel that, most assuredly, flash-blinded them. It was intended to stun, but the light did himself and Eliza better by giving them a moment to scramble behind a stack of boxes.

She hated being pinned down even more than being frustrated. The room was spacious, brick and lacking any way for either of them to get around their attackers. They could hold them off, but sooner or later these Eastman rotters would have reinforcements.

That was when one of the men behind the barrels let out a scream like a child who had seen something terrifying.

Wellington looked to Eliza. "Bettina?"

"Only way to find out," she said, emerging from cover with her pistols drawn.

One barrel was knocked over, revealing a man on his knees, begging Bettina in a language that sounded... Italian? The other fired his own gun in spite of the supernatural apparition floating above them both. Eliza's own aim was superior as her shot found its mark, knocking him back.

The poor ghost looked bemused. "I don't understand what he's saying."

Eliza shrugged. "He says you are his sister back from the dead. He is asking your forgiveness for... throwing you down a well."

Bettina looked embarrassed. "All I did was appear out of the wall and he... I thought... well, it's one of my Halloween tricks you see."

"*Arresto!*" Wellington snapped, bracing the rifle against his shoulder.

The man turned his panicked gaze to the Ministry agent, but got kicked back by the shot coming from the rear.

"Behind you!" Bettina cried, swooping over them to the guard Eliza had wounded.

Eliza shoved Wellington behind the cover of the crates just as another shot rang out.

"Told you having a ghost on our side would be useful," Eliza said as she rolled up to one knee. "Wonder if the Old Man would consider recruiting some. Must be quite a few kicking around the Tower of London."

"Eliza D. Braun, you are quite a piece of work, you are," he chuckled, glancing at the Mark X's transformer.

"Still charging?"

"Not a word about the experimentals, Eliza," he huffed. "Not one!"

A clatter rose from the far end of the warehouse, and a blast of sound and light erupted. Bettina flew over them and disappeared into a tower of crates.

"Street gangs," Wellington began, his eyes wide, "armed with antispectral weaponry?"

"Not what you would expect," she said, daring a peek from their cover.

Before she could get a count, the two spheres flew high overhead. *This is going to sting,* she swore inwardly on recognising them at a glance.

Stunners. Ministry issue.

Both exploded with a high, deafening scream and a light even brighter than the blast from Wellington's Model X. Over the echo of the stunners and the whine in her ears, Eliza heard the door they had come through swing open and strike the brick wall again. There was gunfire mixed with low-frequency thrums. The commotion raged hard and furious, but only for a few seconds.

Wellington blinked as he pressed his fingertips to his ears. "Bloody hell, those stunners are nasty."

"They're meant to be," Eliza said, shaking her head. "You may have to lead me around a bit. I'm just seeing a lot of grey and black blotches at the moment."

"Now I think," the voice said, his accent filling her with dread, "all those nasty rumours about you two are true."

"Just. Lovely." Eliza groaned. "My headache has an Australian accent."

Bruce Campbell propped a steaming hand cannon against one of his massive shoulders while casting a glance over the other. Brandon had a knee buried in the wounded guard's back while he secured the man's wrists. Stepping free of their cover, Eliza could also see a small pile of Usher agents by the warehouse's open bay. Bruce was a cracking shot, so she was certain some of them were dead. Others were unconscious, no doubt, from the stunners.

Usher agents. Dammit.

"Now what did I tell you about rather awkward social discrepancies, Lizzie?" Bruce chided her. "We're supposed to be working together."

"We're not supposed to be working here at all, Agent Campbell," Wellington offered.

"Rather!" Brandon said, pointing at Wellington. "We're trying to make sure we keep the 'secret' in secret agents, eh wot?"

"And with all the ballyhoo you two are kicking up over this Jekyll character," Bruce said, looking at Wellington, "you're putting us all in jeopardy."

"Oh come off it, Campbell," Eliza said with a snort. "Our operations are bound to overlap as Jekyll's business and Usher's are two peas in a pod."

"Heavens above..." Bettina said as she emerged from the tower of crates, "what hit me?"

"Are you having a lark?" Bruce gasped, raising up his hand cannon. The fog slipping from its various pipes and hoses cascaded down in thick wisps, disappearing into the shadows.

"Oh now that's clever," Brandon said, his smile bright. "You've employed a ghost! Tell me, what do you pay her?"

Wellington and Eliza exchanged a quick glance between one another before returning their attention to Bruce.

"Miss Spinnett is... more of a consultant than an employee."

"Is that how you are getting around the Fat Man's rule when it comes to working with ghosts?" Bruce asked, lowering his gun.

"I prefer the term 'agents of unique æthereal backgrounds' if you don't mind," Bettina replied coolly.

"Agent Spinnett is assisting with the Jekyll investigation, and that is on a need to know basis."

Bruce's eyebrows raised. "Oh, so *now* we are working on the 'need to know' protocol, are we? You're playing this one fast and loose, even for you, Lizzie."

"You have no idea," the Eastman thug by Brandon grunted.

Everyone turned to look at the wounded man struggling to sit up. Brandon grabbed him by the scruff of his coat and helped him upright.

"Got something to share, then?" Bruce asked.

"Right coat pocket. Don't worry. Nothing tricky in there. Well, not too tricky."

Bruce gave a quick nod to Brandon, who fished a small billfold out of the guard's coat. He flipped it open and went ashen.

"Right then," Brandon said, passing the billfold to Bruce. He glanced at the wounded Eastman, cleared his throat, and looked over to Wellington. "How's that cat of yours, by the way? Alice keeps him locked up in your apartment these days, yes?"

"Ah, Archimedes?"

Brandon nodded enthusiastically.

"He is... he is quite well."

"Great, wonderful," Brandon replied with a tight smile. "Such a fine intellect for a feline, and a grand taste in bourbon."

"Oh, for the love of... " Bruce grumbled.

Eliza looked to Brandon, then to Bruce. "What?"

"Our friend here," Bruce said, motioning to the gang member with his billfold.

"Friend?" Eliza asked, snatching the wallet from his hand.

She flipped it open and looked at it with Wellington. The longer they stared at the credentials, the more they willed it to change under their gaze, the more she believed today was a terrible day to be a Ministry agent.

Agent David Tarkington
Office of the
Supernatural & Metaphysical

CHAPTER THREE

⇥⇌⇤

In Which a Harrowing Chase Comes to an End

"Well, you have put me in a devil of a position."
Doctor Basil Sound's eyes narrowed on the two of them, and even after all these years of being on the receiving end of this glare, Eliza still felt as though she were disappointing her own father.

The only difference now was that Eliza did not solely receive the look Doctor Sound had perfected with her.

As he rose from his chair, his hands crossing behind his back and tapping against one another while agents-in-training passed by the window overlooking the Whiterock estate, Eliza glanced at Wellington. He was biting back an opinion of some description, she was sure of it. When she returned her eyes to Doctor Sound, she couldn't help noticing additional grey at his temples, a few more lines etched into his face. It was a strange bit of irony—considering the man's ability to monitor and manipulate time and space—he could not stop from growing older. In fact, it seemed to be happening faster.

Perhaps that was why, since the trouble at the queen's coronation, her feelings when being held to account before him had changed. She still remembered arguing with him after the incident in Budapest in '93. Then there was Paris in '94. Twice. Prussia. Operation: Darkwater. The list knew no end. Then came the Antarctica Sanction that had led to her demotion. It had also led to a partnership—and then something more—with the man at her side. She was no longer sure if it was truly a disciplinary action or part of his intent to correct the anomaly in his timeline.

"We were doing our jobs, sir," she said, her skin prickling.

"Is that what you call what you were doing? I would call it breaking the rules and regulations of the Ministry."

"It is rather our forte," Wellington said softly, and she shot him a sideways smile. It was quite adorable that he was attempting to take on half the blame. When they'd first met, he certainly would have done no such thing.

Sound crossed back to his desk and rapped a knuckle against its polished surface as he bit back, "Then next time I should jolly well let you talk to Chief Highfield, and explain your unauthorised operation in his country."

At the mention of Chief Luther Highfield, Eliza recalled the Director of OSM from their previous mission in America. A man of grand stature and someone she would prefer not to tangle with, despite the allure of his dark gaze and striking handsomeness. She considered herself thankful not being an agent of that organisation. Eliza could see herself getting in trouble *on purpose*, just to share space with the man. She pushed the dalliance aside, taking Wellington's hand and facing her current disciplinary infraction. No explanation would satisfy the heads of both departments as to why she and Wellington had withheld status updates during their investigation into Jekyll's whereabouts.

"*Operations,* if you want to be more precise," Wellington returned. "I only see Agent Braun and myself for this reprimand, but I notice Agents Campbell and Hill absent. Are they not being held accountable?"

"Their mission stands on the shoulders of Mechamen compared to yours, Agent Books. You would do well to remember that."

"Ah, yes, of course," Wellington huffed. "Wouldn't want to upset Lenore."

Sound adjusted the spectacles on the tip of his nose. "Beg your pardon?"

"That's the codename for Usher," Eliza said, "according to our OSM contact."

"Yes, your OSM contact. Let's talk about Miss Bettina Spinnett," the Director began. His face settling into a still mask, but his eyes gleamed with rage.

Eliza cleared her throat and glanced over at Wellington. He was staring forward, his gaze focused on an object sitting on Sound's desk. "Well, sir, we were hot on the heels of Jekyll. We needed to use any and all resources at our disposal."

"Even if those resources are forbidden by the policies and procedures of this organisation?"

Wellington barked a dry, mirthless laugh, and shook his head. What had gotten into him?

Eliza tried not to stare. "We were in the field, and a snap decision was required. We enlisted Agent Spinnett on account of her... unique set of skills."

Wellington was always better with words than she was. In fact it was her ill-picked phrases in a similar situation to this that were responsible for her being initially demoted to the Ministry Archives.

Sound huffed through his moustaches. "Need I remind you that enlisting a spectral entity for field operations is not what we do here? Such meddling goes against every law of God, nature, and science."

"Says the man who owns a time machine," the voice from beside her stated coolly.

Eliza could not be certain if Sound was staring at Wellington as incredulously as she was. Where did *that* come from?

"It seems," Sound began, adjusting his glasses on his nose, "that your investigation has become something of an obsession. At least, for one of you. After what happened in India, I can certainly understand why. Jekyll and your family, Books, have a past, as we discovered together at the Water Palace. I believed it would have granted you an advantage." He took a seat at his desk and flipped open a folder before him. "Instead, it is affecting your judgement in the field, and you are no closer to capturing Jekyll. We simply can't have that."

The old Eliza D. Braun would have jumped at that suggestion, but the current one could see where he was coming from. Worst still, it made perfect sense. They had not been sloppy, Eliza remained convinced of that. This was more about the downward spiral that some cases follow, similar to Harry and the Rag and Bone Murders. This whole conversation was giving her perspective on just how out-of-control this matter had become.

Wellington sat up taller in his chair. Hopefully, he was also seeing what she was. "Are you suspending us, Director?"

Sound peered at them over the top of his glasses. "Campbell and Hill need to conclude this Ragnarök business before we can progress in your own apprehension of Jekyll. OSM is now on high alert, and according to Agent Spinnett, well aware of his presence in America. We will keep our respective active agents on the lookout, but for the time-being, I believe you both deserve a rest." He touched one of his temples and smiled. "Some time to give the grey matter a bit of a respite."

"Sir," Wellington insisted, "as we speak, he is taking his madness to deeper, darker depths..."

"And we have more than just two skilled agents here at the Ministry of Peculiar Occurrences," Sound stated, now turning his attention to the file before him. "So, take some time. Relax. Enjoy yourselves."

Neither one of them moved.

Sound never looked up from his papers as he added, "If you're unsure, that is an order."

Wellington leaned forward, but Eliza placed her hand on top of his. "Understood, sir."

Doctor Sound knew them both well—perhaps better than anyone outside of each other—so his expression wasn't entirely convinced, but what could he do?

"Very well then, Doctor Sound," Wellington said, returning to his feet. "We will see you in seven days' time."

"This is a leave of absence, Books." Sound clicked his tongue and reached for a fountain pen. As he noted points in the report open before him, he continued his thought. "I will see you in, say, a month's time. Perhaps longer." He then looked up and smiled. "The Empire is rather large. Surely there is one place you would care to visit?"

Wellington glanced at Eliza. "I can think of one."

"Anywhere but there," the director said with a low growl in his voice.

"We will find something," she assured him, forcing a smile. "Thank you for your time. Come along, Agent Books."

They had only taken a few steps before Sound spoke again. "I feel the need to remind you of one thing, Books and Braun." They turned to see Sound standing before a wall of cabinetry behind his desk. Pulling down one of its leaves, Sound revealed the strange clockwork device, the chrono-model that had once been in his office at Miggins Antiquities. "We're nearing the blackout. Somewhere, sometime soon, the chrono-model will stop."

Wellington took a step forward, his eyes locked on the fragile looking device. "So the events of the Diamond Jubilee didn't fix the timeline?"

The director adjusted one of its many tiny dials, shaking his head. "One might have hoped they would, but the disruptive event is still there. Nothing has changed." The concern in his voice was evident and Eliza didn't like that one little bit. "This is why Usher's Ragnarök takes priority over the hunt for Jekyll. I believe Ragnarök may very well be the dark event that brings an end to all things."

"Perhaps it is not an event," Wellington suggested. "Perhaps it is a person."

Eliza didn't dare utter Jekyll's name, but she thought it. Whatever was disrupting this precious timeline of Sound's, it wouldn't surprise her if it was that nefarious scientist.

The director nodded. "I have considered that possibility, but Time does not work so... linearly—otherwise, the end of the Maestro's scheme should have set things right." He motioned for them to take a closer look at the chrono-model. "See this arm? Something will occur that will cause this to drop. It locks the entire device, and then the Age of Darkness I escaped begins. The only way I can describe the manipulation of timelines is likening it to a game of chess played on a variety of dimensions. The timeline could be affected by one person, a megalomaniac. It could be an event, one of a grand scale like the Diamond Jubilee." He folded up the complicated device and tucked it back in the wall. "I believed the Maestro to be both, but I was mistaken. So being completely honest, I have no idea what will trigger the chrono-model."

"Nothing like not knowing when an Apocalypse will befall the world to keep one on their toes."

"I want you to be aware of this event rushing towards us. Remain vigilant." He took his seat once more and let out a long sigh. "It seems our only hope is to fight it when it comes. Now go, enjoy your rest. We will be in touch."

After a moment of tense, awkward silence that Sound ignored, Wellington nodded curtly. "Very good, sir." He opened the door to the office and motioned for Eliza to join him.

As they walked away in silence past her desk, Miss Shillingworth gave them a gentle smile while another man waiting to see the director rose to his feet. His girth was considerable, and he had a moustache a walrus would have been proud of. When he took his bowler off a vast expanse of forehead was revealed. For a plainly dressed man there was something stiff about his bearing.

After he disappeared into Sound's office, something clicked in her head. "Was that the Prince of Wales?"

Wellington looked a bit befuddled, but then his own eyes darted in that very same direction. "I do believe it was."

Together they turned and walked away. "I thought he was in hiding," Eliza whispered. "The queen did attempt to have him killed after all."

Wellington shrugged, opening the door to the lift. "With Her Majesty free of Jekyll's influence, the danger may have lifted." He glanced around them before adding in a hushed tone, "Also, in her rumoured physical condition, he may be needed for more pressing matters."

The weighty matters of the succession however were not for the Ministry to meddle in; there had to be another reason for the Prince's presence. It was a niggling question that would haunt them through their enforced holiday, she was sure.

Once the lift finished its descent, they made their way to the Archives almost on instinct. They might have been told to take a break, but there was no way Wellington was going to pass up a chance to inspect his original project for the Ministry.

"You don't suppose the Queen will pop her clogs soon, do you?" Eliza asked.

Wellington's eyebrows shot up. "Rather a blunt question, Miss Braun, but one can only wonder what sort of withdrawal she suffered from Jekyll's treatments." He squeezed her hand. "Let's see the state of the Archives and then pack."

Once the Archives of the Ministry of Peculiar Occurrences was housed in a giant warehouse under Miggins Antiquities right next to the Thames, its massive analytical engine powered by the river itself. However, when the Maestro destroyed Miggins, the Archives had also fallen—at least, the physical space. Thanks to Sound's time machine, most of the files were saved. Still, Whiterock's basement was not as big as the original, and there had been some argument who would take on the massive responsibility and outstanding standards Wellington had established. The Ministry had over fifty years of case files and artefacts to house, and these rescued records managed to squeeze quite comfortably into his family's former wine cellar and storage rooms.

"I still can't quite wrap my head around all this," Wellington confessed as they reached the bottom of the stairs, and looked around the new Archives. "I used to pretend to be exploring ancient Druid caves down here. Father would be quite cross with me if he ever caught me down here."

"And your mum?"

"She would play along. My colleague in the field, determined to assist in helping me find the lost relic of my expedition." He smiled warmly. "Or, a nice red to go with the evening dinner."

Eliza let out a slight sigh and pulled her hair back into a working woman's bun as she approached the dumb waiter that led to the director's office. "Funny how this contraption would have sent wine and spirits up to the top of your home once upon a time. Now its requests and completed case files for cataloguing from Sound's office. Far nicer than that bloody chute."

"Rather. Every time a case file landed in that basket I would flinch. Especially when it was from..."

"Campbell," they both said in unison.

Eliza clicked her tongue. "His handwriting is appalling."

"Toddlers' doodles are calligraphy in comparison," Wellington added. He then kissed her lightly on the mouth. How she loved it when he was spontaneous. "So, let's see how my modest replacement to the analytical is performing."

She watched Wellington trail over to the latest iteration of the Archives' analytical engine: designed, engineered, and installed based on his specifications. "So, how did they do?"

"It's still working," he admitted. Was there a hint of begrudging respect in his voice? It was similar to one he'd built in London, just smaller. "Axelrod and Blackwell appear to have followed my instructions to the letter. I understand they had to install a new power source. Quite ingenious—geothermal power, similar to what we saw from the Phoenix Society." He spun around to face her. "Absolutely no telling them I used the word 'ingenious' in reference to their work."

She snapped off a tiny salute. "You can trust me."

His mirth receded the longer he looked at the new engine, a hint of melancholy etching itself on his face. She suspected what he was thinking; the Archives might have his touch on it, but it wasn't his anymore. As an active field agent he was forced to give it up. With everything they'd been through in the last few years, he'd shed a lot of his former life. Eliza knew the sensation intimately—she'd experienced the same thing when she left New Zealand. The only way she kept her own loss in check was not to think about it, but now here he was face-to-face with it.

She tried to distract him. "You know Axelrod and Blackwell were not the only ones behind the analytical engine's construction?"

"Oh?"

"Yes, I failed to mention that a recent recruit took a keen interest in the project and showed quite a disposition for the sciences."

"We have been in the field. How did you hear of this?"

"Alice told me"

"Alice?" Wellington glanced at the machine, then back to her. "How would your maid—?"

"Miss Eliza, Mr Books!" Liam's face appeared around the corner of one of the stacks.

Eliza blinked. She hadn't seen the Ministry Seven for months, and now she was reminded that the clock was ticking on their childhood. His face had gone from rather round, to a more adult square jaw, and the spectacles on the tip of his nose gave the young boy a far-too mature look.

Wellington looked like someone had stood on his toes. "Liam, what on earth are you doing here?"

The young man gave him an odd look and then straightened to his full height. "Been working on fulfilling the office of Archivist in the Ministry."

"I didn't even know you could read," Wellington blurted out. Eliza slapped him on his shoulder at this slight to Liam's character.

However the youngster didn't seem to take any offence from it. "Nah, I could, but not very well. Miss Shillingworth says I am a good study though. And this science?" he began, motioning to the engine. "I see why Verity enjoyed it so much. Bloody fun putting that together, it was."

Eliza smiled, thinking, *now there's the Liam I know.* The lad's Cockney accent was definitely toned down. He was doing what the Seven did best: fitting in.

"How are the others?" she asked.

"Oh, makin' do." Liam ruffled his hair. "Most of us got apprenticeships within the Ministry. All well an' good, all except Christopher and Serena. They're..." He must have seen the concern knotted in her brow as he stammered a bit. "Well... they're not so happy about moving out of London. They thought Whiterock was just a place to lie low. Now we seem to be... you know... " and he motioned around them, "layin' down foundations and such."

"Quite," Eliza responded.

Christopher was the eldest of the Seven, so Eliza wasn't surprised the changes bothered him. Serena, however, was a bit of a shock. She might have expected the young girl to bounce back a bit better. Even though Phantom Protocol had driven them out the city, the House of Usher was on the rise. It was never a safe place, London, for the Ministry Seven, but on account of their association with Eliza, they were assets. That meant the danger was far worse, more imminent.

Wellington cleared his throat. "And you are enjoying it here, in the Archives?"

Liam shrugged, as his hand dropped on the keys of the analytical engine. "Gotta say at first I didn't care for it, but once we got this engine in order I started to come around."

It did not go unnoticed by Eliza that Wellington flinched at that, but she tucked her fingers around his and gave them a reassuring squeeze. He nodded and smiled—perhaps a fraction stiffly.

"Well, I am glad of it. Perhaps the Archives might not be the most adventurous assignment, but I enjoyed it a great deal. Quite the challenge, and essential to the operation of the Ministry." Was she imagining it, or did his eyes get a little glassy as he spoke? "But everything must change. I'm happy to see you find a place."

"A little less adventure seems like a mighty fine thing," Liam said in a low voice.

The young man's sober look was a reminder that it wasn't just she and Wellington affected by recent events. The Seven had lost one of their members and seen London torn apart. She would have liked to talk with them about it all, but their own pursuit of Jekyll had sent her off within weeks of the Diamond Jubilee's clean-up. As street urchins, they had seen plenty of horrors. The Ministry had always offered them a chance for a taste of adventure in the streets and abroad. The events of the Jubilee, however, were a very different matter.

Wellington and Liam shared a look, and Eliza saw in them the same thing: terrible childhoods overcome, battles won.

"Perhaps we should go," she suggested to Wellington. "Leave Liam to his work, and we can pack."

Wellington nodded, absently touching the knot in his bowtie. "Yes, that sounds like a grand idea."

They went back up the stairs, Liam's gentle humming of a music hall ditty growing further off until they emerged on the main floor of the manor.

"I think he will do very well," Wellington commented, though from her angle she could not see his face.

"He has changed a lot, matured quickly," Eliza agreed, "and as we know, the Archives is a place of sanctuary."

He didn't offer any additional thoughts on the new Archives, and she knew better than to press the matter. Wellington was still at odds with not contributing to the reconstruction. The important thing was the new Archives appeared to be in safe hands with young Liam.

As they continued down the corridor to the main staircase, Wellington let out a long, almost contented sigh. Whiterock had been his childhood home, full of terrible memories and haunted by the ghost of his maniacal father. Now it was bustling with the activity of the Ministry. The kitchens further down the hallway were putting forth tempting smells of roast meat, and Eliza supposed soon the recruits would be enjoying their repast in the grand dining room, now lined with far more utilitarian benches to accommodate everyone. Ascending to the second floor, they could hear the rumble of earnest conversations between field agents either returning from or about to embark on assignments.

Yet here amongst their fellow agents was not where she wanted to be. Tugging on Wellington's arm, she whispered, "Race you home!"

It was hardly a fair challenge as she was wearing her preferred attire of trousers and a short jacket. Even as practised as running in heels and a corset as she was, she would never have beaten him. His hazel eyes lit up with a sudden burst of his competitive nature just before they barrelled down the hallway. She managed to get a good start on him, bounding up the first set of stairs before his longer legs stood him in good stead on taking the lead. They nearly collided with Agent Peter Atkins in their sprint, his stack of papers threatening to topple as Eliza slid around him. Wellington stopped to steady the man and his workload, his kind deed granting her an advantage once more.

"I say—cheating!" her partner yelled up to her as she raced on.

Wellington soon made up the ground again, her elbow to his ribs no avail as they raced down the final hallway towards large, ornate doors. Eliza's palm slapped onto the maple first, a proclamation of her victory.

"Now just a moment," he said, resting next to her and crossing his arms. "I would at best call that a tie."

After considering him for a moment, Eliza decided kissing him was a far better option. Then she drew back and touched one of her fingertips to his nose. "Just admit it: I won."

His eyebrows raised, but he smiled. "If it means that much to you, fine... *I won.*"

Before she could kiss him once more in spite of his impertinence, the door opened, and they both sprawled across the floor.

"Mr Books! Miss Braun!" Alice said with a twist of her lips. "I thought you two were the Seven children with all that noise!"

He flushed an adorable shade of red. "It was very much Miss Braun's idea."

Alice shook her head. "Well, either way, it is good to see you. Come in, I think you will like what I have done with the place."

Eliza and Wellington entered the master chambers with some amount of trepidation. Though Wellington had given the Ministry free use of Whiterock, he had not given up the grand master wing on the third floor. After the Diamond Jubilee, it was not just the Seven who had decamped to the Yorkshire countryside; both Eliza and Wellington had given up their houses in the City. However, the physical move itself was left in Alice's capable hands. How she would manage to fit out two people's residences into one—albeit large—floor of a country manor had been worrying to Eliza. She wasn't married to her home, but she had over the years collected some rather nice things.

"Oh Alice," she said, staring around, "you've done a marvellous job."

Wellington too looked rather surprised and delighted by what she had done while they had been in the field. The sitting room was full of a mixture of their treasures. The Venus sculpture she had acquired from a dealer in Brussels. His favourite rug in front of the fireplace. The picture of his mother above the mantle.

And there, sitting on the overstuffed chair Eliza considered a favourite reading location, was the cream-coloured fluffy shape of Wellington's cat, Archimedes. He raised his handsome face with the gold eyes and let out a little chirrup of welcome.

While Wellington went to pet him, Eliza gave Alice a hug and kissed her cheek. "Thank you so much, Alice," but then her smile fell as she considered the toll. "How are you able to manage all this and still continue with your own field training?"

The maid smiled and shrugged. "Nowhere near as complicated as getting the Seven to that safe house in France. Now *that* was a challenge."

"And are the Ministry chaps all treating you well?" Eliza tilted her head and squeezed together her eyebrows into what she hoped was her best furious stare. "Because if not I can go down there and knock some heads together."

"Oh, the lads and lasses are fine," Alice replied. "Though that Shillingworth bint gave me a spot of bother in the beginning, but we've come to an arrangement. She doesn't come up here and give me orders and I don't blow holes in her skirts when on the range." The maid tapped her right leg, which rang out hollow and metal. So—the shotgun was still in her prosthetic leg.

Wellington shot her a glance, but didn't seem to dare to get in the middle of that conversation. Eliza thought that was a very wise choice.

"So are you in for a bit?" Alice asked, and the tone of her voice suggested she hoped the answer was 'yes.' Still she had been Eliza's maid for long enough to know the answer she would most likely get.

"We have orders to take leave. Indefinitely," Eliza replied. She chewed the inside of her lip before adding, "The Director believes we need some time to rest, think things over."

"If you want my opinion," Alice whispered, glancing over her shoulder as if someone was lurking in the shadows, "you should keep going until you hunt that bastard Jekyll down. He's no match for the likes of you or Mr Books here."

"He is proving rather elusive," Wellington said, petting the purring Archimedes.

"Then I'll put the kettle on," Alice said. "We have all the modern conveniences up here. A cup of tea will set you right, allow you to consider potential scenarios and likely hideouts as you pack," she offered with a sly wink. Then she bustled off, with only the slightest of limps in her gait.

Eliza rubbed Archimedes' chin, which he lifted for her to access. "I am not sure even tea can fix this."

It disturbed her to see that Wellington looked to be in total agreement.

CHAPTER FOUR

In Which Dark Delights Are Indulged

Wilber Inversill tried to relax. Considering the circumstances, considering the breath-taking woman before him, grabbing hold of that calm was elusive. If he could just do that, then perhaps she would feel it too. Their eyes communicated so much to each other at the moment. Barely a word needed to be uttered. If she understood him in this silence, then perhaps his own calm would carry over to her.

When she stepped out of from behind the screen, his breath jammed in his throat. She wore breeches that were more like jodhpurs. The form fitting pants showed off her fine toned legs, causing his base instincts to ignite. At first she cast her eyes downward, but then glanced up at him. After a long, silent moment shared between them—she began to turn in place, as if she were the tiny ballerina in the open jewellery box, dancing *en pointe*. As the music box continued its sweet melody from the darkness, she slowly slid her hands across her hips and buttocks. With fingers splayed and palms pressing into the fabric of her breeches, her gestures remained languid. The whole thing was a dream to him, but he found the crimson curls that cascaded down her shoulders, framing her sweet face irresistible. She was a nymph from the faerie-realm, crossing the Veil to be with him.

Wilbur took in a long, slow breath, terrified that his deep draw of the warm air might shatter the serenity of the moment. If all he heard was the music box, then he knew there would be no cause for concern. If only he could sit still enough, he would maintain this illusion. When he shifted in his seat, he did so as quietly as he could. The sound of his own suit rubbing against the fabric of the fine leather chair he occupied was deafening to his ears.

Still, the music box played on, even when she stopped her turn. The blouse she wore would have been better suited for a man. In fact it was proper button-up shirt, admittedly with the top three buttons undone; and in the candlelight of their boudoir, shadows flickered and frolicked along the curve of her breasts. She was nothing like his wife.

He pushed the thoughts of home and family to the farthest corners of his mind. While the notion of mind reading was nothing more than purest poppycock reserved for carnivals and back parlour trickery, Wilbur did not want to leave anything to chance. Who knew what was possible?

She took a few more steps closer, her wide eyes never leaving his. There was no questioning it—she felt the same as he did, and that bought a tingle underneath his skin. Fire raged in his blood, and yet he dug his fingers deeper into his chair's armrests. The sweet smell from the candles—*was it vanilla?*—made him slightly dizzy, but he remained where he sat. The time was not right. He had to wait.

The woman dropped to her knees, and like a cat, she slinked across the floor towards him. Wilbur grew more and more uncomfortable, most especially in his crotch. His body betrayed his higher moral standings and ached to have her lips on his own. He longed to feel her breath against his flesh, hot and delicious against his skin. Maddening as this all was, a part of Wilbur knew it would be delightful.

Her fingers fumbled with the buttons of his shirt. On freeing the fourth button, she pushed the fabric open. Her fingertips tickled the hair running across his chest, and his breath shuddered in his throat.

"Does this please you?" she whispered.

Oh yes, it did. Wilbur did not want it to do so, but it did. And if he lied...

"Yes," he stammered. It was something of a small miracle he could speak at all with his emotions lost in a maelstrom.

"I want to please you," she said with a gasp, her touch turning from a caress into a slight tremble.

She wouldn't look up at him. He needed to see into her eyes. It was strange how he drew strength from her. It made no sense, but he did, and he longed for that connection.

"You will," he assured her.

Wilbur let go of his chair and put his arms around the beautiful girl. She was so lovely, so delicate. She should not be here. He didn't even know her name, but there she was. With him. Tumbling deeper and deeper into this darkness.

He pulled her closer, and when her lips touched his skin, he gasped. He had hoped his moment of ecstasy had not been too loud. Wilbur swallowed through the sudden tightness in his throat and nodded. His hand absently stroked the back of the girl's head and said again, "You will."

She finally looked up at him, and he smiled. He hoped the gesture offered her something.

"Tell me your name."

The *snap* of the music box made both of them jump, and the tears that she had been holding back crept free of her eyes. He kept his gaze locked with hers, but his silent imploring was not enough. He hoped the slight shake of his head was discernible.

"You know her name," the gravelly voice insisted from the shadows of the parlour. "Don't you?"

"Why, yes," Wilbur said, trying to calm his breathing. So long as he didn't see their host, he would be able to keep his semblance of bravery intact. "Of course I do."

"Say it," the monster growled.

"Beg your pard—"

Each word grew in their tenor. He was getting angry. *"Speak. Her. Name."*

Wilbur nodded. He wiped the woman's tears away and tried to make his smile appear strong, confident. "You will please me, Eliza. I have no doubt."

A soft *click* from a latch, and the music box began once more.

"She is beautiful, your Eliza, isn't she?" asked the monster.

"Yes," Wilbur replied. "Yes, my Eliza is quite beautiful."

The music box played for a few notes, uninterrupted, and then the monster spoke. "Touch her."

He took a moment and traced the curve of her breast with the back of his fingers. Her skin was softer than he imagined. If he wasn't already married to another, had they not been under the watchful eye of this perverse creature, he would have found this encounter tantalising. His body thrilled at the prospects of what the evening would offer. Even his rational mind could not suppress base, animal instincts. Perhaps he did want this complete stranger in a carnal fashion. Perhaps his physical reactions to her was a betrayal of everything proper in society.

That did not change the fact that they were both prisoner to a madman, and their fate rested in this little pantomime they performed for his pleasure.

"Does this please you, Eliza?" Wilbur asked.

The girl nodded quickly.

"Now," the monster sighed. Wood creaked as he leaned back in his chair. "Consummate."

Wilbur wanted to look at the monster, wanted to refuse crossing this last boundary between himself and this stranger. If he were to see the beast, all notion of reality and sanity would disappear. The gentleman he had met in the pub had been so kind, so charming. No indication of this bizarre macabre play Wilbur and this girl were creating for the Doctor's pleasure.

He looked to the girl and gave her the slightest of nods. If they led the monster along with this charade, and found the right moment to act, they might just live through the night.

It was at least a hope.

CHAPTER FIVE

In Which Our Dashing Archivist and Colonial Pepperpot Are Called Upon

*S*alcombe in April was particularly lovely. Not too hot, not too cold, and provided it was not raining, it was the perfect sort of weather for some brisk exercise. Certainly, there was plenty of that to be had in this sleepy corner of Devon.

"Coming from me, Wellington, this may shock you," Eliza grunted, "but you are quite mad."

Several hundred feet underneath them both, the English Channel stirred languidly. The waters were particularly blue when observed from this height, but the horizon was not quite clear enough to see their French neighbours. Wellington continued a few inches upward. Hand up. Left foot. Right foot. Push from the legs. Secure a hold on the left hand. He looked around and exhaled. *Breath-taking,* he thought, taking in the jagged coastline they were currently climbing.

"We are supposed to be relaxing!" Eliza called out as she also ascended in the same fashion. Albeit with less confidence.

Wellington slid one of the pneumatic spikes up along their safety rope and placed it where his right hand had been. When he pressed its head, the spike let out a short quick *ffpop!* before securing itself into the rock. Leaning back into his rope, he called down to Eliza. "Do you mean to tell me they do not have mountains in your hemisphere?"

Eliza shot him a rather nasty look. How he did enjoy goading her like that. "I will have you know New Zealand is home to the Remarkables, the Craigie Burn Range, and of course, Mount Cook."

"Mount Cook? Why does that sound familiar?"

Wellington's smile faltered a bit as he watched her hands fumble for purchase. Eliza grunted through clenched teeth as she tucked her legs underneath her and pushed upward. "That is where Douglas trained for his summiting of Mount Everest. I trust you remember Douglas Sheppard?"

Right. That one he deserved. "I would love to make the threat that I could cut your safety line and let you fall to your untimely end, but I'm concerned you may not need my help in that."

"Truth be told, Welly, I only covered the basics of mountaineering when I was on a probationary period with the Ministry." She grimaced as she pulled herself upward. From the coil of rope across her chest, she slid a similar spike up to the rock, pressed the head with her thumb, and with a *ffpop!* the spike was secured. "That was years ago and I do not recall Mount Ruapehu being this vertical—and we didn't have these Mountaineers helping us along."

Wellington let out a snort. "Hammering in spikes by hand?"

"Believe me, I was a certified expert at hammering in spikes by the time we summited."

"Nothing wrong with sharpening the skills, Eliza, wot?"

"But Sound did say he wanted us to relax."

Wellington motioned around them. "Don't you find this relaxing?"

"I might, if we were on one of those boats floating by. You know? Those boats, hundreds of feet below us."

She was now eye-to-eye with him, her cheeks ruddier than usual.

"A bit further, darling," Wellington said, giving her his best smile.

Eliza inclined her head. "If it were anyone else…"

He stole a kiss from her, cutting off her words and earning a little, soft moan from her. That maddened him, and Eliza was fully aware of this.

The kiss would soften the blow of what he was about to offer. "One piece of advice: Three points of contact at all times." Wellington pulled on his safety line to bring himself closer to the rock. He called out as he placed his right foot on a rock jutting out to one side of him. "Right foot. Left foot," he said as he tucked his left foot into a small space in front of his stomach. "Right hand," he said as he stretched his hand above him. "And push." He left Eliza several feet underneath him as he lifted himself upward. Once his legs had straightened, and only when he was steady,

Wellington released the stone face in his left hand and moved it up closer to him. "So long as you maintain those three points…"

"You climb your way…" Eliza huffed as she looked for footholds. She paused. "My apologies, Welly. Give me a moment."

He looked back down at her, his free hand slipping back to the grappling gun holstered on his hip. "Everything all right there, Eliza?"

"This terrain is… well… Ruapehu has slightly different footholds." She placed her left hand above her, then lifted her left foot up, placing it and the inside of her leg flat against the rock.

"Well, it's a volcano, yes?"

"Luckily for us, slumbering but not quite sleeping," Eliza quipped as she tucked her knee into her stomach, and pushed with her legs while tightening her grip on the rock underneath her left hand.

Strands of unbound chestnut hair danced across her forehead and face. Sunlight suddenly hit her on this ascent, revealing the deep red traces in these wayward curls. He smiled on thinking that this was why he liked challenging Eliza. He would miss the fire in her eyes and that wicked smile of hers and sometimes goading her would kindle that. Not that he did not also enjoy the contentment in her face when she slept next to him. The peace her face reflected when they were close, her smooth skin against his…

"Wellington…"

Eliza had covered the distance quite easily between them.

"See?" He smiled at her. "Child's play."

"You are quite the randy tomcat, aren't you?"

"Whatever do you mean, Eliza?"

"I know that look in your eye, Welly," she said, before engaging another Mountaineer into the rock face. "I wonder if teaching me something new or proving me wrong does not serve as some kind of aphrodisiac with you."

"Perhaps I wanted you to pass me in our climb," Wellington said, keeping his eyes on Eliza's posterior, "to enjoy the delightful view."

"Actually, I passed you," she said leaning back expertly, giving Wellington that wicked smile he did so love, "so I could return the favour."

She was easily ten feet in front of him now, so she would reach the cliff's edge first.

That suited him fine. He would have the final word, regardless.

He had managed to pull himself up another five feet when he heard Eliza make the discovery. "Oh! Welly! This is *DELIGHTFUL!!!*"

My skills are adequately sharpened, he thought, drawing the pistol from his hip. *I'm ready for lunch.*

The pistol fired its hook up to the edge above him. Giving his safety line enough slack, Wellington engaged the winch. His stomach lurched as he was hoisted up to the cliff's edge. Catching the edge of the rock extending overhead with one hand, he swung gently there for a moment, even after his second hand got purchase overhead. He found leverage for his right foot, but completing the climb became all the easier when Eliza took hold of his right arm.

"You have outdone yourself this time, Wellington Thornhill Books."

"Tosh," he returned with a slight laugh. "The Director said he wanted us to relax, so that is what we shall do."

"But how do you get all this up here?"

"A very large, efficiently stuffed backpack, and modern technology. These two innovations make our climb a trifle," he said, freeing the grappling hook from the rock face.

Wellington holstered the pistol, and turned to face Eliza who was walking around the setting, clapping her hands together. Between them was a complete luncheon with a fine white wine chilling in a small bucket at the centre. It had been quite an effort to be sure, and he would probably nurse a somewhat tender back the next day... but for the smile on her face, it was all worthwhile.

"The chicken should still be warm," Wellington said as he took a seat on the picnic blanket. "I paired it with a white wine. A *pinot gris* is what you prefer, yes?"

"You spoil me in every way," Eliza said with a little curtsy.

"No, I understand that if I cock up anything, it should not be..." he paused as he pulled the cork free of the bottle, took a quick sniff from the open end of it, and nodded, "... the wine. Now come sit and join me. That climb must have given you quite the appetite."

"Rather," Eliza said, finally taking a spot opposite him.

For a moment, there were only sounds of wind skimming along the grass and the soft tearing of chicken as they tucked into their private, scenic luncheon.

"All right, now I am relaxed," Eliza said, taking a sip of wine as she stared out over the channel.

"Then my mission is not only complete, but a rousing success." Wellington lifted his glass and extended it to Eliza. "Here's to following the Old Man's orders."

She nodded, touching her glass with his. "Without question, and to the letter."

"That climb of yours was hardly to the letter," a voice said from behind them. "You looked as if you were struggling there a bit, Miss Braun."

Eliza and Wellington shot looks over their shoulders. *"Doctor Sound?"* they exclaimed in unison.

"This is a bit of a surprise, I am sure," he admitted, leaning into his walking stick.

"As you can see we were not expecting company; we only have two wine glasses," Wellington said, taking another sip.

"We were under the impression that we were on mandatory leave," Eliza said, with a slight note of annoyance in her voice.

"And those *were* my orders," he said, looming over the idyllic setting. He motioned with his hand at the picnic and smiled warmly. "I must say this is very romantic."

"It *was*," Eliza seethed. "You certainly did not find us with our Ministry rings, seeing as we left those behind once ordered to take a holiday. So how did you do it?"

"Very astute of you, Miss Braun," Sound stated without answering her question. Instead he pointed at their plate. "Oh those cucumber sandwiches look delightful."

"I wouldn't believe for a moment that Alice would reveal our destination," Wellington said to Eliza. "She will make a fine agent to the Ministry, but she's loyal to you first."

"That she is, and that loyalty is not broken, I assure you."

Eliza shook her head before asking Wellington, "You didn't tell Bruce we were coming to Salcombe, did you?"

"Why would I tell Agent Campbell of our holiday plans?" he blurted. "It's not like we are ending the work day over pints at the pub."

"Besides, Campbell is still in the field."

Wellington could plainly see their Director was enjoying flummoxing them.

"That rules out Hill as well," Eliza said, polishing off her wine. She immediately refilled her glass as she thought aloud, "I didn't mention anything to Cassandra, not that I had an opportunity to do so."

"My, it's a bit like a Sherlock Holmes mystery, eh wot?" Sound's eyes widened as he motioned to the bowl of fruit. "Oh, those grapes are quite tempting. Would you mind?"

Wellington took the small bunch and offered them up. *"Bon appétit."*

"Merci," the director said, popping a few off their stem and into his mouth.

She glanced at her glass, half full of wine, and continued to pour, muttering, "We. Can't. Win."

"Give up?" the director asked, a gleam of victory in his eye.

Eliza crossed her arms and glowered, so Wellington had to be the one to concede. "Yes," he said, "yes, we do."

The director shrugged. "Your protégé Serena does love to talk about you."

Wellington was a little surprised, but the Ministry Seven had rather made themselves at home at Whiterock, and it wasn't as if their location was a state secret.

"So am I to assume," Wellington said, holding his own glass towards Eliza. He could hear wine pour as he continued, "that we are being called back in?"

"I have an æthergate waiting for us, yes." Sound looked a little upset at not being offered a glass.

"An æthergate?" Eliza asked with a crook of her eyebrow. "You must be desperate."

"We were a hazard to Ministry operations and reprimanded for it. Not officially, but strongly encouraged to take leave. And now, you have *personally* come to call us back in?" Wellington toasted the director. "And here I thought there were more than two skilled agents at the Ministry of Peculiar Occurrences."

Sound glanced at them both for a moment before giving them a curt nod. "I suppose I have brought this upon myself, but yes, I need you in the office. Now."

"Would you mind if we finished lunch first?" Wellington asked, glancing hopefully at the sandwiches. It had been rather a bother getting it all up here.

Sound tossed the remaining grapes over the edge of the cliff face and tightened his grip on his walking stick. "Yes, I do." He no longer had any laughter in his voice, and Wellington understood the jovial director was now long gone.

Eliza flicked her eyes to one side, and they shared an understanding. In such little ways had they learned to communicate in the field. It worked as well with Sound.

If he was being curt, it had to be serious. Luncheon was quite wasted, but such was the lot of an agent.

CHAPTER SIX

Where a Last Resort Is Employed

"Alms?" her voice croaked. "Alms for the poor?"

Her hands trembled, her fingertips stinging with the morning's cold. She took another deep breath, the smell of Florence's nightwater filling her nostrils. They'd rinse the drains soon, and the tantalising odours of fresh-baked bread and brewed coffee would replace the stench. Visitors from other countries would walk the streets, peruse the shops, examine wares they offered, and dine at the various restaurants. That was still hours away though. Mornings belonged to the working class, those labourers and businessmen, scurrying off to their work places. In this narrow alleyway, she'd found a spot, and even picked up a few coins from passers-by.

Examining the people walking around she did see a few tourists out though. They probably wanted to get going early before the crowds started. Watching carefully, she hoped the kindly foreigner who had become a regular past this spot would appear. He never hesitated to offer her coin. Many of the locals gave her disdainful looks for begging. She was, after all, the reflection they did not care to see. She embodied the less fortunate side of their country. With all the struggles Italy had been through, generosity was tempered with cold logic. *If you have the strength to beg for money, then you have the strength to work.* Maybe for a few more days, they would tolerate her presence at this spot. She had already been there for three weeks. It was high time for her to kick herself off the ground to find good, honest work. That was the Italian way.

Today was different though; her heartbeat raced when she spotted his flawless top hat high above the other pedestrians. He was very distinctive; standing a full foot taller than the Italians, and wearing a sharp, tailored black ensemble.

Strangely enough, she suspected he knew how important he was to her, how her survival had become reliant on his generosity. Perhaps he perceived his coins less of a charity and more of an investment—one he could use in the future.

"Alms for the poor?" she begged, lifting her hand up a fraction higher.

"Good morning, love," he said to her with a crooked smile. This was the first time he actually talked to her. She always hoped he would stop for a moment, but to actually speak to her? "I do hope these coins are a help to you," he said, dropping money into her open palm.

"May God bless you and keep, sir," she managed.

"There is no need for that," her benefactor returned, looking to either side of him. Pedestrians were milling about, paying no heed of either one of them. Strange how in such a public place, the two of them shared a modicum of privacy. "Your state is one of man's greatest tragedies, and whatever has fallen upon you, I can only say I am truly sorry."

"Thank you, sir."

"I have noticed you here for some time, and I want to help beyond this morning's meagre offering." The gentlemen leaned in even further, closer to her than he had ever been. "I work for people that can help. If you are willing, perhaps we can assist one another."

"God bless you, sir," she said looked up into his eyes. His face grew even paler as recognition flashed across it. "So long as you are willing, Brother Streeper."

The coins in her palm clattered against the sidewalk as one hand slapped around his wrist while her second hovered over his pulse point.

"One tap," she warned him, "and ten minutes later you collapse from a stroke."

He did not make a move. Brother Streeper knew not to challenge her in this matter. She was mistress of poisons and toxins. She understood what they would do and how quickly they would take to kill.

"Now then, you will be so kind as to help me to my feet." She moved the needle closer to his skin. "Do take care, lest I slip."

"As you wish, Madame del Morte," he replied.

With his free arm, Brother Streeper reached underneath Sophia's elbow and gingerly lifted her up. She motioned with her head to the alleyway. They slipped deeper in between the stone buildings, far away from pedestrians' eyes. She wanted her time with the House of Usher completely and utterly void any distraction.

Sophia released her grip and took two steps back, holding her hands up in surrender. "As difficult as you may find this to believe, I mean you no harm."

Brother Streeper reached into his coat and pulled out a "Crackshot" that Sophia did not detect. Impressive, considering the bulk of the Wilkinson-Webley creation. The compressors hissed as he took aim at her forehead. "Tell me why I should not pull the trigger here and now."

"Because my death will bring down the House."

His fingers flexed around the handle of his pistol. He wore the uncertainty in his gaze much like his suit from the House. It was evident, pronounced, and fit him like a glove. Sophia remained quiet. She had nothing to offer him in this moment. If he killed her, it might well put her out of her misery.

Streeper took a step closer, his face still reflecting a little confusion. "I would imagine killing you, would move me several steps up the Usher ladder. You have quite the price on your head."

"Something we share in common," she returned.

"What do you mean?"

"I do have a bounty on my head from the House of Usher, that is true. Just as the House of Usher has a bounty on it from the House of del Morte."

She was surprised, if not flattered, by the shock and sympathy that crossed Brother Streeper's face. Perhaps he believed blood truly was thicker than water, that a family's bond and commitment to one another was stronger than the brotherhood. "Your family marked you as a target?"

"Those who survived Usher's onslaught hold me responsible. Had I not overheard my own Nonna and sisters talking, they would have brought me before a tribunal. I would have stood before *mia famiglia* and held to account for what they believe I caused."

"To some extent, it is you fault." Brother Streeper wore a slight sneer. Sophia lifted one eyebrow in response to the insult. For someone so caught off guard, he had found his courage somewhere. "Usher never forgets. You killed our own. You broke a contract."

"Oh, that again?" Sophia rolled her eyes, emitting a soft groan. "If you wish to talk semantics, we can, with the contract in front of me. As for those in your order that I killed—" Sophia shrugged, "—they knew the risk they faced. If not, then they were fools."

"So why reach out to me? You know of my standing in the house. Merely a footman. What sway will I carry?"

Sophia nodded, looking him up and down for a moment. This much was true. Streeper had served as a liaison between her and the House of Usher. It was something of a surprise that he had not accompanied Alexander that fateful night at her hotel in London.

"All it would take would be one æthermissive, and the House would send someone to collect you."

"Ah, but you I have dealt with before." A shudder passed through her body as she added, "The last emissary the House sent unsettled me. Greatly."

Brother Streeper fussed with the lapels of his suit as he paced between the two buildings. Occasionally, he glanced up at her, perhaps searching for some sort of tell that would let him know her plan.

Sophia's patience was wearing thin, "If I wanted you dead, I would be talking to myself at this point."

"So, you reach out to your old contact Ronald Streeper, not by appointment but through deception. Then you ask for asylum in the House of Usher, the very organisation that has a price on your head." Brother Streeper stopped in his pacing and closed the distance between them. "Why would I want to work with an assassin cast out of her own family?"

Sophia refuse to flinch at how close he was to her. Any man drawing this near to her would either be trying to steal a kiss or, for the more foolhardy, tempting her to bed. His breath reeked, teeming with some sort of early morning gunpowder tea. Typically British.

"Consider this, Brother Streeper, I alone found you in the streets of Florence, and managed to get you in this alleyway. Imagine what an army of Sophia del Morte's, all of them sworn to vengeance, could do." She tipped her head back, smiling ever so slightly. "Without my help, you will never see them coming."

Those words did sink in with Brother Streeper. With her limited-to-scarce resources, Sophia was able to track down a member of the House of Usher. It had been her good fortune that the one she found was a former contact. Her deception had been long and patient, just like her family's would be with the House of Usher. They would begin with small underlings; runners first, then, known associates. Because there were still twenty or so of her family remaining, they would be able to accomplish far more in a shorter amount of time compared to her solo operation. She knew what they were capable of, and she had to make sure to get into Usher first.

She could see the same conclusion was becoming apparent to Streeper's mind—he wore it on his face.

"How do you propose to proceed?" he finally asked.

Sophia dug into her filthy rags, searching for a small satchel she wore at her hip. "I need you get in touch with Mr Badger."

"You want *Badger* to bring you in?" Streeper barked a dry laugh. "You are aware that he is the one that issued the order against your family?"

"The del Mortes, or at least what is left of them, is no longer my family. They are hunting me. If they are after me, then they are most assuredly stalking Badger." She pulled from her tattered dress the object she had wrapped up in her Nonna's handkerchief, the last reminder of her grandmother. "It is imperative that I see Badger gets to safety."

Streeper's gaze narrowed. "Quite the tale you tell, Signora."

"You have no idea," Sophia said, opening the kerchief for Streeper to reveal the contents within it, "the depth of this tale."

Streeper's eyes grew wide. True, it was quite the story, but there was merit embedded within it. His answer would be true test of trust between them.

"I will have to make few queries. I know he was receiving a new carrier from the Americas." Streeper shook his head, his eyes staring at what rested in Nonna's handkerchief. "This complicates things, you realise?"

"Dear Ronald," Sophia began, folding up the handkerchief to stuff back into her satchel, "complicated things will not matter one bit if Badger is dead. Whatever you need to do, whoever you need to contact, do it now. I will be where you found me this morning, where you have found me every morning for the past three weeks, and then you will give me orders." Sophia threw back the shawl over her head, hunched over, and took on the semblance of an old beggar crone, homeless and destitute in the streets of Florence. With the creak back in her voice, she said, "If tomorrow comes and goes, so will I. If that is the case, then I wish you good luck. You will need it."

With her walking stick tapping ahead, Sophia went from the alleyway back into the busy streets of Florence. She gathered up what few belongings she had and disappeared into the flood of her fellow countrymen set on their morning rituals. It was now up to Brother Streeper. Either he would appear the next day, offering her a purpose, or she would remain a ghost walking among the living in the streets of Florence.

Sophia stopped at a street corner and dared to glance out from under her cowl. *Mia dio,* she prayed silently, *please do not fail me.*

CHAPTER SEVEN

In Which a Mad Scientist Plays a Game

After seeing the damage the æthergates did to members of Nahush Kari's Ghost Rebellion, Eliza was less than thrilled to step through one herself. She had to remind herself that the ones Kari took advantage of were not true æthergates, but shoddy imitations of what the Ministry and Usher battled over in the depths of the Atlantic.

A knot formed in her stomach when she saw the swirling circular rift with Doctor Sound's Whiterock office just visible on the other side.

"Come along," he said, beckoning her and Wellington to follow him.

Eliza couldn't help her expression tightening into disapproval.

Wellington squeezed her hand. "This sort of travel is an unfortunate side-effect of our service to Queen and Empire, darling."

"This and the hypocrisy are just too much. Wasn't it just last month, he ordered us to go on leave?"

"Circumstances have apparently changed." With a tug on his coat lapels, Wellington walked past her towards the portal. "No time to be a slugabed, Eliza. *Avanté!*"

Now she was alone in Salcombe, and making the jump herself. Safety was once again being left behind. It might have taken close on three weeks, but they'd finally found comfort and relaxation, and now they were just giving it all up.

"Fine then," she grumbled to no one before stepping into the void.

A tingle ran across her skin, the fine hairs along her arms rising, a rush of blood in her veins. *Maybe this isn't so bad,* she thought.

That very moment, the sensation of her insides being yanked forward while simultaneously being shoved backward fell on her. She came close to losing her lunch within the æthergate. Who knew what that would do? Nevertheless, she resisted her body's demands, and pushed forward through the bizarre maelstrom of energy and light. It all was all over in a matter of seconds; and when Eliza stopped moving, she was on the other side of the portal and in Doctor Sound's office at Whiterock.

She did not recall stumbling but when the world slipped back into focus, Eliza found herself in the arms of her lover. Wellington gave her a warm smile and asked as delicately as he could, "So, how's the stomach?"

Eliza nodded and held up a single finger. Taking a few deep breaths, she risked speaking. "I think my previous repasts will stay put."

"Excellent, better constitution than mine. Fortunately, Doctor Sound had a waste bin at the ready. I owe Miss Shillingworth flowers or perhaps a modest tea setting in exchange for taking care of that."

"She adores a good Willow pattern," Doctor Sound suggested as he walked over to his desk. "Now, if you please..." He motioned to two empty chairs in front of his desk.

Wellington and Eliza took their respective seats as Sound sipped from the teacup that was waiting for him. He gave a pleasant nod at its taste, then shifted dossiers around on his desk. Just audible outside were the sounds of the latest batch of new agents practising their *ju jitsu* on the bright green lawn.

The director's face adjusted into his tell-tale scowl which he usually wore in response to a taxing case, and Eliza breathed a bit easier. Even though summoned back from leave, it was reassuring that they were not being called in because they'd done something unseemly or worse.

Granted, she enjoyed being unseemly with Wellington, and while on holiday they'd made up for lost time. She let out a muffled sigh as the director addressed them.

"This came from Scotland Yard two weeks after you'd left for Devon," he said, sliding one of the dossiers over to them. "The man's name was Wilbur Inversill. The lady's name, Esther Simmons."

The man wore a beautifully tailored suit. *A rather fine cut,* Eliza thought. He also had spectacles as well as being groomed in a most gentlemanly fashion. Unfortunately, the man's clothes and face were stained horribly by the gash in his neck. His body lay twisted at an odd angle, but Eliza noted his bowler was much like the way his spectacles appeared—straight, neat, and clean. Not a drop of blood on the lenses or hatband. He was holding the hand of the lady at his side, her throat also cut in a brutal fashion.

"The angle of the man's body is odd," Eliza noted, tapping the photograph.

Doctor Sound peered at her from over his spectacles. "How so, Agent Braun?"

"Well, for starters, his body appears to have dropped where he fell from blood loss," she said, motioning across the photo from top to bottom, "but after he fell, someone had flipped him over. He landed face down, but died on his back."

Wellington, studied the image over her shoulder. "Yes, post-mortem he has been turned, otherwise there would have been more blood on the carpet. His suit is stained more than where he landed."

"And look at his arm here. His right is at a straight angle. That had to be posed."

"Very astute, agents," Sound said.

Eliza followed the man's arm over to the woman. The corset she wore transformed her hips, waist, and bust into an attractive hourglass figure; the cleavage created bordered on the scandalous. Even more eyebrow raising were the tight breeches she wore. It was a style and a fashion Eliza could appreciate.

"So they were lovers?" Eliza asked.

"From what the Yard tells us, they were complete strangers. Both happened to be in Paris at the same time. He resides in the Wimbledon area. She was from Cornwall. Just embarking on a holiday, tragically." The director deposited another dossier on top of the one opened before them. "Now, this case. Lucius Northall and Isabella Bradley. Again, seemingly total strangers. Found dead at a train station in Plymouth. He was a construction worker. She was a rather influential haberdasher, quite the seamstress tycoon it seems."

Eliza opened the file and gave a slight gasp.

The couple were holding hands, their throats torn in a similar manner to the other couple. Their fashion almost identical. He was wearing spectacles and a bowler, again both touches immaculate. Her corset was very tight, with her breasts on display.

"The bowler and glasses," Wellington said, leaning forward, "have been put on post-mortem. That hat is far too big for him."

Sound offered another dossier. "Lawrence Tarkington, a banker from Wimbledon. The lady, Zylphia Jenkins. Schoolteacher."

This time, the couple—still wearing the trappings of a woman of adventure and a man of a proper British upbringing—were almost in flagrante. He was behind her, holding the woman in what would be an eternal embrace. Both had suffered the same fate: throats cut, heads twisted at unnatural angles.

However the man's eyeglasses and bowler showed very little blood. He could not have been wearing them at the time of death. They were obviously placed there after the deed was done.

"Finally," Sound said, opening another dossier. "Edwin Carlyle and Lulu Summers."

Again, captured in an embrace of death, their necks a mangled mess.

This time, Wellington jabbed at the image. "I say, I have a brown jacket just like that. In fact I have a bowler and eyeglasses similar to those. Interesting how the gentleman is always taller than the lady, and she is notably short in stature."

Eliza looked at the other cases and then began reshuffling the photos, organising them by date. "Wilber Inversill, Esther Simmons. Edwin Tarley, Lulu Adele." *Please, God, let me be wrong,* she thought as she placed the third photo next to Tarley and Adele. "Lucius Northall and Isabella Bradley. Lawrence Tarkington, Zylphia Jenkins."

"He's spelling our names, isn't he?" Wellington said in a low tone.

Dammit, so he saw it, too. "Yes."

"We were called in on the third murder. I had my suspicions based on the clothes they were wearing," Sound admitted, "but my hunch...?"

"Wilber, Edwin, Lucius, Lawrence... Esther, Lulu, Isabella, Zylphia..." The words came out of her dry throat, and she could not stop the thought flashing through her mind. "They are meant to be us. All of them. Jekyll is baiting us, killing people he can get to instead of us."

"Jekyll?" Sound asked. "How can you be certain?"

"Look at the photos, Director. Only one person would come up with something so depraved." Eliza glanced up at Sound and added, "It would not surprise me if there were evidence of sexual intercourse between..."

Doctor Sound's complexion went ashen.

"Good God," Wellington whispered.

"God has absolutely nothing to do with this," Sound replied darkly.

Eliza's gaze focused on the images, looking for details that she knew Jekyll would include. "Seems that we so upset the mad doctor that he wants us to continue the chase."

"What are you looking for, darling?"

Her head shot up. Wellington focused on one photo. "Darling?" she repeated.

"As far as Doctor Sound is concerned, we are still on mandatory leave on account of disciplinary action. He can sod off for all I care in the wake of this."

"I *am* sitting right before you," their director grumbled.

Eliza moved her hand from one photo to another. "Jekyll would not stage such a tableau without giving us a bread crumb to follow. He wanted us to figure out that he was on the move. He wanted us to follow him, of course. But there would be something Jekyll would offer—not as blatant as this."

"True, I think Jekyll was considering our efforts less of a pursuit and more of a sport. And then the director took us off the case…"

"His gallivanting seemed diminished, didn't it?"

Sound cleared his throat. "Consider your reinstated status as my apology. It seems the mad doctor is, indeed, keen on you both nipping at his heels."

Wellington smoothed his moustache. "Here is where Jekyll's ego will prove the death of him. He wants us so badly on his trail that he has actually foreshadowed what he is planning."

"Another murder. This time, a gentleman with a name that starts with 'I' and a lady with 'A'. Complete strangers." Eliza chewed her bottom lip. "Unless he decides to change that detail."

"We should put nothing past him," Wellington said.

Eliza leaned forward, then pointed to something in the photo before her. "Director, do you have a magnifying glass?"

"Actually, something better," he replied, opening a drawer to his left.

The monocle looked sturdily built, but then, housing so many other lenses, it had to be. Suspended from its side were additional multi-coloured lenses, but Eliza could not even begin to guess their functions. She secured the eyepiece against her right eye and experienced a bit of vertigo as everything on that side was suddenly magnified to the point of distortion.

"All right there, Agent Braun?" Sound asked.

"Yes, just a little…" She placed her hand against Wellington's chest. "Well now, that's quite a sensation, now isn't it?"

"Just focus on the picture, and when you are ready, close the other eye, relying only on the *magnomonocle*."

"Yes, quite," Eliza said, bracing herself against the table. She closed her right eye and pressed a thumbnail against the detail in the original photograph. "Let's try this."

Switching dominance from left to right, Eliza could now see everything magnified, albeit so extreme, that the image was fuzzy. She turned back the magnification until the detail took on a more discernible shape. Daring to experiment with this new technology, she slipped one of the lenses into place. It was the red one as the hue spread across her field of vision, but details jumped from the image.

"I see it now," she said, adjusting the zoom of the magnomonocle. "It's a ticket. For the Underground."

"How can you tell, Eliza?" Wellington asked.

"It's the bar-and-disc symbol. And the destination was St Pancras. Welly, would you please?"

"One step ahead of you, Eliza," and underneath her finger slid another photograph. The second murder scene.

"Now you wouldn't be so thick as to put the next crumb in the same place? You're too clever for that," she whispered as she worked across the photograph. "There, underneath Summer's right boot heel. Another rail ticket. Standard fare. Plymouth." Eliza lifted her hand free of the photo. "Wellington, go on and put the Paris murder underneath my hand." The image slipped into her grasp. "So, Boston to London. London to Pancras. Pancras to Plymouth. Plymouth to Paris. So now Jekyll is destined for..." She paused. This time, in the waistcoat pocket of Jenkins' outfit. "A ticket for that new hypersteam that runs between Paris and Constantinople?"

"The Orient Express." Wellington looked up to the Director. "That madman is on the Orient Express."

"You realise it is a trap." The Director leaned back in his chair and fixed them both with a stern gaze. "Jekyll wants you to rush after him. He wants you on the chase in the hopes that you will make a mistake, giving him a chance to remove you both from service. Permanently."

"We know Jekyll wants us dead, sir," she began, "What is the alternative? We can't let innocent people continue to be his message to us. If we don't take this bait, he'll happily just keep killing."

Sound's eyebrows drew together as he glowered at them. "I should send a team with you—"

Wellington held up his hand, and Eliza's heart sank. "I am sorry sir, but we can't do that either. Jekyll has shown almost superhuman abilities to detect a trap. The only way we can set one for him, is to walk into his."

Her rebellious nature was definitely rubbing off on him.

Blowing through his moustache, the director gave a reluctant nod.

Just as they turned to leave, Sound spoke. "Before you go haring off, a moment of your time. I harboured concerns we might end up at this point. Luckily, I was already instituting a new policy for agents in high risk assignments. Right now, that would be you." Pressing a button on his desk, he spoke to Miss Shillingworth outside. "Send her in."

The bright smile of Agent Ellie March was the first thing Eliza noticed, and she couldn't help but smiling back. They'd last seen the young blonde agent, in India, and so it was nice to see her at Whiterock looking as happy as a child on Christmas morning. She'd obviously landed on her feet.

"Agent Books, Agent Braun," Ellie said, putting a surgeon's bag on Sound's desk and opening it. "It's wonderful to see you, and to bring you the latest from Professor Axelrod."

Wellington straightened up, pulled at his lapels, and glanced at the corners of the room as if the professor would pop into existence. "He's here?"

Ellie shook her head. "Unfortunately, no. He sends his apologies for not being present today."

Sound cleared his throat. "The laboratory explosion last week?"

The young woman shrugged as if there was nothing exceptional about that. Anyone that worked with Axelrod eventually got used to the multiple brushes with death.

Though he was not in the room, his presence was felt when Ellie withdrew two large syringes from the bag. The grin on her face was almost familiar.

"I worked with the Professor on this." She sounded so proud.

Now it was not just Wellington who was worried; panic threatened to take hold of Eliza too. She was fine with needles, but when they contained a concoction from Axelrod, she started to get nervous. As long as Axelrod stuck to making machines he was manageable, but with syringes and all that they implied anything could happen.

Then her concerns turned to Wellington. Immediately, her hand interlocked with his. She knew the lingering effects of Doctor Jekyll's experiments had left him with a healthy hatred of the needle and the mad scientists that tended to go with it.

"Director," she said evenly, "what exactly are in those pokers that Agent March is waving around?"

Sound cleared his throat. "Well, as you can attest, our Ministry rings and the current ETS has proven unreliable—especially when agents leave them behind. A problem you are well aware of." She knew she was blushing, and Wellington too. "Also with the ETS compromised during our tangle with the Department of Imperial Inconveniences, we can no longer trust the system. We need to track our agents with something that cannot be taken off, destroyed, or 'hacked' was the term Professor Axelrod used."

Wellington cleared his throat again. Eliza knew he needed a drink. "You mean you are going to inject us with an *æthertracking* solution."

"Professor Axelrod sent his assurances this is all perfectly harmless," Ellie said waving a syringe in each hand for emphasis.

Wellington looked as if he were about to faint. "You are asking me to trust one of Axelrod's creations in those sodding great needles?"

Ellie put the syringes back in the bag. "The professor worried you might have these concerns. If you don't care for needles, I also have it in another form."

Eliza was almost afraid to ask, but she did anyway. "And that would be?"

She rummaged around in her bag and pulled out a long rubber glove and a capsule the size of a croquet ball. "A good old fashioned suppository!"

"I am beginning to see why Axelrod picked you, Agent March," Wellington said in a very dry tone.

"The needle it is then," Eliza said as she removed her jacket.

Wellington rolled up his sleeve and presented his arm. "For Queen, Country, and Empire, safety first."

"How long does it last?" she asked, clenching her right hand into a fist.

"A fortnight, maybe three weeks at most." Ellie tilted her head. "It depends on how much exercise you get. Works through the body a little faster when in an excited state."

Eliza forced a smile while considering visits to Whiterock's gymnasium, perhaps later in the evening. "All right then."

After a few moments of prodding and pricking, both Eliza and Wellington were effectively "tagged" and offered small icepacks for their multiple injection sites.

"Well now," Sound said, "I won't bother asking you to be careful, since I know that would be a waste of my breath, but I will implore you to send word through the usual channels if you confirm Jekyll's presence. With the formula flowing through his veins, you may still need backup."

He flipped through a small organiser on his desk and produced a card. "Please, I am asking you as your friend, not merely as your superior. Now, make preparations while I see to arrangements. You leave in twelve hours."

The way he delivered this request surprised Eliza. Was their director quite himself? He didn't look it, and now he didn't sound it.

She actually dared to pat his hand as some kind of comfort. "We remember India, sir. We won't make that same mistake again."

Even to herself, it was hard to tell if those were only words or if she really meant them. Eliza supposed she would truly find out when the time came.

CHAPTER EIGHT

⇢⇛○⇚⇠

Where Agents of the Ministry Set on the Hunt

Bruce Campbell excelled at many aspects of the Ministry's operation. Sharpshooting, although he was known to go wide with some of his range targets. Disguise and infiltration although he was so broad-shouldered and carried such a distinctive chin and jawline that no camouflage could conceal. Research and investigation, although if he relied entirely on his own intellect, what would Lizzie and Books do with themselves?

Fisticuffs? Now there, Bruce was unparalleled, and he really enjoyed a good go-around with a fellow combatant.

Much better than dealing with people directly, and he knew himself enough to understand it was not his forte. No, it was better that someone else handle those delicate matters.

Early on in Bruce's career, he was investigating a little old lady in Auckland convinced that a sea dragon was hibernating in her estuary. She was hysterical; blubbering without stop, her nose leaking like a sieve. Luckily, back then, he'd had Junior Agent Eliza Braun to take the lead. It was one of those rare times he'd was thrilled to have her about.

Right now—although he would never admit it out loud—he wished Eliza were with him in this stark, bleak interrogation cell, consoling this American gent sitting across from him, now out-blubbering that little old lady from Auckland. Still, he did have his partner to rely on. When their subject let out a muffled wail into his handkerchief, Bruce glanced over to Brandon and jerked his head. This wailing gentleman should fall under the Canadian's particular set of skills.

Brandon looked at him in a panic and shrugged.

Bugger—there went that idea.

Bruce motioned with his head once more before clearing his throat, loud enough to be heard over the man's sobbing. "Mr Harker, both I and my partner here understand your worry. If it were my wife, I'd be as concerned as you."

"Concerned?" David Harker squeaked. *"Concerned?!* Sir, I don't know how concerned husbands are in jolly old England when someone kidnaps their wives, but I am *distraught!"*

Bruce wanted to tell this cloth-eared git he was Australian, not some pommy bastard. Instead, he bit his bottom lip and took a deep breath. "Sir, I can only imagine how difficult this situation is for you, but as you have pointed out so keenly, my mate and I are not from these parts."

That was when Brandon put his arm around Mr Harker, or at least tried to. The way Brandon's arm flailed and trembled around the American, David Harker's tailored suit might have been made with lava fresh from Krakatoa itself. "Just start from the beginning, ol' chum, so we know what we are getting into."

Brandon offered the American a kerchief which Harker drenched with tears in a moment. Still it plugged the dam a little. After a quick sniffle, he dabbed at his eyes and looked up at Bruce. "My beloved Virginia and I got married just over a year ago. She is my love, my life, my soul—"

"Yeah, mate," Bruce said with a nod and a sigh, "the water pageant you're giving us here corroborates that."

"We were in New York for only a few days. I had some business to attend to. Virginia and I were keen on taking in some of the sights, so we were in Central Park, and that was when..." David struggled to catch his breath. "When..."

"So it was in Central Park, was it?"

"We were crossing Gapstow Bridge, and Virginia said to me, 'I am feeling a bit peckish. Would you get me a snack from that lovely man over there?' She pointed out a vendor who had candied pecans. So I went to fetch her a snack. You ever tried these candied pecans? They have a sweet crust roasted on the outside of them..."

"Oh, I know the snack," Brandon said cheerfully. "Quite tasty. And as pecans are fantastic for protein. Well, most nuts actually..."

Bruce dragged his hand down his face. "Brandon..."

He looked between Bruce and Harker bemused for a second, before nodding, and once more patting the distracted man's back. "So you got the snack, you turn around, and..."

"And my beloved," Harker choked out, "had been taken."

Bruce rubbed his chin. "No sign whatsoever? You're suddenly in Central Park, completely alone?"

"Only myself and the nut vendor. The park bench I left her on was vacant."

Bruce continued to jot down his thoughts in a notebook, a trick he picked up from Books that had been proving rather handy. He sat back in his chair, focusing on his notes concerning the unsteady Harker.

"I don't know about you, mate, but I could use a cuppa." He looked around the interrogation room. "I wonder if they have any tea here?" Bruce stood. Brandon also moved to get up, and but Bruce pushed him back down by the shoulder. "Would you like anything, Mr Harker? Tea? Coffee? Beer?"

"I just... want my Virginia back," he blubbered in reply.

"Yeah, 'course you do. I'll be a minute, Brandon."

Before his partner could ask, Bruce was outside in the hallway. He rounded a corner and entered an observation room. The man watching was even more impressive in the flesh, and Bruce had heard plenty of rumours about him. Luther Highfield, Chief of the Office of the Supernatural and Metaphysical, walked up to the one-way window and narrowed his dark eyes on David Harker. He was a broad African-American gent, as well dressed as any who visited Saville Row. In all respects he looked more the senior officer than Sound ever did.

"So, Agent Campbell, your thoughts?" Highfield's deep, gravelly voice echoed in the room.

"Honestly? The bloke is hen-pecked and then some." He paused. "You got that saying over here?"

Highfield examined the Australian before nodding. "If that is his only offence, we can let him go. His story checks out, and we don't think he's a suspect."

"Already? Is that how you all at OSM run investigations? One interrogation and you think—"

Chief Highfield strode closer to Bruce. "It may surprise you that the Office is involving you in this case, but I assure you that you are here as our guests. Do *not* test the limits of that hospitality."

Now with Chief Highfield standing only a foot or so away, Bruce felt small. Extremely so. His usual attack plan with the Fat Man would not work with this one.

Bruce found his throat was a little dry. "Of course not, Chief Highfield. So, why did you bring us into all this?"

Highfield rubbed his jaw and shot him an unsettling smile. "I have three reasons this kidnapping is more appropriate for the Ministry. Reason one, this case falls under your jurisdiction as Mrs Harker was, before her marriage, Virginia North. A British subject. Since we are already investigating four other kidnappings, it wouldn't hurt to have you in on this one. Means I can reassign my own agents."

"Reason two?" Bruce asked.

"In our preliminary questioning of Mr Harker, it seems that they were about to embark on a trip to Italy. We received confirmation this morning that her ticket was, in fact, used at Liberty Harbour Aeroport. The woman holding said ticket matched Virginia Harker's description."

"Really? This morning? Sounds like you are on top of this."

"These kidnappings are similar to each other. Worryingly so."

Bruce's brow furrowed. "Same time of day? Or same location?"

"Same time of day, same location, and even the same nut vendor."

He leaned forward. "You're saying these were arranged kidnappings?"

"Even down to the wife asking their husbands to pick up the cinnamon-baked pecans. They have all said the same exact thing: *'I am feeling a bit peckish. Would you get me a snack from that lovely man over there?'*."

Highfield glanced up at him. "See the thing of it is, we've had agents searching through Central Park and we've never found any pecan merchant. Not even one."

"If this is true, then that means this wasn't a kidnapping."

"Exactly, Agent Campbell."

Bruce shook his head. "So, what are we looking at here? Wives looking to start a new life sans husbands, or some sort of scheme wherein if the wife doesn't comply, harm may befall the family?"

"That's for you to dig up," Highfield said, "I look forward to working with you, as opposed to cleaning up after you've been on a mission here."

Bruce held his hands up in surrender. "My investigation was on a need-to-know basis, Chief, and your counterpart—my superior—wanted to keep it that way."

"Yes, he did, didn't he? I will have a word or two with him about that." Chief Highfield inclined his head to one side. "Would you care to reveal why you are here in the United States, as a professional courtesy?"

"I can only say it is an investigation." Through the mirrored glass he saw Brandon rocking David Harker. His partner's gaze jumped all around the room. He looked to the massive mirror and mouthed *"Help!"* as Harker trembled in his awkward embrace. "I think I need to go in there and rescue my partner."

Highfield nodded. "That was the answer I expected. Sound has his people trained well and does love his secrets."

"He does indeed." Bruce tucked his notebook back into his coat pocket. "So you will also understand, our training dictates we do not undertake any new assignments without orders from our superiors."

Highfield reached into his coat pocket and produced what looked like the printout of an æthergram. "You mean, like this? Received it before you and Hill arrived."

Bruce snatched the order out of Highfield's grasp. He whispered a few choice words under his breath. Was the Fat Man serious? "Very well, Chief Highfield. We'll be glad to help you out."

Against Highfield's ebony skin, his smile flashed bright. "Then good hunting, Agent Campbell."

With a derisive snort, Bruce returned from the observation room to the interrogation room. Brandon looked relieved as his partner gave Harker a final pat on the shoulder before breaking the embrace and taking a seat opposite of him. Bruce waited for Harker to catch his breath before taking a seat.

"Mr Harker, I can tell you're rather rattled by all this, but the Ministry will not let it stand."

"We won't?" Brandon asked, giving him a sideways glance.

"No," Bruce insisted, holding up the folded orders and passing them along to Brandon, "we won't. Her Majesty's finest are on the case. In working with OSM, we have uncovered a lead." He gave Harker's shoulder a gentle squeeze. "Don't you worry, mate. We will not rest until we find your lovely Virginia."

"No, we won't," Harker said, dabbing at his eyes. He took another shuddering breath, then straightened his jacket, "When are we under way?"

Brandon's head jerked up from the orders he had been reading. "I'm sorry, Mr Harker?"

"When are we under way?" Harker said, an edge now present in his voice. "I spoke with my banker before I arrived. I have the necessary funds in place to bankroll this venture of ours. I will not tolerate simply waiting in the wings while my beloved Virginia is in someone's nefarious hands."

"Now just a moment," Bruce managed through clenched teeth, squeezing the man's shoulder a hint tighter. "We're trained to handle this sort of situation. We can't guarantee your safety…"

"Agent Campbell," Harker said, shaking off Bruce's hold and rising to his feet, "I will have you know that I graduated with top marks from Virginia Military Institute. I can hold my own in the trickiest of situations, and will not accept any answer in the negative. This is my life, my love, my Virginia, and I intend to see that I am the first face she sees when we find her."

This was not really happening. Was it?

The door behind him opened a crack. Chief Highfield poked his head into the interrogation room. His smile infuriated Campbell. "And this is the last reason I am being so accommodating, Agent Campbell." With a wink, he added, "Do give my regards to my British counterpart."

Bruce let out a long, slow breath, before turning back to look at the determined David Harker. Doctor Sound must have a good reason for sending them to follow this lead of kidnapped wives. At least, he hoped he did.

"Right then." Harker said, looking between the two of them, "Where do we begin?"

This mission was already off to a delightful start, but it looked like they could at least afford good booze on the way.

CHAPTER NINE

·⊶⊰⊜⊱⊷·

When the City of Love Welcomes Our Agents of Derring-Do

Once Eliza and Wellington had cracked Jekyll's enigma it was a rush to pack their bags and prepare for another nerve-racking æthergate trip. The usual travel lines were out of the question as Jekyll was not playing by the rules. Yet why would he? The man was an utter cad, not to mention a bit cracked.

So in the midst of all this, the youngest of the Ministry Seven, the diminutive Serena, confronted Eliza and Wellington. She looked up at them, feet planted, a glower carved deep into her usually sweet face.

"I'm coming with you."

These were the first words she had spoken to either of them in quite some time. The young girl had been making a real effort to avoid them. Eliza had done the same when she was about her age when her parents were not paying her enough attention—at least in her mind. While the Brauns had a parcel of children and a pub to keep an eye on, she and Wellington had a madman loose in the Empire. None of these things made any difference to a child.

Eliza had bent down, placing a gentle hand on her shoulder. *"This is far too dangerous, Serena. We'd be distracted with worry for your safety. It would probably get me and Mr Books killed."*

Serena stared down at her feet for a moment and then looked up. *"Since the hullabaloo at the East End, everyone's found a place in the Ministry."* Then her face scrunched into a sour expression. *"Except Christopher, who's done found a bottle to crawl into at the local pub."*

Wellington had looked over to Eliza, and she caught in his expression a reflection of her own confusion. She could say nothing in response to that. It was true. All the boys from the Ministry Seven had landed quite nicely on their feet, save for Christopher. The eldest of the Seven wanted no part of the Ministry even though he was offered a position. He'd discovered the limits of his desire to serve Queen, Country and Empire. He had made noises about finding passage back to London, but the last anyone had heard, he had found a comfortable corner in the Hunter's Horn, the local pub of Hebden Bridge. He did odd jobs around the town to cover his thirst and modest means.

That had left Serena. Not even ten, and she wanted a place in the Ministry.

"I'm sure you could find a place to help out here," Eliza had told her, but those words were not very convincing. Serena wanted to be involved the way she had been in the streets of London. *"Alice could use some help in Whiterock, or perhaps you could assist in the kitchens. Only for a little while until you're older."*

"But Miss Eliza, I'm just as good at infiltration as Jonathan and Jeremy. Better, even!" Serena had crossed her arms before adding, *"I can complete that escape room challenge in the West Wing in half the time it takes both of them."* Eliza could still remember how surprising that was, along with how proud she was of the girl's skill.

"Now, Serena, you understand the kind of work Mr Books and I do. It's dangerous."

"I know," she insisted. *"I saw that when we tangled with that Dottie Diamond tart. Then there's what happened outside St Paul's. I ain't no fool."*

"But that was different, that was in London. You don't know Paris like that. We can't take you with us, because we need you to be safe."

"I don't want to be safe. I want to be like you." Serena said.

Those words struck hard, and Eliza didn't have any answers for the girl. On one hand she was proud of Serena's determination, but on the other she was afraid. Was this how Eliza's mother had felt when she had taken her own post at the Ministry?

Instead of answering her, Eliza hustled Serena into the care of Alice, who offered up as much tea as the situation warranted. The tearful girl continued to follow them about, and had watched in silence as they finished their packing, headed to the staging area in R&D, and prepared to take their brief trip across the channel to Paris.

Just as they were about the depart Whiterock, Eliza had reached out for Serena, only to have the child run off, sobbing.

That memory haunted Eliza even as they entered the æthergate. When they arrived in Paris, her mind was still in a fog.

"This city is rather beautiful isn't it," Wellington said, as he leaned against the white stone balustrades of the Pont Neuf, and stared down at the bustle of the tiny river craft below. "A real pity we won't get to see more of it."

It was a chilly blue-grey day, so the usual bustle of pedestrians on the bridge was muted. The tall cream and white buildings nearby loomed over them somehow.

Eliza shivered. Wellington might be waxing lyrical on the beauties of the city, but to her, it was a city marred by Jekyll. That monster had brought them here and made Serena cry. Their circumstances took away the joy of the city. Soon enough they would board the Orient Express, provided Wellington's plan panned out. The æthergate had granted them a full day in the City of Lights, but not necessarily for enjoyment. They were here on business, and that was not the way she wanted to see Paris with Wellington.

Her gaze went from window to window. The itch on the back of her neck reminded her that the villainous doctor could be standing at one of them at this very moment. She hadn't realised how much comfort she got from Jekyll's isotope trail, but with Axelrod's and Blackwell's tracking solution gone from the madman's system, he could be anywhere and they wouldn't know it.

Yes, though leaving Serena in tears had been difficult, it had also been the right choice.

Huddling a little closer to Wellington—this was the city of love after all—she squeezed his arm. "Don't worry, we'll be able to enjoy it one day. Right now, Jekyll wants us to follow his trail of carnage. To what end God only knows…"

"True, but such hubris may be the man's undoing," Wellington said, casting a gaze off in to the horizon. Eliza looked up at him, "Dr Jekyll does have rather a small opinion of our intellect," he said, his breath rising in front of his face. "And a rather too large one of his own."

"You're saying that's how we'll catch him?"

"Indeed."

Eliza shook her head. "All of this doesn't matter because the Orient Express is completely full. We could not get tickets."

"Yes, I am aware of that."

"We could take the place of some staff, but the train is so exclusive that the servers all know each other. Intimately. The sudden arrival of two unexpected waiters would be sure to draw attention."

"That it would."

Eliza dealt Wellington a quick, light jab to his ribs. "What's your game then, Books?"

"As I said to you back at the hotel," he chortled, rubbing the spot she had just poked, "this is a nut that I might have a way to crack."

Yet from their walk from the hotel to this scenic bridge, he had not revealed to her how he intended to do this. For an archivist there was a surprising touch of the showman in him.

Motioning with his head for her follow, they wandered to the end of the bridge, their feet now touching the Île de la Cité. Surrounded by the Seine, Eliza allowed her mind to wander through memories of Paris, both when she'd been a solo agent and when she had worked with Harrison Thorne. Her dead partner still haunted certain places of this beautiful city—for her, at least.

Her eyes met with a street-vendor who, from his proper posture and bright smile, had rather hopefully set up his little stand near their footpath. In the summer he probably did well with all the lovers strolling by the river, but on this chilly, overcast day it was only Wellington and Eliza. The warmth of the square oven underneath the vendor's wide umbrella was tantalising, drawing them both in. Even agents on the hunt needed sustenance. Eliza's sweet tooth was already sending commands, and before Wellington could reach for his wallet, she had stepped up and ordered them both chocolate crepes.

The vendor smiled at them through his grey beard and spooned a ladle of mixture onto each of his two hot plates. He then flipped up the brass cover of the control panel. Watching the skillet as the batter poured in from slim faucets suspended over the hot surface, he manipulated levers and dials as the open skillet pitched and spun. A flip of another switch, the skillet folded onto itself with a quick hiss, creasing the thin crepe in half. The vendor's elbow flipped another switch on the panel, and the skillet folded itself again once, then twice, turning the crepe into a triangle. Another loud hiss, and the crepe slid through a shower of powdered sugar sprayed from a small arc before slipping into a paper bag.

"*Très bon!*" Eliza said, taking the crepe for herself.

She loved to watch artisans work, especially when manipulating such clever gadgets as this. She also loved food.

They were in the middle of Wellington's own snack being created when a member of the *Préfecture de Police de Paris* stepped up and ordered one as well. It was not surprising since the Place Louis Lépine right behind them on the island housed the prefecture, but Eliza took notice when Wellington stiffened. The look he gave her partner was long enough to read the signs: he knew him. Immediately her fingers drifted to the pounamu pistols concealed under her jacket, just in case. Her gaze flicked over the approaching officer's sharp uniform, shiny silver buttons, and his rank. A Commandant, so very high ranking to be out getting his own crepe. He was carrying a suitcase, with no distinguishing details about it other than it was bulky.

"Even drab weather as this cannot ruin Paris," he said, setting the case down at his feet, "but if you were indulging in crepes, you could have at least waited for me, Wellington."

"*Bonjour, mon ami, Louis. Ça me fait plaisir de vous voir.*" The smile on her lover's face was genuine, and his Parisian French flawless. He shook hands, and for a fleeting moment, Eliza might have thought he was about to hug the man. However, Wellington's English reserve outplayed this Frenchman's warmth. He stepped back and gestured to her. "May I present—"

The man with the perfectly combed moustache and impeccable bearing took her hand and brought it to his lips. "The redoubtable Agent Eliza D Braun. Commandant Louis Renault, at your service. A pleasure to meet you."

When she glanced at the crêpe vendor, he tilted his head. "Oh, George? Do not mind, he is one of mine."

"One of your—?"

"Miss Braun, the French Police are only as good as their information." He nodded to the vendor who handed him a crepe. "George sees quite a bit in his day-to-day vending, I assure you, and he is a trustworthy gentleman."

"And you know Wellington, how?" She couldn't help but ask. As far as she was aware, he'd lived a sheltered life in the archives.

Louis' eyes sparkled. "Ah, now that would be a very long story, and I am afraid you do not have enough time. Let us just say it involved *Légion Étrangère*, a card game, and a lot of wine." His grin faded. "Unfortunately you will not be having time for sport like that—not with whom you are chasing." His face folded into an angry scowl. "Jekyll has been a thorn in our side as well."

Paris was rumoured to be where Jekyll had retreated to straight after their tangle with the Ghost Rebellion in India. From the expression on Renault's face, he had not left the City of Lights unscarred.

Louis examined his snack. "So, Wellington, am I to understand you believe Jekyll has returned to Paris?"

He nodded. "In a fashion, yes. We have to find a way to get on board the Orient Express."

The policeman's eyebrows raised. "Leisure, or hypersteam?"

"Hypersteam."

Louis spread his hands. "It is the maiden voyage for the new service. There are famous people taking advantage of their expedited adventure. Attention from the press. Hardly lends itself to dark operations..."

"Louis?"

The officer gave Wellington a sour expression. He did not like that Wellington was spoiling his building of suspense. "It was no easy thing." He opened his jacket and removed two slips of paper. They weren't tickets.

Wellington opened them and then glanced up. "Really, Louis?"

Eliza looked at Wellington, who opened the papers before her. Her breath caught in her throat. "Police? You want us to pose as *police?*"

The Frenchman shrugged, even as he polished off his crepe. "There was no way to get you in as a guest, or on the staff, but we have five police officers stationed on the train. I have proper uniforms for you both," he said, motioning to the suitcase. "The Orient Express is an expensive piece of technology, and its passenger list reads as a who's who of affluence and intellect. We must protect them."

"Will you be joining us?" she asked.

"It would be a lovely journey, I am sure," he said, brushing his hands together, before motioning around them, "but who would look after the jewel of Europe?"

"I see," Wellington said, with a knowing nod. "You think Jekyll will make things rather nasty, don't you?"

Louis dismissively waved his hand. "Nothing you cannot handle. I will only get under your feet."

Wellington glanced across at Eliza, and she smiled. "It wouldn't be the first time we have pretended to be from another agency. Say thank you to your kind friend, and we can be on our way."

Louis wiped the chocolate from his immaculate little moustache, and grabbing hold of Wellington, kissed him on each cheek. "I have informed the other three officers that you are special agents along to help. Their names are on that piece of paper. I do hope you don't cause them too much trouble."

The twinkle in his eye suggested he wouldn't mind if they did.

He took hold of her hand and kissed it once again. "It was a pleasure, Miss Braun. Please take care of Wellington—even if he can be a bit of a—how do you say, dry stick?"

Her lover straightened, adjusting his cravat, but any retort was cut short when Louis pulled out his pocket watch and tapped it. "I think you will have to hurry if you want to get to the Gare de l'Est on time."

"Thank you for your help, Louis," Wellington said, picking up the suitcase. "Please give my love to Adèle and *p'tit* Louis."

Worried that he was about to get into a long farewell, Eliza yanked him out from under the awning, and towards a row of taxis. She knew the streets of Paris well enough to understand that it was going to be a run, even for the two of them. They found one of the new Hummingbirds, a beautiful piece of vehicular design, running on electricity. She didn't allow Wellington a chance to even suggest they take a moment to admire.

Right now their game was, most assuredly, afoot.

CHAPTER TEN

⋆⇨⇦⋆

In Which Our Dashing Archivist and Colonial Pepperpot Uphold the Law of the Land

"Come along, Eliza," Wellington whispered, "otherwise someone will most assuredly—"

Eliza glanced to either side, yanked him into the small alcove after her, and stole a long, deep kiss from him. Oh, he did love these moments of impetuousness, but now wasn't the time for such affections. Still she must have loved the look of him in the uniform.

With his lips pressed against hers, Wellington could have broken this kiss at any time, but he was certainly not complaining about the situation. Truthfully, he too was in need of a moment's respite.

Despite that, Wellington pulled away and looked at his lover dressed in the trappings of a French police officer. "Someone will most assuredly see us."

"It's Paris," Eliza replied, glancing back to the steady traffic of travellers trying to make their schedules, "and no one batted an eyelash as we changed in the back of the taxi."

His smile went crooked. "True, but now we are undercover and incognito, so let us focus on that." With that, he motioned back to the terminal.

"You are no fun at all, you know that, Welly?" Eliza said, her lips forming a pout as they continued on their way.

"Yes, I know, I am such a 'dry stick' when engaged on a case."

"A case the director ordered us off."

"And then put us back on, darling. The alternative to Doctor Sound remaining steadfast in his decision would have meant more innocent blood spilled, now wouldn't it?"

"There is that," she admitted.

The bustle of trams, vehicles, the shrill whistle from a conventional train, and endless currents of people filled the grand station, as light filtered through its magnificently large half-circle window. Together Eliza and Wellington made their way past platforms, flower vendors, and PortoPorters, but everyone parted almost instinctively for them. Whether it was out of respect or fear, no one stopped or delayed them even with all the foot traffic in the Travel Centre.

Descending the fine marble steps leading to Platform 20, Wellington and Eliza left behind the chaos of the public and entered the posh, exclusive grandeur of the upper-class. This new hypersteam brought the famous Orient Express into a new age. Scarlet banners hung from columns inside the station, while beneath a tumult of onlookers—those important enough to see off the guests of the hypersteam, but not quite influential enough to find a seat on it—gathered. At least they could catch a glimpse of the luminaries of society as they boarded.

"Now that," he whispered, halting halfway down the staircase, "is a marvel."

While hypersteam travel was no longer ground-breaking as a technology, the Orient Express' version introduced innovations that would completely change the landscape of transportation, analytical engines and navigation. Wellington had heard rumours that this model, the OHX-1, could reach speeds of over one hundred miles per hour. Possibly, one-hundred and fifty miles per hour. The OHX-1 was more angular than other models of hypersteam, while recycling pipes needed to create the hypersteam's super-heated fuel were smaller and better insulated, creating a higher pressure for additional propulsion. He traced the lines of the OHX-1 around to the ornate, elegant passenger cars behind it. If what he had read about the Oriental Hypersteam Express were true, then the cars contained amenities and creature comforts that rivalled the White Star Lines' Trans-Pacific airships.

"Darling, do be careful, lest you start drooling."

He shook his head and chuckled in spite of himself. "My apologies, but this?" He motioned to the OHX-1. "This is unlike anything ever seen before and considered somewhat risqué for the exclusive and staid Orient Express."

Eliza motioned him toward the train, and they resumed their descent to Platform 20. "Risqué is rather my speed."

He chose not to reply to that little trap. After time together he was getting good at spotting them.

Closer to the Express, regardless of their uniforms, both Wellington and Eliza had to push through the crowd. When they broke through, they found a higher-ranking officer who motioned for the two of them to join him. This sergeant issued various assignments to their fellow officers until it was just the three of them.

"You are friends of Louis?" he asked.

"Oui, sergeant," Wellington began, *"Je m'app—"*

"Please," the superior said, "speak English. I am sure your French is flawless. And that is what gives me concern. Also, the less I know of the two of you, the more deniability I have."

Wellington paused, glancing at Eliza who shrugged, then turned back to the sergeant. "We are indeed friends of Louis. Sergeant...?"

"Petit. Sergeant Petit, and you need access to the passengers?"

"Yes," Eliza said, "we believe a madman may be amongst the guests."

Petit raised one eyebrow. "And the reason I am just finding out about this is..."

She cleared her throat. "You had a series of brutal murders a few months ago. A string of prostitutes, yes?"

Petit's eyes went wide. "You know of the Ghoul of Notre Dame?"

"We've read the case file from the Préfecture."

He stared down from one end of the train to the other, and his complexion grew paler by the second. Wellington saw his problem; the beautiful and famous were being funnelled through a maze of roped off areas towards the OHX-1. Petit shook his head. "Of course that monster would choose the Orient Express. It is a bouillabaisse of influential targets."

Eliza followed his gaze and gasped, talking hold of Wellington by the wrist. "That's Douglas Keating," she whispered to him, motioning with her head to a smartly dressed dark-haired man carrying a small valise. Well, smart until you reached the man's head which sported a hat that would have dwarfed Wild Bill Wheatley's in comparison. "The cattle baron from Texas."

A blonde lady, in a glittering green dress that accentuated her fine form followed him, though from the distance between them they didn't appear to be a couple. However, in the way she touched the man's back and laughed along with him, they knew one another. "Ashe Robbins," Eliza added, "the famous actress."

Wellington attempted to look impressed at the celebrities from America, but his own excitement welled up to the surface as he recognised, "Professor Henrietta Falcon, the scientist from the Brunel Institute! She is revered around the world for her engineering breakthroughs. Quite amazing to see her out of her university. I wonder if she had a hand in designing the OHX-1?"

"And that is Jean-Pierre Dubois, the French Ambassador, and he is talking to..."

"...Mustafa Solak, the renowned poet," Wellington finished. "Many call him the Shakespeare of the Ottoman Empire."

"Scientists, politicians, artists, and robber barons," Sergeant Petit went on, his voice now rather dry. "All of them are in terrible danger."

"Quite." Eliza glanced across the crush of people before turning her face towards the train "Any sign of him, Welly?"

"No, but the longer we are out in the open like this..."

"True," she said before turning to Petit. "Perhaps we should take our place on the Express as your officers?"

The sergeant nodded. "Follow me."

A brass band struck up, playing cheery selections that distracted the crowd. As the three of them slipped on to the Express, the crowd's adulation and the band's overtures were muffled by the train's lush interior. Passing through car after car, Wellington noticed each of the luxurious sleeper units was labelled with its occupant. Professor Falcon was in the room next to the Texan cattle baron. They finally came to a stop in a car with only two doors visible, the one before them marked *"Privé"*. Petit opened the door to reveal an immaculate office with a desk centred before a wide window.

"Welcome to my base of operations," he said before motioning to another door to the left. "Through there, the two you will attend to passengers' needs and complaints."

"Where are the other uniforms going to be?" Eliza asked, leaning forward to peer at a large diagram of the Express mounted on the wall behind the desk.

Petit pointed at various cars. "We will be stationed at each end of the sleeper sections at night, and then during the day patrolling the parlour and viewing cars."

"Weapons?"

"Standard French issue Moussin-Elard 504s with variable settings, set at half-pressure on last inspection." Petit looked between them and shrugged. "We don't want to melt holes in the OHX."

"Especially with these somewhat temperamental engines," Wellington said, raising his hand a fraction as if he were afraid to break in. "One shot through the hull and the best result would be a stranded train. Worst case..." He mimicked an explosion.

"You seem to know quite a lot about the OHX," Petit noted.

"He reads engineering publications... for fun. I'm more of a Brontë girl, myself."

"Then we shall have to avoid the worst case, Mr Brooks," Petit said with a violent bobbing of his Adam's apple. "So what is your plan once we are under way?"

"Mingling," Eliza replied.

"As police officers?"

"Both as uniforms and undercover. Hiding in plain sight as it were," Wellington explained. "This may make our job a bit more difficult, but it will mean we can move freely among the passengers."

"You talk as if you are travelling with the common folk," the police commander chuckled. "You forget that you are with the elite. They will expect you to see to their every need. Mostly those needs will be about as deadly as wiping their bums after a visit to the loo. You will not find the assembled here as accommodating as those in third class." Petit took a seat behind his desk, glanced at the clock in the wall, and then turned to the paperwork on his desk. "I will have a full manifest sent to your quarters. Now, off with you. The Express departs in roughly fifteen minutes, and I will expect you to make at least one round of the train before you return here." And with a wave of his hand, Petit was done with the two of them.

Wandering out into the corridor with Eliza at his back, the environment began to settle in with him. For the next few days, this testament to technology and luxury would be their world. Jekyll had to be hidden within the passenger list, and in between tending to the passengers' demands, they would also be a line of defence. It was a matter of finding Jekyll before anyone else died.

Pausing at a junction between cars, Wellington looked around at the details surrounding them. They had travelled on many hypersteam engines in their time, but those models were utilitarian compared with the OHX-1. Care and thought was evident everywhere, from polished gleaming brass to ornamental rivets. From where they stood, they observed finely dressed porters loading luggage into a rear car—nothing as common as portoporters for this exclusive crowd. Only human hands would handle *their* particulars.

"This machine is exquisite," Wellington muttered, managing to keep his outward countenance that of a disinterested police officer as opposed to the expression a clankerton would wear.

Eliza twisted her lips. "For the cost of the tickets, I should hope so."

His eyes lingered on Eliza's lovely profile, and he let out a muffled sigh. No, there would most likely be no time for romance on this most romantic of trains. Their priority was to apprehend a mad doctor as quickly as possible, for both their and the passengers' sake.

CHAPTER ELEVEN

-·→≡◯≡←·-

In Which a Battle of Wits Is Engaged

Mrs Hyacinth Thanderbaum in 2D complained again about the amorous noises coming from 2B.

Mr Alex White protested that the configuration of his shower taps was far too complicated—though why that should be a matter for the constabulary, Wellington had no clue.

Miss Octavia Flattery insisted that someone find out where her Scottish Terrier's favourite toy had disappeared. It was apparently diamond-shaped and worth a pretty penny.

This was all on Day One.

The only comfort was Wellington and Eliza had, so far, remained unnoticed and unrecognised. Their gamble on being in plain sight was working rather splendidly. While they stood watch in the dining car or walked the occasional patrol along the length of the train, conversations between passengers continued without interruption. They were, in a sense, invisible, like servants.

Day Two, however, would present a very different sort of challenge.

Eliza entered the office in a smart, stylish morning outfit—a conservative tweed blazer and matching skirt against a bright yellow blouse—and straightened her hat. Wellington saw it in her face; it was giving her trouble. Always a dangerous move for a piece of headwear.

"All right there, darling?" he asked after a moment of watching her fidget in the mirror.

"It's rather frustrating," she began through clenched teeth, "that I've managed to put together this outfit, and my hat refuses to remain where I want it." She then spread her gloved fingers wide. "And these do not make pinning it in place any easier."

"Allow me," Wellington offered, stepping free of his desk post.

A smile fluttered on Eliza's lips. "You look rather smart in brown."

He smoothed out the lapels of his own suit. "I do, don't I?" Taking the pins out of her hand, he waited for Eliza to position the hat where she desired it to sit. As he worked in pins between the hat's fabric and her hair, he asked, "Any new leads this morning over breakfast?"

"Did you know, that soap is the most important instrument in the medical profession, ranked alongside with the scalpel?" The tension in her voice that of an individual ready to crack under the stress of tediousness and boredom.

Wellington nodded. "Is it now?"

"Oh, yes," Eliza said, sounding like a scream lurked behind her calm words, "straight from the chiselled jaw of Barton Linton, the sole heir of the Linton soap empire. The man possesses the same amount of charisma as his familial product."

Wellington swallowed a snicker as the final pin slipped into Eliza's hair. "There you are, darling."

She closed her eyes, took a deep breath, and when her brilliant blue eyes flicked open, a somewhat too bright smile flashed at him. Yes, he was certain the heir of the soap empire had come a hairbreadth from being strangled with the rope from his own product. "And what is your agenda for the day?"

"I was going to try to dig a bit with the Castles."

"Frederick and Ida?" Eliza barked a laugh. "And I thought Barty was an undertaking."

"They seem like charming people..." Wellington cleared his throat. "From a distance."

"Yes," Eliza agreed, "like, say, that between London and Mars?"

"Oh, come now..."

"What makes you think they know anything? The Castles are older than dirt!"

"We should never question the knowledge of our elders," Wellington stated. "And our elders do love sharing it."

Eliza crooked an eyebrow but then a smirk crossed her face. "Rather clever, Welly. Rather clever."

The sergeant's office door opened, and Petit appeared, his gaze on the coffee pot only broken by a quick glance to the two of them. *"Bonjour, Monsieur, Mademoiselle,* today is your day in rotation?"

"Yes, it is," Wellington said, checking his reflection in the mirror one last time.

"Nothing new then, I take it?"

"Since leaving Vienna, we have been doing our best to work through the manifest and passengers when assembled."

"And with over fifty across these cars, the trip is going to go by rather quickly," Eliza offered.

"Indeed," Petit replied. "So who will you be talking with this morning?"

"The Castles."

"Good luck with *them*," Petit sighed gloomily whilst pouring himself a cup.

With a tight smile, Wellington exited the office and made for the dining car. Through the window in the door, he observed many seated patrons, while one or two tables remained vacant.

At the farthest end of the car, he could just make out the elderly couple he needed to question.

Frederick and Ida Castle sat with their backs to the opposite door, but occasionally flicked glares at those younger than they were—which was everyone. The old man never took his bowler hat off, even when eating or meeting a lady. Wellington had observed this terribly rude behaviour on his innocuous patrols of the train. Still, Frederick was dutiful to his wife, whom he pushed around in a rickety old wheelchair.

No one on this train was short of a penny or two, so he could only imagine that the Castles, despite their fortunes, leaned toward the miser's side of the upper-crust.

"Once more unto the breach," Wellington whispered, opening the door and preparing for battle, or as some liked to call it, breakfast.

While his outward expression exuded a dull familiarity with his surroundings, Wellington remained in awe, once again, of the luxurious touches of the Express. This dining car reminded him of a London gentleman's club; all done up with dark brown wood-panelled walls, and lush red lounge chairs. They were set up in either pairs facing each other or, at the junction, slightly wider tables for four, which suited his purposes rather well. He stepped aside for the highly polished automaton delivering coffee and tea to the small handful of people enjoying late breakfast. As he moved to the rear of the car, his eyes went from passenger to passenger, gleaning as much information as he could.

Amelia Chase and her twenty-year-old daughter, Molly, were sitting opposite each other. Chase the Elder tapped Molly on the knee, and she slipped over to sit on the vacant chair tucked to one side. The Chases would eventually become part of the investigation, as everyone here were potential leads to Jekyll, but they also filled Wellington with dread. Molly was an only daughter, and gossip said Mrs Chase had thrust her before every eligible bachelor the previous summer and winter, and showed no signs of stopping. According to newspaper columns that Eliza was addicted to, Mrs Chase's efforts had been for naught. This meant the young girl was now being thrust before *married* men. Hard to believe, but being set up as a mistress to some wealthy so-and-so was preferable to having Molly become a spinster. Though, with her head bowed hands clasped, the poor girl didn't really seem the mistress type.

His eyes darted over to Professor Henrietta Falcon, lighting up a cigar as she eased back into a chair, her attention on a book of complex computations. From the look on her face, she found her morning read rather amusing. Her head shook gently from side to side as she picked up her pen and made notations within its margins. *A published work,* Wellington wondered, *and she's offering corrections and notations?*

The closer Wellington drew to Ida and Frederick Castle, the more he understood exactly what Sergeant Petit meant. They were not attracting many visitors, seated as they were in the farthest reaches of the dining car, where the rattle of the train on the tracks was loudest. Their countenances didn't help in making them approachable, either.

Frederick Castle, a baron of the growing "personal security" industry, dressed in the height of fashion... from twenty years ago. He had sandwiched his jowls in between two stiff collars and regarded Wellington's approach through a pair of watering blue eyes. His wife, Ida, slumped in her wheel chair, fought to stay awake. The chair lacked any of the advances Wellington's invalid father had possessed, even though the Castles were rich enough to have afforded one. The squeak from its wheels going up and down the corridor was one of the few irritations on the Express.

The miserly eccentric and his dutiful wife were hardly unique in the Empire—in fact, it was rife with their sort. From the much-feared Mistress McTafferty in her highland estate subsisting on boiled beans, to Kevin Moncrieff, who lived in a boarded-up house in Highgrove, while his banks earned more and more each year, there were always those who made money only to hoard it. Even with the current state of affairs, Wellington still preferred mad scientists over such skinflints.

Still, needs must.

"Good morning," Wellington offered cheerily as he took a seat opposite of them. He smiled what he thought might be his best smile—the one Eliza said she found charming.

The Castles fixed their eyes on him and did not return his greeting. This welcome to their table was as stony as Avebury Circle itself. If Wellington hadn't been on Her Majesty's payroll he would most likely have attempted to slide under the table. The longer Ida stared at him with her beady eyes, the more Wellington preferred her slumped in slumber.

Time to hide under the cover of a persona. Eliza had been telling him how it was the bit of their job she enjoyed the most—well, second only to blowing up things. Slipping into a role that wasn't quite her, using all of her wiles against the most recalcitrant of people. Eliza had a rather extensive portfolio, Wellington had discovered, of identities—or legends as they were referred to in the Ministry—that she spent many hours developing and perfecting. No wonder she had been so cross when Wellington had cast her in a moment's improvisation as a mute when they faced the Phoenix Society. That had not gone over so well.

"Lovely day, isn't it? Nothing quite like a morning's repast to start off a day, yes?" Wellington asked as he took off his bowler and laid it on the chair next to him. The weather was always a good opener since everyone had an opinion on it. Surely even these two.

Surely.

Frederick's lip curled, revealing an ugly row of broken teeth. It was a heartbeat later that Wellington caught a whiff of fetid breath. *Wealthy enough to ride on the Orient Express,* he thought, *but not enough to keep their teeth in good order. How predictable.*

Clearing his throat as he laid a napkin across his lap, Wellington focused on Ida. Hopefully, a sweeter disposition awaited him there. "Madame, in the spirit of this breath-taking adventure to the Ottoman Empire, you surely must let me push you to the Observation Car. The mountains we are passing through are quite—"

"You're planning on stealing my wife, are you?" From another man's lips the sentiment might have come across as a light quip, but Frederick Castle's words accompanied by the hard slap on the table that turned a few heads in the dining car came across as a prelude to a duel.

Wellington's gaze darted to Ida, who had still not spoken a word. Her own cold, suspicious glare, spoke volumes. Her head receded amongst the many layers of clothing wrapped around her, like she was a tortoise in distress. No one would ever imagine her being stolen away in such a fashion—could they?

Frederick's fist striking the table made him think again. Wellington noted the large size of the old man's mitt, the rows of black curly hair in sharp contrast to his pale skin. This man would have made for a wonderful brawler in his younger days, and perhaps in present ones too.

Not that he wanted to test that theory. "No-no-no," Wellington said quickly, waving his hands in the air. "As lovely as your wife is, my dear fellow, I can see she is quite smitten with you."

In truth Ida had not removed her gaze from Wellington to anywhere near her husband. He had never understood the expression 'if looks could kill' until that very moment. Mrs Ida Castle was practically poisoning him with her gaze.

This wasn't really going as Wellington had imagined it.

Sweat was now breaking out on his forehead, trickling down his neck. Was it his imagination or had the room suddenly got far too hot? "Perhaps I should start again? Orville Isaac. I am in construction and real estate. Thought I would meet some of my fellow adventurers and share stories over tea. And you are...?"

"No one of concern, especially to you, sir," Mr Castle replied, his voice turning positively into a growl. "We hate tea. Almost as much as unexpected, *unwanted* company."

Well then, that settled that. Interview done.

"I crave a pardon," he said, rising, and jamming his hat back on his head. "I won't trouble you further."

He tried to make sure he didn't break into a run to get away from the Castles' table. He had only made it a few paces before the husky, exceptionally polished accent stopped him in his tracks. "Bad time of it, then?"

Wellington looked down to see where the query came from. He was standing next to Professor Henrietta Falcon, the smoke from the end of her cigar lazily slinking upward from its bright orange tip as she rested one hand on the book on her lap.

"The rich, I have found, tend to be a little harder to crack than those of more humble backgrounds." She looked up and a strange dizziness almost overcame him. The woman was mature, late thirties or even early forties, but the darkness in her eyes, and raven hair wrapped in bun all created a striking impression that caught him completely off-guard. "You're too kind, is your problem. Pleasantries are not always the best way in."

There was something in the way she enunciated her words. Her speech punctured the air, but it suited the sharp lines of her cheekbones. She did resemble the predator whose name she bore. Lifting the cigar to her lips, she took a slow drag from it before leaning back in her chair and exhaling. The sharp, sweet smoke only made Wellington's dizziness worse.

"Perhaps I misjudged the Castles as the affable sort," he confessed.

"I would find such a miscalculation from a man like you unexpected, and even a bit disappointing."

Wellington blinked. "I'm sorry?"

"You strike me as a man of intellect," she said, her mouth bending into a crooked smile.

"Well, I usually am." He shrugged. "I suppose the axiom of the ancients is true."

"Which one would that be?"

Wellington attempted to mimic her grin. "No one's perfect."

She stared at him, sizing him up just by looking into his eyes. From a distance, Professor Falcon demanded admiration and respect, but up close, Wellington found her to be most formidable.

After a short lifetime of fighting to keep his balance while maintaining eye contact, Falcon offered him her hand, "Professor Henrietta Falcon, from the Ada Lovelace Centre."

He took her hand, but could not stop from his brow creasing. "Not the Brunel Institute?"

"No longer," she said, gesturing for him to join her. "That particular institution is much like this train and its guests." She flicked slightly with her head back to the Castles. "Full of the most annoying, irritable people on God's green earth." Wellington cast a glance over to the couple, but Henrietta simply took another puff from the cigar. "I wouldn't worry about the dear things hearing me. Both are quite deaf."

Wellington blinked. "Deaf?"

"I could state the obvious, that Frederick is a cheap old bastard who won't even offer his valet a shilling for his troubles, and that Ida's wheelchair should wheel itself to the grave, and yet…" Henrietta craned her neck over her shoulder. Wellington followed her gaze to where the Castles sat. Ida was asleep once more. Frederick was busy scraping the last of the meat off the chicken's bone. "See? Deaf as wooden planks."

"I tried to be pleasant, at the very least. So… *rude!*" Wellington said with a huff.

"Or simply inconsiderate. They don't bother. They have what they believe a good life and damn the world around them."

"And you?" Wellington asked, catching the attention of the automaton before turning his gaze back to Professor Falcon. "What do you believe you have?"

Falcon crooked an eyebrow, then leaned forward to gently rest her elbows on either side of the open book. "Cutting to the chase, are we?"

"No, if I wanted to cut to the chase, I would ask what made you move from Mechanical Design to... what are they calling that science at the Lovelace Centre again?"

"Quantum Engineering," she said, smiling brightly. "But something tells me you already knew that, Mr...?"

"Orville. Isaac." Wellington gave a slight nod to the book between her elbows. "And I did know that, yes. The notations in this already published book you have here indicates that you are about to begin work on your sixth book."

"Seventh. I handed my latest to the publisher just before I packed for this little jaunt."

The automaton arrived with the tea, and Wellington watched the machine perform effortlessly. It did not seem to struggle with its balance as the train rocked back and forth in its rhythm. He glanced over to Falcon, who was still staring at him. "One of your works, I assume?"

"The internal gyroscope system is mine, yes, and so is the voice and motion recognition programing and the overall design of the *automosteward*. I do think aesthetics should matter."

Wellington raised his cup to Professor Falcon and then winced.

"I cannot take claim for the tea recipe, however," she said, sliding to him the bowl of sugar cubes.

He gave a slight nod and then said to the automosteward, "Breakfast Number Three, if you please."

"Yes sir," the synthetic voice replied before turning towards the kitchen. "Your name and Passenger Identification, please."

"Orville Isaac," he returned. Wellington then reached into his coat pocket and pulled out his ticket, assigned to him by Petit. "Passenger 0422."

"Thank you, Mr Isaac. I will make certain the toast is to your liking."

Wellington watched the automaton walk away before turning back to Falcon who was enjoying his reaction to the innovation. "I take it the name and identification is..."

"... for the kitchen staff so that a passenger's specific tastes or requirements are always met. Your toast, for example."

"I do prefer it to be more of a golden brown and soft, yes."

Professor Falcon gave a slight nod. "Those details matter to a passenger. The automosteward also uses passenger references for the train conductor, in case of additional charges to your fare," she said, motioning to her own cigar.

"Brilliant, that is," he said.

"So, Mr Isaac, you asked me a moment ago what I think I have," she began picking up her cigar. She went to puff, but paused and then motioned to the vice. Wellington gave an assuring nod, and she proceeded to smoke. He had expected this woman based on her reputation and character in interviews to be quick witted and clever, but he did not count on the woman being this seductive. "I believe it to be a sense of adventure and wonder."

"I would imagine that is expected, considering our current mode of transportation?"

Henrietta chuckled. "The OHX-1 was hardly inspiration. More like evolution."

"I beg to differ. Hypersteam travel is an incredible feat, even though it is now expected in train travel. To combine all the luxuries of the Orient Express and the innovations of hypersteam all so seamlessly?" He shrugged as he stirred two cubes of sugar into his tea. "That is a touch of brilliance."

"Maybe you are not perfect, but I was right: you are a man of intellect and intelligence. Rather refreshing."

Wellington didn't try to fight the blushing. Being referred to as "a man of intellect and intelligence" from a mind as brilliant as Professor Henrietta Falcon was quite an honour. He cleared his throat and finally asked, "Refreshing, you say?"

"My colleague and I could see at the departure ceremony the calibre of travelling companions. Politicians, stage celebrities, business tycoons. Not what you would expect to be passionate about the sciences."

"I could easily be that average passenger," Wellington offered.

Professor Falcon leaned back in her chair to take a drag of her cigar. "Tosh, don't be so absurd. You're a man passionate about knowledge. It's in your vocabulary, and in your eyes."

Wellington chucked. "Must be quite the skill you have there, Profes—"

"Henrietta."

Wellington took another sip of tea. "Must be quite the skill you have there, Henrietta. Anyone else on this train strike you in such a similar fashion?"

"Well now, Mr Isaac, I can assure you, I do not invite all men to my table as you have been. Not even my associate from the Lovelace Centre, and he's a fine gentleman."

"As you said—sometimes, it is most difficult to find a like-minded adventurer to share with." Wellington managed to tear his eyes away from the professor to see the automosteward approaching with his breakfast. The scent of eggs, ham, and toast—perfectly prepared—tickled his nose.

"Perhaps, if you attend tonight's soirée, I would meet a gentleman such as yourself and make an introduction."

"Is this event in the parlour tonight?"

"A chance for Her Majesty's subjects and cultural authorities from all of Europe to share drinks and chit-chat, yes. Tonight, at seven." A strangely playful smile crossed her face. "Are you saying I have convinced you to attend?"

"I was not planning to do so, but yes, it sounds most delightful. And I am anxious to get to know my fellow adventurers."

"I don't even think this lot are bold enough to be labelled tourists. They intend to stick very close to the itineraries the Cook agents have meticulously designed for them, and that includes the closest restaurants that cater to their sensitive palates."

"I take it you do not adhere to such conventions?"

"Burned my itinerary before arriving to the station," she said with a self-satisfied smile. "If I am to journey beyond the Empire, then I want to experience it all, free of the trappings Her Majesty is so fond of assuring her citizens are always omnipresent."

Wellington nodded. "Then I am indeed most fortunate to be at your table. You do not seem to be the kind to suffer fools lightly."

"So, tonight. At seven." Falcon then stood and slid next to Wellington's teacup her card. "Do not be fashionable. I prefer promptness."

With the slightest of nods, Professor Falcon gathered up her book and notes, and continued back towards the passenger cars. Wellington was certain he was watching her with the same fascination as he did with the automosteward. He turned back to his breakfast, but not before making eye contact with the Castles. They were glaring at him.

Wellington looked back at his breakfast and then took up the announcement card of Professor Henrietta Falcon. Quite the turn of events.

Dropping a third cube of sugar into his tea, Wellington gave the brew a few stirs, then raised his cup to the crotchety old couple.

Bugger off, you wankers, he thought with a smile. *I have plans tonight with a scientific legend.*

CHAPTER TWELVE

⇥⇤

In Which Gentlemen of the Ministry Attempt to Mend a Broken Heart

"That's the most ridiculous thing I ever heard!"

"You mean to tell me," Brandon Hill began, his jaw somewhat slack out of shock, "in all the years of butting heads with the House of Usher, you never heard about the code names for their regional directors?"

Bruce gave his Canadian partner a rap on his shoulder. "Mate, you understand me better than anyone in the Ministry. I just need to be told what must get done, and who I need to punch."

"Well, that's who we're contending with here. The bloke goes under the moniker of Mr Badger."

"I hate bloody badgers," Bruce grumbled. "Little bastards live underground but jump out and chew your toes given half the chance."

Brandon shot him a look from under one arched eyebrow. "You know *nothing* about badgers, Bruce. You just don't like Italy."

The Australian rubbed his nose and looked around the street market of Assisi. It was a sunny day in the province of Umbria. Everyone was having a fine old time buying cheese, artichokes, tomatoes and what have you. The olive skin, raven locks, and tantalising curves of the locals almost made the trip across the Atlantic worthwhile for Bruce.

Almost.

David Harker was as miserable and insufferable as Bruce feared. Even the slow ascent of the airship *Cloud Dancer* made him lose his lunch while his complexion fluctuated between green and yellow.

And if Bruce had to hear about how "his darling Virginia" was in such a state of fright *one more time*...

A muscle in his jaw twitched, but another Italian beauty—this one with a body and a face that would have made Venus jealous—caught his eye. She smiled and dared to wink at him.

"Whatever they feed the locals here sure does make for some good-looking people," he admitted, allowing his smile to widen.

"I shall not debate you on that," Brandon said cheerily, buffing a bright red apple he had purchased from the market. "Italy is a place of beauty. Music. Art. Architecture. Produce."

That last item ripped Bruce out of his flirtation. "Come again, mate?"

"Look at this, will you?" Brandon asked, holding the apple up to him. Admittedly, the fruit was bigger than his fist. Impressive, to say the least. He took a deep bite out of the shiny apple. "Oh, and what of the technology? If only Da Vinci were able to see this brave, new world we live in."

"Are you purposefully not noticing the bits o' jam here in Umbria?" Bruce watched as Brandon took another large bite. "How's that fruit, mate?"

Brandon shrugged, sending bits of apple in every direction. "I have tastes, like you, but they are more..." He thought a bit through his exaggerated chewing until his eyes widened. Seemed that he found the word he was looking for. "Exotic."

"More exotic than the women of Italy?"

"Well, there's exotic women of Italy, and then there are those *exotic* women of Italy. Women that are as dangerous as they are alluring.»

Bruce cocked his head to one side, but he deduced what Brandon was on about. "Good Lord," he whispered, shaking his head. His partner, regardless of the way the two of them get on and the results that they brought back to the home office, was sometimes completely off his nut. "The del Mortes?" Bruce asked in a hushed voice. "Are you mad?"

"We can all dream, my friend."

Casting glances left and right, Bruce leaned in even closer. "How many of them have you seen?"

"Only a few, at a distance," Brandon replied with a slight sigh.

"You're lucky, mate. Close up, they're pretty. I mean, gorgeous. Ravina and I tangled with one another in Kenya. Monica... yeah, Monica, quite a looker, that one." Bruce paused, taking in the somewhat dopy grin painted across Brandon's face. His partner was completely and utterly clueless. "Something else that is quite pretty? Angel's Trumpets."

Brandon furrowed his brow. "Angel's Trumpets?"

"Wait... this is something you *don't* know?"

"Oh, when it comes to botanical matters, I'm afraid I am far from a green thumb."

"Well, let me enlighten you about this little plant from home. Angel's Trumpets. Beautiful little buggers, they are, all yellow and orange, like those Daylilies but maybe not as big."

"Oh, they sound delightful."

"That they are, and the scent? Just loverly." Bruce crooked an eyebrow at his partner. "They are also highly toxic. You eat these seeds or brew up a bit of tea with those leaves, and you'll be dealing with headaches and maybe some disorientation… if you are lucky."

"And pray tell what if you are unlucky?"

"Paralysis and death." Bruce gave a little nod before adding, "That is the del Morte family in a nutshell."

Brandon's shoulders slumped. Was he going to give up like that?

"Now hold on a moment!" He chimed in, as Bruce expected. "Sophia del Morte helped us with that trouble at the Diamond Jubilee and, according to scuttlebutt at the office, assisted Eliza and Wellington in India last year."

Bruce replied with a derisive snort. "I am sure she had her own reasons. Kind of difficult to do something out of the goodness of your heart when you don't have one."

Brandon went to take another bite out of his apple, but he froze. "Well, bugger me," he whispered. "Looks like our recruit doesn't understand the notion of working in shadow."

Turning to follow his partner's gaze, a choice curse fell from Bruce's lips on seeing David Harker, dressed in such a manner that he stood out in the Marketplace. He might as well have a giant banner that read *"I am a cloth-eared git bumbling his way through Italy. Please rob me!"* suspended over his head. Harker's suit was spotless white. Not a muted cream or even a soft white. Bright white. The accompanying hat he wore, a simple boater's hat, was much like his suit—spotless, free of any sort of wear—as if purchased only a moment ago.

This would have been enough to push Bruce and Brandon's efforts into disarray, but to top it all off David Harker was passing out paper leaflets to anyone and everyone walking by him. The man might as well had lit a bonfire in the middle of Assisi's town square and danced naked for all to see.

"Bet I can guess what he's giving out to Italy's great unwashed," Bruce growled as he came to his feet.

His stride devoured the distance between himself and Harker. With a loud *snap* that made the man jump, Bruce snatched the flyer free from his hand. What Bruce saw and read there was no surprise. The artist he had hired had done a good job of rendering David's "Sweet Virginia". Bruce could tell that since he'd had her picture shoved in front of his face so many times by her blithering idiot of a husband. The word "MISSING" stretched across the top of the flyer, filling the top quarter of the page. Underneath the portrait was Harker's name, the hotel he had booked for them all, and contact information.

"Mr Harker," Bruce began, crumpling the flyer in one hand but paused.

"Are you mad?!" was the phrase perched on the tip of his tongue, but he had to proceed very carefully. The tosspot was not only bankrolling this entire mission, but he had the blessing of both the Ministry headquarters and the Crown itself. Bruce had to employ diplomacy on this matter—not one of his greatest skills.

"I understand you are..." and he ground his teeth as the flyer crinkled in his fist, "... distraught over the disappearance of your beloved. Believe me, you made that quite clear during our voyage here. But you cannot—"

"What do you mean, I cannot?!" Harker blurted, wrenching the flyers away from Bruce's grasp. "My finances that are funding this English-American venture. All it would take would be one æthermissive and I can assure you the newswires will find my story most compelling."

Brandon came up behind Bruce in an attempt to smooth the waters. "Mr Harker, we are trying to find your wife. Nefarious sorts have taken her from you..."

"And I am intending to raise awareness, and recruit as many people as will hear me to aid in our search for my dear Virginia."

"Exactly," Bruce replied, "and you are recruiting complete strangers, any one of which could be working with the kidnappers."

Harker looked around, his puffed-out chest deflating. Not completely though. "You can't be certain of that."

Brandon grabbed the remaining posters out of his hand. "The point is, neither are you."

"This is how operations work, mate," Bruce said, leaning into Harker. "These people have no idea we are here. The more we can work in secret, the more of an advantage we have over them. If they become aware we are here, we'll be chasing their dust. So, burn these flyers and we do this *our* way. Low profile. Undercover. Ya' understand?"

"I... paid a rather hefty penny to have them printed," Harker stammered.

Brandon glanced at the flyers, looked back to Harker, and shook his head. He started back up the stairs of their hotel.

"You want to be a part of this job, feel like you are entitled to be as you are picking up the bill, then fine. Sign the check, tag along, but you do things *our* way."

Once Brandon returned with nary a flyer in sight and Harker brought to heel, the three gentlemen walked a little further down the street, dodging shoppers and toddlers. Bruce's gaze darted from building to building, his cursory glances meant to look like those of a tourist's, but for his own part, he was not enjoying the architecture so much as he was watching for sightlines. It was impossible to judge how much damage this plonk head had brought to their operation.

"So you have some idea where in Umbria my beloved is being held?" Harker called over the surrounding din.

Both agents turned to stare at him. "You mind speaking a little louder because I'm not sure the merchants in Florence heard you," Bruce said in a low voice.

"Florence?" Harker chuckled. "That's miles from here."

"Bruce," Brandon broke in with a dark look, "I'll slip on ahead whist you train our Junior Agent here."

"That might be for the best." As Brandon walked away, the Australian could tell his partner was done with Harker. Brandon might have a slow temper, but once it got going, it was a terrible thing.

With a touch of his finger to his lips, Bruce beckoned for Harker to follow.

After a few minutes of bobbing and weaving through foot traffic, the two men stopped in front of a pink-coloured building, no different to those around it. Bruce didn't find the dwelling characteristic of Usher. They usually preferred something more dark, brooding and opulent. Anything gothic really.

"This is the first step in finding your beloved, Mr Harker. Within these humble trappings is a defector from the group we believe are behind your lovely's abduction."

"Just a moment—you *know* who abducted my sweet Virginia?"

Right, how do we broach this subject? The House of Usher was a secret society. Granted, organisations like his, OSM, Section P, and others were well aware of them, but to avoid panic and paranoia, his superiors kept that knowledge from the public.

Except now the public was standing within punching distance.

"Mr Harker—David—" Bruce began, "what your government's agency and my government's agency do are not very different. We handle cases considered too unusual for the authorities, and this means we have dealings with nefarious individuals."

Harker swallowed hard. "Nefarious?"

"Oh, yeah. The worst, and right now, I'm about to meet with one of their lot."

"Are you..." Harker swallowed again. "Are you sure this is safe?"

"Bloody hell, trust me will you? I won't let so much as a hair on your head get harmed."

Harker gave a sharp nod before releasing the breath he was holding. "Very well. What would you have me do?"

Bruce lead him into the foyer of the building where, as his good Australian luck would have it, a bench was open. "I want you to sit here and keep a sharp eye while I go and have a chat with this *scallywag*." Harker was the sort that would enjoy feeling as if he were contributing to the intrigue. "Keep watch and I'll yell if I need any help. All right?"

Harker gave a nod and dropped into a position on the bench that he must have believed communicated casual.

Bruce entered the lift and began his ascent. Inside, the building was quite simple and clean. The checkerboard tile had a high polish, the walls were smooth, and the wooden doors gleamed. Hardly the kind of setting Usher tended to prefer. However this informant of his was not the run-of-the-mill Usher operative. He preferred a more comfortable setting for his business. Today, this meeting was happening as he had uttered one word capturing his and Brandon's attention: Ragnarök.

Usher had been keeping this operation Bruce and Brandon had uncovered in Russia close to the vest, but they had tripped up using the ticket Virginia Harker had purchased with her husband for Italy. Thanks to the photo that Harker always carried, it was easy enough to find she had picked up a train ticket from the Florence Travel Plaza, her destination from New York. From Florence, she had grabbed the first train destined for Assisi. While Virginia was well-educated, she was not fluent in Italian. That made it easier to identify a lone female tourist attempting to find her way through the countryside. Considering this trail left behind, it was like the House boys weren't even trying.

This convenient trail ran cold once they had arrived in Assisi, so now the clock was ticking in earnest.

His informant surprised him on mentioning Ragnarök when Bruce had asked about Virginia Harker's kidnapping. The staged disappearances OSM had been contending with and Ragnarök had something in common, and Bruce's informant was eager to share with him what he knew.

With that weighing on his mind, Bruce exited the lift but froze by the third step. In the corner opposite something moved. Drawing a modification-free Bulldog, he slid into a corner and waited. It could be a House boy. It could also be some old lady wrestling with her groceries while trying to manage the door.

One way to find out.

He waited for the shuffle to still, and that was when Bruce dragged his foot across the floor in a slow scuff, then tapped his heel three times.

Nothing.

Bruce repeated the gesture. *Scuff. Tap. Tap. Tap.*

A voice from where the sound came from asked, "Bruce?"

Lowering the Bulldog, he let out a slow exhale. After a peek around the corner, he found Brandon folding up some metallic device and stuffing it into his satchel. "How in the blazes—"

His partner grinned and patted his bag. "I used these claws of R&D's to climb up here." For some reason known only to him, Brandon was always eager to try out any of Blackwell's or Axelrod's creations. It was as close to a death wish as an agent could come in Bruce's opinion. It was the only thing he shared in common with Wellington Books: a healthy distrust of those two *clankertons*.

"So how experimental are those things?" Bruce asked. "They even christened?"

"Not yet," Brandon said, the eagerness in his words threatening to overwhelm him. "You think they would let me name them?"

Bruce gave him a shrug. "With our R&D geniuses, anything is possible."

"That it is, mate. That it is."

"How are we for tactical surroundings?"

Brandon motioned for Bruce to join him by the window. He gestured to the surrounding structures. "Foot chase across the rooftops might be a bit of a challenge with the sharp angle of the roof. Main concern is that chapel," he said pointing to a tall bell tower jutting over the village's modest skyline.

"Great," Bruce grumbled. "Perfect sniper location."

"But the good news: no sign of being watched, at least from the ground."

A sudden shift in wind carried with it the comforting scent of bread baking and succulent meats on an open fire somewhere. Bruce fought the sudden urge to sneak away for some pasta and a glass of wine. He had developed quite a taste for Italian food even if he had to watch his back for the del Mortes to get the good stuff.

"Why don't you make for that belfry, mate. I'll give our contact here a right and proper shakedown."

Brandon gave a curt nod before asking. "What about our unexpected guest?"

"He'll behave." Bruce motioned back to the lift with his head and added, "I've got him keeping a watch on the lobby."

Chewing on his bottom lip a little, Brandon looked back and forth between the lift and the window he had just scaled up to meet with his partner. "Even that might be too much."

"Don't you worry, mate," Bruce assured him. "I've brought him to heel. We treat him like a diplomat or HVT and make him feel like he's an active part of our little ballyhoo. Right?"

Brandon screwed his face up. "High value target or not, I don't like it. He's... unreliable."

"He's the money right now."

"I'll go back the way I came," he grumbled, pulling out one of the metallic, chain-mail gloves from his satchel. "You've got your Ministry ring on?"

"Of course," Bruce said, holding up his hand. "Why?"

Brandon sat on the windowsill, placed his hands on the exterior, and lifted himself out into the open space. "I overheard a rumour back at R&D when I picked these gloves up. Something about replacing them."

"With what?"

"You really wouldn't like it. Enough said."

The agents shared a little salute. "Enjoy yourself, mate." Brandon's smile brightened before Bruce took a few steps forward and pointed at him. "Not too much, though."

By the sudden, deflated expression on Brandon's face, that little suggestion had been necessary.

Bruce smoothed out the front of his waistcoat and approached the door of the apartment where he would meet his informant. Something did not feel right about this. Up until now they had communicated through dead drops and coded messages, having only "met" in a back alley a few blocks from this building. The informant had disguised his voice in this introduction and never left the shadows. This would be their first face-to-face. Previously this informant had offered up reliable details of smaller operations. With the mention of Ragnarök and an actual meeting, Bruce was certain his man on the inside would be expecting safe passage in exchange for information.

With David Harker along for the ride, this simple defection would prove difficult.

Finally deciding now was as good as the next moment for his approach, Bruce knocked twice. Paused. Knocked three times.

His grip tightened on the handle of his gun, but a muffled voice responded. "Good. You're alone, Campbell."

How did he know that? Bruce›s thought scattered as he glanced up to see the metallic snake, its smooth, featureless glass face bending towards the opposite direction of the corridor, then back to him. "Outside of the Remington-Elliot in your coat, any other weapons I need to worry about?"

"You only have to worry about what I'm carrying," Bruce pulled his hand away from his lapels, "if you are intending to double-cross me. That's not in the cards today, is it, mate?"

The latch pulled back, and Bruce nudged the door open, its low creak sending a chill up his spine. It was far too bloody quiet in this building for his liking. He watched as his Usher mole, Adolfus Maine, backed up, a modified shotgun in his grip, pointing at Bruce's chest. The weapon's indicators cast soft green light against the man's trigger hand.

Only when the door closed behind him did Bruce dare to speak. "The raven comes in the morning."

The young man's back stiffened, but he looked Bruce up and down before replying, "But not if the lion gets him first."

This was the first time Bruce had laid eyes on Adolfus Maine. In fact he wasn't even sure if that was his informant's real name.

Maine couldn't have been more than eighteen years old. A scruffy attempt at a red beard resided on his rosy cheeks and wrapped around his chin. The glasses he wore were another feeble attempt to make him look older, but were about as a successful as the facial hair.

His Adam's apple bobbed as he examined Bruce, but he lowered the shotgun. "Are you all there is?" he said, his eyes darting to the door as if he expected a horde of agents to burst in.

"Only me."

Moving very slowly, his hands open and facing Maine, Bruce slipped up to him and flipped the safety above the trigger. The indicators switched from green to yellow. Now, the bloke would not shoot a hole in the floor.

"Look, mate, I'm all you need." The boy turned pale. A change of tact was in order, or Bruce realised he might have to change a nappy. "Rest assured, I'm not alone. Alright? Got an agent across town in the church and got a bloke downstairs."

His informant looked him over again, but this time he nodded. Holding out his hand he said, "Argus Tinsdale. Thank you for making these arrangements on such short notice, Agent Campbell."

"Argus Tinsdale?" Bruce asked. "Not Adolfus Maine?"

Tinsdale barked a dry laugh before flipping the hood up over his head. He now looked like a well-dressed monk. "You didn't think me foolish enough to use my actual name when turning over secrets to the enemy?"

"Makes sense, now that you mention it." Bruce cleared his throat. "It's good to meet you face to face."

Tinsdale walked in a strange, serpentine pattern around his parlour. "You are far older than I thought you were, Agent Campbell."

Bruce was about to return his own thoughts on Tinsdale and his age, but froze as he took in the boy's dwellings. For such a young pup, Argus Tinsdale had quite the opulent lifestyle. This was the kind of apartment that would have made Eliza D Braun green with envy. Deep, dark colours, textures that promised only the finest of comfort and quality, and various works of art, both paintings and sculptures, that spoke volumes of Tinsdale's breeding and education.

"Nice bit of tinker at the door," Bruce said, motioning to the odd surveillance contraption. "Very clever."

"Invention is a bit of a hobby of mine. Some people say I am far too clever for my own good. Sometimes, I think they are right. Sometimes."

"Got to hand it to you, mate," Bruce said, continuing his way into the apartment, "you are certainly..."

"Stop!" Tinsdale snapped.

Bruce froze and followed Tinsdale's frantically waving hand to his own feet. Bright white tape outlined a border of some kind. They were some distance from the windows. "Am I right in assuming these are the boundaries of possible sightlines?"

"So long as you stay within these boundaries, you should be safe."

Taking a generous step back from the lines, he asked, "What exactly did you do for the House of Usher, Mai—sorry, Tinsdale?"

"I ran their accounts."

"So you're one of them number blokes, balancing the books, making sure payroll goes through, that sort of thing?"

"Yes."

Quite the prize, especially considering the boy's age. "And you're what? Eighteen? Sixteen?"

"I'm nineteen, thank you very much!"

Bruce shook his head. "Pardon me then." Walking around the borders of the sightlines, he peeked through a break in the curtain. "Well, for a numbers bloke, you're quite the cautious one."

"With the new management and what I know, I have to be."

"How long were you with Usher?"

Tinsdale cleared his throat. "They recruited me while I was at university."

"University?"

"I entered at fifteen. I've always been talented with mathematics. Usher took care of my parents so long as I made sure the books were in order. Not a bad life, really."

"While I'm sure your story is fascinating, that's not what brings me here."

"Ragnarök," Tinsdale choked out the word. When Bruce arched an eyebrow at him, he went on. "The House is aware that the Ministry found some things in Russia late last year, but they are moving on with it, regardless."

"And what is 'it' exactly?" Bruce leaned forward. "Because we've been looking ever since then to find out what Ragnarök is."

Tinsdale motioned to a table tucked away in the corner of the parlour. At the sight of the modest tea setting, Bruce's stomach growled. "Nothing good."

"Not a tea drinker, myself," he said. "But I could go for a bite to eat." He took a seat opposite of his informant and started stacking cucumber sandwiches on a plate. "What do you have for me?"

"Ragnarök is the brainchild of the new Lord of—no, he calls himself the Chairman," Tinsdale corrected himself as he poured a cup of tea.

"And who would that be? Mr Badger? Mr Fox?" Bruce waggled his eyebrows as he reached for the tea. "Mr Ostrich?"

The young lad shot Bruce an icy stare. "When you reach the heights of *Chairman*, anonymity is no longer allowed."

"So what is this bloke's name?"

"Herman Webster Mudgett, but he insists on being referred to by his alias. Dr Henry Howard Holmes."

"In my experience, names like that signal you're dealing with a tosspot." Bruce took a quick sniff of the tea he was about to sample. He hated tea, but if it kept his informant talking, that was all that mattered.

"Holmes is the reason I am leaving the House. That, and Ragnarök."

"Must be a massive operation if this Holmes fella is pushing it along, despite our Russian operation. You got munitions and weapons development there, human trafficking in the United States from what OSM insinuates. What's going on here in delightful Italy, I wonder?"

"Research and development," Tinsdale said simply.

"What kind?" Bruce said, before the growl of his stomach sounded again.

Tinsdale motioned to Bruce's sandwiches. "Agent Campbell, why are we talking when you are on an empty stomach. Please, tuck in. I will get you properly caught up once we finish our tea and are safely underway."

Bruce glanced down to the plate in front of him. It wasn't the pasta dish he was craving earlier, but these nibbles would tide him over until he could eat properly.

Only when he picked up the top cucumber sandwich with two fingers did he notice the soft glow rising and falling from his Ministry ring's stone.

"Mind if I pick up an extra cushion?" Bruce asked in an even voice. "This chair isn't suiting me."

"Help yourself."

Rising from the table, Bruce nodded to Tinsdale as he meticulously buttered his scone. The pillow was within reach, but Bruce knew he would never make it when he heard the soft scrape of a chair leg against the floor.

His left hand shot out as he turned and slapped hard around the Remington-Elliot Tinsdale was now brandishing. With the pistol pointing away, Bruce drove his right hand up into the boy's elbow, bending and breaking the arm in one strike. Gasping for breath, Tinsdale went to scream, but Bruce stopped it by breaking the poor sod's nose. Now Tinsdale was struggling for breath. With the right arm useless, Bruce slipped around and grabbed the nape of the boy's neck. He swept the informant's legs out from under him, driving the lad's face into the large pillow of a chez lounge. Tinsdale kicked and bucked, but Bruce simply braced his knee into the informant's back and pushed him deeper into the cushion. The muffled scream turned into a rattling gasp, and Bruce only pressed harder. Shoes that had scrambled for purchase now scuffed out a weak, worn effort. Then Tinsdale was still.

Bruce didn't move. Not for another few minutes or so.

And there goes any hope for a smooth operation, Bruce thought glumly as he pulled himself off the dead man. Combing his hair back with his fingers, he took in a deep breath and swallowed back his distaste. Tinsdale was not even twenty, and Bruce had killed him. He needed a drink, but he did not want to chance anything in here. Returning to the table, he waved his ring hand over the tea setting. The cucumber sandwiches, the salmon sandwiches, and the biscuits. Only the scones and tea failed to make his ring blink. Yeah, Tinsdale was a lad, but he was also ready to kill Bruce. Premeditated like.

He took another look around the room. No doubt someone would be here soon, especially if Tinsdale didn't send word that there was a corpse in need of Usher's attention.

Bruce crossed the parlour for the informant's desk, open to the world with no semblance of security. *Why would he lock it? Tinsdale expected to murder me with cucumber sandwiches*, Bruce thought. His hand paused over a blank pad of paper while his gaze darted from corner to corner of the desk. Tinsdale had a few notes scattered across part of this roll top. Grabbing a pencil, Bruce drew from the pad its last entry. Tearing it free of the pad, he stuffed it in his pockets. A quick check of the desk drawers yielded a black book only a little larger than his hand. It was full of notes and numbers.

This would be more for Brandon's expertise.

Bruce returned to Tinsdale's body and started rifling through his pockets. A set of keys, a wallet, and a small scrap of paper, folded only once. He glanced at the writing.

Gargoyle

With a final glance around the flat, Bruce closed the door behind him and began his descent down the stairs.

When he emerged from the stairwell, Harker sprang to his feet. "Any word on my Virginia?"

Bruce shrugged. His answers tumbled out like running water pouring out of a pitcher far too fast. "Possible lead. Need to follow up on it. Talk as we walk. Let's go."

"Mr Campbell? What is—"

Bruce grabbed the man's arm and dragged him out into the afternoon sun. While Harker looked about him and kept returning his confused gaze to Bruce, the Australian simply kept his eyes forward and his stride strong and confident.

He had to hope his partner had not been observed on his trip to the bell tower of Assisi. From now on he had to assume, all eyes were on him and his irreverent Canadian partner.

CHAPTER THIRTEEN

Wherein a Monster Strikes

"You look stunning," Wellington said.

Eliza glanced at herself in the mirror, turning slightly. The evening dress was a recent purchase from her last visit to London. The black patterns which wound and twisted their way along the dress and its train were quite lovely while the plunging neckline was very daring. Oh, how her mother would find this look scandalous.

"I sincerely hope in this fashion I can hold a candle to the formidable Professor Henrietta Falcon," she said pointedly.

Usually when Wellington blushed, she found it charming. Endearing, even. When he did it at the mention of this academic's name, though, she found it insufferable. "Eliza, I am sure you will find her as impressive as I did when we meet her tonight."

"I can introduce myself as a kindred spirit or perhaps as an old friend," she said, crossing the room to pick up her modest purse. The weight of her Ministry-issue pistol gave her much comfort. "You did rather go on about her this afternoon."

Wellington cleared his throat. "I did... yes..."

"In quite excruciating detail, I might add."

He dodged that barb by taking stock of himself in the mirror. Eliza made a note in her mind to put Professor Henrietta Falcon at the top of her suspect list. Out of spite.

"Ready, are we?" he asked.

Staying mad at Wellington was nigh on impossible, she realised as she took his arm. "Very well. Into the belly of the beast we go."

They proceeded towards the dining area of the hypersteam in silence. Outside was darkness so heavy and absolute that only the lights from within their train reflected back to them. Eliza glanced at their strange, transparent reflections against the train's long black mirrors. *We do make a fine couple,* she thought, squeezing Wellington's arm.

He looked around them before he asked her in a hushed voice. "No sign of Jekyll today?"

Eliza twisted her lips. "I was careful, though having to mingle with the passengers, I expected the worst. Still, I didn't see him. If he's here, he is keeping his head down."

"I have been combing the passenger manifest," Wellington said. He took a breath that made his entire body shudder. "We're trying to eliminate possibilities, but it is taking too long. We're only a day or two out of Constantinople."

"I know, Welly, I know," Eliza reassured him, although the same inconvenient truth gnawed away at her resolve. The madman's combination of barbarity and brilliance she found most unsettling. "Perhaps he's using another kind of cypher for his name. A play on words, a name from his own past..."

"What's in a name," Wellington said, his words punctuated with a mirthless laugh. "A rose by any other name would smell as sweet."

Eliza rapped him on his shoulder. "If you insist on quoting Shakespeare, please, anything but *Romeo & Juliet*. I found Juliet to be rather dim if you must know."

"Which of his works do you prefer?"

Eliza tilted her head. "*Much Ado About Nothing*. A rather charming romance if there ever was one penned by the Bard."

That earned her a sincere smile. Dressed as he was in his own finery, an elegant dinner jacket of the finest cut with a crisp white bowtie and a waistcoat, the smile was the last detail his outfit needed.

They approached the door to the train's parlour. On the other side of the ornate glass pane, opaque and featureless figures milled about. The scent of fine tobacco tickled Eliza's nose, and her mouth watered.

"I could go for a cigar myself," she said wistfully. "Lead the way, Orville."

"With pleasure, Angelica."

Opening the parlour door, before them was a less formal, more relaxed version of their boarding ceremony in Paris. The influential, the powerful, and the famous were now merely people, all sharing stories, opinions, and observations on the world. Perhaps some of them were discovering unexpected commonalities while others were testing their convictions.

Whichever it was, one thing was sure; it was an impressive tableaux of prestige.

Jekyll could well have regarded it as a delightful feeding ground.

"Mr Isaac!" a voice called from across the room to their right.

Eliza mustered up a smile she hoped would read as charming and affable and turned to look at Professor Henrietta Falcon. She couldn't help crooking an eyebrow at what the academic was wearing this evening. Perhaps she underestimated the woman as the eye-catching red dress she wore was a delightful union of silk and lace, her own neckline challenging Eliza's in scandalous depths. The colour was also labelled inappropriate in these social circles, but Falcon wore it with confidence.

"Frederick-Worth?" Eliza asked, motioning to the professor's dress.

"Why, yes, the man did leave quite the legacy, did he not?" Falcon turned on Wellington to demand, "Mr Isaac, your thoughts? It is rather bold and daring for a woman of my academic profession, but I would argue that my femininity is just as worth celebrating as my scientific achievements. So, why hide it? From the looks of your wife's tastes in fashion, I would think she is in agreement." Falcon turned her attention to Eliza. "Or does Mr Isaac keep you in a gilded cage, as do most men with their sweethearts, and allow you to shine only when it suits them?"

Her crooked eyebrow inched higher. *What, my dear Lady Disdain, are you yet living?*

"My dearest Angelica, is a woman of her own accomplishments. I am most fortunate to have her in my life."

"And what do you do, Mrs Isaac?" the professor asked.

"I'm a writer," Eliza stated, "and in between publications, I engage in competitive target shooting."

Falcon's eyebrows raised. "You are?"

"Oh yes," Eliza said with a tilt of her head. "I'm quite a crack shot."

"I would love to test your mettle. Perhaps we could find a range somewhere in Constantinople?"

Eliza blinked. "That... that would be lovely."

"Your husband here was quite vague with your plans at the end of the line."

"Angelica is researching a novel, so I am taking some time from my own work to assist her."

"How very supportive," Falcon said with a broad grin, "and what are you writing?"

"Scientific Romance," Eliza stated as Wellington blurted out, "Spy adventure."

Falcon looked to each of them, her smile widening. "Crossing genres. How exciting."

"Perhaps drinks are in order," Wellington said, taking Eliza's arm and threading it through his own. "Professor?"

"Delightful, Mr Isaac," Falcon replied. "I want to hear all about your book and the research therein."

The three of them made for the bar where Eliza took quick stock of the OHX's special guests. Mustafa Solak held court at a corner table, and from the gestures he was making, she gathered he was reciting poetry. She also caught sight of Douglas Keating. He gave his luxurious moustache a gentle stroke before smiling and raising his glass to her.

Eliza was about to return the smile but instead went cold. Keating was alone. Ashe Robbins was nowhere to be seen.

Esther Pimms. Lulu Adele. Isabella Bradley. Zylphia Jenkins...
Ashe Robbins.

A drink appeared behind her which she snatched up and took a deep swallow. The burn of bourbon—a particular spirit she did not care for—jolted her back, and her eyes darted around the parlour.

"Angelica?" Wellington said, appearing at her shoulder with a glass of wine for himself and some kind of clear liquid intended for her. "I believe you snatched up Professor Falcon's drink."

"From the looks of her, she was in need of one. Never mind," Falcon said with a grin as she took the tumbler out of Wellington's grasp, "I was in a vodka sort of mood, anyway."

Eliza toasted the academic and, against her instincts, took another swig of the American spirit. How proud Bill Wheatley would have been of her.

"Angelica," Wellington asked, the concern in his eyes more than earnest, "are you not well?"

Eliza looked around them and glanced at Falcon. Sod it if she knew, her life was at stake along with everyone else. "Wellington, I know who is next."

She watched as he went pale. Falcon lowered her drink from her lips and glanced between them. "Perhaps you are drinking that bourbon rather too quickly, or did you call your hus—"

"Professor Falcon, time is of the essence. My name is Eliza D Braun, and this is Wellington Thornhill Books, and we are agents of Her Majesty's Ministry of Peculiar Occurrences."

"We are searching for a madman on this train, have been for days now," Wellington added, before taking hold of Eliza's hands. "Who's next?"

"The actress. Ashe Robbins. 'A' is next for my name, and she is not here."

"Are you certain of that, darling?" Wellington asked.

Eliza looked at him with her head cocked to one side. "An actress missing a chance to shine in a social setting? You saw how she was dressed at the train station."

He went to answer, but swallowed instead. "I... I didn't pay much attention to her if you must know."

"I did not find her particularly appealing in that colour."

Both Eliza and Wellington turned to the professor. She had forgotten the intellectual was standing there, and from the look on her face, she was not at all put off.

"So, we are to have a bit of an intrigue on this journey, are we?" she asked taking a sip of her drink.

"Professor, what we do is rather dangerous," Wellington said. "I must insist that—"

Professor Falcon kicked back the vodka, not flinching in the slightest. "Mr Books, have you ever hunted tigers across the Serengeti? Or have you scaled Mt Kilimanjaro, and on your descent shouldered your Sherpa when he's broken his ankle? Or have you bungie jumped from an airship over the skies of Auckland?"

Wellington's brow furrowed. "Bungie jumping?"

Eliza rapped his shoulder with the back of her hand. "It was all the rage when I left New Zealand." She leaned in towards the professor. "What we are about to undertake is not something to tick off an Adventurer's Club To-Do List. This man is a monster. Literally."

"The person we are chasing," Wellington added, "is killing random strangers and spelling out our names. He is up to 'A' in Eliza's name. With me, he's up to 'I'."

"Ashe Robbins, the actress," Professor Falcon said, "and you are now wondering about the 'I' and who is not here."

"We have not found Jekyll anywhere amongst the passenger list, so we have no idea if he has found his next target."

Falcon pursed her lips. "How did you have access to this list?"

"We've been masquerading as French Police assigned to the Express."

"Jekyll could be travelling under an assumed name," Eliza offered.

"So, you believe this Jekyll chap has been spending the journey looking for his next victims?" Falcon asked, her eyes glittering.

Something about that question made the idea of Jekyll interviewing close to seventy-five passengers within three days ridiculous. Twenty-five people a day from the moment they departed the Travel Plaza? Even for Jekyll that would be insane and easily noticed.

"Of course not," Eliza muttered. "That would be rather silly, now wouldn't it? And when you put it that way, how did we bloody miss this?"

Now it was Wellington who inclined his head. "Eliza?"

"Think on it, Wellington—you have three days to find two victims amongst over seventy passengers. So who has access to the passenger manifest?"

"Security," Wellington replied. "The Conductor and Stewards."

Eliza circled her hand like an impatient wheel, urging him to think faster. "And?"

Wellington shook his head, but the professor took Eliza's arm. "The staff. In particular, the *kitchen* staff."

"The automostewards," Wellington said with a triumphant grin. "They take your name and ticket number and deliver it to the kitchen."

"Each passenger, delivered to you, literally on a silver platter," Eliza added, feeling like a total dunce.

Falcon's mouth opened as if to ask something, but she stopped and frantically started searching the parlour. "Mr Books, do you happen to have the time?"

Wellington slipped out his pocket watch. "Twenty minutes after seven."

"Who are you looking for, Professor?" Eliza asked.

"Dr Tomlin," she said. "Doctor *Ignatius* Tomlin. Ignatius is my colleague from the Lovelace Centre, the colleague I mentioned to you earlier this morning. He is far more punctual than I, and he told me this afternoon that he would be joining me tonight at a quarter past seven, here. He's late."

Eliza's heart kicked in her chest. Her fingertips itched for her pounamu pistols as she asked, "Why that particular time, Professor?"

"He had a few computations that needed his attention, so he was unable to join me for dinner. To make up for it, he promised to join me for drinks."

"Dr Tomlin was taking his dinner early in his cabin, wasn't he?" Eliza saw the answer in Falcon's face. "Cabin?"

"Second car. Cabin 24."

Not tonight, Jekyll. It ends now. "Time to go, Welly."

"Right behind you, darling," he said. "Professor, you should—"

"—join you?" Falcon interjected, bending back her wrist. From the sleeve, a small pistol slapped into her open palm. With a quick hiss and a crackle, a transformer spun up. "But of course."

Eliza slapped two hands over the pistol and pushed the professor's hand down. "Professor," she hissed, "are you mad?"

"No, just prepared."

Wellington gave a little chortle. "I had no idea Quantum Engineering was such a dangerous profession."

Falcon winked at him. "If you are not in danger as a professional scientist, you're not pursuing the sciences right."

"And exactly what is this contraption of yours?"

With a smirk and a waggle of eyebrows, Falcon replied, "Something I've whipped up in my laboratory. Theoretically, I know what it could do, but I'm not so concrete on what it can *actually* do." She leaned into Eliza's ear and whispered in such a way that caused a trickle of electricity to slink down her spine. "Why don't we find out together?"

An experimental. Lovely. "Keep this mechanication of yours concealed until we can get out of here. Now then," Eliza said to each of them, taking a deep breath before continuing. "Jekyll may be preparing his next tableaux in Cabin 24, so we need to move."

Wellington nodded before bolting for the door.

"I was going to say *inconspicuously* but..." Eliza motioned with her head for Falcon to follow.

"Is Mr Books always this impetuous?" Falcon asked.

"Perhaps not the word I would use," Eliza said through clenched teeth. He was up ahead, moving quickly through the train. Reaching into the folds of her dress, she slipped her pounamu pistols free. "Concerning Jekyll, though, his judgement can be questionable."

Through the door window, she saw he'd come to a halt. Eliza and Falcon entered the car just as he kicked at the door to Cabin 24. A blood-curdling scream worthy of any fine *grand guignol* came from the cabin.

Over the cry came a man's voice, shrill and panicked as well. "We're in here! We're in here!"

"Mr Books," Falcon called, holding up her dubious sidearm. "Run."

Wellington disappeared through the opposite car door as Falcon pulled the trigger.

The sound assaulting Eliza's ears defied reason. Wondering where the bass drum, Gatling gun, and screaming hyena had come from, she finally realised this aural madness came from Falcon's palm-sized pistol. The beam emitting from its muzzle split, creating a field of wild, swirling energy when it came into contact with the wall. As Falcon turned at her waist, the crunching of wood and grinding of metal drowned out the odd, rattling thrum-scream. Luxury and elegance tore asunder, removing the wall completely and revealing a diorama of what was happening in Cabin 24.

Then, the crunching of wood and metal stopped.

The screaming ceased.

The calls for help went quiet.

"So *that's* what it does," Falcon said, eyeing the diminutive pistol with delight.

In Cabin 24 Ashe Robbins was dressed in high boots, a revealing blouse, and tight-fitting breeches. Around the actress' waist was an ill-fitting gun belt with toy pistols that had green handles. Her cheeks had a good amount of rouge on them but there were lines of black running through it. She had been sobbing. Sharing this macabre stage with her was a man about Wellington's height, or at least made to be so, with books secured to his shoes in a slapdash fashion. The suit he wore swallowed him whole as did the bowler. If Eliza had not known there was a grown man wearing the suit, she would have thought it was a child playing dress up.

It was when Wellington emerged from the far door of the car that the director and sole audience of whatever was transpiring between Miss Robbins and Doctor Tomlin picked himself up from the floor. He was clutching what remained of the high back chair he had been sitting in. Tendrils of smoke rose from the man's scorched shoulder as he spoke her partner. "Ah, Wellington," Jekyll spoke cheerily, "come to enjoy the show? We were about to get to the good part."

He turned to face Eliza and Falcon, and from behind her, the adventurous professor let out a gasp that was part exclamation and part shock. Jekyll's chef's frock sported modest stains from the night's repast, but there were also a few smears that Eliza recognised straight away as blood. That did not bode well.

"Ladies…." Jekyll smiled an impossible smile. Teeth that were far too long and far too sharp for a human jaw, grew more visible as the corners of his mouth stretched further and further back towards his ears.

Instinct took hold, and Eliza's grip on her own pistols tightened, but she caught a movement in the corner of her eye. With a quick, hard shoulder check that would have made a rugby back quite proud, she knocked Professor Falcon over, thwarting her shot intended for Jekyll. This was not Eliza saving Jekyll, but an apprehension. They needed to take him alive—however that might go.

He inclined his head towards Wellington, still at the opposite end of the car. So they at least had him confined between the two of them; his chemically enhanced strength and agility against Eliza's and Wellington's aim.

Could the chase be—

The mad scientist's eyes locked with hers and his smile stretched a fraction more, and that was when her eyes caught sight of the small box in his right hand.

Of course, she thought. *If he had access to the passengers, he would have access to the crew. All parts of it, including...*

"While I am not a cook, I am a rather clever gent as you both know," Jekyll said, his over-pronounced words sending spittle everywhere. "I garnished the conductor's food with something special, something quite unique. So unique that it could prove hazardous to his health if he does not receive an antidote." From his jacket's inside pocket, he held up a small vial of red liquid. He set it on a small table nearby, then held up the device resting in the palm of his hand. "That antidote will mean nothing if I throw this switch, however. Access to the engine will lock down completely. You might get through the door with some effort, but not before the Express comes into Constantinople like a gigantic bullet fired from a gun." Over his shoulder, Jekyll called, "Wellington, be a good lad and join the ladies."

Eliza's eyes went to her partner's, but he gave a fractional shake of his head. *Not yet.*

Jekyll gave a hard, dry laugh. "Keep your hands up where I can see them, if you please. I know Arthur raised you as quite a resourceful lad."

Wellington put his hands up to frame his face, his footsteps silent as he slipped by Jekyll. The madman's gaze never left Eliza's, his eyes fixed on her hands. If she even tried a shot, he would have thrown that switch.

"Very good," Jekyll said as Wellington passed by, countering him. He winced as he did so. He was hurt. Good. "Let us not do anything hasty, yes?"

A scream followed a rush of flesh, a decision made independent of any counsel or authority, as Ashe Robbins threw herself at Jekyll, wrapping her diminutive form around the monster's forearm. The unexpected jolt caused him to drop the trigger. It clattered along the floor, just close enough to Wellington for him to scoop it up.

Jekyll roared as he swung his arm back, lifting the actress off her feet. She soared back into the now-open cabin, and the mirror her body struck crunched on impact, shattering the reflection of the enraged fugitive. Robbins' body crumpled to the floor as Jekyll sprinted for the door where Wellington had been.

Ye gods, was he fast.

"Falcon," Eliza said, "get that antidote to the engine room."

Muttering a choice curse or two, Eliza sprinted past Wellington, making chase down the length of the OHX-1. Jekyll must have known how this had to end, seeing as they were running out of...

Oh. Damn.

She took aim and fired. Jekyll stumbled into the door frame, and his head reared back just before he pushed himself forward. Maybe she had hit that mangled shoulder. Impossible to tell through the broken glass of the door ahead, but she had caught him somewhere.

"Alive," Wellington reminded her as he dashed past. "We need him alive."

"Thank you for the reminder," Eliza gasped. "Nearly slipped my mind."

They now entered the crew quarters, and Jekyll was still ahead of them, his shoulder covered in blood but doing nothing in slowing his pace. The mad scientist slipped through the final door with enough time to lock it behind him.

Eliza pulled back the hammer of one of her pistols.

"Save your bullets," Wellington said, his stride widening as he drew closer to the door.

"Remember. Manners." Eliza said, stepping back. "Knock first."

He stepped up to the door, took in one long, slow breath, and Eliza caught in Wellington's eyes that dark stare she had once been on the receiving end of in India. His kick shattered the lock and lifted the door off its hinges. "Knock, knock, Dr Jekyll," he called into the luggage car.

Two steps in and a harsh white light blinded them both. Eliza's hair whipped her face, and her mouth suddenly watered. A thick tang of copper assailed her nostrils, tempting to take her down to her knees. She knew this sensation all too well, and amidst the assault on her physical senses, she also felt a growing dread. The haze receded from her eyes enough for her to see the electroporter swirling before them, its self-contained tempest devouring Jekyll. He disappeared just before the gate collapsed on itself and snapped shut, leaving singed suitcases and lockers rocking side to side in its wake.

Bracing herself against a stack of crates, she rested her fist against her hip, let out a long breath and waited. She couldn't imagine what Wellington was thinking in this moment.

"Perhaps..." she began.

"Do not start, Eliza."

"I would rather not fight about this."

"Neither would I."

She sighed. "Do you think the Old Man is right?"

Wellington frowned. "About what?"

"That we are too close to this. Too close to Jekyll."

"You think we are *letting* him escape?"

"I think," Eliza said, chewing on her bottom lip, "we're being careless."

"I think not," came a polished accent, sharp and insistent.

Both Eliza and Wellington looked back to the where the door swung on damaged hinges.

"Before you ask, the conductor and I had a rather one-sided conversation. He should be administering the antidote to the engineer as we speak," Professor Falcon stated. "Now, I believe you two should take a moment to tell me all about this clever little intrigue you have pulled me into. Why don't we start with the man who used ætherdimensional manipulation to escape because that intrigues me greatly."

CHAPTER FOURTEEN

In Which a Genius Devises a Clever Plan

Electricity once thrilled him to the core. Something about that strange metallic scent made his mouth water and the hair on his arms stand on end. It intoxicated him like a fine scotch or brandy. That signature odour of raw power conjured and controlled by Man was more than just the smell of innovation. It was the smell of success. The smell of money.

Electricity had been the innovation that made him who he was: the brightest scientific mind in the world. In the truest sense it defined him—and certainly not that mad Tesla fellow.

Now, the electricity in the air turned Edison's blood cold, caused his heart to hammer against his chest, and made his palms sweat. From the sharp tang, it wasn't a Shocker on the blink. The scent was his captor returning from the hunt, and Edison knew there would be something new for him to do.

The simple act of sitting up in his bed activated the two Shockers standing guard in his room. Their eyes turned from green to yellow as both metallic heads swivelled in his direction. Once they had acquired their target, their bodies followed suit. Their odd movement of head first, body after was unsettling—a flaw he had left in deliberately for just that reason. However, now that *he* was the prisoner, Edison made a mental note: the independent movement between head and body had to go. He'd make it more natural next time.

When the lock to his room disengaged, the Shockers' eyes went from yellow to red. Edison took a deep breath, tried to imagine himself somewhere other than a dungeon in Paris. With the Shockers on high alert, any sudden movement—even the most remote sign of a threat—and they would strike.

"Security Protocol HJ EH 101," a dreadfully familiar voice boomed out.

Dr Henry Jekyll entered Edison's quarters and glanced only for a moment at the surrounding automatons. Once the sentries' eyes returned to the amber "Caution" glow, he turned to face Edison. "Thomas, how are you today?"

Even with the Shockers powered down, Edison was still in defensive mode. He did not care to feel the Shockers' wrath. Dr Henry Jekyll's? Even less.

Still, it was better to play to the man's volatile ego. "As good as a captive can be," Edison replied. "Considering that I can only see this room and the adjoining bath, it is just another delightful day in Paris."

Jekyll chuckled. "Captivity has done very little to blunt that wicked sense of humour of yours, but I fear I have neglected my responsibilities. It has been some time since I came to check on you."

"The Shockers; protocols in tending to my dietary needs are adequate. Except for Epsilon over there. He keeps burning my toast."

The Shocker farthest from the door flashed its eyes between yellow and blue, its internal gears seeming to clatter in an almost angry fashion.

"Ah, yes, Epsilon." Jekyll walked up to the trembling Shocker and rapped a knuckle against its head. "On the blink. Literally. An engineering matter beyond my own scope, so I turn to your talents in this field."

Edison held himself to the edge of the bed. "I'm going to need very specif—"

"I have all the tools you will need. The Shockers are quite the creation, but very high maintenance," Jekyll said, motioning to the adjoining room. "If you please?"

Edison was trying to grasp what stunned him more: that Jekyll was actually trusting him with maintenance on the Shockers, or that he actually used the word "Please."

As he slipped out of bed, his eyes never left the closest automaton. Though its status was in safe mode, its head continued to track Edison's every move. The other, Epsilon, on the other side of the room, hesitated, but followed him. Once the inventor entered the parlour, two of the three Shockers activated. The Shocker closest to the window, a Shocker that Edison designated as Beta, remained dark. Beta would only activate if another Shocker were to fail. He glanced over his shoulder at Epsilon and noticed the unit was limping.

Jekyll was correct: the Shockers were one of his finest innovations, and they were designed to be high maintenance. One of his more ingenious strategies. A commission from the Pinkertons for these automaton enforcers would be lucrative, since after the prototype, they were inexpensive to create. The real money with the Shocker would be in maintenance though. Outside of himself and a select few technicians that worked for him exclusively, no one else understood or were successfully able to maintain and repair his mechanised security guards.

"Alright then," Edison said once he reached the centre of the parlour, "let's take a look at you, Epsilon."

Edison opened the metallic French doors built into the Shocker's chest. Lights blinked on and off, gears clicked and kept time just as a heart would, and a number of small chassis continued to rotate without fail.

"I was hoping this be something simple," Edison said. "Pop open the hood, look at the engine, see what's wrong."

Jekyll clicked his tongue. "Mechanical Engineering can be a fickle mistress." He motioned to another room that held a long table. "Would it help if you use the table?"

Edison glanced into the dining room, looked back at Epsilon, then back to Jekyll. "That would be most appreciated. Yes."

Jekyll motioned for a sentry to approach. "Do assist Mr Edison; carry his tools into the dining room."

"Follow," Edison spoke in a monotone to the malfunctioning Epsilon. It took a few seconds before the unit attempted to walk. That must mean a problem in Epsilon's internal gyroscope, or something in one of its relays. He directed the Shocker to lay down on the table. Its legs extended, inch by inch, until its knees were flush with the table surface. The knees bent back, lowering itself onto the table. Its legs then retracted to their normal height, and then the automaton was prone.

Jekyll looked to the other Shocker, Alpha. "Just stand there," he said, "Keep an eye on Edison."

Alpha's head turned to face backwards, and the automaton walked in a reverse direction to the far corner of the dining room. Once there, the head swivelled back to a normal, front-facing position.

"I can trust you to bring Epsilon back to proper functioning form, yes?" Jekyll asked.

Edison crooked a single eyebrow. "I am fully aware that you've turned my machines into bombs, and they will go off if I reconfigure their programming or internal mechanics in any way. So making it functional is my top priority."

"Excellent," Jekyll said. He beamed with newfound vigour as he rubbed his hands together. "I knew I could count on you. Otherwise, it would be…" With his mouth he mimicked the sound of an explosion, wiggling his fingers as he spread his hands apart. "You really want an entire city block on your conscience, even one as shallow as yours?"

An insult was on the tip of Edison's tongue, but he thought better of it. One word could turn this man into a wild beast, and he still had not figured out that what his triggers were. "I'll get this Shocker up and running in no time."

"I know you will," he said. "Feel free to begin. I just have a few things to collect."

Opening up the Shocker, Edison examined the various mechanical arrangements, in particular the central gyroscope. Catching it pitch and spin in a wild, erratic manner proved his deduction correct.

Edison looked up from Epsilon, ready to tell Jekyll what was wrong when he paused. He had a line of sight between the dining room to the kitchen. He saw Jekyll over the sink, tending to a nasty burn that stretched from the top of his shoulder all the way down to the middle of his forearm. Some sort of high-energy oscillator discharge must have brushed against him, perhaps when he was in his alternate form or somewhere in between. Someone had gotten close to Jekyll. Far too close for the maniac's liking. That must have been what brought him back here. He needed somewhere safe to lick his wounds. The mad doctor must be experiencing vulnerability, which meant he would be taking extra precautions in any further outings to protect himself.

If self-preservation so preoccupied him that might mean he would consider other matters a lower priority.

Turning his attention back to Epsilon, Edison began formulating a plan. It would have to be a clever notion to get past Jekyll, but that was Edison's speciality. Clever ideas.

"Dr Jekyll," Edison called, still hunched over Epsilon's open chest, "a word, if you please?"

Jekyll was buttoning his shirt back up as he walked into the dining room. "And how is your patient?" he asked.

"The gyroscope. Catastrophic failure, I am afraid," Edison began. *Don't seem too eager,* he thought to himself. *Remain calm. Do not suggest anything too…dramatic.* "The lack of balance is what is causing the programming failure, and its limp. Eventually, Epsilon will suffer a disconnect in the unit's oral sensor. Without a gyroscope, internal mechanics are out of calibration, in turn wearing out vital systems."

"But you can fix it?" Jekyll asked.

"If I had caught it in time, yes, I can. I need to remove the gyroscope, see if I can repair it or need to replace it," Edison said, and then he motioned to the Shocker's head. "The internals are damaged, though. Some of these things I can repair without a problem, but there will be other systems that may require some… improvisation. That includes the gyroscope."

Jekyll's expression was exactly what Edison thought he would see. His eyes grew a shade darker. "That… sounds complicated."

"To someone who isn't an engineer? Yes, I am sure it sounds like it. As I am working with limited resources, and you need all the Shockers in service, I'll whip up a solution. It may require adding new components to this unit's internals."

Jekyll took another step closer to Edison. Even though the mad doctor was a full foot shorter, the man's demeanour was enough to trigger Edison's flight response, but Edison summoned up his courage. He did not budge.

"You said you could fix it," Jekyll insisted.

"And I will," Edison returned, "but, as you said, it is complicated. I'll put in a small subroutine that will prevent any further decay to the internals and will make allowances for any possible adjustments I need to make to the gyroscope."

"A subroutine?" Jekyll followed Edison's gaze. He was trying to read him. Edison had sat at tables with some of the most powerful men of industry. Jekyll was terrifying, but not cut of the same cloth as those robber barons. Edison stared back at him as Jekyll asked, "And what exactly does this subroutine do?"

"This subroutine will override any sort of interference caused by the gyroscope falling out of sync with the Earth's gravity. Both will keep the automaton balanced, thereby reducing wear and tear on the mechanics."

"Why not simply change out the gyroscope?"

"I could, if I had another gyroscope handy. I don't. Neither do I have an internal gyroscope for a Shocker lying around in my shop, nor can you go down to the local hardware store and pick one up for me. While I can keep the Shockers running with these…" He motioned to the unfurled collection of fine tools. "… the worst-case scenario has sadly come to life. I can attempt to repair and realign the gyroscope, but it will need some type of…" He thought long and hard for the best word to use instead of "sabotage" which would have triggered Jekyll. "… alternative solution. Hence, the subroutine. This will enhance the electric brains signal pick up any fluctuation in the drivers. To do all this, I need a small boost hooked up to the automaton's brain."

The madman's gaze was something out of a nightmare, but Edison steeled himself. Jekyll's eyes, void of any emotion, any empathy, any decent intent, stared down into Edison's soul. "How fast do you think it will take for you to put something together?"

Edison looked around the room, slowly. He could not afford to look anxious in any way. His eyes landed on a desk outside the dining room. Slipping away from Jekyll, he picked up a notebook lying there, and began jotting down numbers as he returned to his captor. "I could probably have something ready within an hour, possibly two."

"You have half an hour. One more second and I cannot guarantee your patient will not explode along with the other Shockers."

Edison would need to work quickly, and he hated that. He preferred to deconstruct, take time to understand how something worked, and then put it back together. For this clever scheme, there would be no testing, no numerous ways to get it wrong until he got it right, no tinkering or fine tuning.

This would be his only opportunity. "I will see what I can come up with."

Jekyll stepped away from Edison, turning to a mirror to adjust his tie. "Oh, I hope you find a solution, because I need him operational. If I am short staffed I'm afraid I'll have to be here more. I think that is something neither of us would like, don't you agree?"

"I certainly do," Edison grumbled.

"Good." With that, Jekyll slipped into his coat, wincing as he did so, returned to the mirror, and began to preen over himself. "You better get started then."

The subroutine would do just as Edison promised. It would boost Epsilon's brainpower and provide a stronger connection with its gyroscope, which Edison could fix and have up and functioning within a mere twenty minutes. The subroutine would also, at random points of the day, transmit a simple Morse code signal. The signal would be silent but strong enough for anyone listening to hear the message Edison sent: C.Q.D.

He would have to prevent the subroutine from transmitting until Jekyll left, but the other Shockers would remain blissfully unaware.

Now, all Edison needed was for someone—anyone—to be listening.

But how would they breach the door without triggering the Shockers?

One challenge at a time, Thomas, he thought to himself at his makeshift worktable. *One challenge at a time.*

CHAPTER FIFTEEN

⇥≡⇤

In Which Our Intrepid Agents of Derring-Do Are Joined by a Learned Scholar

By the time they had disembarked from the Oriental Hypersteam Express in Constantinople, Wellington's anxiety was under control. Instead of wanting to down an entire bottle of whiskey, alone, in the confines of the hypersteam's parlour, he simply wanted to have a single scotch, provided it was three fingers deep and neat.

Cool logic was his saviour, delivered by their new partner-in-mischief, Professor Henrietta Falcon. They'd saved two lives, even though the brave and somewhat fool-hardy Ashe Robbins would not be treading the boards anytime soon. Her shoulder was dislocated and her arm broken. *"All those years in stage combat,"* Robbins had jested, *"and it is on my vacation I break my arm."*

Now Wellington took in the foreign and unfamiliar surroundings stretching before them. Constantinople. A city with a colourful history and patterned by intrigue.

After so many failed attempts to catch him, it was hard to stay optimistic that this time would be different.

A lit cigar appeared before him. The smell was enticing. "Here, Mr Books," Professor Falcon offered with a crooked smile, "It should calm your nerves. Does mine."

"Thank you," he said, taking it from her fingers. After a long drag, the sweet taste of the smoke did seem to relax him a bit.

"Ever been to Constantinople?"

"No," he said, taking in the bustling crowds, the rows of buildings pressing on one another as they led to a solitary spire in the distance.

"It's been a spell since I have been here, to tell the truth," Eliza said, coming up behind them. "It does have its own charm."

"Indeed," Professor Falcon turned to Eliza, "If you are in the market for adventure, Constantinople is the city of choice."

"Very true," Eliza replied before stepping closer to Wellington, her voice dropping to a volume meant only for him, "but adventure is rather difficult considering our circumstances. Married couple? Again?" Eliza sighed, taking the small cigar out of his hand and enjoying a puff. "Why can't I be your mistress sometimes, Welly? Far more my speed."

He tried not to flinch. He enjoyed the benefits of cohabiting with Eliza, but the aristocratic part of him was still a little conflicted about it. However, he certainly did not want her believing he thought of her as a mistress.

"Married couples attracts far less attention," he said under his breath.

"But such a cover sets a tone for a dull outing, does it not?" Professor Falcon added.

"The idea is *not* getting noticed," Wellington insisted, taking the cigar back. "We are to blend into the surroundings, either as tourists or lovers on holiday."

"But sometimes normality attracts attention in itself," Falcon countered. "The friendlier sort may wish to strike up conversations with you, ask intimate details and the like."

Wellington took another drag from the cigar before asking the question he suspected he might regret. "So what sort of legend would you create around us?"

Professor Falcon looked up, as if she were reaching into a creative corner of her brain, while slipping her arm into Eliza's own. Her pale fingers came to rest on the other woman's shoulder, while her smile grew a hint darker and more mischievous. "I was thinking of you as a travelling philosopher, a radical scouring the world for validation of his anti-social beliefs. And we are your concubines."

Wellington blinked. "Concubines?"

"Yes," Falcon said, with a lift of her eyebrows. "You are travelling to study the ancient arts of carnal desire so that Free Love could truly transform the world into a Paradise here on Earth."

His one glance at Eliza told him he would find no ally there. She said instead, "I love the sound of this."

"As you would be far from the prudish sensibilities of our beloved England," Falcon went on, "you are a pariah, ensuring you that no one would dare broach a conversation with you."

Now the ladies united against him. Another puff from the cigar, and Wellington tossed the vice to one side. Falcon was right. The smoke had left him quite returned to a state of calm.

"Right," Wellington stated tersely, much to the bemusement of both of his companions, "I think, instead, we should stick to the original legend with one diversion. We are all from the Lovelace Centre, travelling together to consider opportunities abroad."

Eliza looked around, and her mouth twisted into a grimace. "Not to cause any undue concern, but what of your colleague, Profes—?"

"Henrietta," she insisted. "If we are to be working together, I insist we drop the formality."

"Good luck with this one," Eliza said with a snort, motioning to Wellington.

"As for my esteemed colleague, Doctor Tomlin has asked to return home for some much-needed rest. I think that was more than enough excitement for him."

Wellington nodded. "So, he does not care for the peaks of Kilimanjaro or the..." His brow knotted, as he asked Eliza, "Exactly what is bungee jumping?"

"It's where you secure a thick elastic rope to your ankles and throw yourself off a bridge or a platform of some kind suspended over a deep ravine. The rope snaps you back safely when you reach the end of it." Eliza stared down at her shoes when she added, "When you're an island nation at the farthest edge of the Empire, you learn to make your own fun. Many of the Polynesian tribes have been doing it for generations."

"Mr Lambert?" A dark-haired man, dressed in a beautiful tailored suit and a stylish scarlet fez, addressed them from the shade of the train station's awning. At a distance, he didn't look much older than Christopher, the eldest of the Ministry Seven, but as he came closer, the tiniest flecks of grey came out in the man's goatee and beard. These hints of time only granted him additional refinement. "Mr Hannibal Lambert?"

"Yes," Wellington said, answering to their cover. "So sorry to have kept your waiting. One of the stewards spilled a pitcher of water as the train was coming in."

The stranger nodded. "Indeed, one must always take care not to slip on the slick brass."

Pass phrase confirmed. This was their contact.

"Mr Aydin Tilki, I presume?" Wellington asked.

He nodded, giving his hat a slight tip to them all. "Yes, I am your guide in Constantinople." He lowered his voice and glanced over his shoulder. "Our mutual friends in London secured my services for your time here."

It was a little galling to need a babysitter, but as Sound pointed out in their last communication from the OHX-1, the Ottoman Empire was deep into a special kind of turmoil. Everyone, even disinterested parties like the British Empire, had to proceed with caution. Distrust of France, Great Britain, and Russia was high. Sultan Abdul Hamid II was cosying up to the Germans, so if he found out the Ministry was carrying out operations in his city, the repercussions would be severe.

Mr Tilki's dark gaze travelled to take in Professor Falcon, and he raised one eyebrow in Wellington's general direction.

"Yes, there has been a slight… alteration… in our operation," Wellington began, his pleasant smile struggling to remain so. "Adyin Tilki, may I introduce Henrietta Falcon of…"

"The Ada Lovelace Centre," he said, taking her offered hand with both of his as if she was made of the fragile crystal. "Your work on the positronic analytical dynosphere is astounding." He kissed her hand, then continued his thought. "Perhaps even mind-opening."

Falcon looked taken aback by the sudden attention. "You know of my research into self-aware analytical machines?"

"Science is my passion, and a friend at the Ministry pointed out your work to me. It is an honour to make your acquaintance." He looked back and forth between Wellington, Eliza, and the professor. "So, exactly how did this come to be?"

"Perhaps we can debrief you," Wellington began, motioning to the Travel Plaza, "as we proceed to our lodgings?"

Mr Tilki secured their minimal luggage, arranged for it to be sent ahead to their hotel, and ushered the three of them out of the Plaza and towards the street. The heat of the day, Wellington feared, would be reaching its tightest grip on the city in an hour or so. He preferred to catch his breath in the coolness of their lodgings straight away.

"I have secured rooms for you at the *Pera Palas Oteli*," Tilki said, urging for them to follow him through a break in the traffic.

"A fine establishment," Professor Falcon stated.

"One of the best hotels in Constantinople," Eliza agreed, "so, not what I would call a low profile."

"Not all is what it seems," Tilki said with a bright, confident smile. "The Palas is one of the few European-style hotels in the city. If you stayed anywhere else you would stand out. Besides," he added, leaning in towards them, "the hotel has a wonderful series of secret tunnels."

Eliza returned the grin. "So we go in as tourists, and then immediately head out in disguise?"

"But," Wellington asked, still not ready to believe in their good fortune, "how many know of these tunnels?"

The man spread his hands. "Only a very small group in our little community of spies and street criminals. I do not see how your mad doctor would even if he has been here for a span of time."

Wellington's shoulders relaxed a little. Maybe their luck was taking a turn for the better. After all even if Usher had knowledge of the Palas' tunnel network, they would not have shared it with Jekyll. From their intelligence, the mad doctor had burned that bridge most effectively. Without those valuable connections, he'd have no insight to the spy community.

In Constantinople, Tilki and his network gave them a chance.

Their contact gave a slight shrug. "You should know this city is a very old and complicated one. I was born and breed in Constantinople, and I still do not know everything about it. However, I assure you I know it better than a madman sheltering here for only a few months. Rest assured, we will find him."

Falcon took a measure of the man. "You seem confident, Mr Tilki."

"The city only gives up her secrets reluctantly. You have to work many years before you know even half of them. And please, call me Aydin."

He looked so earnest that a pit opened up in Wellington's stomach. Except for the Ministry Seven, earnest individuals who helped them seemed to meet untimely ends. And even the Ministry Seven had discovered they were not impervious. He would rather not have this one's death on his conscience.

Their hotel was not far from the Travel Plaza, and despite a plain stone exterior, the inside opened into a beautiful courtyard, with lush plants and a bright, tinkling fountain at its centre. It relieved Wellington to find it several degrees cooler in the lobby and courtyard than outside, yet he knew they could not enjoy the beauty or luxury of their hotel.

"Aydin," Falcon began, "do you think there are any vacancies remaining?"

"There should be," he replied.

"Excellent." After giving Wellington and Eliza a quick glance, she asked, "You will inform our colleague here about our new legend, yes?"

"Of course," Wellington said, clearing his throat before adding, "Henrietta, darling."

Eliza failed to stifle a laugh as Henrietta made for the Registration desk. "Henrietta, *darling?*" Aydin asked.

Eliza motioned to the formidable professor. "Our recruit has altered our legend. It is rather... creative."

Aydin nodded and smiled. "She is an original, that is most certain." He reached into his jacket and handed Eliza an envelope. "The case summaries you requested. Every strange occurrence in the city for the last month, and a layout of the 'network' underneath the hotel. If you need any additional information, I can arrange to have dossiers pulled for you."

Henrietta walked back to the three of them. "Lodgings secured, directly across from my companions."

"How fortuitous," Aydin chuckled. "In your room," he said to Wellington and Eliza, "I took the liberty of providing a wardrobe that will make you less..." He cleared his throat, then added, "... outstanding."

"Men's clothes for me while on covert operations?" Eliza asked.

"As per the Director's missive," he replied. He bowed to Henrietta. "A pleasure. Do have a care with these two. I will meet you later tonight at the agreed location."

With that he left them standing alone in the luxurious lobby of the Palas. Henrietta appeared ready to burst.

"I believe we should retire for a moment," Eliza offered. "Just a chance to freshen up."

"Shall I join you in an hour or so?" Henrietta asked.

"Two hours, then give our door a knock."

The three of them took the lift to the fourth floor and retired to their respective rooms. The suite was large, simply furnished in white, but the décor remained the height of luxury. The window looked out over the courtyard, and Wellington fought the desire to indulge in a nap. Delightful as it would be to surrender to a moment's respite in Eliza's arms, the idea of Jekyll loose in the city terrified him to no end.

Removing her hat in one swift movement, Eliza flopped on the bed and let out a long, slow sigh, before rolling over and propping herself up on her arms. "My hotel was much seedier on my last visit to Constantinople."

Eliza seldom talked about her past missions, and Wellington was in desperate need of a diversion. "What were you doing here?"

She shrugged. "I was an escort to the British Ambassador because of a threat from Methuselah's Order, but it turned out the intelligence was all wrong. They were actually in Baghdad." A wicked smile flickered across her lips.

"And something happened?" Wellington asked, dropping a kiss on that curved mouth.

"Oh, remembering how upset Bruce was, stuffed into a dinner jacket while Brandon was having all the fun in Baghdad."

He chuckled at that.

Still, now was not the time to revel in it. "No time for fun," he said, and instead spread the case summaries in a semi-circle around Eliza.

Dragging a chair closer to the bed, he propped his feet on the far edge of it and stared at the sheets.

"Point taken," Eliza said, pulling pages closer to her.

First off, the local reports, especially for summaries, offered far more detail than he would have expected. Wellington slid two summaries closer and began with the one on his right. His eyes wandered over to the report to his left, and the similarities between the cases leapt off their respective pages. The victims were all young people, men and women of the poorer parts of the city. The photographs captured all too well the victims' last moments etched on their faces.

"Are all of them are like this?" Eliza asked.

"I asked Mr Tilki for specifics, and sadly, he was able to deliver."

A gentle knock came at the door.

"I believe," Eliza said, her words deep and throaty as she smiled wickedly, "that is the third in our party. And she's early."

"You encouraged her."

"I like the way she thinks," Eliza purred.

"Last night, you wanted to gouge her eyes out," he whispered.

"That was before I met her," she whispered back. "You're right. I absolutely *adore* her!"

He glared at her, took in a deep breath, and answered the door with a smile. "Professor Falcon," he said, ushering her into the room.

"Henrietta," Eliza cooed, propping her head against her hand.

"Wellington, Eliza," Henrietta acknowledged each of them. "I know we agreed to taking some time, but to be honest, I was finding it somewhat difficult to clear my mind."

"Grab a case summary and dive in," Eliza said, motioning to the various documents strewn around her.

Henrietta raised her eyebrows as she helped herself to two cases. "He's certainly been making himself at home."

"This is not just Constantinople. Paris, New York, Trondheim," Wellington replied, his expression growing more and more forlorn with each city he named. "Bodies and other experiments all abandoned for us to find later."

"Ah yes, the augmentation trials you told me about." Henrietta let out a long, slow sigh as she browsed over one of her cases. "I remember my early days at university when I was searching for my scientific passion. In the Biology Wing, there were whispers of bettering the human body. Not just through conditioning, but actual augmentation; changing the design of the body on a cellular level. It was all very..."

Eliza's brow furrowed. "Very... what, exactly?"

Henrietta bit her bottom lip before offering, "Sacrilegious." She looked at both Eliza and Wellington. He gathered Eliza's expression was as stunned as his own. "I dare say you were not expecting such an answer from a scientist. However, even though I have seen much of this world, I also nurture a strong belief in faith. I think it keeps one's moral compass true. In the sciences, it is too easy to begin believing one's self God."

"Well, Doctor Jekyll took these quaint notions and applied science to the mind as well." Wellington pulled out from one of his suitcases Jekyll's ledger. "From what we gather, at least in the beginning, Jekyll was trying to isolate human behaviours. In a sense, he was attempting to bring desires to heel. Violent. Affective. Analytical. Sexual. He wanted to give people full command over their mental faculties."

"Sounds like discipline and self-control," she said, extending her hand to Wellington. He gave her the ledger, and she began looking through it.

"As you can see, Jekyll wanted to go beyond that. He wanted to gain complete mastery of the human mind, to turn emotions on and off at will."

Falcon placed a free hand on the pages open before her. "What of these notes here? It looks as if this partner of Jekyll's was on a breakthrough." She leaned in an inch closer and read, "Arthur?"

Eliza looked at Wellington. He gave her the tiniest of nods, and a slight smile.

"Arthur Books," Wellington said. "My father."

Henrietta looked up from the ledger. "Your father worked with Jekyll?"

"You can now understand why we are so invested into this matter."

"And may I ask what your father brought to this madman's work?"

"Physical conditioning. My childhood was unconventional."

"May I, darling?" Eliza asked. Wellington shrugged as he crossed over to the window overlooking the courtyard. "Arthur Books and Henry Jekyll concocted a physical and mental conditioning designed to be something of a lifestyle. Strict diet for the wife, and eventually for her new-born child."

"These gentlemen kept a very complete logbook," Falcon said, reviewing earlier notes from the ledger.

"Also there was 'training' once the child was ready and able." Eliza looked over to Wellington—it was his story after all.

"My mother would have none of it. Hard to know if she discovered my father's ultimate goal, or if he refused to let his wife dictate what he could and could not subject his son to."

"What was the purpose of all this?" Henrietta asked.

"I was to be a template for a new age of existence, a next step in evolution. My first application was to be something of a super soldier for Her Majesty's Empire."

Henrietta closed the ledger and handed it to Eliza. "And…?"

Wellington tugged on his waistcoat. "I ended the experiment."

The professor considered Wellington for a long moment before returning to the summaries in hand. "I take it after you did so, Jekyll remained in touch. Kept an eye on you, to see your progress free of supervision?"

"Actually, I believe I was fourteen at the time," Wellington said, a sigh escaping him, "my father and Doctor Jekyll had quite a row. I am still uncertain of the details, but after that, 'Uncle Henry' no longer visited."

"And you never heard from him again?"

He shook his head. "Not until India, last year."

Henrietta set aside the case summaries, and stepped back, crossing her arms as she looked at the string of murders. "So why come out of hiding in such a dramatic fashion?" She motioned to the files. "This is not a man who wants to keep a low profile. He wants to be found *now*."

"We've been so concerned with catching Jekyll," Eliza said, her eyes now going from summary to summary, "we never asked what he wants."

"At the Water Palace he told me something," Wellington said, taking a seat, "something I did not mention in the report. Jekyll wants to finish the experiment. He wants the two of us to carry on what he and my father set out to do all those years ago."

After a pause, Henrietta nodded. "A most terrifying thought, to be sure."

"We need to find him in his hunting ground and stop looking for his den."

"Like in our first mission together?" he asked, recalling that very different time. "That factory where the Rag and Bone murderer was picking victims?"

"Think of it, darling. Even for someone like Jekyll, finding victims carries with it some danger. He must have an area where he knows the streets, and the people that walk them. He has to be comfortable to strike."

"Like a lion who roams his territory."

Eliza nodded. "Monsters have them too."

"An intriguing thought you have there," Henrietta said, "but this monster is cunning. He will want us to come to him, to his territory. You told me earlier on the train of his taunts. Undoubtedly he will have traps and tricks ready for our arrival."

"This means I will have to exercise my most loathed virtue." Eliza grumbled. "Patience."

Wellington went back to the valise where he kept their field essentials. Pulling out a folded up piece of paper, he pushed the case summaries aside and unfurled it to reveal a map of Constantinople. Now would have been an excellent time to have Aydin with them, but perhaps he would play into this developing strategy of theirs later when it came time to find a vantage point.

"Now comes the part of serving Her Majesty in the Ministry that I do not care for. Thinking like a madman," Wellington said with a dry throat. "Constantinople is hardly small, but we must find the best hunting territory."

Henrietta leaned in, pointing to a region of the ancient city. "What about Fatih?"

"I know that area," Eliza said. "It's damn near perfect for the likes of Jekyll."

"Speaking as a newcomer to this corner of the world, why would this suit Jekyll?" Wellington said, moving a magnifying glass over Fatih. "The streets appear to feed into the area, but is it of high elevation? What specific advantages would it offer someone like Jekyll?"

"It offers him an abundance of victims," Henrietta replied. "Fatih is the Grand Bazaar of Constantinople."

"Locals, adventurous tourists, even those looking to hide." Eliza reached over to the jumbled stacks of Aydin's case summaries and sifted through them. "Two cases here, the deceased are unknowns. Fatih would be the place, or at least a good starting point in trying to find Jekyll."

"So," Henrietta began, "what's the plan?"

Wellington pinched the bridge of his nose, screwing his eyes shut as exhaustion crept over him. "We go there around dinner. We have to rest, arm ourselves mentally as well as physically. We pick a vantage point and hold it during the night see if we can't find our lion."

"We have no guarantee he will strike tonight."

"You forget, Henrietta," Eliza said grimly. "We denied him an exquisite kill on the Express. Jekyll will be craving tonight."

"A very good point."

"We need to get elevated," Eliza said, returning her attention to the map.

"It would be good if we had eyes lower to the ground as well," Henrietta offered.

"So how do we keep in communications with one another?" Wellington asked.

Henrietta smiled, looking between them. "It is most fortuitous that you happen to have an engineer within your ranks."

"Go on," Wellington said.

"As I was travelling with my associate, I had devised these portable recording devices using the same technology as with *æthermissives* to send finished recordings between each other. The devices themselves are no bigger than a woman's evening handbag, but easily concealed. I could convert them to transmit across the æther to one another instead of sharing recordings."

"Their weight?"

"Perhaps a stone at most."

Wellington nodded, pacing a few steps with the occasional whisper to himself. He pointed to Henrietta. "Make them lighter. And have the microphone be small. Something we could conceal in the cuff of a sleeve. And we will need a third device."

"I can manage that," Henrietta said.

"I will contact Aydin," Eliza said, "and let him know our new plan. Then see if we can get in a few hours of rest."

"After that we find a good spot to wait for a predator," Wellington added with a wry grin.

Eliza walked over and kissed him on the cheek. "No, darling. What we are hunting is so much worse."

CHAPTER SIXTEEN

In Which the Enemy of My Enemy Is My Best Friend

His eyes darted to the timepiece in his hand, and then to the clock by the bar. His lunch appointment was late.

Filippo Rossi, known by the House of Usher as Mr Badger, rapped his fingers against the smooth surface of the table, trying to relax. While Argus Tinsdale was many things, he was always punctual. He also demanded it of his colleagues and even his superiors. Tardiness was, according to Tinsdale, the height of unprofessionalism. Only his spectacular results afforded him the chance to talk so arrogantly to members higher up the House's hierarchy.

Tinsdale had incredible inside knowledge of not only the Ministry, but of many world government operations. It was unclear how he obtained his information, but Filippo suspected the younger man was playing all sides of the Great Game. He could be posing as a double agent, but it had never been proved. He'd never put a foot wrong, until today, when he was late.

Filippo took a sip of his wine, a fine vintage from a vintner loyal to the House. This year had been exceptional. He'd intended the bottle of wine to be something of a peace offering to Tinsdale. Since the man's arrival in Italy, their encounters were best described as prickly. At Holmes' insistence he'd been brought in, which meant he was drafted into the Ragnarök operation.

Damn it, man, Filippo thought, topping off his glass. *There are plenty drafted into this grand plan of yours. Do not tempt fate with too many mouths.*

He'd never dream of expressing that thought to Holmes. The Chairman— as Holmes preferred to be addressed—believed in accountability. It would be accountability that returned the House to power. As much as Filippo hated to admit it, the results were now being seen. It was not all bad as Filippo's success in Italy had him in Holmes' good books. The House was reclaiming its previous influence, due in part to Ragnarök.

However, only a few in the House were fully aware of what exactly Ragnarök was.

His angry reverie was interrupted by a hand turning the wine glass reserved for Tinsdale right-side up. Filippo watched stunned as the stranger poured himself a glass, only halfway, and returned the bottle to his side of the table. Taking a seat opposite of Filippo, the newcomer removed his hat and smiled.

"G'day, mate."

The stranger had the trappings of a gentleman, but his boisterous salutation and smug countenance contradicted his fashion sense. This was definitely not Argus Tinsdale.

"Signor," Filippo began, clearing his throat before switching languages, "I must—how do the English say it—crave a pardon?"

"The Poms may say something like that, but you've got a problem: I'm not from Pommyland." When the great ox smiled, it made his chin seem even larger. "That's just the first of many problems you're going to have tonight, mate."

Looking around the café, Filippo struggled to stop the corners of his mouth from twitching. "Sir, I must ask that you leave before I have you removed from the premises."

"Yeah, that's another one of your problems. Those blokes supposed to keeping an eye on ya..." The man took a generous sip of the wine and waggled his eyebrows at its taste. Apparently, that was a sign of approval from wherever he came from. "Those boys are enjoying a wee lie-down. A little nap so we can have some undisturbed conversation."

Filippo's eyes flicked to his walking stick. He could upend the table and then draw the sword from its concealment.

"Now, maybe you're thinking of some crafty way of doing me in, but then you will never know what I'm on about... Mr Badger."

That got his attention. He took another look at the stranger. He was not with the House, and yet he had his code name with the Board? That could only mean... "Tinsdale?"

The man clicked his tongue as he lifted his glass in a toast. "Poor sod. Afraid he's not making this little rendezvous, as he's feeling under the weather." He went to take a drink, paused, and then added, "Six feet under the weather, if you get my drift."

Filippo's throat tightened. This was precisely what he had warned Holmes about. "Whom do I have the pleasure of addressing then?"

"Campbell's the name. Bruce Campbell. Proud citizen of Australia and agent of the Ministry of Peculiar Occurrences."

"Mr Campbell, I am but a humble cog in the great machine."

"How about we cut through the song and dance, mate, because... Italy? It's hot. Bit too sultry if you ask me. Not as awful as Cloncurry, but then again... not many places are." Bruce set his wine aside. "So before I bid a farewell to your quaint little country, you're going to tell me everything you know about Ragnarök."

Filippo frowned as he filled his own glass with wine. "I'm afraid my knowledge of Norse Mythology is a bit foggy. I did not pursue history while at university."

Campbell threw back his head and laughed, his bright teeth almost blinding in the afternoon sun. "Yeah, yeah, Norse Mythology. That's a good one, mate. Guess what I studied at uni?"

This lummox attended university? Standards must be quite low in Australia. "I cannot imagine."

"Boxing." Campbell pressed his right fingers into his left palm, and a soft cascade of pops followed. He repeated the other side. "My teachers considered me a natural. I even earned me a few Golden Gloves in Oz and Pommyland."

"Well done."

"I'm pretty proud of it. And the best part?" he said spreading his arms wide with a quick flick, before resting his hands on opposite corners of their small table. Filippo could not deny the lummox provided an imposing figure. "It's a skill I get to apply to my chosen profession. Quite handy, right?"

Such a lout could not intimidate him. Filippo glanced up and down the street. None of his guards or attendants were in sight.

There was, however, a police officer strolling down the cobblestones. He licked his lips and considered a foolhardy idea. All he needed was a moment's distraction, enough to get away while Campbell dealt with local law enforcement.

"Now that would be quite the thing to explain to your boss," Campbell said, back to considering the wine in his glass. "I'm sure he, she, or however you lot run things at the House of Usher, will be curious why you involved a copper. Especially when they hear my own story and see my credentials."

"All false, I have no doubt," Filippo said with a curl of his lip.

"To your eye, sure, but to a bloke wearing out his plates of meat, I bet he will have us all down at the constable's station for a nice little chit-chat, one even nicer than this one. How you going to explain why the police officers in this fair town all know about Ragnarök." Campbell picked up the bottle and made ready to top off his own glass. "Now, when he walks by, I suggest you give a good laugh, like we're mates having a grand ol' time, eh?"

The policeman got closer, his stroll without care. He even stopped to chat with the local florist for a moment. He was new. Filippo did not recognise him. While he did have allies in the police department, Holmes was adamant that any Usher associates involved with Operation Ragnarök were personally approved by him. Recruits could talk, then questions would happen.

"Ragnarök," he said, turning back to Campbell. "A name heard by chance, or perhaps scribbled on a scrap of paper. Your information is obviously circumstantial. Innocuous, at best."

Campbell held the bottle over his glass and gave him a wry smile. "Can you afford to take that chance, mate?"

Filippo watched as Bruce began tipping the bottle, the wine slipping out and filling his glass. The footsteps of the young police officer were now right next to him.

His laughter prompted Campbell to join him in the mirth. Filippo stole a quick glance at the police officer whose smile widened at the sight of two friends enjoying a laugh over what looked like excellent wine. Still chuckling, Campbell went to pour the remains of the bottle into Filippo's glass, but he waved his hand and shook his head at the gesture.

Bruce sighed. "So, you were going to tell me about your little caper."

Taking a deep breath, he followed it with a drink of wine. "In my time with the House of Usher, through my own ascent to the Board, I've been involved in many operations, but nothing on the scale of Ragnarök."

"Well, good for you," Campbell said, unimpressed.

"Ragnarök is not an operation you can chalk up as yet another scheme from the House. This operation is massive. Even I do not know all of its working parts, save for the fact that its success relies solely on the Italian operations that I, as you may have deduced, am in charge of. The only one who understands this operation to the last detail is our new Chairman."

"Chairman?" Campbell said, rolling the wine glass in his fingers. "Thought the Lord of the Manor was in charge of you lot?"

"We were, but the House fell under..." Filippo cleared his throat and shrugged. "... new management. This is his brainchild, his grand scheme to return the House of Usher to its rightful seat of power."

"Quite the undertaking. So if you can't tell me all about Ragnarök, why don't you give me the humble contribution from you all here in Italy."

Filippo fidgeted in his chair. He had to find a way out of this. If his part in Holmes' plan were to falter, that would mean he faced the same fate as Mr Bear. After Brother Streeper's report on what happened in Russia, Bear had been swiftly and bloodily replaced.

"Where is my darling Virginia?" came the shrill, frantic voice from the street.

Filippo turned to see the man emerging from the combination of mechanised and pedestrian traffic. He was tall, lanky, and dressed in a fine tailored suit. He looked like an English tourist, one of many that Italy suffered from the British Empire; only this one, instead of brandishing a phrase book held a gun. It was not modified in any fashion—just a simple Bulldog. He aimed it at Filippo.

The shot made him jump, but it was the sparks against the sidearm that made him blink. On seeing Campbell, large as he was, move from their table to this pale tourist still shaking his hand where the gun had once been, Filippo considered himself twice as lucky. Had he tried for his cane, the Ministry agent would have been on top of him.

Instead, Agent Campbell was on top of the stranger, tackling him as something cut through the air and shattered a planter tucked by one of the wrought iron support beams of their café.

Snatching up his walking stick, he calmly began his exit.

"Bugger me," Campbell swore from behind him.

That was Filippo's cue to sprint.

In his mad dash for the kitchen, he dodged and shoved aside various kitchen staff. Filippo shouldered through the back door, slamming into the opposite wall of the alleyway. Salt and pepper hair blinded him for a moment, but combing back the veil with his fingers, he pushed hard against the wall, launching himself down the alley and into the street. He knew this Assisi intimately, an advantage he intended to exploit. Filippo barrelled his way into a boutique, slipped behind the desk and into the back room, where another door led to another alleyway. He looked to his left, then back the opposite way, then once again to his left. Foot traffic, a few cars, but no sign of that Ministry agent.

Keep moving, his instincts screamed. *Keep moving.*

The heat encouraged a more leisurely, slow pace to the village, but Filippo sprinted through the streets, tossing others who were oblivious to get out of his way. One man grabbed him, earning a quick, hard kiss from Filippo's walking stick against the skull. The crowd parted from him as if his assault on the stranger had been a stone dropped into a millpond, the ripples expanding from the point of entry. Filippo's escape was unhindered for the time being as he ran for a sweet shop just across the street. His entrance was so forceful, the door's window shattered. Again, over the calamity of the customers and shop owners, he ran behind the counter, burst through the back door, turned a corner, and stopped, his fine shoes scuffling against the stones underfoot.

Where did this dead end come from?

Filippo turned to see a gentleman, also in a hurry, round the corner. He, too, shuffled to a halt.

"I say," this stranger said with a gasp, "you put on a right good chase."

His grip tightened on his walking stick.

The man held up a wallet. Filippo recognised it immediately. "You dropped this. In the…uh…." He took another breath, and shook his head. "That boutique. My Lord, but you are fast. Did you participate in those new goodwill games a few years back? The Olympics?"

He took a few timid steps closer. One more, then leaned from where he stood and snatched it out of the man's hand.

"You're welcome," the stranger said, wiggling his fingers as he shot Filippo a disgusted look. "Should be fortunate that you didn't take my hand with it."

A quick peek into the wallet revealed all his money present. Perhaps he was a tourist, and an honest one at that. The accent was not quite British, but of a dialect he could not place. He scratched his dark beard as he removed his hat and fanned himself. Whatever offence he might have given, must have passed as the stranger smiled at Filippo. Quite friendly, all of a sudden. His dark eyes looked up and back down the alleyway. The stranger appeared genuinely concerned for him.

Confirmation of this came quickly after the thought. "You all right then?"

"Yes, yes, I'm fine."

"You don't sound it."

"I am." Filippo fished into his wallet and produced a few notes. "For your trouble, signor. You are most honest."

"Ta," he said. His round cheeks glowed with delight on receiving the gift. "That is mighty kind of you. I say, you lot here in Italy are quite nice and all."

He nodded. He went to leave, but the stranger placed a gentle hand on his shoulder.

"And your food? Dear Lord, your food, oh how I will miss your food."

"A tourist then?" Filippo asked.

"In a manner of speaking."

The hand that was on Filippo's shoulder bent back, and a Remington-Elliot slipped into the stranger's hand as he stepped clear.

"Now I suggest you drop the walking stick and come with me," he stated, the dark eyes no longer friendly.

"You're with the Ministry?"

"Brandon D Hill, at your service." He glanced at Filippo's cane. "Please, don't make me ask twice about the stick."

For a fleeting moment, Filippo considered lashing out. It would be a gamble, more so for this one than for the Campbell chap. This one wasn't the bruiser the Australian was. This agent was cunning, perhaps more dangerous. If Campbell was a great gorilla, this one was something akin to a leopard.

"A gentleman's agreement?" Filippo implored. "The stick is quite expensive—one of a kind."

"The walking stick? Or the sword inside it?" He winked. "Got one at home just like it."

He ground his teeth until they hurt, then released the stick, allowing it to fall with a clatter.

"Excellent. Now, slowly, you're going to stay in front of me, and we're going to meet with my mate, Bruce," Hill said, stepping back to grant Filippo a bit of space.

"Charming fellow."

"That's one word for him. Off we go then."

Filippo had only taken a single step when he heard something cut through the air and slap against Hill. The agent lurched forward, his free hand snapping to the nape of his neck. He tugged at something, and pulled free a small, dark dart, no more the length of a finger.

Looking from the dart to Filippo, Hill's dark gaze was now glassy, distant. "Stings a bit," he managed before crumpling to the ground.

Gathering up his walking stick, Filippo prepared to resume his mad dash through Assisi, but froze on seeing the woman at the corner. Where had she come from?

"Mr Badger?" she asked, her eyes as black as the hair pulled back in a tight bun from her striking face. Lips rich and dark as the blood going cold in him twitched back into a pleasant smile. "Wonderful to finally meet you."

"What—?" was the only word coming to him in his rising state of panic.

"We have no time," she said, taking him by the wrist and pulling him towards her. "The Ministry is on to you. We must go, and we must go now."

"I don't—"

"We go. Now."

With another tug on his arm, Filippo stumbled forward. No longer running, the head of Usher's Italian operations walked towards what he could only imagine would be a safe haven alongside his unexpected saviour, Signorina Sophia del Morte.

CHAPTER SEVENTEEN

⇢≣⇠

Wherein Our Agents of Derring-Do Track a Monster

"I fear I am not very Turkish looking," Wellington grumbled to his reflection.
As promised Aydin had sent up a collection of local clothing, and out of that pile Eliza had chosen loose grey trousers for Wellington to wear. These salvar were worn by both men and women in the Ottoman Empire. Over that she had layered a shirt, pale green vest, and a dark blue robe. Then on his head she placed a scarlet fez, which she draped with a thin white scarf. Glancing down at the long socks she'd pulled over the salvar, he wondered that even with all this, he still couldn't pass as a local.

In this disguise, he was just a pale Englishman wearing pyjamas several sizes too large.

"I haven't finished yet," she said, resting her hand on his shoulder, "but do remember the more daring of Her Majesty's subjects are perusing the bazaar tonight. They often put on local clothing and try to blend in with the locals."

"The so called 'exotic' is a worldwide fascination, I suppose," he muttered. Hearing himself, Wellington wondered if he was growing curmudgeonly the longer he worked in the field. Granted, he hadn't been in the field *that* long—maybe he was just getting long in the tooth. "I watched one soldier too many lose themselves in such places, so forgive me if I sound..."

"Like a grumpy old man?" Eliza chuckled. "Well, remember that even life in London is far from a storybook fantasy. Think of all the Seven have faced. The Empire has its fair share of iniquity, too. The only reason its citizens seek it in such far-flung places is that here it's exotic."

Wellington had to agree. "And less likely people you play bridge with spotting you."

Eliza stood back and eyed him. "Indeed, now I think we both need a little more in the way of beards."

He blinked. "Beg your pardon?"

Eliza had a polished mahogany case that Wellington had seen in their apartments in Hebden Bridge, but never seen what was in it. His eyes widened when she opened the lid. Doing so, activated a sequence that unfurled a three-mirror array, turning the small case into a portable vanity. The inside of it turned out to be full of make-up that would have made a stage actor jealous. Alongside multitudinous sticks of makeup mimicking many skin tones, were several beards of varying hair colours, and a selection of rubberised noses. *No wonder that case was so damn heavy,* Wellington thought, *she's got a whole theatrical company in there.*

After much consideration of the contents, Eliza beckoned him over, then opened the lid of a narrow tin to reveal a thick and curly black beard. "I think this one will suit you quite well."

After examining it for a moment, Wellington pressed the opposite tips of the beard into his sideburns as Eliza worked to secure the rest of it under his chin and around his lips.

When finished his new fashion mostly swallowed up his face.

Eliza tapped another tin. "I have a handsome light brown one for me, but I need to give you a little something more."

Wellington shuffled his feet wondering how much further his lover might go down this particular avenue.

Picking up one of the finely carved noses with a Roman curve to it, she held it before him. "Do you know, Welly, changing one's nose completely alters the whole face."

At least she wasn't coming at him with a knife. "I would suppose it does…"

Using a small paintbrush, she applied some rubber glue to the inside of his new nose.

He took her hand. "Now this will come off?"

Pursing her lips together, she didn't even bother answering. "You're hopeless, darling."

After she pressed on, just like that, he had a new nose. It was strange, particularly when he took a breath through it, but when he examined himself in the mirror, he could hardly recognise the reflection. Only his hazel eyes were familiar.

Wellington stroked the construction carefully with one hand. "Always contemplated growing a beard this long, now I know how it will look if I do, but the nose I suppose I can't manage."

Eliza nodded, but then gasped on looking at the adhesive. "Think you could get used to it, then?" She held up the tiny vial in her hand. "Wrong kind of glue. I don't think it will come off now?"

"What?" he squeaked.

Her chuckle betrayed the prank at his expense. With a wink, she turned to her own reflection and set about applying her own beard and nose combination. From the matching tin she had a well-trimmed brown beard that also covered much of her face. Within a few minutes, his lover would be as unrecognisable as he was.

The thought crossed his mind that if Jekyll killed them tonight, they would give the local constabulary quite the mystery when unwrapping them. The authorities would have a devil of a time working out what had happened, but that was too dour of a proclamation for him to share with her.

A knock came at the door. Eliza gave Wellington a nod as she finished up her application.

Picking up his Remington-Elliot, the compressors hissed to life as he crossed to the door. "Yes?" he asked, standing to one side of it.

Henrietta's voice filtered through the door. "Mr Books? Just wanted to be certain you were heading to bed."

He opened the door a crack to give her preview of what lay within. She gasped, before letting out a long breath and a chuckle as he let her into their room. Once he shut the door, Henrietta spoke in a hushed voice. "That is an exceptional disguise. Well done." Wellington noted she'd dressed in the clothing of a Turkish lady, with a green salvar, blue robe and a simple scarf draped over her head.

"You look prepared too." He gestured to his face. "But I can't take credit for my own appearance, this is Eliza's art."

Henrietta raised one eyebrow in appreciation.

"Give me a moment," Eliza said from the cover of her portable vanity, "and if you need anything, I will gladly assist."

Wellington stroked his new, larger beard. "I believe she has missed her calling."

"I've always considered myself a thespian at heart," she offered, turning back to finish her work. "However, my performance is more directed towards seeing another sunrise as opposed to favourable reviews from critics."

Eliza was always lovely in any attire she chose to wear, and nothing had changed. Her long immaculately trimmed beard made her cheekbones even more defined, and her blue eyes were remarkable against the strong nose she'd given herself. Eliza D Braun made quite the beautiful young man.

Examining herself in the mirror, she fussed with the beard until it was as she liked it.

She broke away from her reflection and returned to their luggage. "Well, now to clothing. Luckily the size of the fez allowed me to work in holsters for a pistol, and I have a large bag for rifles. Also, as Wellington and I are men, we can carry curved swords. Aydin was kind enough to include one for each of us."

After they had buckled those on and stowed as many pistols as could make Eliza happy under their flowing robes, there was nothing else to do but begin the hunt.

The three of them, checked the hallway, and slipped into the corridor quiet as a family of church mice. At the end of the hallway was the servant's entrance, from there they descended to the basement level where a shift of hotel staff were busy with laundering guest clothes, linens, and other creature comforts of the Palas. Once here, Aydin's map became their guide.

"According to this," Wellington muttered to the ladies, "the entrance to the hotel's tunnel should be at the back of the supply cupboard. Behind those linens." He motioned with his head to a row of bedsheets hanging from a line.

"I love the smell of fresh laundry," Eliza said in a light tone as they moved piles of towels and linens to access the exit. "Reminds me of my Mum." She let out a little sigh as she pressed open the low door at the rear of the cupboard.

He didn't know what to say to that since he had lost his mother young. As he ducked into the cubbyhole, he idly wondered what Mrs Braun was like and what she would think about him. On this particular mission, it seemed rather unlikely he would get the chance to find out. Again, he didn't mention that dark thought to Eliza.

"Very telling, the odour of burning clothes does the same for me," Henrietta remarked.

That was a statement just begging for further investigation, but they didn't have time, so he let it lie. In silence, they descended the neatly constructed but narrow stairs in the walls, to reach an underground tunnel leading from the basement to their guide, Aydin.

"Good evening, agents. Let me be the first congratulate you on your appearance. The reality is superb. A fine group," he said, smiling. "With you all here, I take it the map is serving you well?"

Wellington glanced at it. "Looks like this takes us at least two blocks away from the hotel. If Jekyll is watching that should give us enough distance to avoid his notice."

"I hope so, but let's be cautious just in case," Eliza replied, adjusting her fez a fraction.

He shot her a glance from under a raised eyebrow. "Was that really Miss Eliza D. Braun suggesting caution?"

"I thought it might be worth a go."

"Will the wonders of Constantinople never cease?" Wellington quipped.

"A little less cheek from you, Books."

"In your disguises this is quite charming," Aydin noted.

Henrietta glanced between them. "Well, while I am in favour of romantic tension, perhaps we should continue this delightful bit of melodrama at the Bazaar."

Wellington adjusted his belt. The loose trousers, much like the false nose he wore, were taking some getting used to. "A bit of a surprise to find you here, Aydin. Can't trust us alone then?"

"Not at all," he returned, drawing what had to be a modified Bulldog, "I just thought you might need a little backup."

"The more weapons and eyes the better," Henrietta said, "and having a guide is always better than a map."

"Then follow me," and Aydin took the lead through the tunnel.

Only a few minutes had passed for the four of them before they emerged into an alleyway off a main thoroughfare. They proceeded into the flow of people with not even a glance from the surrounding crush. A casual passer-by would have taken them for a group of friends perhaps—as long as they kept to the edges of the crowd.

Constantinople was a city of great energy, and no little confusion—both which tended to go together. It was, Wellington knew from his boyhood studies, also one of enormous history and culture. Before the Ottoman Empire, it had been the Eastern City of the Roman Empire. Before that it had been Byzantium. So there were layers upon layers to the streets they now walked, which reached back beyond the time of Christ. He would so have loved to explore that historical aspect rather than the villainous one they pursued.

Around them were the locals going about their work, but also a fair number of travellers. Europeans mingled with Arabs and Russians. Chinese traders haggled on street corners. It was indeed where east met west and did plenty of business.

"Don't become distracted," Aydin said, leaning over and whispering in his ear. "And speak English, no matter what happens."

"English?"

"Consider the marks for business here," Aydin replied. "We as merchants want to be as accommodating as possible. We will be practising our mastery of your language openly here. The better our English, the more commerce we see."

Wellington blinked. "Marks? Don't you mean customers?"

Aydin shrugged. "Poh-*tay*-toe. Poh-*tah*-toe."

Their guide led them deeper into the city where the main flow of people congregated, with both portoporters and mules laden with goods to either side of them. Wellington spotted a tram with words he recognised on it. *Büyük Çarşı.*

A surge of pride in his Turkish rushed through him, even as Aydin jerked his head to indicate they should get on. All four of them leapt on board the bulging tram and held on near the back as it rattled and jerked its way through the press of people. It was worth the few coins to avoid all that.

Wellington was excited to be approaching the Grand Bazaar. He'd read about it from the safety of London, but he had never imagined seeing it. Nestled between two mosques, the Grand Bazaar had over twenty gates which led to more than sixty streets. As they pulled up to the Beyazit stop alongside the main gate, he realised they had a daunting—maybe even impossible—task ahead of them.

People streamed in under the white stone arch, which was as ornate as anyone might find on a castle. All the people on the tram bustled off, and the crowd carried the four of them along through the entrance.

Once through Aydin motioned them away from the foot traffic. They pressed close to each other to one side of the stone arch, far from any curious eyes or ears. This innocuous corner was their own quiet sanctuary from the madness of the incredible market sprawling before them.

Wellington's expression must have said it all. Aydin inclined his head, a feigned modesty in his tone as he told them, "I know you probably were expecting stalls, awnings, and a few lonely buildings scattered about. We call the Grand Bazaar *grand* for a reason."

"Every street has its speciality, so there is a method to the madness," Eliza said, her hand brushing against Wellington's, steadying his nerves with a touch.

"Booksellers Gate, Silver Row, and Women Clothiers Row, are just on the other side of the gate," Falcon offered, unintentionally rubbing rock salt into the open wound that was his pride. Usually, he was the one in the know, but presently he was the odd man out. "I must confess I had forgotten just how massive the Bazaar is."

Aydin smiled. "No need to worry, I have already found us the perfect spot to observe the whole marketplace. Stay close."

A simple request, but once they moved away from the safety of the wall, Aydin's request quickly became one of the labours of Hercules. So many people, so many scents that he could only identify a few: cardamom, cumin and paprika. The rest were a cloud of rich earthy tones that made his mouth water to imagine what culinary purposes they could be used for. From every possible angle came voices, calls for his attention, pleas for his business. The Bazaar exploded before him with colour from fabrics, from rugs that could also pass for works of art, while the sun's last rays made the embroidery threads of gold and silver twinkle like starry skies ripped from the heavens.

The main streets that they worked their way towards had no stalls; they were far grander. Some sellers had the whole building with their front door open wide, wares stacked high and hanging from every surface. Others had smaller stalls in large communal buildings, which Aydin steered them away from.

Jostled back and forth, Wellington found his eye being caught at every possible moment. Sapphire blue glass from threads of mosaic lamps. The ruby red of stacks of pomegranates cut open and gleaming. The mountains of Turkish slippers in turquoise, amber, and indigo.

How on earth could they hope to find Jekyll among all this? So many things and people crowded together competing for attention?

Wellington took a breath and remembered what Eliza had told him in their briefing. The missing were not tourists, they worked at the bazaar which closed at ten o'clock. Soon the shoppers would get herded towards the exits.

If Aydin meant to find them a hidey hole before then it would have to be soon. None of the shops had back alley access; the vendors all went in and out from the front.

However, several shops stood two stories tall, and must look out over the rooftops of the other buildings. He jerked his head up towards their window and Eliza nodded. The nearest was one selling shoes and soft textiles. The owner, a grey-haired and hunched gentleman, haggled over the price of a bolt of silk with a pair of French tourists. A younger man, most likely his son, was keeping a close eye on the passing people, just in case one of them wanted something. It was how most merchants worked since haggling could get intense, and no one wanted to lose out on making the most money.

Aydin approached the younger man and spoke to him in Turkish in a low tone. He glanced over at his father, but then held out his hand. He pressed what had to be lira into his palm before gesturing them to follow into the shop itself. Seemed that the son was happy to make a little money on the side as long as his father didn't see.

He showed them to a staircase to the top floor. The young man did not follow for too long, darting back to the marketplace before he got noticed.

"Should be a nice view," Aydin said. "You take a position up there. I have another location at ground level for Professor Falcon; a spice merchants right at the corner. The bazaar will be closing in half an hour, but we will stay on and find this villain of yours." His expression was fierce and bright. Wellington hoped that meant they would meet with success.

With a nod to their recruit, they separated; he and Eliza to climb the stairs, Henrietta and Aydin to supply support from street level. At the top, they found a large window that had a magnificent view across the tiled roofs of the bazaar, the sun setting in waves of scarlet and ochre before them.

Eliza set about unpacking their rifles. "Plenty of good angles up here, and a nice view of the smaller streets."

"Yes, quite."

She glanced over at him. "We're going to get him this time, Welly. We are."

Looking into her determined blue eyes, he could almost believe it. His throat went dry "Just be careful. I couldn't take losing you."

Her hand clamped over his and squeezed. "You won't, and I won't lose you either. Come on, with Aydin and Henrietta helping us, I am optimistic about this."

The sun began to sink, and he shaded his eyes against the glare. "The more the merrier. If hunting a mad scientist with super human abilities can be said to be merry in any fashion."

Her little chuckle relaxed him. Perhaps she was right and tonight they would have Jekyll in their clutches. Then they would celebrate with champagne.

CHAPTER EIGHTEEN

Where Mistress Death Makes an Offer

The door slammed behind Filippo, making him jump. Sophia del Morte didn't seem to care, pushing by him, making for the windows overlooking Assisi. She scanned the street below as well as the windows opposite before yanking the curtains shut.

He took a step, and Sophia rounded on him. "Stay precisely where you are!"

The assassin went to the other window, repeating the ritual of checking foot traffic and sight lines. When she yanked the final set of curtains closed, the room descended into ominous darkness.

"Sit," she spoke over her shoulder.

Filippo slipped out of his coat and took a seat on the couch, fumbling with his hat. He watched the ghostly woman, dressed in what would have been better suited for an adventurer, go to this apartment's cellaret and open one of its crystal decanters. The faint scent of almonds tickled his nostrils, so it had to be Amaretto. She poured two glasses without looking at him.

The black outfit made her practically invisible, except for the faint gleam of her olive skin when she moved. It was impossible to ignore the menace she exuded, especially when she handed him the drink.

"Graziei," he muttered before bringing the glass to his lips, but he paused. The del Mortes were not just known for their knives and guns.

Sophia shook her head. "Suit yourself." Taking the glass out of his hand she poured his drink into her own before taking a generous gulp. A shudder ran through her once it had passed her lips. "There. Happy?"

Slightly mollified, Filippo nodded.

"I did not save you just to kill you, and I would not ruin a perfectly good amaretto by putting poison in it."

"No, no you would not," he said, trying to keep his voice steady.

Sophia tilted her head and smiled. "Granted, I can understand your concern. After all, you are Usher, and Italy is your responsibility, Mr Badger. We both know it was you who gave the order to have my village executed."

Again, the glass stopped short of his lips. He desperately needed the drink, but Sophia del Morte had named the elephant in the room. Now, the question was how to avoid being trampled by it?

"If you're convinced of my involvement in the destruction of your family," he began, his hand fighting a slight tremor, "why are you helping me?"

Sophia threw back the sweet liquor and took a seat opposite him. Her lips pursed, relaxed, and then pursed again. She looked as if she were chewing on her own thoughts but needed one more taste of the amaretto before continuing. After a third sip, she went on.

"My family holds me responsible for what happened. I was, after all, the only del Morte doing business with the House of Usher." She shrugged. "Of course, I knew the risks, but I thought you all were more easily managed." Her smile was tight as she looked at Filippo. "Obviously, I underestimated the House's tenacity."

"Yes, you did," Filippo stated, regaining his calm and taking a drink of the sweet liquor.

She watched him with a falcon's focus. "Well, my hubris came at a cost. I am now a pariah to my own family."

Filippo had done worse in his time so he was not at all sympathetic. "What a shame... no more family Christmas dinners for you."

"It is a bit more worrisome than that. What remains of the del Morte family is now hunting me."

Filippo set his glass down before him, considering Sophia's words. She was a marked woman to Usher as well, but he had not been in favour of it. The del Morte's—particularly this one—were not to be idly disturbed. Like a pit of vipers, they were best left alone.

Sophia del Morte had already proved she was the embodiment of death. In one evening, the House lost some of their best when a failed abduction turned deadly. Even though it was expressly ordered throughout the ranks to avoid the assassin, standing orders within the House was that if an opportunity arose to eliminate Sophia del Morte, they should take it.

His mind wandered to the sword in his walking stick. This was clearly an opportunity, but it was hard to calculate the risks at this moment.

"So, it would seem that you are in need of an ally?" Filippo asked.

"So it would appear."

The amaretto was finally calming his nerves. He glanced to the covered windows and tapped his glass with his fingertips. Out in the streets of Assisi were three agents of the Ministry of Peculiar Occurrences, and they sought more information about Ragnarök. That they knew the name of the Chairman's passion project was unsettling, and he could not afford to assume these agents were bluffing.

He took another measured sip as he contemplated Sophia del Morte. This woman had a reputation for many things, but not for generosity or charity. "To be blunt, *Signora*, may I ask what exactly you want of me?"

"I need you to get out of this city. With the Ministry onto whatever endeavour you are undertaking, you may have to close down operations in Assisi."

Filippo let out a low chuckle. "This town is simply a gateway to my current project. However, with their presence here, I need to get to Rome straightaway."

"Then I will get you there safely," Sophia stated as she took a seat next to Filippo. "When I tell you to move, you will not question me. If I tell you to hide, you will do so. You will, my dear Mr Badger, have to trust me." She emphasised the point by brushing the hair off his face. He managed not to flinch.

"Just like that?"

Sophia crossed her legs, twisted her lips into a smile, and let out a long breath. Up close all of these actions were quite riveting—and that also terrified him.

Filippo polished off what remained of the drink before leaning forward and fixing his gaze on Sophia. "And in exchange for this, what will you ask from the House of Usher?"

"You said it yourself—an ally. I request sanctuary."

He raised an eyebrow at this. "Sanctuary?"

"Yes," Sophia replied, adjusting his collar. "I want asylum within the House of Usher. I assure you, for that I will make the arrangement very much worth your while."

This ought to be amusing. "How so? What could you possibly offer me or Usher? Your unending servitude? Since we have plenty of that from others, we have no need of yours."

Sophia laughed, her expression folding into derision. "No, of course you don't." She spun her empty glass in her fingers. "I intend to deliver unto Usher the whole del Morte family. They have deemed the House and all its associates a priority."

Easing back into the couch, Filippo glanced at the windows. He wanted to look over his shoulder at the door, but what good would that do?

"I am the only thing standing between you and their wrath. So it would seem, we need each other."

Filippo swallowed hard on that bitter truth and wondered if she had more Amaretto available, or if there was enough in the world to make this more palatable.

CHAPTER NINETEEN

◆⇌⇋◆

In Which the Last Person You Trust Becomes Quite the Reliable Chum

Brandon Hill lay prone on the bed, a cloth bag packed with ice resting across his forehead.

David Harker sprawled across the couch, his white suit stained with dirt and dust from being tackled.

Bruce stood between them, at a loss for words, save for three. *What. Utter. Wankers.*

Taking in the ridiculous comedy for another moment, Bruce went to their suite's bar and poured himself a whiskey. He wasn't sure what kind it was. It was clear. It smelt strong, and that was good enough. This was not two fingers' worth, or even three. This one was a whole fist.

He glared at the other men as he poured. "I cannot believe, you two morons can take a simple operation and turn it on its ass."

It was Harker who protested—or at least he tried. He sat up and let out a small yelp.

"All right then, let's start with you." Bruce took a swig of the clear alcohol, and shuddered as it tore down his throat. Good God, what lighter fluid were they drinking in this hotel? "Why would you pull a gun on our contact in the middle of the street in bloody daylight?"

"Have you ever loved someone so deeply, so completely, that they become your life?" Not waiting for Bruce to answer, Harker blathered on. "Whatever you may think you know about love, I can tell you that my darling Virginia is all that and so much more. That cad knew where my light and love is being held, and you were taking far too long!"

Bruce fixed him with a hard look. He had no sympathy for the bumps and bruises he had personally dealt to this idiot. "Well, not sure if you know this, but we are supposed to work *in secret*. This means avoiding socially inappropriate behaviours like shooting a man in a restaurant!»

"Mind speaking louder, you git? Don't believe the French couple two floors down heard you clearly enough," grumbled Brandon.

Bruce spun around. "Alright then, Canuck of Action and Adventure, Master of Monkey Knife Fighting, and Spring-Heeled Jack of All Trades, explain to me how you allowed someone to get the drop on you!"

"The attacker snuck up behind me! Not like I have eyes in the back of my head," he snapped as he pressed the ice harder against his forehead.

The real trick in being a secret agent, at least for Bruce, was to expect things to go to pear-shaped. No matter the skill of the agent or the plan you have thought out to the last detail, realising things can go completely sideways keeps you on your toes. The leader of the Italian branch of the House of Usher had been within his physical grasp, but now they were even worse off. They had no indication of Virginia's whereabouts, or why Usher even had her meeting Badger in Umbria. This whole operation had eroded into a dog's breakfast, and since Bruce was the lead on this case, it would be his head on a plate.

"Your afternoon's antics set us back months," Bruce said pointedly at Harker. "Now that Badger knows we're on his trail, he will go underground. One thing he won't be doing for certain is staying in bloody Assisi!"

"My intentions were honourable," Harker mumbled.

Bruce let out a loud *"Pfft!"*. "If you were looking to help Virginia, you've done the complete opposite."

"Now, now, Bruce, go easy on the poor chap."

This was months of surveillance, research, and investigation, all lost on account of that tosser, Highfield, getting in the last word with them for running operations in New York without approval. "Bringing this bloke along with us was nothing more than OSM's idea of a joke. With this stunt of Harker's, our trail on Usher has gone—"

A knock came at their door. Bruce drew his Remington-Elliott and made it two steps before stopping at where Harker now sat. "Not. One. Sound," he whispered to him.

Taking a place to the right of the door, Bruce gave his voice a gravely rumble akin to someone just roused from a deep sleep. "You'd better have a good reason to be waking me up."

The voice from the other side of the door was muffled, uneasy. "Sorry to disturb you, sir, but a note has arrived for you."

Bruce placed the pistol's muzzle against the door, while with his free hand opened the door just enough to reveal a pale, nervous bellhop. "Did you see who delivered it?"

"Sorry, sir, but it was dropped off by parcel post. Our delivery boy was just paid to take the note from sender to here and delivered it with utmost secrecy."

Bruce yanked the door completely open. "Did the note bearer ask specifically for Bruce Campbell?"

"No, sir. The note is addressed and intended for your travelling companion, Brandon Hill."

Bruce grabbed for the folded note from the bellhop, but paused. The young hotel associate was wearing gloves, a standard for a hotel of this status. Damn. He was just going to have to risk it. Bruce spread his palm and motioned for the bellhop to place the note there. As the bellhop gently placed the parchment in Bruce's open hand, the Australian peered at it, trying to see if there was anything on the outside of the paper. "Mind if I ask a silly question?"

The young bellhop perked up at the offer. Maybe he was hoping for a chance to get back into Bruce's good graces. "Anything you like, sir, within reason. "

Bruce brought the note up to his nose and took a few sniffs of the paper. Nothing out of the ordinary, save for the smell of paper and ink. "The bloke delivering the note, did you happen to notice if he was wearing gloves like you?"

"Why would a postman be wearing gloves?" The bellhop chuckled. "After all, he is handling packages, sifting through envelopes, and, of course, delivering the mail. He wouldn't be able to hold onto anything."

"Did the postman look sickly at all? You know, like he was poisoned?"

The bellhop's cordial smile faded. "Poisoned? We don't see a lot of poisoning in this line of work."

Bruce glared at the bellhop, and the fellow shrank back. So he knew his expression had to be terrifying. Brandon was always better at putting on a cordial look. "Just answer the bloody question."

"I am confident in saying the postman was not wearing gloves."

Bruce nodded. That was going to be as good an answer as he was going to get. "Fine then. Thanks for the delivery."

"Will there be anything else, sir?" the bellhop asked, extending his hand, ready to accept a small token of appreciation.

Bruce glanced at the cupped hand and then looked up. "You expecting a tip, mate?"

He responded with a weak smile and a shrug.

"Right then," Bruce said with a nod. "Your tip: always wear gloves when accepting anything from strangers. You never know where it's been. Now, bugger off."

With that, Bruce slammed the door shut.

"What was that all about?" asked Brandon, as he pulled himself up from the bed.

Bruce still hadn't fully touched the note resting in his palm. He carried it across the room as if it were a ticking bomb. Considering how things had progressed for them so far in Assisi, this letter could do just that. "You got that whatchamacallit Axelrod and Blackwell cooked up in R&D for us? You know, the thingamajiggy that can apparently detect poisons?"

Brandon winced as he hobbled over to the dresser which stored their clothes and a few of their weapons. Third drawer down, he pulled out a polished wooden box that could easily hold a loaf of bread and have a bit of room to spare. It took up the centre of the small table in front of Harker, and with a few flips of locks from opposite sides, the lid split open to reveal a wild combination of miniature boilers, pipes, and hoses, all connected to a long, central vent running the length of the box. It had at one end, gauges, lights, and switches that controlled whatever this contraption did. Brandon was prone to reading the instruction manuals from Axelrod & Blackwell—Bruce was not. His partner flipped three of these switches, coaxing a soft, constant hiss from the machine, just audible over the clicking of cogs and gears inside it.

"I don't understand," Harker said, watching Bruce carry the note over to Brandon. "Why all this theatre?"

"Considering nobody knows we're here except for the Ministry and that there are people that would be happy enough to see us dead?" Bruce lifted the note into the sunlight, looking for any residue that might glisten. "This was a letter, delivered anonymously, and specifically to Brandon, shortly after someone attacked him, probably from the House of Usher. I would rather err on the side of caution."

Brandon pulled out from the right lid of the box a set of tongs and waved the letter through the steam.

"So how's it looking, mate?" Bruce asked. "Is that whatsitsname doing what it's supposed to be doing?"

"If you mean the *toxitector*, yes, it is working, provided there are no toxins to detect on this note that is." Now the scent of caramel and nutmeg tickled Bruce's nose. His eyes jumped from the thingamabob to the note itself. The paper did not change colour, smoulder, or react in any sort of manner to the surrounding steam. "If R&D were correct we should have seen something on the paper by now. This note looks clean."

"Right then," Bruce said, freeing the note from the tongs' grip. "Let's see who is reaching out to us."

He turned the note over. It was strong beige parchment, folded again and again on itself and sealed with wax. The insignia imprinted inside the seal revealed nothing to Bruce. It was not a crest from a country or government office he recognised. Crossing the room, he went to the hotel desk and fetched out a small magnifying glass.

At first glance it appeared to be nothing more than a red rose, but on closer inspection, the petals were actually various instruments of death. Curved blades. Firearms. Bullets. Instruments of an apothecary's office. And, from what Bruce could guess, other plants that could be poisonous.

No, Bruce thought, *if this is who I think it is...*

Bruce cracked the seal and unfurled the note. While Axelrod and Blackwell's doohickey hadn't detected any toxins on the outside, there was no guarantee there wouldn't be something special waiting for him within. The handwriting was neat, concise, and quite elegant. After reviewing the message, Bruce's knees went a touch weak. He took a moment to gather his wits, straighten up, and then start reading aloud from the very beginning.

My dearest agent Brandon D. Hill,

I regret in subduing you in such a common manner. I meant no offence and I hope you can forgive me.

I also hope this message reaches you safely, and that you realise this matter involving the House of Usher is strictly professional. Knowing you and Bruce as I do, I understand why you would report Mr. Badger and my whereabouts to your Ministry superiors. In fact I am counting on it.

Mr. Badger and I are heading for Rome – which part, I am not yet certain. Whatever Usher operation you are investigating, you must look in that city. I will not interfere in your business unless it involves an extraction for Mr. Badger in which case it will become problematic. Please do not make it so. I would so hate for this to become ugly.

I know there is not much trust in our profession, but I hope my actions for agents Books and Braun speak for themselves. Thank you for your attention.

Yours sincerely,

Sophia Del Morte

Bruce handed the letter to Brandon. His partner read it wide-eyed—then again, before looking up. "So," Brandon began, a slight smile crossing his face, "this gives me hope?"

"About what?"

"Maybe Sophia del Morte has taken a fancy to me? Quite nice of her to apologise like that, ain't it?"

Bruce considered for a moment that his jaw might actually clatter against the floor. "She's not asking you for an evening out on the town, mate."

"But," Brandon said, his smile brightening ever so slightly, "there could be a chance!"

Bruce crossed his arms over his chest. "And what about that Anouk bird? Did you not learn anything from that period of your life?"

"This is a problem when you meet someone as passionate as you. Yes, it was a rather painful separation period we endured…"

"Brandon, she tried to kill you."

"We were in love."

"She tried to kill you with a moose-throwing trebuchet."

"It was *true* love," Brandon insisted. "Harker here can understand that, can't you, mate?"

Harker blinked. "I'm sorry. Did this Anouk woman throw a moose at you?"

Brandon waved his hand dismissively. "Anouk and I have a complicated relationship. Sophia del Morte is different. Sharing a repast with her would be instructional… a purely professional meeting of minds."

Bruce swallowed back a groan. His partner may have been one of the most skilled agents in the Ministry, but he just wasn't playing with all his marbles. Not at all. "Sophia del Morte. You were taken out in the street by Sophia del Morte. You wouldn't survive a dinner with her."

"That first statement isn't quite true." Brandon lifted a finger as if he were to about to bestow sage advice on to Bruce. "She *knocked* me out. She did not *take* me out. If I had been taken out, we would not be talking."

Bruce went to respond, but could not find the words. Brandon was absolutely right. Sophia del Morte was the type of assassin who did not leave anything to chance. If she wanted Brandon dead, then he would be dead. Instead she had gone to great lengths to make sure he got this message. How long had she been watching them? How long had she been in Assisi?

And what was that whole business with Mr Badger? Was Sophia del Morte working for the House of Usher once again? That would be nothing short of a stunner on both sides. According to rumours, Sophia and the House suffered a falling out. Falling out with any of the del Morte clan only led to many, many deaths.

"You got a point there, mate," Bruce admitted.

"It would seem that we have not only Usher to worry about, but Sophia del Morte as well."

A voice across the room chimed in, startling them both. "Did you lot read the same note?"

Bruce and Brandon both looked at each other, then turned to David Harker who was brushing off his jacket. "That note was an apology. A rather eloquent one if you don't mind my saying."

"Actually I do mind," Bruce stated. "The lady behind this letter may seem polished and refined, but she's a cold-blooded killer. Make no mistake, mate. If you see her, you're dead."

"Gentlemen, I do perceive that this woman is a killer of the highest order, but re-read the letter." Harker hobbled over to where the decanters sat. Bruce had not seen Harker partake of any libation since their trip, but as he poured himself a healthy snort, the toff continued, "This is an apology. Perhaps I am being presumptuous, gentlemen, but skilled assassins would not necessarily send such letters after subduing one of their opponents."

"She wants something," Brandon stated pointedly. "We are not completely daft."

Harker shook his head before taking an unmeasured gulp of whatever whiskey he had chosen. "Read the note again. She is *apologising* to you. There are no direct threats against you, or Mr Campbell. She has offered you a destination. She is keeping you gentlemen in the loop while extending a professional courtesy regarding this Badger fellow. Allow her a wide berth, and you can carry on with your endeavours.»

Bruce and Brandon shared a look at one another. The Australian would never admit it, but he was absolutely right; del Morte wasn't interested in them, or their mission. What was her game?

"What do you think, mate?" Bruce asked Brandon.

"Well, first, what they say about the broken clock is right." He looked down at the note again. "And second, we need to book passage to Rome, with the fastest transport we can find. If we can get a head start on Badger and Sophia, we can get a lead on Virginia."

Harker's face brightened at the prospect.

"Pack your bags and polish your rosaries," Bruce said as he looked at both men. "Seems like we're paying the Pope a visit."

CHAPTER TWENTY

Wherein Danger Lurks
Around All Corners of the Sacred City

His knuckles brushed the wood once again. "Are you in there?" Filippo paused to look up the hallway and down from where he came before leaning closer to the door and knocking again. "Signorina del Morte, are you awake?"

This was their fourth day together, their second in Rome. As it had been on their travels from Assisi to the capital city, Sophia del Morte slept like the dead. Several mornings and one afternoon, during their trip to Rome, Filippo went to rouse her from her sleep. Those attempts were no different from this morning's.

Perhaps she was keeping odd hours in order to watch over them while on the road. Maybe, on account of her chosen profession and lifestyle, she did not sleep well at night.

Filippo broached the subject once with Sophia, attempting to make light of the fact she was not a morning person.

"My sleeping habits are not your concern," Sophia had stated. *"Remain confident that I am keeping an eye on you, as well as assuring our safety."*

Filippo remembered bristling at that as he was aware he'd traded being the Ministry's prisoner for hers.

"So exactly how am I supposed to conduct business, Signorina?" he had asked her.

"*I suppose you will have to be flexible.*" She took several steps closer to him. Filippo could still recall the extreme discomfort he experienced the nearer she got. While Sophia del Morte was a striking woman, he was aware her ruthlessness matched her beauty and grace. "*Even if I am asleep, you are not to leave your room. Your safety is my priority.*"

"*For that, you have my unending gratitude.*"

"*Do not mistake my dedication, Mr Badger. Your safety is my passage into the House of Usher.*" She had fixed him with a hard, cold look. "*You are in Rome. A city* mi famiglia *knows very well, and they are all out for your blood. Do not test your luck against their abilities.*"

During their trip from Assisi, this new condition of hers had made things inconvenient. Once in Rome, managing current operations were nigh on impossible. He needed updates from his subordinates. He required status reports from his operatives. He had to make certain that his part in Ragnarök was still progressing forward. Smooth, and by the numbers. That was how things had to go.

With one more breath for courage, Filippo knocked—this time, louder. That should have roused her even from the deepest of sleeps. "Signorina del Morte, answer this door immediately!"

The silence threatened to smother him. Filippo surrendered to the compulsion to look up and down the corridor yet again, but it was empty. Everyone else was already about their day—unlike him.

No. Today would not be a waste. He could no longer wait.

Retreating back to his adjoining room, he checked his reflection in the mirror. He missed the creature comforts of his home and offices, and the privileges of his standing in the House of Usher. All these things were only a few city blocks from where they were staying, but they might as well have been in Rome, Iowa. He could only hope that the Ministry agents he had met were still in Assisi, chasing their tails, while they had escaped to the Sacred City.

Escape, Filippo thought, shaking his head. *I would have fared just fine had I not been cornered by that other* bastardo.

He adjusted the suit's fine pressed cuffs, checked the collar, and let his fingertips run the length of his cravat. These little touches were all that remained of what he had come to expect from life. Topping his dark suit with a fine black derby and stroking his moustache with the back of his finger, he gave himself a nod of approval in the mirror. He was ready to head out.

The sunlight glinting off his silver Usher ring signalled that, yes, he would indeed be able to conduct business today without interference.

Taking up his walking stick, Filippo Rossi set off for the streets of Rome. He planned to obey only one of Sophia's commands: send no *aethermissives*. This was totally sensible as any communication could tip off the Ministry. Sophia and Filippo needed to take advantage of their confusion and build a distance between them.

Æthermissives could also tip off any operatives of the del Morte family. They were hunting Sophia. If he believed Sophia's tale, they would take down any Usher brothers and sisters they could.

Pulling the lift gate shut, he pressed the call button for the lobby. During the slow descent he checked the availability of his sword. The blade was still plenty sharp and easily removed from the cane scabbard. He regretted not having the walking stick that doubled as a small rifle, but since their flight from Assisi was so unexpected, all he had was what he was wearing.

The lift shuddered to a halt. Sliding the gate back, he opened to door to the lobby, and grasped at how difficult this all was. Within seconds, Filippo took in the location of every seated couple, assessed sight lines for potential snipers, and memorised every detail in passing of the hotel's elegant receiving area. Over a decade before his own field training had been exceptional, but he was older now and horrendously out of practice.

So many potential threats—and this was only the hotel lobby. He had not even seen what waited for him outside.

While the English took pride in their London and the French held Paris as the Jewel of Europe, Italians revelled in the majesty, history, and pageantry of Rome. Civilisations had risen and fallen all from this one city. Now it was the centre of the House of Usher's grand scheme that would, according to their Chairman, change the world, bringing the vision of their founders to life. Filippo had to make certain, beyond any shadow of doubt, that his part in Ragnarök remained on schedule, remained perfect. Every success, every setback, conjured memories of Bear.

With his head down, Filippo slipped into the afternoon pedestrian traffic, working his way through the city. His gaze occasionally jumped to the windows of surrounding buildings, brief glances of potential vantage points. Though, if Filippo were to catch a glimpse of a rifle muzzle or the glint off a scope's optics, it would be too late.

From the shadows of a canopy, Filippo saw his destination: a haven in case of impending or unexpected storms. The Raven's specialty, although they carried books from all over the world and of varying genres, was collections of poetry. A tiny bell overhead announced his arrival; and from the midst of bookshelves, a young, dark-haired woman smiled at him as he entered the establishment. Her eyes darted to another woman—this one a patron—taking stock of what The Raven was offering.

He slipped between two rows of books and ran his finger across the spines. He stopped on a book that covered the rose varieties of the world. Considering his outfit, he could pass himself off as a man of academic study, provided no one realised he was in the Gardening section. The customer continued her wander through the store, stopped for a moment at the collection of 17th century poets, picked up the volume, and thumbed through it. She nodded, then went to the shopkeeper to finish the purchase.

Filippo waited for the patron to leave, then he approached the counter.

"May I help you?" asked the shopkeeper with a fetching smile.

"Yes, I am looking for a collection of poetry. Something dark, something menacing."

"Did you have a poet in mind? Shelley? Polidori? Anyone in particular?"

"I'm trying to remember the line," and then, for an added effect to his spy craft, he sighed, offering the shop girl an awkward smile, "and forgive me if I butcher what I can remember, but the writer had a line that started with something about midnight. 'While I pondered weak and bleary'…?"

The shopkeeper gave a little titter. "No, no, no. It isn't bleary, it's weary."

"Oh," Filippo said, "so the verse goes: Once upon a midnight dreary while I pondered weak and…?"

"Weary," she said with a nod. The confirmation that everything was clear. "Weak and weary."

"That's it!" Filippo said, relaxation easing to his body for the first time in days. "Do you have any collections featuring this poet?"

"Will you follow me?" she said walking out from behind her counter. "I think I have what you need in the back room."

"That would be lovely."

The shopkeeper flipped her sign hanging from the door from "Open" to "Closed" and with a warm smile beckoned for him to follow.

Tension ebbed away as he left behind the mundane bookshop and stepped into another world—one he was familiar with. An æthermessanger sat in one corner of this back office, silent but waiting for word from the Chairman. At the desk where one would expect bills and invoices from publishers, he recognised at a glance many notes and dossiers concerning operations in Rome. It was most comforting to come in from the cold and return to the protection of the House.

"Finally," he breathed.

The shopkeeper smiled. "You kept us on edge since Assisi."

Filippo frowned. "Whatever do you mean?"

"Your communications with the House stopped abruptly—it was a cause for some concern."

"Understandable." Filippo looked the girl up and down, then asked, "Doesn't Giuseppe hold this post?"

"Usually yes. I am his right hand if you will." She gave a slight tilt of her head. "My name is Angela."

Filippo nodded. It was not uncommon to see women rising in the ranks now, part of the Chairman's new approach to the House of Usher. He used the del Morte family as an example of how lethal, cunning, and efficient, women could be when in positions of power and authority.

"And where is Giuseppe?"

"Called away to oversee another operation."

"Not Ragnarök?" Filippo asked.

"No, the House will not sit on the laurels of a success, so we are planning for what's next." She arched an eyebrow. "Unless your silence is a cause for concern. You are still on target, yes?"

"Of course I am, woman," he snapped. "Just because I went silent for a few days does not mean there's a problem."

Angela bowed her head, her expression faltering between annoyance and contrition. "I take it this is a simple check-in then, and you are advising us that all is well?"

"Not entirely. I ran into a complication while in Assisi."

"Complication?" Angela stiffened. "I do hope you have more details than simply a *complication* behind your sudden silence. Especially at this crucial phase...."

Filippo bristled at her condescending tone. While this was all part of Holmes' new vision for the House, he was *still* in charge of this region. His mood had not improved with being on the run, unable to notify anyone. "I am well aware of that." He took in a deep breath and tried to quash the growing animosity. "Please inform the Chairman that I am safe, but communications for a time will be limited."

"And, Mr Rossi I presume you need an updated status report on operations here in Rome?"

"Yes," Filippo replied, "that would be lovely."

She moved back towards the desk, and that was when Filippo drew the sword out of his cane.

Angela spun at the first sound of steel rubbing against the scabbard. Filippo had no idea where the gun came from, but one was in her hand. Perhaps she'd had it tucked up her sleeve, but before she could bring her pistol round to bear, he flipped the cane scabbard up and struck the weapon hard, knocking both it and the shooter to one side. He managed to leap out of the concealed office and back into the bookshop before she squeezed off a shot.

Crouching low, he worked his way through the shelves. He could hear Angela still in the concealed office, along with the clicks of a safety being disengaged. From his quick glance, her pistol had been a standard derringer, something simple to conceal. What Angela wielded now sounded much heavier, and far more lethal.

"Filippo," Angela called sweetly, "why the sudden change? Aren't we all part of the same House?"

"If we were, you would've called me by my proper title, Mr Badger. True names are for confidants. I knew Giuseppe—but not you."

"Very clever." Angela's voice grew closer. Filippo crawled in the opposite direction. "You know, I prefer eye contact when I speak with people. Why don't you stick your head out so I can see you, and then we can talk properly?"

His silent crawling now became a noisy scamper, but he still managed to keep the cane in one hand. As he scuttled between shelves, he wished The Raven had been a bit bigger. The space in front of the door was open, and he just knew she would be waiting for him to make a break for it. While he struggled with the handle, she would shoot him in the back.

Filippo paused and listened. A board creaked. Working his way back to his feet was not quiet; his old bones popped defiantly, each crack threatening to surrender his hiding place. He rose slowly from his position, daring to peer through the breaks of the shelves towards the door. Turning to his left, he caught a glimpse of Angela and the impressive sidearm she now brandished.

Filippo ducked as bullets struck the shelf of books where his head had just been. Bits of paper rained down on him as he ran in a crouch towards a different shelf. From behind, he heard a confident stride closing the distance. The Raven's door banged open, the bell above announcing the entrance of a patron who chose the wrong day to ignore the sign on the door.

Two more shots rang out, followed quickly by the grunts of a body struck by bullets. Something hit the floor. Something heavy. At least one person, Angela or the stranger from the street, was down.

"Badger," Sophia del Morte called out. "Dammit, Badger, where are you?"

This time Filippo did stick his head out and breathed a sigh of relief when he saw Sophia del Morte standing in the middle of the bookshop. He took two steps and then froze. He had seen plenty of dead bodies before, but poor Angela struggling for air was a pitiful sight. Blood bubbled from her chest where a bullet had struck.

Filippo glanced across at Sophia. "This was a safe house—a trusted place."

Sophia gave a slight shrug. "I wouldn't expect you to know my sister. You never did business with her."

"She is a relative?"

Holstering her pistol, she motioned to the dying woman on the floor. "This is Lucinda. Her specialty is—was—infiltration. Somewhere in here is your true contact. Probably stuffed in a closet. Hold her wrists down."

Filippo did as he had been told. He would no longer question a del Morte, even as she covered her sister's mouth and nose.

"Lucinda was always one of the prettiest of the del Morte sisters," Sophia began, even as she pushed back the poor woman now struggling to breathe. "If I'd had my way, I would simply slit her throat or shoot her in the head. However, I know that my Nonna always prefers an open casket for her family."

In his younger days, Filippo had been responsible for many deaths by many means. Poisons. Beatings. Once he'd dropped a gargoyle on a priest's head. In many cases though, it was more about character assassination than an actual corporeal assignment. He had never assisted in a killing like this. Lucinda struggled and kicked against his restraint while Sophia's hand covered her nose and mouth. It was the whimpering that made him his stomach twist into a knot. Thankfully it slowed and stopped altogether.

"You just killed your own sister," Filippo said sombrely.

"Aren't you the perceptive one?" Sophia sneered.

"I do not understand…"

The hand came at him like a whip and knocked Filippo to one side. A thousand needles burned on his cheek, and welts rose where she had struck him.

"I told you not to leave your room without me," Sophia snapped.

"I had business to attend to."

"That nearly cost you your life." Sophia stomped over to Lucinda's feet and grabbed her by the ankles. "Had I not been here, you would be dead. Is your business really worth your life?"

Filippo searched for an answer, but instead he remained enthralled by the sight of Sophia del Morte dragging the bloodied mess that was once her sister away. She took her behind the counter and into the office. She handled her own flesh and blood so callously—void of all emotion.

After a moment he followed her. "If I was Lucinda," Sophia began, her voice steady, "then where would I put Giuseppe?" Spinning around she opened the cloakroom door and a body fell out with a thump. His throat was cut from ear to ear.

"There he is," she said with a smile. "So what gave Lucinda away to you?"

Filippo cleared his throat. "My name. She called me *Mr Rossi* and not by my proper moniker within the House. A field operative wouldn't know such things."

Sophia looked around the office her gaze falling on a large ottoman. When she opened it she found several folded blankets inside of it. "We can pop her in here."

"And then we contact Usher?" Filippo asked.

She tilted her head. "Perhaps, when we are ready to leave Rome."

Now this madness had gone far enough. "This is your family! This is your sister, your flesh and blood, a bearer of your family name! How can you be so cold?"

"You do not understand, Mr Badger," Sophia stated the tenor of her words carrying as much emotion as a stone. "The del Morte clan stopped being my family the moment they turned against me. There is to be no mercy."

Filippo let that sink in; she was being honest. The truth was within the ranks of Usher, she might have a chance at safety. She'd have resources, and support from other Usher brothers and sisters.

"How did the del Morte clan find out about The Raven?" Filippo asked. "Does that mean they know might know we are at the hotel?"

"If they knew that, we would already be dead. Other del Mortes have worked for the House, so it's not surprising they were aware of this place."

After a few moments moving blankets, Sophia placed Lucinda in the ottoman and paused. She muttered a short prayer, then brushing off her hands, Sophia turned to him.

"If Lucinda was here, then we should assume that all safe locations have been compromised. Can you conduct your business quickly from here?" She motioned to the silent aethermessenger sitting in the corner of the office.

"I believe so," Filippo replied.

"Very well then," Sophia said, pulling back a flap of leather from the brace around one of her wrists. Underneath was a small timer. "After thirteen minutes, we must go. It will be a challenge to get you back to the hotel, but I think we can make it. Beyond half an hour, I cannot guarantee that my family will not show up and cause a scene."

With a frantic nod, Filippo scrambled for the aethermessenger. He flicked three switches behind its large glass screen and sat patiently as the device's inner mechanisms spun to life. Within a few minutes, the screen would go black, and then he would be able to conduct business.

He would see the successful conclusion to Ragnarök.

CHAPTER TWENTY-ONE

In Which Shadows are Chased

It wasn't the first time Eliza had experienced the drudgery of staking out a location, but this one had a special frisson to it.

Wellington sat a few feet away, tucked into the growing shadows. His eyes, like hers, were covered by Starlight goggles. She observed him in similar situations before, but this time she knew he felt it too. Her body was tense and had been that way for a long time.

The business in the bazaar below had tapered off. Silver and gold merchants, jewellers and craftsmen, had already locked up for the night. Streams of shoppers funnelled towards the main doors and bid good night to the remaining merchants before the market's doors were locked. As the gaslights sprang to life along the main thoroughfares, the back alleys began to get darker by comparison. Now the only people left within the bazaar were shopkeepers and workers. They moved about in a much more relaxed manner, closing up their stores and chatting to each other over the day's events.

Watching them, Eliza could guess some had families to get home to, while others did not. They had normal lives, and now she started to think she might envy them for that a little.

Wellington shifted in his place, leaning forward into the dark, and adjusting his Starlights. Eliza turned and fixed hers on the direction he was looking.

The spark flared on the small device secured on her shoulder, and from the light came a voice.

"Overwatch, this is Shadow One." It was Aydin. He was somewhere in the streets, milling about with the shopkeepers. "All clear. Shadow Two, report."

"Shadow Two here," Professor Falcon responded. "All clear."

Once the spark disappeared, Eliza touched the top of her *electrocomms* and spoke into the spark she created. "Overwatch here. Well done, Shadow Two. I dare say, you're a natural."

The spark disappeared, but then reappeared when Henrietta spoke. "Very kind of you to say, but my heart rate is rather elevated at present."

"Maintain radio silence," Aydin interjected. "Eyes open, if you please."

Eliza would have retorted, but he was correct. This was an operation, and while Henrietta Falcon's presence was unorthodox, it was not the time for social pleasantries. They were hunting a madman, and everyone—even the unexpected agent in their team—needed to focus.

"You must commend Aydin's professionalism," Wellington spoke from behind her.

"I'm trying to offer Henrietta encouragement."

"Offer it when we are back in Hebden Bridge, safe and sound, with Jekyll as our prisoner."

Eliza glanced over her shoulder at Wellington. He looked quite unnatural in the moonlight, his eyes dimly lit by the screen glow of the Starlights. "Are you sure of that tactic, my love?"

"He's no good to us dead," he replied flatly.

"Are you wanting him for Ministry matters, or personal ones?"

Wellington took a moment before answering. "Bit of both."

A little smile crossed her lips. "How I do love your honesty."

Eliza eased the tiny lever on the left lens upward, increasing the aperture of her goggles, then twisted her frames to bring the two men in her field of vision into focus. The men were featureless figures in her Starlights closing the shutters of their shop. No one else appeared in that particular alleyway. The merchants were taking their time, pausing to chat and share conversation. From their postures and gestures, it must have been a good day of commerce. *Well done, gents,* she thought.

Flakes that could almost have been mistaken for sunlit dust or a snowdrift slipping free of a mountaintop caught her eye. Some sort of debris was falling from above the two shopkeepers. Eliza followed the trail of dust upward into the rooftops, and there a shape was moving. A familiar shape.

Her fingers nearly broke the top arm of the electrocomm as she pressed down to open a channel. "Shadow Team, I have contact. Repeat, I have contact."

Eliza swallowed hard. There was no mistaking the lanky shape sporting a top hat. Even from this distance, it was obvious he was transforming, taking full advantage of the shadows. Jekyll in full control of his mutation was an unsettling thought. However, more so was the grey shape undulating and distorting within her specs. Jekyll's mastery of the transformation was such that he could summon his darker nature while examining the young men below. The once gangly man was now a leviathan, bulging with muscles, standing at least eight feet tall. Eliza looked to the two merchants closing shop, neither aware that a horror loomed above them.

"Target confirmed," Wellington stated in his own comms.

Henry Jekyll positioned himself like a jungle cat, preparing to pounce upon the young men. Eliza perched her Starlights on the top of her head, and raised her rifle, mounted with its own Starlight scope. Through the optics—its crosshairs surrounded by numbers flipping back and forth—she centred Jekyll, compensating for distance and possible wind currents. With a final, long exhale, Eliza squeezed the trigger, and the sniper rifle only nudged her. The limited recoil was another reason this particular rifle was a favourite of hers.

Through the scope, Eliza watched Jekyll's massive thigh explode from the shell's impact. Much as she wanted to kill him, they needed answers—though splattering his brains all over the tiles would have been gratifying.

Jekyll fought to keep his balance, but his teetering and the crack of the sniper rifle had alerted his prey. They ran into the night, calling out for help. That lost kill would upset Jekyll greatly. Good.

"I think we have his attention," Wellington said, "Now let's take the blighter down."

He was up and through the window before she could even attempt to stop him. The roofs were curved red tile, but there were firm ridge-lines made of brick that provided decent footing. She wasn't about to let him tangle with Jekyll by himself. She secured the rifle across her back, snatched up her satchel, and ran after him.

"This is Shadow One," Aydin's voice crackled from Eliza's shoulder. "Target is using the rooftops. Moving southwest."

"I've got him," Henrietta said, and then three successive pops came from the comms, quickly echoing in the real world.

Eliza struggled to keep up with Wellington as she was carrying considerably more firepower than he was. Still, he was within sight as they both leapt from one roof to another. A third leap, and a tile slipped from underneath her foot, but she had kept her balance forward. She stumbled a few steps before looking up to see Wellington bounding from rooftop to rooftop while Jekyll lumbered in the lead.

Rapid gunfire thundered, and just ahead of Jekyll a veil of debris kicked up.

"This is Shadow One," Aydin spoke from their comms. "I have the target sighted. I think he's turning around."

Jekyll was indeed doing so. He now faced Wellington and Eliza.

"Yes, thank you," Wellington replied in his comm unit, "we can confirm that."

"Have a care, I would imagine up close that hulking ox is quite nasty."

Jekyll's distorted face twisted, his lips curled into a snarl.

"I think Jekyll can hear you, Agent Tilki."

"So, Little Wellington," Jekyll said with a grunt, "this is where we dance once again? In the Constantinople moonlight, with your lovely lass at your side. How sweet."

"So he wants to take a stand, does he?" Eliza asked, setting her haversack in front of her. "Fine. I brought an old friend for this very moment."

Axelrod and Blackwell had been somewhat hard to pin down on improvements in their offerings from R&D. Many times her requests had received the reply, *"The device does what we intended it to do, ergo it needs no improvement!"* but Eliza was adamant on a particular weapon from the two clankertons. Katherina had been waiting for an upgrade since she had first rescued Wellington from the House of Usher in Antarctica. The high-velocity, high-calibre hand cannon that was barely a step under a grenade launcher had blown the doors of his interrogation room to a nice effect.

Now, with improvements finally made, it was time for her to be let loose again.

"Give me some room, darling," she said, bracing the arm holding Katherina against her chest.

Wellington blinked. "Is that—?"

"Yes."

Jekyll snorted just before charging at a dead run towards them, the wound not seeming to hinder him in the least. With a toss of her head, Eliza drew aim and fired. Katherina's kick was just as she remembered.

Jekyll took the full force of the shot directly to the chest. It stopped him in his tracks, sending him back a step or two. Jekyll coughed once, twice, then resumed his charge. His monstrous form was the definition of resilience.

Intent on making her point, Eliza dealt Jekyll two more shells in quick succession. His chest rippled from the points of impact, and this time he staggered back several steps, but he was still standing. He roared in outrage, but the roar ended with the monster choking to catch his breath. That made her smile.

Jekyll glanced at both of them, then changed tact. Instead of coming at them, he turned and made a run for the edge of the rooftop.

"Bugger me," Eliza swore, lowering Katherina as she countered his run.

"What?" Wellington asked, keeping pace with her.

"Katherina didn't stop him, but she did take the wind out of his sails." She just needed him to stand still. "He's getting tired."

"If he's getting tired, that means…"

"He's not attacking."

"Weren't you pestering Axelrod and Blackwell to enhance that thing?" Wellington bellowed waving his hands towards the weapon.

Eliza lowered the weapon. "They did," she said over her shoulder before raising Katherina.

It had to be now.

Eliza engaged the switch labelled "Hail, Mary" by Axelrod. The hand cannon hissed just before she took aim. She allowed herself a little lead before pulling the trigger.

The shot lifted her off her feet and sent her back into Wellington. They both tumbled over, but they managed to see the round slam into Jekyll. The giant teetered, and he tried to lean forward, but there was no stopping his massive momentum. Jekyll's form was slipping, both in footing and shape.

His right foot slid into the night, followed by the rest of him.

Jekyll screamed as he fell. Both of them scrambled to their feet and only took a few steps before there was a massive crash. They reached the edge of the rooftop to see Jekyll sprawled out in the street beneath them. He was still conscious, but barely.

Eliza's comm went live as she saw Jekyll sit up. "Shadow One, Shadow Two, move in!"

He must have heard one of them to his right as he turned in that direction, but someone leapt out of the shadows and struck him in the neck. It looked as if Jekyll were about to backhand the attacker, but instead his arm went limp and he fell back with a dull thud against the street.

"Overwatch, this is Shadow One. Sedative delivered," came the breathy report of Agent Tilki.

Words were hardly adequate. All she could feel was the wide grin on her face, and the sweat running down her spine. Her partner was not smiling, simply staring down at the doctor as if he was about to bolt at any given moment.

Wellington turned to look at her. "The enhancement?"

Eliza motioned to where Jekyll had fallen. "There you are. Axelrod and Blackwell finally deliver."

Their chase was at an end, and now they would find out if all the trials they'd been through were worth it.

CHAPTER TWENTY-TWO

Wherein the Thunder from Down Under and the Eccentric Canuck Get Out to the Country

"You sure about this, mate?" Bruce asked, lowering the Starlights from his eyes.

"Sophia's note said Badger spends a lot of his time here," Brandon replied with a shrug. "It's a remote farm on the outskirts of Rome, but how this all ties into this Usher project I don't know."

Bruce cast a glance over to Harker. He squirmed around in the new dark suit they'd got him. His new attire did not thrill him, but it wasn't like they had much of a choice in clothing for him. His wardrobe's colour palette leaned heavily towards the extremely bright, and while he had four linen suits in the height of Italian fashion, they were not practical for spies engaged in covert operations.

Ignoring the twitch in his jaw, Bruce growled, "If I told you one more time how smart you looked in the new suit, would that help you stop fidgeting?"

Harker looked at him with a sour expression. "I assure you gentlemen, I will not be a hindrance to you in this crucial time."

"Famous last words," Brandon grumbled.

"I am a quick study, I will keep my distance as you two approach the farm. I will not interfere. I will not, in any way, attempt to insert myself into your business." Harker took a deep breath, and Bruce swore he saw the pale Italian moonlight catch tears welling up in the man's eyes. "I want to make certain one of the first things my sweet Virginia sees is my face. I just wish I was better dressed for it."

Here we go, Bruce thought.

Brandon held up a single finger in front of Harker. "The moment you put any of us in peril, I will subdue you, put you in a wardrobe, and collect you like luggage later. Ya' follow?"

With a crooked eyebrow, Bruce glanced at his partner. He relied on Brandon to be the more level-headed of the two of them, now, there was the distinct taste of tension in his words.

"Stick to the plan, Harker. Maybe that little del Morte crow has been good to us so far." Turning to the farm, he brought the Starlights back up to his eyes. "But that doesn't guarantee anything."

Brandon nudged him in the shoulder. "Now, now, Bruce, are you still having problems trusting our girl, Sophia?"

Did he really say that? "A little something about 'Our girl Sophia' you need to remember—she's an assassin. Ministry agents are singing with the angels on account of her. She helped Books and Braun *once*. Doesn't make her a friend."

"Just saying," Brandon said with a shrug. "Sophia has no reason to trust us either. What does she have to gain in helping us?"

"A question for the ages," Bruce mumbled, scanning the farm from one end to the other.

They had only been in Rome for a day when the latest message from Sophia arrived to their hotel. She'd mentioned how Badger had made contact with the House, meaning they were aware of his presence in Rome. Sophia also mentioned Italian operations for Ragnarök had been established outside the city, in this quaint little corner of the countryside. The odd part about Sophia's letter was how imperative she made Badger's contribution to the House. It was as if Badger believed he alone was Ragnarök.

At first appearances, the farm was nothing out of the ordinary. The buildings on the property were one storey, simple rural constructions. Instead of one larger barn towering over lower-lying structures, this farm had three. Unique, but not unusual. What was unusual, however, were the moonlight towers still blazing at one o'clock in the morning. In his experience, cows did not need reading lights.

Another strange detail were the farmhands that walked the perimeter. They should all be doing whatever farmhands did of an evening. The Starlights couldn't offer any more details about them on account of interference from the towers, but from the way they moved, Bruce was certain: these were armed farmhands. If he knew anything about the House, and he certainly did, their weapons were most likely some kind of modified shotguns. If he was wrong, and they were rifles, hopefully they weren't as a crack shot as that intriguing Russian sharpshooter, Ryfka.

The whisper was far too close to his ear. It was not Brandon. "So, Mr Campbell, when are we off?"

The agent turned his head to Harker. Any closer, and the two of them would be kissing. "Step back, you tosser, I didn't need a bloody reminder that you stuffed yourself with garlic ravioli." Whatever spasm overtook Harker—Bruce couldn't be sure if it was a nod, a shrug, or something in between—he backed off. "Guards are still making the rounds, and they're keeping to the intervals rather regularly. Like in Russia. These houseboys are a whole new breed. Liked it better when they were a little lax, but those salad days are over, I guess."

Brandon brought the Starlights back up to his eyes, and Bruce did the same. "What about there? Westward quadrant. Watch."

Through the specs, Bruce observed two ghostly figures approach one another. They exchanged a nod and walked past one another. Feet became yards and then hundreds of yards. They reached opposite corners of the barn before stopping, turning, and pausing at the end of their walk. They stayed like that for another fifteen minutes before repeating the movement.

"That window of opportunity is tight, if we take them out, we would be on the clock. They might overlook one guard missing. Call of nature, or some such. When *two* guards go missing from the same perimeter that's gonna get us unwanted attention."

Brandon cleared his throat. "This is the part of the plan you are not going to like."

"What do you—" The words caught in Bruce's throat, and the Starlights came down so quick, he worried he might've shattered one of its lenses. "You can't be serious, Brandon!"

Brandon shrugged. "I'm open to alternatives. Presently, I am not seeing any other."

Bruce looked over at Harker. "Tell me that when you attended University, you participated on the athletics team."

"Wasn't much for sport, a spot of tennis here and there."

The twitch in Bruce's jaw returned.

Harker's brow furrowed. "What's the problem, gentlemen?"

"See the two guards standing on the west side, closest to the barn," Bruce said, handing Harker his Starlights. "They pass one another, we are going to have to sprint from a hiding place to the door."

After a moment, Harker passed the Starlights back to Bruce. "I do not see what the trouble is."

Brandon was now scanning the perimeter for some way to get a little closer. "Awful lot of ground to cover. We could belly crawl for a bit before running."

"Lesser of two evils, mate, we will have to manage. So here's how this is going to play: Brandon and I are going to run to that barn, get the door open, and then you are going to run like the devil himself is chasing you. Don't look at the guards, don't look behind you, just run."

Harker swallowed hard, but Bruce saw it in his eyes. He understood this was life and death.

Bruce slipped the Starlights into his haversack and shouldered it. "Time to stop talking about this, let's go."

The three men stuck close to the tree line, pushing on to reach the closest point of the forest to the barns. Bruce motioned for Harker to lie low, as he and Brandon, their bellies pressing into the grass, began a slow crawl across the wide, open field. The doorway the two men passed, Bruce hoped, wasn't secured in any way. If it were, Harker would have to get back to the hotel, and report the farm's location to the Ministry. That would be expecting a lot, he knew.

Maybe it was the excitement and tension of the moment that made every slide, every slip against the grass, sound as if it was a John Philip Sousa March. Now they were close enough to see in the moonlight the grain of wood within the barn wall. They watched the two guards close in and pause.

Why they stopping? Bruce's hand slipped into his coat, and he pulled out a modified barker. *Do they see us?*

They weren't close enough catch any words, but it was clear they were having a conversation. A small flame flashed between them, and cigarette smoke surrounded one of the guard's head.

Bruce shared a look with Brandon. Was it time to improvise a Plan B?

Brandon motioned with his head to the guards. The second guard was smoking as well, and after a few more words, they nodded to one another before resuming their walk along the barn perimeter. Bruce counted the steps. They needed a little more distance. *A few more steps,* Bruce thought. *Just a few more...*

Bruce pushed off the ground, got to his feet, and made his way for the door, Brandon pounding alongside him. When they reached the barn and glanced back, to see the guards still walking in opposite directions. They had made it. Now came another test. Bruce held his breath and pressed against the latch trigger. The bolt lifted free from its hinge, and the door swung open without effort, save for a soft, tiny squeak. Both men slipped into the barn. Now, time to pray for Harker's ability to mimic Mercury himself.

The Australian nearly yelped when Harker appeared only a few steps away from them. Bruce thought he might have pulled a muscle in his neck from swallowing his small, short scream. Brandon tugged at his partner's coat, and Bruce grabbed a handful of Parker's jacket before everyone ended up yanked into the barn. As badly as he wanted to slam the door, Bruce had the wherewithal to ease it shut.

Once secure, Bruce turned on Harker, whispering, "Exactly how long have you been behind us?"

"I told you I was a quick study. I saw how you crawled on your belly across the field, so I figured it couldn't be that hard. My cleaning bill will be ridiculously high, I know that. But I could have never made that distance, not even at my fastest."

Brandon clapped Harker on the back. "Well done."

"I have to admit, good job, mate."

Harker looked around the barn—at least what they could see of it—then back to where they came in. "I caught a glimpse of the door handle. It's a rather rudimentary lock. Seems a bit odd."

"Odd how?" Bruce asked.

"There's no handle on the inside, so the door secures from the outside. If you are trying to keep something hidden why not lock it from the inside? And with something for more complicated?"

"What exactly are you on about?"

"What I'm on about is that this locks from the outside. Whoever is behind all this, these doors are designed to keep something *in.*"

Bruce and Brandon both shared a glance. Maybe they were rubbing off on their unwelcome guest?

Bruce peered ahead into the barn's darkness. "No standing on ceremony. Let's locate Virginia, find out what we can about Ragnarök, and get back to Jolly Ol' England *tout de suite.*"

As agreed upon, Bruce and Brandon took a full five-step lead on Harker. The deeper the three of them pushed forward into the barn, the more they discovered its unconventional layout. While the outside suggested spaciousness and the reek of hay and cow shit, this barn had none of that. Instead it had been segmented into small rooms, able to contain two or three people at a time. A strange antiseptic smell hung in the air and grew stronger as they crept forward.

"Are you certain we can't stay in Rome a day or two?" whispered Brandon. "Just so that Sophia knows we appreciate what she's done for us?"

Bruce froze in mid-step, before rounding on his partner. "You're dreamin', mate. Tell me your dreamin', or tell me that I am asleep and having a bloody nightmare right now."

Brandon was about to say something, something Bruce knew would make him upset, but Harker had come up to them, gesticulating forward.

Ahead of them was a long row of taut, thin linens, suspended high enough to give whatever was happening behind them a modicum of privacy. Still, with the cloth shields up, these areas were lit in such a fashion that shadows moved along them like a Far Eastern puppet show. The tall shadows were three doctors who surrounded someone prone on a bed. These doctors milled and fussed about their patient, checking bottles suspended over their head, recording what they saw on clipboards, and conversing in hushed tones between one another. It wasn't until one shadow in the centre stepped aside that they realised the figure in the bed was pregnant, the woman's belly so swollen that she looked fit to burst.

Harker's eyes bulged, but he didn't make a noise. Bruce motioned with his head to a nearby room. The three of them shuffled into the closet and closed the door quietly behind them. Brandon was already looking around, as something overhead grabbed his attention, while Harker steadied himself against the wall.

It was their guest who broke the silence. "Why are these cads examining a pregnant woman in the middle of a farm in the middle of nowhere? What sort of place *is* this?"

"Ministry of Peculiar Occurrences," Bruce stated. "It's all in the name, mate."

From one side of the room, Brandon let out a delighted *"Yes..."* as he started to dig into one of the storage shelves. "I was hoping that Australian luck of yours would come through." His partner tossed him what looked like a physician's clothes. He glanced at Harker. "I think you should hunker down here? You would be safer hiding than wandering with us into a dangerous situation."

The other man shook his head defiantly. "I have come this far. Find me a set as well."

It was obvious the git would not take no for an answer, so Brandon complied.

"So you didn't do sport in university, what about amateur theatrics?" Bruce asked.

Harker slipped into the coat. "My peers considered my interpretation of Romeo quite moving."

With a stethoscope clipped around Harker's neck and a clipboard tucked under Brandon's arm, Bruce led them back out into the barn. They now walked with more of a purpose if not a slight swagger. So long as they acted as if they were supposed to be there, no questions would be asked. From the looks of the silhouette they had seen, the presence of three more doctors could go unnoticed.

Rounding the corner, they watched the silhouette of the woman being rolled away on a gurney.

"Let's see where they take her," Bruce whispered. "Look... doctorly."

Brandon whispered gibberish to the two of them as he "read" off his clipboard. His partner did relish a good role. They turned another corner to catch sight of an orderly pushing the woman further into the barn. The patient looked asleep. Perhaps that was best. The walls disappeared, and the barn opened to a central, spacious area. This space was far more characteristic of what a barn should be, wide and open for everyone to see what was inside.

"Doctors," a gruff voice called from behind them.

The three of them turned around to see a foreboding man dressed in black. An Usher Houseboy. A big one. His mates, standing behind him, were openly brandishing Lee-Metford-Tesla rifles. This would not be—

"Finally, security," Harker said, stepping clear of Bruce and Brandon. "Where the hell have you been?"

Oh dear God, Bruce thought.

"I'm sorry?" the Usher operative asked.

"We requested a security detail over an hour ago, and no one has followed up with me," Harker insisted. "Have some free time on your hands now, do you?"

The operative was now looking to the three of them, his skin blanching somewhat. "I'm... sor-sorry, Doctor, but I didn't catch your—?"

"We reported during our shift change that we sighted something odd in the forest. Movement of some sort. Didn't look like wildlife as it was walking on two feet. I was expecting to hear from someone on this matter, and no one replied." Harker looked at each of them, before asking, "So, have you investigated?"

"Um, Doctor..."

"You haven't? Bloody hell..." Harker stepped even closer to the Usher henchman and drove a finger into the man's broad chest. "Do you have any idea the scope of this project? What will happen if we fail? What if what we saw were agents of... let's say... the Ministry of Peculiar Occurrences? What then?"

The henchman nodded before turning to his mates. "Round up all security teams. I want eyes on the forest perimeter now!"

Once they were alone in the corridor, Bruce placed a hand on Harker's shoulder. "Well done, mate."

He smiled. "Improvisation always was a strength of mine. Let's see what those cads were protecting."

Occupying five rows of beds, six deep, were women, all of them hooked up to a variety of machines. Whatever these devices were, Bruce could only hope their function was kinder than how they looked. These mechanical monsters were a variety of tubes and coils reaching from a central core like the tentacles of an octopus, attached to the women either in the arm, left breast, or womb. The three of them continued deeper into this bizarre, macabre spectacle, some women looking up from their books to smile and nod. One sat up in her bed and smiled as she made eye contact with Bruce, whispering *"Doctor?"* as he walked by. Some were asleep, but they were in a fitful state as their faces twitched in either pain, fear, or both.

A metallic groan came from Bruce's right, compelling him to take a closer look at what these women were hooked up to. Whatever the machines were churning, the luminescent liquid visible through the device's portholes was green, and a heavy warmth emitted from every machine. Bellows rose and fell as the constant *click-click-click-click* kept time with jets of steam that occasionally burst hard and quick from vents. Solutions swirling in glass containers hung from metallic trees and, like the many tubes that slinked from the machine to various places on the body, ran from the bottles to each patient. Every woman was in a different state of pregnancy, some barely showing while others looked as if they were ready to give birth any minute. Bruce noticed something each woman shared in common: the largest of tubes coming from the mechanical churn connected to each woman's belly.

"Bugger me," Bruce whispered. "This is a farm all right. This is a breeding farm."

"But, mate, what are they breeding?" Brandon asked, motioning to the green goo stirring in the small engine.

"David?" a voice from behind them spoke softly.

"Virginia!" Harker blurted out, his voice carrying across the barn. "My darling Virginia!"

The two agents frantically looked from one side to the other. Perhaps now was a good time to take off the frocks, as they were inhibiting access to sidearms, but so far, no alarms had sounded. Best keep the deception alive. They turned to see a petite blonde girl, grey eyes reminiscent of storm clouds, and round cheeks that had a natural blush to them.

In fact, for a kidnapped woman she looked in top health.

"David, what are you doing here?" Virginia asked, her brows furrowing. She was working on a cross-stitch, but it dropped from her fingers on seeing her husband.

"Why you silly thing, I came here for you. You had disappeared, and I couldn't do anything but follow after."

Virginia without any expression of relief, happiness, or elation on her face instead narrowed her eyes. "I thought the note I left was quite specific."

Hold on, Bruce thought. *What did she say?* "You left him a note?"

"I beg pardon, but who are you?"

"My name's Bruce Campbell of the Ministry of Peculiar Occurrences. We're here to rescue you."

Virginia's eyes went wide then shot back to Harker. "You brought the Ministry of Peculiar Occurrences here? To rescue me?" Now that was definitely a glare. "I thought I was very clear!"

"What note?" Bruce demanded, a knot in his stomach developing.

"Oh, my sweet darling Virginia," Harker began, completely oblivious—perhaps blissfully ignorant—of the accusation in her voice. "I've read that letter. I read it several times. I knew it wasn't you. You must've written it under duress."

"I wrote it under five minutes, but I think I was very clear."

Harker began showering her face with quick kisses. "See, you're in a terrible state, no doubt from whatever strange concoctions they are pumping into your system." Harker motioned to the mechanism pumping its bizarre concoction into her arm and still-flat stomach. "Come home with me, my sweet, darling Virginia, and you'll be right as— "

David Harker never got the opportunity to finish what Bruce assumed was a well-intentioned thought. Virginia grabbed the hose connected to her arm and ripped it free. The needle, decorated with rivulets of her blood, was visible for only a second before she jammed it into David Harker's eye. If the exchange between Harker and his wife were not enough to alert the guard, the sight of David Harker with a needle protruding from his right eye socket, making it cry luminescent, green tears, and his gasping for breath would. The shock on his face was something to behold too.

"Your darling, sweet Virginia," she spat, keeping herself within David's field of vision, "has never felt more alive until now. I was going to be part of something revolutionary. A new and completely mad world, plunged into darkness. So, of course, you had to come along and bungle the whole

thing!" With each of her words this sweet, young woman was transforming in front of him. Bones popped, welts sprung all along her skin, and her eyes went from a light grey to a brilliant emerald.

Virginia screamed and grabbed Harker's throat. She sunk her fingers into his flesh and tore his throat out as easily as one would grab a pint from the bar. He'd been coming along so well, but now he would never have the chance to improve any further. Poor bastard.

"Bloody hell!" Even as a seasoned agent this turn of events caught him off guard.

"We have to go!" Brandon said as Harker's body dropped to the ground.

The expression on the poor bloke's face was one frozen in shock and surprise. There was no help for him now.

"Good idea!" Bruce agreed, even as he caught Virginia's blood-soaked face turning in their direction.

The two agents dashed for the end of the row, additional screams of alarm and primal rage filling the air with each step.

"Right," Bruce shouted over his shoulder. "Nearest exit…"

"Not quite yet, partner," Brandon returned.

"Come again?"

"If I would ask myself, *'I am a collection of important documents implicating the House of Usher's management of a breeding farm. Where would I be?'* and I really had to think on this…"

"Brandon!"

"Take a left at the end of this hallway!"

He did as instructed and saw two Houseboys coming at him.

"Fists up, mate!" Bruce called before breaking into a guttural howl and launching his right hook down on the lead Houseboy.

He knocked the man's jaw out of joint, but Bruce's following uppercut did the man's nose in as well. He let his momentum finish the job as all two hundred pounds of him slammed into his chest. Bruce heard Brandon's scuffle start up as he hit the floor. For now, he was on his own.

Bruce gave the Houseboy two quick punches to his face and held the third one back to see if it was needed. This guard was done. Time to check on…

A dark figure in front of him toppled back, and there stood Brandon, sheathing his favourite hunting knife. "Straight ahead," his partner said, motioning forward. "Then up the stairs."

"Stairs?" Bruce resumed his run, not knowing what to think of Brandon's instincts, but sure enough, a wooden staircase appeared out of the dark. "Up?" he asked.

"Up!"

The two thundered up the staircase, skipping every other step as they climbed higher and higher to an upper floor of the barn's second level. The stairwell ended at a door that Bruce opened with his shoulder.

He looked around him. "How did you—?"

"That's your problem, Bruce," his partner scolded, as he began looking around the open office overlooking the barn. "Sometimes, research pays off. Barns of certain styles and builds follow a template. Convert it to serve as a medical facility and there will be some alterations to that template." Bruce could now see through the wide window that this office could not only look into what was happening in the centre section of the barn but also in the small examination rooms they had seen earlier. None of the rooms had roofs to allow that. "When we were changing, I noticed our closet had no ceiling. After a few minutes, I could make out this observation deck. If it was what I concluded it was, then there should be..."

Bruce was about to start stuffing files from every desk into the haversack when he paused. Against the far wall was an analytical engine. "Think you can get this up and running?"

"Let's take a look." Brandon flipped a few of the device's switches, and the screen before him blinked to life. "Interesting." He clicked a few keys and nodded his head. "Oh, very interesting."

Glancing down, Bruce watched the screaming harpies below in the barn's main holding area, with various Houseboys and medical staff struggling to calm them down. From the floor, one Houseboy looked up and pointed at him. "Brandon, our time is about to get a little short. Mind telling me exactly what is so enticing?"

"There is a lot of information here. Timelines. Project objectives. And… oh, lovely." Brandon chuckled. "Looks like I have an organisation tree here of who is in charge of what departments."

"Fantastic! Print this stuff up and…"

"Slow down, Bruce. If you want me to print all this data up. We can, but it's going to take some time."

"How much?"

Brandon looked at the screen for a moment. "Five hours… maybe six."

Bruce shot a look at the window, then back to his partner. "We got maybe six minutes before it's us versus the Farm's security. So, options?"

"We can shut down the engine, disengage the connections, remove the drive." Brandon pointed to a curved, metal handle protruding from underneath the machine's housing. "Right there."

"Do it."

Brandon typed, but whatever he had entered into the machine, it did not have the results he wanted. Brandon's cursing and the hard buzzing sound from the engine itself were an indication of that.

"Talk to me, Brandon," Bruce said, as he drew out from his haversack a Bulldog.

"The analytical engine recognised the sequence for what we want to do, but it is requiring a passcode to initiate it."

"A what-what?"

"Passcode. Similar to what we use when we are meeting contacts and we use a code to confirm who we are? Analytical engines can sometimes have an extra layer of security. We need, according to the screen, an eight-character passcode." Brandon dug into Bruce's bag to fish out his pistol. "Bugger it. We got to go. Whoever designed that analytical engine was a right clever gent. Far too clever for me. Maybe even far too clever for Books himself."

Bruce blinked. A right clever gent? Like Tinsdale. "Eight letters, you said?"

"Characters. Could be letters, or numbers, or a combination of both."

Going to the keyboard Bruce started typing. Brandon stopped his hand.

"Mate, if you get this wrong, we don't know what will happen," Brandon's grip tightened on Bruce's wrist. "This level of security, it could erase the drive in the best-case scenario."

"Trust me."

Bruce finished typing the word he had found in Tinsdale's office. "If I'm right, it was a zero, and not an odd 'O' in there."

"What?"

The clicks and whirs coming from the analytical machine came to a halt. The screen went dark. Then came a series of hard, sharp pops as steam erupted from behind it.

"I... I think you did it. But how?"

Bruce grabbed a hold of the drive. "Gargoyle. Courtesy of our far-too-clever deceased double agent in Usher." The drive slid out of its housing. "Get back to the hotel, call the Italian police on this operation, and..."

"Blimey," Brandon whispered from the observation window.

When he joined his fellow agent, he watched with the same fascination the odd display playing out before them.

Red lights were slowly blinking while Usher security and medical personnel were working against the wild women to get them either out of their beds, or wheeling them out of the barn. They were scrambling to escape.

A chill crept under Bruce's skin. Mr Badger shouted out some kind of order, and at his side was Sophia del Morte. She was aiding the evacuation. Her frantic gestures paused on making eye contact with Bruce and Brandon. After glancing at Badger, she mouthed a single word: *Run!*

"Mate, what do they know that we don't?"

"Well I did say 'best-case' security measure was to erase the drive." Brandon swallowed. "Worst-case, I would imagine, could be a self-destruct sequence. Even if you safely disengage the drive that sort of measure would be used…"

"Bugger me."

Brandon made for the door and glanced back. "Last one to the hotel buys the rounds?"

Bruce followed close on his heels. "We'll drink to the memory of the poor bastard Harker, provided we haven't mucked around for too long here. Now move!"

CHAPTER TWENTY-THREE

Where Old Fears Are Faced

"Damn them all!" Filippo exploded as they entered their safe house.

"Keep your voice down," Sophia scolded, closing the door behind them.

His prison might be a specious apartment, but it had begun to feel like a coffin. When Holmes found out that the Farm was destroyed it might well become one. *Accountability,* Holmes had told them all in a very serious tone.

"We do not need our neighbours growing curious," Sophia reminded him as she secured the door's final lock.

Filippo turned on his heel and stuck his finger only an inch from her face. He did not need this woman chiding him as if he were some petulant child. "I will carry myself in whatever manner I see fit, nosy neighbours or otherwise. You're not my mother. You're not the Chairman." He knew full well this woman could kill him that moment, however with the Ministry's destruction of the Farm, he had nothing more to lose.

Sophia might want him to take her to the House, but that would mean certain death now. The loss of the Farm was an immeasurable loss to the Brotherhood and possibly put the entire venture in jeopardy.

"Ragnarök depended on my success here in Italy, and now thanks to the Ministry, we are ruined." He ground his teeth together as he entered the darkened parlour. "What am I saying? This is worse. Far worse than that."

"Calm yourself," Sophia replied, her tone almost gentle. Turning up the gaslight in the room she slid her hands across his shoulders. "This is merely a setback to you and the House."

Was she actually attempting to comfort him?

He shook off her touch like it was a creeping spider. "You are talking about things you know nothing about, woman." He took a seat on the couch and ran his fingers through his hair. On reaching the back of his skull, Filippo balled his hands into fists. "I must think of something to tell the Chairman."

"We must find and exploit the advantages of tonight's loss."

"Advantages?"

"Yes. Focus on what you were able to save, and what you learned, as opposed to the loss," Sophia said, sitting next to him.

"You think we can simply negotiate our way through this quagmire?"

"I have faced far worse. You are making much ado about nothing."

She just did not understand—and why would she? It had been years since she'd served the House, so she couldn't be aware of the recent changes. "I have no doubt, Signorina del Morte, of your persuasive skills, but I assure you, Holmes is neither easily swayed nor manipulated."

"Holmes?" Her lips twisted, and the skin around her eyes drew into tiny lines as if something was not to her liking. It was very different to her usual mask of calm.

"Our new chairman. Henry Howard Holmes."

What happened next shocked Filippo to the core, and that was quite an accomplishment after tonight's events. Clasping her hand to her chest she leapt up. It was almost as if she were about to succumb to the vapours. She quickly collected herself, but in that fleeting moment, Filippo saw another side to the deadly assassin. Fear. He saw fear overcome Sophia del Morte.

Smoothing her dress, she took a deep breath, and then with wide strides made her way to their humble kitchen. Sophia returned with a pair of glasses and a bottle of wine she'd brought to the apartment a few days before. Once she drove the spike into its cork, she yanked it free with a resounding *pop*.

"So, when did Holmes assume leadership of the House of Usher?"

"Just over a year ago," Filippo replied, as she poured two generous glasses. "Shortly after the events in London, Holmes led his own coup for the position of Lord of the Manor."

"Let me guess. He made sure it went uncontested."

A muscle twitched in Filippo's jaw. The mixture of savagery and calm determination with which Holmes had taken over was something he would never forget. "You know him?"

Sophia took a rather long, slow drink of her glass before replying. "Just before the Diamond Jubilee, I requested asylum with the House of Usher.

They sent me an emissary. Holmes." She stared out into nothing for a moment before taking another gulp of wine. At this rather reckless pace, she would be in need of another bottle soon. "I saw what he was when I first met him. If I had gone with him that night, we would not be having this conversation. The fact that *he* is in charge of Usher changes things."

Holmes was the embodiment of a necessary evil. The previous Lord of the Manor had become a doddering fool. Holmes rightfully took his position, which he rechristened as Chairman. In the past year with him at the helm, Usher had returned with a vengeance. Once again it was a respected and feared organisation as it had been decades ago. They were back to working in the shadows, pulling strings unseen to general society. The cost of this aggressive rebirth for the House of Usher, though, had come with a high body count.

It was not just reserved for those outside the House. Everyone had to be accountable. The price to pay for failure was the same for him as it was for a simple operative on the streets. Holmes did not tolerate botched operations. Filippo thought it was a worthwhile cost for Usher to return to what it had been, no longer the laughingstock it had become.

Except now it was his turn to be held accountable.

"You're not the only one put off by Mudgett." Filippo admitted. Sophia's brow furrowed at that name, so she didn't know quite everything. "His real name. Herman Webster Mudgett. I had my contacts in the Americas do a bit of digging."

"Interesting."

"By the time we unified against Mudgett, he had already ingratiated himself with the Lord of the Manor—which he took masterful advantage of."

"He can be very charming when he wants," she observed, staring into her glass.

Filippo laughed. "Indeed, and we had already invested a good amount in him. A body double. A prisoner swap. Manipulation of the press when the body double insisted he was innocent. We rescued him from the hangman's noose and he in turn turned the House into his property."

Sophia slid the second, untouched glass of wine closer to him. Filippo stared at the wine, enjoyed its bouquet at a distance, but did not reach for it.

"Really?" She rolled her eyes and took another sip.

He was in need of some decent wine, and he could tell from the label that it was a fine vintage. Still, he was no fool. This was Sophia del Morte, after all.

She proceeded to pour a portion of his wine into her glass. Handing him back his glass, now considerably less, Sophia drank. After a moment, she fixed a hard gaze on him. "I rescue you from the Ministry, from my own flesh and blood, and yet you still believe—even when we find ourselves in this grand disaster of misfortune—I am on some blood vendetta for a family that hunts me?"

Filippo examined his glass. The nose on this vintage was apparent, and he could appreciate its complexity, its fruity, earthy scent. This woman was certainly dangerous, but she needed him. She needed Usher. There would be nothing to gain in killing him at this point.

"And might I add," Sophia said, leaning into him, "we are about to face Henry Howard Holmes together with, perhaps, not the best of circumstances behind us. I, for one, intend to savour a good bottle of Italian wine, or two, if we are to be speeding towards our demise."

The woman had a good point.

When the wine touched Filippo's tongue, everything it had promised in its nose was met and surpassed. Along with misfortune, he and Sophia apparently shared this in common: a taste for fine wine.

He held the glass of ruby liquid to the light. "Tell me you have another bottle in the kitchen."

"Since when does any Italian buy good wine one bottle at a time?" Her smile was quite sincere. As she poured a bit more into his glass, she said, "I would have been extremely put out if you had not joined in. I do hate to drink alone."

"Not tonight. So, I take it you have a notion of how we are to win over the House in light of what happened at the Farm tonight?"

"I have an idea or two."

Filippo nodded. It wasn't surprising she had suggestions. It wasn't the style of the del Morte family to act upon a whim. A plan was always in motion.

"Well then," he began, clinking his glass with hers, "a toast to our ingenuity. Let us enjoy this evening of good wine and ways of winning Henry Howard Holmes to our favour."

"Yes, let us do that," Sophia replied, drinking deep to his toast, her eyes sparkling in the half-light.

CHAPTER TWENTY-FOUR

In Which a Snap Decision Carries Consequences

"That rotter gives me the bloody creeps," Eliza seethed.

It had been nearly three days since they'd brought Jekyll out of unconsciousness. He was rather battered about in their apprehension of him on the rooftop—not that Wellington thought that was a bad thing—so this was their first time to attempt to get any information out of him. In fact, it was lucky that Wellington had not been the one to bring him to this interrogation room from his cell. Jekyll might have developed some more bumps and bruises on the way.

Henrietta inhaled smoke from her cigarillo before blowing a long stream out her mouth. The sweet smell covered the dark business before them. "I am in total agreement with Eliza."

Falcon, Sound, Eliza, and he observed the mad scientist in the interrogation room through tempered glass. On their side it was a window, on his, a mirror.

Even getting him through the æthergate had felt like a long time to Wellington, and now having him locked up, he was still on edge.

In his youth, Interrogation Room One had served as a wine cellar. Jekyll might have even come down here with Arthur Books to choose a bottle while discussing their project: Wellington himself. Over the past year they converted it into a reinforced cell to question the most dangerous ne'er-do-wells. A monster like Jekyll could test the design to its utmost, yet at the moment he was his diminutive self, seated, his hands resting on the surface of the small table.

"Yet he has remained this way since regaining consciousness," Sound said, his eyes never leaving Jekyll.

Henrietta leaned forward a little. "He does appear calm. This madness is a very peculiar sort that triggers his physical transformation. I have never seen its like."

Eliza's lips twisted. "Hopefully you will never again. His madness is of his own making. 'Twas a little scientific formula to unleash the potential within—except his was as a murderer."

"Still, he hasn't tried to escape," Wellington said, his gaze raking over the still form of the architect of all his pain.

"Actually, Agent Books, he has been most polite," Sound replied. "No attempt at charging the door. No screaming. No foul language."

"He hasn't asked for anything? Hasn't demanded a right to counsel, the presence of a solicitor?" Eliza asked.

The director ran his finger along the length of his moustache as if the gesture soothed him. "He has remained as stoic and as resolute as a soldier, and I, for one, find it unsettling."

"Considering how verbose he has been before—" Eliza began, but she stopped as Jekyll rose from his place at the small table.

The director went to a small control panel built into the stone frame around the glass window. Though his hand hovered over a large red button, he thought better of it, and threw a small switch which pulsed red.

A little surge of worry rushed through Wellington. "Exactly what is that?"

"Safety measure," he said in a low tone.

"What kind are we talking about?" Wellington was not completely certain if he wanted to know the answer.

"If the cell becomes compromised, it will release pressurised containers of concentrated chlorine and mustard gas."

Henrietta exhaled suddenly. Wellington could not conclude if said gasp was one of shock, revulsion, or excitement.

"Chlorine and mustard gas?" Eliza asked. "That will…"

"I am well aware of the consequences, Agent Braun," Sound replied curtly. "If you look behind you, there are gas masks available for any personnel in this room in case the safety measure are used. Let us hope it—"

He stopped as Jekyll walked towards the window, his gaze roaming from end to end. Wellington watched as Sound's hand inched closer and closer to the pulsing button.

"Hello?" Jekyll's voice through the observation room's speakers sounded so very civilised. Everyone on the other side of the window held their breath. Jekyll spoke as if they were an assembled class of medical students and he, a lecturer. "First of all, thank you so much for the kind treatment and delightful service of... wherever in God's Earth we presently are. I am, however, growing a bit anxious. Cagey, if you will," he offered with a wry grin.

"Sir, request permission to gag our guest before he makes another god-awful pun like that?" Eliza asked.

"Agent Braun, please..." he whispered.

Jekyll tilted his head. "I gather I am within the Ministry of Peculiar Occurrences. I have a very simple request. I wish to have an audience with Wellington Thornhill Books. Provided his schedule allows, of course."

All eyes turned to Wellington, and he felt the full weight of their judgement. Taking a deep breath, he took a few steps closer to the window. If the hand hovering over that switch had been his own, there would be no hesitation.

Sound's voice shattered the tension. "Agent Books..."

"Sir, do not ask to do him this," Eliza implored. "Jekyll knows the inside of the human mind. He's a master manipulator."

Henrietta broke in. "Let me offer my services. I have a number of doctorates that are at your disposal, and might help with..."

"I am well aware of what sort of monster Henry Jekyll is." Sound's eyes narrowed. "However, he seems to have his heart set on speaking with Wellington. It is a vulnerability we should exploit."

"With all due respect, sir," Wellington said through clenched teeth, "have you lost your bloody mind?"

Sound stiffened, and even he wondered at it. Perhaps it was Eliza's influence creeping to the surface, or maybe it was resentment from the Water Palace incident. They called it justice, carried out in the name of the Empire, but both he and Eliza agreed it was anything but. It had been revenge, and a bold display of power. Such displays built empires, and perhaps even helped keep them held together. Sound believed he was showing his power, but since he only knew Jekyll from reports and agents' accounts, he didn't have the whole story. Wellington and Eliza had experienced his transformation into the monster, and they had witnessed what he'd done to the Duke of Sussex. Jekyll had manipulated both Lawson and even Her Majesty.

Above all he was the cause of Wellington's own demons. Even his own father had been in league with him. He was, in short, darkness incarnate.

Wellington's gaze darted to the safety measure. Sound would not be able to stop him. He could end it all, here and now.

"Books, you need to understand the grander scope of things," Sound spoke gently as he crossed to the control panel. "Jekyll should get put down, I do agree on that. However, he is too valuable of an asset to discard. He is key to the events which created you, events that I hypothesise relate to this Ragnarök venture the House of Usher is planning."

Henrietta pursed her lips at those words. "If I may, Director, I have observed this man, and what he enjoys doing. Jekyll is not an asset, he is a monster. By all means interrogate him, but afterwards burn him to ash, and find a deep hole to bury those embers in."

"I knew there was a reason I liked you," Eliza said, leaning over to squeeze her arm.

The director stared at her for a moment, but did not offer any commentary on Professor Falcon's suggestion. "Then let us begin. You have your sidearms at the ready, Agent Braun?"

"Always."

Sound cleared his throat. "I intend to be as accommodating with our guest..."

"You mean, your *prisoner*," Henrietta interjected.

"... our *guest*, as we finally have a lead on why Usher is after Agent Books here." Sound slipped his pudgy thumbs into the pockets of his waistcoat. "I trust you to follow orders, yes?"

"Yes, sir," Eliza and Wellington muttered.

"Very good. Braun, I want you and your firearms at the ready. If Jekyll attempts to overpower Wellington, or even hints at transformation, I want you in there. Am I clear?"

She nodded, though looked none too happy about it.

Henrietta let out a little snort. "Eliza is a force of nature, Director, but if Jekyll does transform, will she be enough?"

"If Braun is incapacitated, and Wellington fails to prevent Jekyll from transforming, we deploy the gas," Sound replied.

Wellington's heart seized in his chest for a moment. "Sir? Are you wanting me to tap into my... talent?"

"Only if necessary," he said. "I have confidence in you, m'boy."

There it was: the full authority of the Ministry of Peculiar Occurrences against him. If he rebelled, his only option would be to resign. In that moment, a chilling epiphany struck him this wasn't just for the Ministry, it was for him too. It wasn't about the House, or Ragnarök. It was about Arthur Books and his original plans.

Jekyll tapped on the glass for attention. "I will just wait here then, shall I?"

Eliza squeezed his hand and gave him a faint smile. Picking up a modest wooden chair from the corner so that he would have somewhere to sit inside, Wellington looked deep into her sapphire eyes. "Do not hesitate."

"It won't come to that," she assured him. "Even if this goes pear-shaped, Henrietta and I are with you."

Henrietta slipped from a holster secured in the small of her back the experimental she had called upon while on the OHX. "Just make sure to duck."

Sound flicked the button to open the door to the outside corridor. With a final glance to Eliza and Henrietta, Wellington walked to the cell door, chair in hand. The guard took a defensive posture as he unlocked the hatch and opened it for Wellington.

Doctor Henry Jekyll sat on the other side of the table, his fingers laced together, the smile on his face warm and inviting. Wellington's legs grew heavy, and a queer thought flashed across his mind. Was this what the lion tamer felt before going into a cage with the King of the Jungle? Armed only with a chair, what chances would he have if the beast were to not to stay within the confines of the performance? No, it would be intellect versus intellect here. The real test would be how deep Jekyll would go into their shared past.

The door shut behind them with a dull thud.

"Little Wellington," Jekyll cooed. "At last. We have some time to catch up."

Wellington was aware Eliza was close, watching from the other side of the glass. He was not alone. She was there. It was a game of psychological chess. He had to say ahead of this one.

Jekyll motioned for him to place the chair across from him. "Please, as this is an interrogation room of some description, let's make use of it." He looked around and his eyes stopped on an exposed beam overhead. "You know, I think I recognise those beams." He craned his neck to look behind him. "And the curvature of that wall there. Are we in your family's wine cellar?" He chuckled. "I do love what you've done with the estate."

"Thank you, Doctor."

"Really?" Jekyll clicked his tongue. "Well, I suppose I outgrew the title of 'uncle' after you ascended into manhood." He traced a small knot in the table with his fingernail, his eyes studying the wood, but he didn't fool Wellington. "I miss those times. We accomplished so much together."

Wellington put down the chair, and sat in it as comfortably as possible. "I admit, I am flattered to have made such an impact on your life."

"Oh, Wellington, you were more than just an impact. You were my life. The apple of my eye."

"And my father's?"

That took the man's knight. There was a flicker of darkness across the good doctor's face, but it was merely that—a flicker. "Arthur Books. Your father was quite the rogue. So respected, so revered in his social circles, and yet..."

"And yet, an utter bastard."

Jekyll locked his gaze with Wellington's. "Indeed, to kill your mother so callously, and with nary a concern for how it would affect you? So cold. So heartless."

Jekyll thought he was being clever. Perhaps that cost Wellington a pawn, but hardly a revelation. "Yes," he said, grinding out that admission. Perhaps it would convince Jekyll this was a sudden realisation. "I often wondered about it."

"I did not agree with his choice to take Lily from you. It is important for a boy to have his mother in his life. Essential, really."

Wellington's eyes never left the doctor. It had not been Jekyll's idea, but he had done nothing to stop it either. *A bit too quick to defend your rook there, old boy.* «Knowing my father as I did, I could see you serving as his moral compass.»

"In so many ways. You have no idea."

"But at the Water Palace, you said something about my father lacking vision, about how he could not see beyond his commission to the House of Usher."

"Arthur, Arthur, Arthur..." Jekyll recollected in a dry whisper before releasing a gruff, dry laugh. "Your father was a vain man. He and I were going to accomplish great things with you, but he could not see beyond this..." Jekyll motioned with a single hand to the air, his gaze somehow looking beyond the cellar walls, "... this empire of your Queen's. It was all about what he could give back to Queen and Empire. What you were? Far greater than that."

"What was I?"

"Evolution, my dear boy. You were to be the next step. For us all."

So there it was, out in the open. He and Eliza had not revealed his involvement in this whole sordid affair, but now Sound knew. He couldn't see the Director's expression behind the mirror, but he knew it would be angry.

He had left his Queen undefended, and Jekyll saw it because his expression had given it away. The doctor clucked his tongue. "Oh, no, no, no. Dear Wellington, did you not tell your colleagues about your intimate involvement in my little experiment?" Jekyll now held the advantage, and he pressed it. "You were such a grand subject too. I did hope, though, that you would see what we were trying to achieve…"

"Which was?"

"Man is, at his core, savage, but often caught up in social morals, appearances and civilities. Yet when are we the most alive? When we take the life of a creature on the hunt? When we are taking a woman, ascending into manhood? When we kill our fellow man on the battlefield? We are creatures of death, of chaos, and of pain. I discovered this in my own work before your father and I focused our attentions on you; and I once struggled to separate the two—man and monster, or what I *believed* to be man and monster.»

"You don't think they should be separated?"

"Never! They should be embraced, but it took me so long to do so. You were instrumental in that, my dear boy."

Wellington shot a glance at the mirror. "You call me that, and yet you look no different from when I knew you in my childhood. I would dare say you look even younger than me presently."

"A convenient side effect of the serum—one I had hoped got embedded in you, but alas, it was not. I had hoped our Manifest Destiny would be born in you." He gave a wry smile as he spread his arms wide. "Because there are advantages to concentrated treatments, as your queen and I discovered."

"But those toxins—"

"Treatments," Jekyll corrected, a slight edge in his words coming to the surface.

Careful. Are you sure you wish to expose your King in such a fashion after making such progress? "The House of Usher seemed rather keen on tapping into that serum you fashioned for Her Majesty and the Prime Minister. Perhaps this is why the House is so obsessed with bringing me in to their ranks."

"Well now, Wellington, you are the key to the serum, after all. Oh, the things they would accomplish with a few hundred of you."

Now the King was flanked. So why did this strike him as too easy? Wellington stayed stock still.

Jekyll shrugged. "Of course there are some side effects. For example, I have limited control. The physical transformation and its wild bloodlust do vex me. That was the problem with the Maestro's serum when he tried to create his own super soldiers. Too concentrated a dosage."

Something about hearing the Maestro's name, the sudden image of his Grey Ghosts rampaging the lower East End in those incredible armoured suits, threw a switch in his head. "You've been trying to replicate the serum. The Duke of Sussex. Queen Victoria. All those people in your ledger. This was never about control. You were conducting a lab experiment, just on a grander scale. You've been working to replicate my childhood!"

"Oh for God's sake, do not be so melodramatic," he scolded. "I am attempting to replicate the results your father and I achieved in a shorter span of time. Arthur and I both recognised the difficulties in having our evolution being a womb-to-the-grave process, and this has been quite the challenge, I assure you." Jekyll shot him a wide grin. "And this is what has eluded Usher for all these decades."

Wellington leaned back in his chair. Something was dreadfully wrong. All this time, he thought himself manoeuvring for a final checkmate in this back and forth with the doctor, but Jekyll was all too accommodating.

"So why did you want to speak with me?" he managed to choke out.

"Simple enough. I wanted to extend the invitation for you to join me." He patted the pocket of his waistcoat and shook his head. "Well, I would check the time, but I know we have both been here for quite a spell. It is high time you and I set forth to finish what Arthur and I put into motion so many decades ago." He shrugged his shoulders and gave a soft chuckle. "Do you think that my intent was simply to rampage through Europe, indulging my own personal desires? That little cypher was merely an indication of what I intend to do if you say 'no' and deny what is, by right, ours."

The cold returned, and this time he swore he could see his breath as he asked, "What are you intending to do?"

"We have a few more things to finish, you and I, and I have no intention of stopping until we take up the mantle of power that is rightfully ours."

Wellington was on his feet, the chill under his skin now replaced with a wildfire triggered by the man's games. He went blind with rage, especially with Jekyll's laughter, but a sense of clarity washed over him, even as Wellington picked up his chair and jammed it underneath the doorknob. It rattled, followed moments later by a pounding from the other side. It didn't matter; it sounded a thousand leagues away.

He did not know how he found himself standing in front of Jekyll. Time was now occurring in wild, erratic flashes of consciousness. The doctor still laughed—at himself, Wellington, or their current situation, that was uncertain. He kept on laughing right up until the moment Wellington grabbed him by the hair and drove his face into the table.

The pounding at the door got louder.

Figures moved frantically on the other side of the mirror.

Jekyll had admitted to him the truth. Even if Wellington had known it all along he needed him to say it.

The doctor laughed as blood poured down his face. "You gave such a grand performance at the Water Palace. I think you have potential still to unlock."

Wellington threw Jekyll's face into the table again. Even with the broken nose and blood dripping from a split lip, Jekyll kept laughing. He would *not* stop.

"Ooh, that one had a bit of vim and vigour to it." Jekyll spat, and a bloody tooth bounced off the tip of his shoe. "You're beginning to surrender to that nature Arthur and I cooked up. Why are you wasting my time and yours? Go on! Show me!"

"I want *nothing* to do with this!" Wellington roared.

Darkness crept from the edges of his sight. His heartbeat thundered in his ears. He tried to take a deep breath, but his chest was unreasonably tight. Jekyll would not stop.

"Stop lying, Wellington!" the mad doctor bellowed back. "You crave this. It makes you realise you're alive. I watched you in India. You were exquisite, why? You embraced it. You embraced it because all this—the Ministry, your archives, that precious darling colonial of yours—are nothing but distractions! I will remove them all until it is only you, me, and the future!"

Everything snapped into a hard, crisp focus. Wellington did not feel a rush of blood, his frantic heartbeat, or his ragged breathing. Only blissful solitude, this exhilarating clarity, and the bloody monster before him mattered.

"Yes. That's my boy! We will burn the world to the ground until we are the only ones standing. We *are* the future!"

Jekyll would be true to his word. He would wipe out everyone close to him, then turn to the innocent, just as he had done in Europe.

When Jekyll smiled at him, a trickle of blood poured from the split in his flesh. "Your father would be so very proud."

The ghost of Arthur Books whispered to him, *My son...*

He would not stop.

Wellington's hands shot forward and slapped against the laughing man's head. His wild laughter ceased as Wellington twisted. There was a distinct *crunch* and then the silence returned. Only for a moment.

Jekyll slumped against the table, then crumpled at Wellington's feet.

A wheezing grew louder in his ears, and it was indeed himself. Every breath hurt. The world teetered underneath him, but he righted himself after a few steps. Bracing himself against the table as he took in another breath. A third. And another. He might as well have just run a marathon. He needed to rest. A drink would be nice as well.

He looked around, his gaze stopping at the limp form sprawled and bleeding out across the floor.

He waited. No clever whisper from beyond the grave. Capital.

Nodding, Wellington pulled himself free from the table, removed the chair from the door, and took a few steps back.

The door flew open, and Sound was the first through, followed by Eliza and Henrietta.

Eliza. His calm. His centre. His world.

"I'm free," Wellington whispered. The declaration earned him a strangled gasp from her. "I'm finally free."

CHAPTER TWENTY-FIVE

In Which Edison Takes a Chance

Jekyll was overdue, and for a man that sometimes appeared to be made of clockwork that was unusual. Edison could set his watch by Jekyll coming by to check on his prized possession.

Yet it had been well over a week, and still no word. At the least, there should have been an æthermissive.

His eyes wandered over to the Shocker he had modified. Every day, a part of him expected the Shocker to become aware of what it was doing, of what it was transmitting. The small box magnetically attached to the automaton's brain continued to use its host as a transmitter. The signal went out at intervals, even going silent on the day Edison knew Jekyll would appear. He wondered, *was there anyone out there listening? There had to be! I am Thomas Edison after all.*

The Shockers continued to keep watch over him, their eyes switching from green to yellow whenever he drew too close. Edison kept his movements deliberate, clean, and slow. There would be no mistaking a hostile overture towards them. He paused before one of the Shockers, and for the first time he noticed how well it was doing its job. When he first designed them for the Pinkertons, the intent was to create an automaton with a sole purpose of seizure and personal protection. However, Edison believed they could do so much more. They wouldn't be just enforcers; they would serve as the deterrence.

A smile cracked across Edison's face. "You outdid yourself, Thomas," he whispered to himself.

The spark jumping from the yellow eyes of the Shocker caused Edison to start. He caught his breath, placing his own hand against his chest. Perhaps he had outdone himself, but that didn't mean the Shockers weren't irritatingly sensitive. While there were plenty of moving parts in an automaton, Shockers could break down if you looked at them funny.

Turning back to look at the Shocker he had just addressed, Edison froze. The Shocker's eyes were dark. No light at all. He looked at the one behind it and saw the same. The two standing by the windows were just like their metallic brothers.

Daring to step closer, he peered into the dark slits where its eyes would be. Nothing indicated that power was flowing. This was not a sleep mode that Edison designed, nor was it some sort of stealth mode. They were indoors, and it wasn't needed.

He dared to touch the metal chest of the Shocker, just for a moment, with the tips of his fingers. The exterior was not hot, nor was it charged with electricity. Putting his hand back on the chest, he leaned into the creation, pressing an ear to the Shocker. While his hearing was problematic on the best of days, the vibrations trembled through his skin. His fingertips and his ear told him nothing. The machine was silent all the way through.

He glanced around the room. This could be just another test from Jekyll. That man loved to play games, especially when bored. Edison had become his favourite plaything.

"I suppose the punishment will be worth the crime," Edison said to himself, giving the Shocker a light push.

With a great clatter, the Shocker fell to the wooden floor. It lay prone and made no effort whatsoever to get up. Edison, his heart racing harder than a winning horse at the Derby, waited for the others to move in. They did nothing.

Before he could make for his room, and throw a bag together in order to escape, he caught the sound of the doors locks disengaging. Frantically he looked around the room for anything that would work as a weapon. If Jekyll were to find him surrounded by dead Shockers, Edison could only imagine his rage.

The coat rack was the only thing not secured to the floor, and sturdy enough to take down an opponent... but Jekyll?

Edison swung the furniture at the person who entered. The rack was heavy, heavier than he first thought it would be, and his attack ended with him stumbling over the rack which had landed against the floor with a dull thud.

Who he saw standing before him was not who he expected. Two other men joined the stranger, all dressed uniformly; long black coats, black gloves, black cravats, and top hats. Their eyes fell on Edison, but their expressions didn't change. Much like their fashion, they were uniform.

Anything this bland, anything this regimented, had to be a government. United States, French, it didn't matter. He was being rescued.

"Thank God," sighed Edison. "You got my signal."

"Mr Edison? Mr Thomas Alva Edison?" asked the closest gentleman.

"Who do you think I am? Fucking George Westinghouse?" barked Edison. "You've been looking for me, I presume, ever since I went missing—nearly a year now? I would assume, if one of America's brightest suddenly goes missing, you would at least have the decency to know what I damn well look like!"

True, this was the government he was dealing with, and their capacity for thought and deduction would not necessarily be at his standards—but this was ridiculous.

"I assume President Cleveland sent you," Edison said.

The three men looked at one another, confused, as well as amused.

"President Cleveland? Of the United States of America? Hiring the Pinkertons to come and find me?" Good Lord, these men were morons! "Alright, if you are not government operatives and not Pinkertons, you are—what—specialised bounty hunters? You are intelligent enough to understand a radio signal I presume?"

"Mr Edison," a voice from behind the agents spoke, loudly enough that even Edison's deafness would not miss a thing, "words cannot even begin to describe what a pleasure it is to make your company."

The phantom that walked into Edison's parlour should not have done so. This was a dead man. The inventor had not been present at his execution, but he had read the papers. He knew all about this ingenious madman. The Murder Hotel—barbaric, twisted, and immoral as it had been—was an engineering marvel. Edison had a rather unpopular opinion among his peers about it all. He thought the murder hotel in Chicago should have been preserved. An astounding amount of thought, planning, and innovation which was worthy of investigation.

"You're supposed to be dead," Edison managed to say.

"Yes, I get that a lot. We have never met, but I've admired your work for years." he said, holding out his hand, " Dr Henry Howard Holmes, at your service."

"I sincerely doubt that," Edison returned. "I take it, this is not a rescue."

"That depends on how you look at it," Holmes said, his grin almost that of an old friend. "I understand you worked for my organisation once before."

Edison frowned. "I've worked with a lot of organisations in the past."

"Yes, you have, but how many ask you to send California into the sea?"

"You are with the House of Usher?" Edison asked, his voice dry.

"Yes, but since you last worked on that particular project, there has been a change in leadership."

Edison's shock ebbed away. He now looked at the killer standing before him with an air of shrewdness. "I take it I'm looking at it, then?"

"That you are," Holmes said, with a slight bow.

"You received my signal?"

"Quite clever," Holmes said, strolling over to the prone Shockers that Edison now wished were in full operational order. Jekyll had told him if anyone were to attempt a rescue operation, they would experience the full wrath of the Shockers. "We stumbled upon the signal quite by happenstance, but then again, when you pick up a signal that reads 'CQD Edison' and the signal is originating from a landlocked section of Paris, it was simply a matter of time—if not a race against factions—to find the source."

"With my own government looking for me, do you really think Usher will simply be able to spirit me away and no one notice?" he said, through a dry throat.

Homes turned, his smile turning into a slight chuckle. "Jekyll has deprived you of newspapers, hasn't he?"

The man did not appear hurried at the least. It would not have surprised Edison if Holmes had taken a seat and asked him to brew up a cup of coffee. He looked completely and utterly at ease.

Edison motioned to the Shockers standing still around them all. "And exactly how did you manage to short out all the Shockers in the house?"

"Ah, yes, quite the innovation." Holmes turned to Edison, his pride obvious. "I knew of a device that I challenged my Usher clankertons to create. Something called an electromagnetic pulse. We detonated it before coming in here. Knowing your propensity for weaponising electricity, I wanted to rest assured no electric countermeasures were waiting for us. Granted, not only are the Shockers inoperative, but so are any and all electric devices within this building. Rather ingenious, this silent weapon. The only way you know it has done its work is that anything electric becomes a paperweight."

The sheer inventiveness of that silenced Edison, which was an achievement in itself.

"Mr Edison," Holmes said, placing his fine black bowler on top of his head, and motioning with his hand to the door. "If you wouldn't mind. I would much rather have a man of your reputation, intellect, and stature walk out of a prison, instead of being carried."

Edison looked to the other three Usher henchmen and knew this would not be a fight he could win. His days of such adventures were long over. "Then I suppose we should be off," he agreed.

"Excellent, old sport." Holmes said, with a brilliant smile. "I am sure we are going to be the very best of friends."

Letting out a long sigh, Edison nodded, and proceeded to walk from one terrible situation to another.

CHAPTER TWENTY-SIX

⇥==⇤

In Which a Hard Decision Is Made

"What happened in there, Books?"

Doctor Sound looked particularly cross, and he had every right to be. Wellington had gone completely rogue and taken the law—quite literally—into his own hands. Then he'd served as an executioner. The director had frog-marched them into his office where no other agents or the clever Professor Falcon would witness his rage.

"Sir..." Wellington said, his hands clenching and unclenching, "I made a choice."

Oh, Welly, Eliza lamented, *no going back now.*

"Is that what you call it?" Sound asked, his eyebrows threatening to touch the top of his forehead. "Because it looked like a cold-blooded murder from where I stood."

"Now just a moment, sir," Eliza broke in. Sound turned to face her, and she wondered with his face that shade of red his head did not explode on the spot.

Clearing her throat, she continued. "There are plenty of times when we kill for Queen and Empire. It is part of the job."

"With my authority—and I most definitely did not give it in this case," Sound said, his lip curling into a snarl.

She had not seen such passion from him since way back when she'd disobeyed orders not to kill Wellington in Antarctica.

Sound's hands clenched into fists. "We are trying to find out what Ragnarök is, and Jekyll could have given us a hint of what Usher was planning. According to a debrief with Campbell and Hill, the House was running a breeding farm in Italy."

"A breeding farm?" Eliza asked.

"The women involved were being administered a serum that sounded very familiar to Jekyll's," Sound stated, his gaze fixed on Wellington. "Now, any opportunity to find out what was going on is lost."

Eliza kept an eye on those fists, just in case. "With respect, Director, you didn't know what this man is capable of. All you saw was the display at the Water Palace. Welly and I have been on this madman's trail for months. *Months.* He was not a menace. He was not a danger. He was a bloody apocalypse outfitted by Saville Row."

"That does not give Agent Books the right to kill him!"

"If he is in danger, then he has to defend himself!"

Wellington's headshake was barely perceptible as he spoke. "I was not in danger."

"You fail to realise, Agent Braun," Sound snapped, ignoring him, "what I am contending with when it comes to Wellington's behaviour. There are members of Parliament that are still uneasy about the incident in Bombay, or did you forget his own countrymen that Wellington gunned down?"

"That was in the *heat—of—battle!*" Eliza insisted. "You cannot hold him responsible for his actions there. They had him pinned down. No reinforcements. The Ghost Rebellion was upon him. If he had not tapped into his talents..."

"Talents that he obviously cannot control," Sound interjected.

"I was in full control of my faculties," Wellington offered, his words only just above a whisper.

Eliza gave a huff as she turned on him. *"Shut it, Welly, you are not helping your case!"*

"He wouldn't stop."

Eliza and Sound stared at Wellington, and she could only guess if the Old Man was seeing what she did. Her love was staring at the edge of the Director's fine mahogany desk as if he had never seen such a thing before. The thousand-yard gaze, though, Eliza recognised as the look of an operative who had just returned from deep cover. Sometimes they came back from the place of horror, sometimes they didn't.

She could only imagine where Wellington was right now. His voice never changed in inflexion or pitch as he spoke. "I had never achieved such a state of... *clarity*... like that. I think... I guess... this was the final step that my father and Jekyll were working towards. They had bred into me all these talents, but the one problem I had was control. I remember times when I served in the military, teetering on the edge of sanity. That would be my indication to pull back. Retreat inward, if you will, while leading the charge forward.

"That was why I joined the Ministry. I knew what I could do, but I could not control it. So I buried myself in the Archives, well aware of what I was capable of, but knowing I could not trust myself. Then I met you," he said, turning his gaze to Eliza. Her heart clenched. "I had to tap into those talents. Far more than I felt safe in doing so because I was always on a razor's edge. In that interrogation room, though, everything was so..." He paused, exhaling a breath that made his body tremble. "Focused. Yes, focused. Colours were vibrant. Sound was clear. Everything in that moment was elevated, heightened."

The room fell into a tense silence. Eliza dared not break it as if he would shatter with it.

"Wellington," Sound began, his anger absent and in its place an odd demeanour that was a marriage of pity and compassion, "what did Jekyll say that brought you to this heightened awareness?"

"It's not what he said, sir. It's what he promised." Wellington looked back to Eliza. "He promised me he would not stop until we claimed what he called our own Manifest Destiny. If I did not fully embrace what I was, Jekyll said he would remove any and all distractions from my life. The Ministry. The Seven." His eyes welled with tears as he said to her, "You. I had been fighting the urge to give over to my talents, but when he swore to take you and..." He took another breath, and then turned his gaze to the window across the room. "At that moment, the world snapped into focus. I had become what my father wanted... and I knew exactly what I needed to do."

"And you were in complete control?" Eliza asked. "For the first time?"

Wellington nodded, but then paused. "No, wait, there was one other time."

"When?"

He looked up at her, and his smile tied her stomach in knots. She wanted to kiss him so badly in that moment, but would have been highly inappropriate.

"Underneath the Havelock Manor. You were unconscious. We were pinned down. I tapped into those talents, and I... I got us out." Wellington gave a little chuckle as he looked over to Doctor Sound. "My father always told me I needed a focal point. I do believe I have it here, do I not, sir?"

"Quite," the Director replied, his tone low and dry.

Wellington looked so frail, and so exhausted, that Eliza wanted to throw her arms around him. He did not want this "talent" as they had called it. It was nothing more than a curse. Wellington's father and Henry Jekyll were hell bent on creating the unstoppable soldier, a killing machine that could blend into British society. He would be the template for future regiments of Her Majesty's military, or perhaps for a phantom army that Usher would unleash upon the world. They'd tried to purge Wellington of his humanity when he was just a boy, but Lilian Books held onto her son. Her husband recognised that and removed her from her boy's life. To Arthur Books, his wife was nothing more than an unwanted variable in an equation he was anxious to solve. To Wellington, she had been lighthouse through a raging tempest.

Now, Eliza had become that lighthouse.

The sudden hard ring from the telephone made her jump. Sound had three telephones on his massive desk. It was the dark red one calling out for attention. Doctor Sound stared coldly at the phone, letting it ring a third time. Then a fourth. At the sixth ring he picked up the receiver and pressed it against his ear.

Eliza could just hear the muffled, electronic buzzing of another voice speaking in the receiver. "Yes, mum," Sound replied with a nod. "Well, we have a development in that matter. Dr Henry Jekyll is dead." Eliza expected the voice to rise in pitch and volume, outraged at this unsanctioned assassination. Instead, the unintelligible voice continued. Doctor Sound's expression never changed. "Yes, mum. That's correct. How did you—" His words stopped abruptly as Sound's gaze went to Wellington Books. "What are their conditions?" The Director's complexion went ashen, and Eliza knew whoever was on the other end of that phone brought nothing but ill to Whiterock. "I see. Then I suppose we shall make preparations immediately." There was a pause, and then, "No, I am certain that he will be completely compliant in this matter." He nodded. "Yes, mum, I will tell him. Believe me, Agent Books is a gentleman of immeasurable character. He will not fail us." He gave a long, slow exhale and then said in a somewhat sombre tone, "God save the Queen."

Doctor Sound replaced the headset into its cradle and stared at it for a few moments. The silence was maddening, and all Eliza wanted to do was scream for answers.

"That was the Countess of Kimberly, Secretary of State for Foreign Affairs. Usher, according to the Secretary, has done the unthinkable. They have broken their silence."

Eliza furrowed her brow. "Yet you don't seem surprised."

"Because this is not my first time standing here, facing this decision." He crossed the office to a more comfortable corner, a table decorated with glassware, decanters, and high-back chairs. "In one instance, Miss Braun, I order you to eliminate the opposition with extreme prejudice," he said, pouring himself a drink. "Another instance, Jekyll was still alive, spirited away to the Arctic Circle and locked away in isolation. We mounted a full assault against Usher. Agents died, but we eliminated the threat, nonetheless. In another, your Ministry Seven mounted a rather clever confidence scheme that bested Usher." Sound took a deep drink from his tumbler, and then fixed his gaze on Wellington. "The last time I stood here, I ordered you to tap into his superior soldier abilities and unleash everything you possessed."

Eliza stepped closer to the both of them. "How many times have you been here before? At this moment?"

Sound took in another deep drink before answering. "I stopped counting after twenty. Every solution I dreamt of—and in several timelines, *we* dreamt of—did nothing to resolve the blackout. My future remained altered, plunged into darkness, and now I find myself with only one remaining option."

A muscle in Eliza's jaw twitched. "Which is?"

Doctor Sound looked to each of them. "We are invited to participate in a prisoner exchange."

"What does that mean?" Eliza inclined her head to one side. She did not care for the conclusion that was dawning over her. "Are you suggesting—"

Sound held up a solitary finger. "Miss Braun, we have no choice. This comes directly from the Secretary."

"And we're supposed to agree to handing over Wellington on account of Usher dropping their card at Buckingham Palace?"

"Usher did not contact us. As I said, we're *invited*—by the Office of the Supernatural and Metaphysical."

"Usher contacted—?"

"The United States government." He polished off the remaining amber liquid in his glass before continuing. "Usher demanded Henry Jekyll in exchange for this OSM asset. The Secretary informed me of this, so of course I was obliged to tell her of Jekyll's demise. Seems that Usher had a contingency plan in case of such a matter. They are demanding we hand over Wellington Books in exchange for the asset."

Eliza let out a mirthless laugh, making Sound flinch. "Oh, that is just mad! You know that at the best they will reduce Wellington to some mindless killing machine answering to Usher. The worst..."

"I am a lab specimen," Wellington said, slumping back into his chair. "Dissected. Catalogued. And discarded."

"You cannot do this, sir," Eliza said, her jaw tightening.

"Yes, he can."

Sound turned to face him, surprise etched on his face. "Wellington?"

Her partner looked up from where he sat. "Sir," he began, "am I to assume this is something you haven't tried in your numerous attempts to restart the Timeline Tracker?"

"I have avoided this option so many times, Agent Books, Agent Braun," Sound replied, his gaze boring into Wellington. "I even tried to alter the timeline before this moment, remove you completely from the equation." His eyes jumped to Eliza and a wry smile crossed his face. "Imagine my surprise to discover that your meeting the indubitable Miss Braun here was, indeed, an immovable point in time."

"I do hate to be predictable," she sniped in return, "but I'll make an exception this one time."

Sound let out a low chuckle. "At this point, I have found myself in some kind of control, or at least as one can be within a timeline. I had concerns that this particular crossroad would demand something dramatic. With each failure..."

"Sod the timeline," Eliza seethed. "You have infinite options, yes? So pick another one!"

"Time does not necessarily work the way theories would dictate..."

"I don't think you hear me, Sound," Eliza snapped.

"I don't think you realise what is at stake, my love," Wellington said to her softly.

Turning to look at Wellington, she glowered at him. "Director, give us the room, please."

Sound cleared his throat. "This is *my* office, last time I checked.»

Eliza did not take her gaze off Wellington. "And you will give it to us."

"Agent Braun—"

"Doctor Sound, are you sure you want my undivided attention?"

"Very well then," Sound returned. "Do take your time."

She continued to stare at Wellington, even after the door closed. For a moment, only the *tick-tick-tick* of Sound's bloody desk clock broke the silence.

"What are you doing?" she asked.

"You're angry. That is to be expected."

"No, Wellington, I am not angry. I am enraged. I am incensed. I am..." She ground her teeth together. She wanted him to know, but she also needed to understand why Wellington was so willing to surrender, to simply give up on them. "... furious."

"Eliza, this is not about us. This is about what is at stake. The world is facing a darkness that compels HG Wells to create the Ministry of Peculiar Occurrences. He is travelling back and forth through time, trying to find one moment within countless possibilities, to avoid whatever this doomsday is."

"Did it ever occur to you that humanity is broken, has always been broken? Perhaps this is a fate that we all are destined to face? Why are you so willing to sacrifice the happiness we have to save the world?"

"Isn't it selfish to bring about the end of days just so we can have some joy?"

"Why can't we be selfish?" she demanded. "Have we not earned a bit of peace by now? We have saved the Empire, and in some instances, the world, from secret societies, mad scientists, and all-around nutters." Eliza shook her hands out in frustration.

He stared at her for a moment, and then replied with a sigh, "This is not how duty works. In our line of work, we're expected to lay down our lives in service to Her Majesty."

"You mean the same queen that ordered our swift removal barely a year ago?"

Wellington waved a hand in the air dismissively. "A terrible counter-argument, and you know it. The queen was not in her right mind when she issued that order."

"No, no. I am done with this. I am tired of always putting my life on the line for an empire that does not give a toss about us!"

"Then why don't you do something about it?"

He asked in a firm enough tone that it grabbed her attention, but there was no anger or malice in his words. Wellington's query had been calm, but his words held resolve she could not ignore.

Turning back to him, she bent to one knee to look in his eyes. "Welly?"

"I am what Usher really wants, we all know that. You. Me. Sound. This has to play out and I must be turned over to them so that you can do what you do best."

A headache began creep behind her eyes. "What exactly is that?"

"Rescue me," he said, tears welling in his eyes. "One last time."

"Wellington..."

The door opened, and Sound marched back into the office. "Agent Books, Agent Braun, we can no longer dally. We have a duty to perform."

"Yes sir," Wellington stated, his eyes fixed on Eliza's. It was the same silent way they communicated with one another in the field, and in the bedroom. She had never had a connection like this with any other man, and she didn't want to lose it. "I am certain we are all clear now in what we need to do."

"Agent Braun?" Sound asked. "Are we—"

"Would you mind shutting it, Old Man?" Eliza yelled, and it felt good.

"Enough of that, Eliza Doo," Wellington said, his words barely perceptible to her, even when she pressed her forehead to his. She became aware of the tears drying on her cheeks. How long had she been crying? Before Sound came back into his office?

"You have to end this, my love," Wellington whispered to her. "You know what to do."

Eliza knew what he meant.

Wiping the tears from her face, Eliza got to her feet and strode out of Sound's office. Everyone and everything passed around as if some surreal nightmare had her in its grasp. Eliza reached the operations room on the main level of Whiterock Manor, Wellington's final words to her echoing in her head. This had once been a ballroom, with lords and ladies dancing to beautiful music beneath the chandeliers. Now it served as the main offices of both stationed agents and agents visiting from other branches of the Ministry. When she came to a stop at her desk, her eyes lingered on the desk opposite of her own. It was Wellington's and from this spot, the two of them had pieced together clues on Jekyll's whereabouts.

"Eliza," came the husky voice of Henrietta Falcon. When she looked up at her, Falcon gasped. She must have been a sight.

"Eliza, what's going on? Where's Wellington?"

She understood exactly what she needed to do, but she would have the narrowest of windows for it. "Henrietta, I may lose Wellington. He is surrendering himself to the House of Usher." Henrietta's eyebrows raised as Eliza struggled to keep her composure. "I know what I need to do… but…" It was difficult to breathe, to think. "… but how to begin… "

Henrietta nodded, pulling another desk chair up to her. She eased Eliza into it and held her hands tightly. "I understand, and I think I know where to begin." She looked to either side of them, assuring there were no agents within earshot. "And we start with Wellington's measurements…"

CHAPTER TWENTY-SEVEN

In Which the Mistress of Death Makes Good on Her Bargain

Filippo blinked once, twice, thrice, when the bag over his head was removed, then he took a deep breath. The dank smell of standing water tinged the air, and a rock ceiling carved by time arched over his head. He couldn't tell if it was gas or electricity illumination, but his new surroundings were a cave.

He wanted to reach up and rub his face, but his right arm would not move. Neither would his left.

In fact, Filippo was unable to move anything. Not even his head.

He desperately wanted to. To his left, breathing, faint—but someone was there. There were several people there. He was certain of it.

Filippo strained his eyes to look as far to the left as possible, and once his eyes could move no further, he tried to force his head to turn. No pain. *Nothing.* Yet, his muscles refused to work. His skin prickled with sweat as his head turned against this bizarre, invisible resistance. Finally, the mysterious people came into view.

Several feet away from him stood a young woman, flanked by three children. From the rags hanging off their bodies, grime and filth decorating their skin, they resembled street urchins in desperate need of a bath and proper clothes. They stared as Filippo not in shock, not in fear, nor in revulsion. They stared at him as if he were a butterfly specimen pinned under glass. These four vagabonds took a full measure of him. Something ran down his temples. Sweat? He trembled. This unseen resistance was taking its toll. He gasped for breath. His lungs burned from the strain, but at least the burning was something.

"You should not struggle," a voice called from somewhere nearby. Words bounced around him in the cavern's echo, so it was difficult to know much of the speaker. Female, definitely. But where was she standing? Only this was certain: the speaker was in control. "You will only injure yourself, Signor."

"Who are you?" Filippo asked, his voice booming against the surrounding rock.

Filippo did not want to panic. Not knowing where he was, nor who these people were, did nothing to calm his wits, but he would not give in to terror.

Footsteps were now *behind* him. His heart pounded faster, and for a moment, there was nothing except for the thrumming of his own blood.

"This must be unnerving, Signor," the voice spoke again. "Please, let me accommodate you."

The sharp *clack-clack-clack* of cogs catching on one another echoed all around him, the sound conjuring images of ancient torture devices used in the Spanish Inquisition. The world began to tip and spin. Filippo still did not *feel* anything but his world moved downward. Whatever restrained him now brought his captors into his field of view.

At the centre of the small group standing before him, was an elderly woman, her hair shock-white save for strands of black peppered throughout. She stood with the assistance of a cane, while at her side was another, much younger woman, dressed head-to-toe in black. She looked tired as if she carried the weight of the world on her shoulders. The younger woman held a doctor's bag.

The old woman rested both hands on the head of her cane, and much like the urchins to his left, she took the measure of Filippo. From the woman's expression prisoners were nothing new. "Mr Filippo Rossi," the old woman began, her diction sharp and deliberate, "your journey was not too unsettling I hope?"

Filippo's brow furrowed. Not too unsettling? What sort of question was that? He screwed his eyes shut as he struggled with the last thing he remembered. Wine. He was having a glass of wine. A fantastic meal on his plate. His unexpected saviour sat across from him, toasting to their plan in dealing with the House. With an idea of what they would do next, he booked flights for them to Toronto where they'd be rescued by the House.

He would put in a good word for her, but that was all. He would not care about her fate once she was handed over. Then...

The dinner was delightful as was the wine, but then he recalled only flashes of memory. Fabric slipping over his head. The sensation of being borne up and placed in a truck or cart of some fashion. His body rocking back and forth as he was being spirited away. Where exactly, he did not know.

Filippo simply needed to keep his wits about him. "To whom do I owe the pleasure?"

The old woman wrung her hands against the head of her cane. "My name is not important."

"It would certainly help, if we are to discuss matters at hand. You have me at a bit of a disadvantage, at present."

"I have *you* at a disadvantage?" The old woman smiled and nodded. "Well now, is this not a most interesting turn of fortunes? Not so long ago, it was you who had me at a disadvantage when you attacked my family. Without provocation."

Filippo considered the ladies and children to his left. His gaze narrowed on the old woman, and his heart continued its frenetic pace. The resemblance was uncanny.

"Nonna?" Filippo croaked out.

Her expression turned sour. "Yes, but you are to address me more formally, not as *mi famiglia* would. Either address me as Signõra del Morte, or Francesca."

Filippo swallowed hard, and now his throat might as well have been full of crushed glass. He was in desperate need of a drink, but he dared not ask a single thing from the matriarch of the del Morte household. He knew there had to be others of the clan nearby.

Why was he unable to turn his head? What was wrong with him?

"Signõra," Filippo began, a tremble in his voice—not the best way to start a conversation with an adversary. *Never let the other side know how terrified you are.* A basic lesson from when he was in the field for Usher. Filippo cleared his throat and started again. "Signõra, I can only assume you have many questions for me."

"Many questions? What makes you think I have any questions? I understand the situation quite clearly. You set the House of Usher against the House of del Morte. You came into our village and attempted to wipe us out."

Filippo took in a deep breath. He had to find some sort of common ground—some kind of leverage. "I know *famiglia* matters a great deal to you. I know that turning your daughters and granddaughters on your own must be difficult. However, when one of your own kills another, I have no doubt you would want to avenge that death."

Nonna leaned in, her cane remaining steady even as she did so. "Go on."

"The one who brought this upon you, the del Morte who betrayed the House of Usher and in turn betrayed your family? I can deliver her to you." Filippo licked his lips, trying to assert control over the situation. "Grant me safe passage to Usher and I will personally pledge all of our European resources in finding Sophia."

"Now why would my Nonna ask for help from the House of Usher," spoke a familiar, luxuriant voice from behind him, "when Nonna knows exactly where her Sophia is?"

Her smile sent chills through him. He was oddly grateful to experience a sensation of any kind at this point. She took a place by Francesca, and the look on her Nonna's face was one of immense pride. She had been his saviour, and eventually, his confidant. This dark Guardian Angel, Sophia del Morte, who had spun an incredible tale of desperation and alienation, but here she was in the bosom of her family.

Filippo went to say something, but paused. The other woman to Nonna's right, the one all dressed in black carrying a doctor's bag, suddenly caught his complete attention.

On a small table next to Nonna, the woman began laying out a wide array of edged instruments. Were these the instruments of her office? Or were they instruments of torture in her hands? Perhaps, a bit of both? In her eyes, Filippo saw burning white heat. Her face did not twist in rage—she didn't even so much as furrow her brow. This quiet stranger regarded Filippo with a gaze that drilled into him.

His attention jumped back to Sophia. "I saw you kill your sister…"

"Cousin," Sophia corrected him. "You saw me kill my *cousin.*"

"Sister, cousin, we do not need to lose ourselves in the semantics of it!" he snapped. "You shot Lucinda twice in the chest, and then you had me hold her down while you smothered her."

Sophia's eyebrows raised as she nodded. *Quite a tale,* her face seemed to say. "A grizzly task, Signor, but you answered the challenge. What you witnessed, however, was not what you believed it to be." She motioned with her hand for someone to step forward. The sweet shopkeeper that tried to kill him the other day, the same shopkeeper that hunted him through the stacks of The Raven bookshop—Sophia's cousin, Lucinda del Morte appeared out of the shadows. She was wearing the shirt she had worn that day, still bloodstained from the shots Sophia had landed on her person.

Theatrics. The entire incident at the bookshop had been an elaborate illusion.

"You were protecting me," Filippo insisted. "You had plenty of chances to kill me. You saved me from being apprehended by the Ministry."

"Indeed, I did. And Signor, believe me, what I told about my standing in the del Morte family was not a *complete* lie," Sophia admitted, motioning around her. "I am held responsible for what happened at Montenegro. I had gone into business with the House of Usher, a sanction that Nonna specifically warned me against, and now *mi famiglia* have become refugees in our own country. This is my responsibility to bear, and I resigned myself to face my fate."

"Isn't this the way of the young, Filippo?" Nonna asked him. "So melodramatic. So ready to fall on their sword for the wrongs they have done when they could just as easily make amends."

"There never was a sanction on Sophia," he whispered.

"To turn family against each other breeds only contempt and dishonour. That is bad for business." Nonna glanced at Sophia and then turned back to Filippo. "Instead, I offered Sophia another option: you."

"Tonight's dinner. That is how you find yourself here, with us," Sophia offered.

He had to keep his wits about him.

He had to remain calm.

He was failing at every turn.

"We drank the same wine, ate the same food," he insisted. "Whatever I had, would've affected you as well?"

Sophia nodded. "Most perceptive, you are quite right. You and I prepared meals together, and we drank from the same wine bottles. Not to say you did not take precautions, at first. I did notice you only moved your food from one side of the plate to the other, drank wine only you purchased. Of course, I observed that." Sophia then took a few steps closer to him, resting her hands against her hips as she stood before him. She'd lured many men to their deaths with her beauty, but now she was less of an Aphrodite, and more a spectre, ready to escort him to the next world. "Did it ever strike you as curious while we were travelling that you were never able to wake me up in the morning?"

Her sleeping habits were infuriating, but what did that have to do with his current predicament? "What?"

"A woman does need her privacy, you can understand that? And in my private moments before bed, I would ingest a good amount of tea brewed from Angel's Trumpets, this rather delightful flower from Australia. Not enough to kill me, but enough that would keep me paralysed. All those times you were knocking at my door? I heard you. Every time. When you set off on your own, I was a little concerned I would lose you."

"But your cousin was at The Raven. How did you find—?"

"My dear Filippo, once I found you in Assisi, the del Morte family set their plan in motion. We have been watching you in secret since we set off for Rome. And yes, you were right—if I wanted agents of the Ministry dead, they would be dead. I had to make certain that I won your trust. While I did so, I built my own immunity to this poison. When you finally believed yourself safe and under my protection, you now find yourself in this position."

The young woman in black, walked over to his left, out of his vision. A lever clanked. The cave filled with the sound of gears, high-pressure motors hissing to life, and wisps of steam slinking from under him to curl over the edge of his table. Looking to his left and right, he saw a long mirror mounted on a mechanical arm extending itself from underneath the slab on which he laid. The reflection that swivelled into view revealed Filippo lying against a featureless slab, only one restraint running across his chest. His arms and legs were free to move if they were able. Contorting his face, he looked at his limbs in the mirror, attempting to move even a finger. Nothing.

"And now I turn you over to my sister, Hortensia," Sophia said, motioning to the woman Filippo saw in the reflection of the overhead mirror. "She will be taking on the proceedings from here."

With a slight incline of her head, Sophia placed a kiss on Nonna's cheek and then started ascending a stone ridge winding up along the far wall.

"Wait," Filippo called to her. "You're leaving? After all this, you're leaving?"

She paused halfway up the stone stairs before turning back to him. "Much as in your Ragnarök, you are merely one cog in the machine. This is only our first step forward. *Ciao, Signor Rossi.*"

Filippo watched her for as long as possible, until Hortensia pulled another lever, conjuring more steam and mechanical clamour. The table underneath him began to move again as the loud *clickety-clickety-clack-clack* of gears and cogs echoed all around the cave. Filippo once again stared toward the rock ceiling, the reflection of his paralysed body mocking him in the mirror overhead.

Hortensia leaned into view, joined moments later by other members of the del Morte clan. The woman he had seen earlier was there, her expression no different. Her eyes were like all the others upon him: curious, studying.

Then Hortensia spoke. Her voice was a contralto—not as intoxicating or seductive as her cousin's. She was far more clinical in nature. "Perhaps you are thinking, Signor, that I intend to abandon my Hippocratic oath. *Do no harm.* I tried to uphold it, you know? I tried so hard, and I still try. Every day. Family, I have discovered, presents an exception to even the most hallowed oaths." She pulled into view the small table with the tools of her trade on it. Hortensia held up the scalpel. "In my time as a physician I have learned that oaths have no meaning if they cannot be tested—at least, when the cause is just."

Dizziness swept over Filippo as he willed his hand to come up and grab the scalpel. He would drive it into her neck and then carve his way to freedom. If only his body were as strong as his will. Then, quite suddenly, sensation began to return. Her fingers running against his chest. His shirt scraping against his skin as she removed it. He still couldn't move, but tactile awareness was coming back.

"You took from our family our means of existence, our means for survival. Now we all must learn our craft over again. Nonna has given me the responsibility of educating my sisters, nieces, and relatives, and I intend to do so." Filippo's breath caught as she stared at him for a prolonged moment before looking up at those gathered around him. "Tonight, with the assistance of Sophia's poison, we have a lesson. We will study in detail the most vulnerable points on the human body." Hortensia looked to each of them in turn. "Shall we proceed?"

They all nodded in unison—even the children.

CHAPTER TWENTY-EIGHT

Wherein Eliza Says Goodbye

A chill in the high desert air wasn't surprising, nor the feeling of loneliness and desolation. Still it was a spectacular part of the world, the Arizona Territories.

Seated in the waiting room of the remote train station, staring out the window, the vast skies scattered with stars called to Wellington. It was a beautiful scene that he enjoyed in silence even though he was not alone in the room.

Eliza left an hour previous to see to preparations, and he found himself glancing at the spot where she usually was—missing her. Even her simmering rage would have been some kind of company.

The others in the room—Bruce Campbell, Brandon Hill, Director Sound and Luther Highfield, Chief of the Office of the Supernatural and Metaphysical—were not so much comfort.

Though this was only Wellington's second visit to the southwestern region of the former colonies, he was familiar it from a rather dramatic moment of Ministry/Usher history. The case involved his Canadian and Australian escorts. With tense shoulders and their silence, they communicated well enough that they were recalling it themselves. This train journey into desert was not their idea.

Wellington leaned back in his seat. "No need to fret, gentlemen, I am certain our friends at OSM have taken precautions. No cataclysmic collisions tonight."

Sound and Highfield stood by the door, talking in low tones and taking little notice of the others. The Chief towered over the Director so that he had to bend down a little. He was as well-dressed as the last time Wellington had seen him. Highfield, a broad-shouldered black man, obviously chose his fashion to compliment both his skin tone and height.

Brandon followed Wellington's gaze and lowered his tone. "That particular mission was a delightful romp."

"I can only imagine."

"If you could only have seen how that ornithopter swooped in and..."

Bruce's eyes were hard as flint. "Mate, save the small talk. We're on a job."

Frowning, Brandon glanced over his shoulder to Sound and Highfield. "Oh, yes, quite." He cleared his throat and offered, "Sorry about all this, Books."

"Tosh, think nothing of it."

He blinked, as if thunderstruck by the sentiment. "Come again?"

"This has to be done. I understand that, and it is for everyone's betterment."

Brandon looked over to Bruce, and the Australian folded his hands and leaned forward. "Are you serious? Books, you're a Ministry agent. A damn fine one even if I've never said it. You have—"

"Committed crimes against Her Majesty's own citizens..."

"You were not yourself," Brandon insisted. "You went a little mad. You have a certain set of skills that need monitoring. We know that now, and you've got it under control."

"I am still a criminal." Wellington let out a sigh. It felt right to admit it. "A liability. Usher has a valuable asset that makes my own unique abilities pale in comparison to the monstrosities he could design. Add to that what insight I could glean on Ragnarök, provided I can break free of captivity..."

"Dammit, man," Brandon snapped. Sound and Highfield went silent as they turned, their gaze towards them. "You are not some bargaining chip. You're one of us."

"That will do, Agent Hill," Doctor Sound stated evenly.

It was a surprise, but the Canadian did not back down. "Which one of us will be next, I wonder?"

"Brandon." At his name he turned towards Eliza who had appeared at the door. Her expression was even sterner than their Director's. "This is bigger than all of us. We have to let it play out."

"Let it...? Are you saying you are all right with this?"

Eliza crossed her arms in front of her. "Considering what is at stake, I am content."

Of course she wasn't. Wellington knew that. She didn't seem at all convinced that what they were doing was right. Still, he trusted her.

"Agent Hill," Wellington said, "I admire your kind words and sense of loyalty, but if you wish to honour me, I would ask that you do not judge the Ministry in this moment. We are all doing what must be done."

The man's expression hardened from crestfallen disappointment to enraged resolve when Brandon's partner chimed in his unwanted opinion on the matter. "As we like to say in the South Pacific, she'll be right."

Wellington cast a glance to his own feet. He really should have polished his shoes before they cuffed his hands behind his back. "Indeed, Campbell, but I have a request for you as well."

"Do you now?"

He motioned with his head over to his partner. "Watch over her."

Eliza straightened. "I beg your pardon?"

"Why would I do that?" Bruce said, his eyes going between her and Wellington. "She's a big girl. She can take care of herself."

"I would never debate you on that point. Be that as it may, I would appreciate the gesture."

Bruce let out a long sigh as he looked over to her and then shrugged. "You know she and I don't get on."

"That's an understatement," Eliza muttered.

"Just..." Wellington clenched his jaw. He knew better than anyone how stubborn Eliza could be. "I'm not asking you to be her best mate or her maid. I'm simply asking that you keep a watch, even if it is a distant one, on her."

Bruce and Eliza both snorted.

A metallic snapping rang through the room. All the agents looked to the two directors. Chief Highfield drew his finger back and forth across the top cover of a pair of Starlight Specs, a quaint new device from the same people that created Starlight Goggles. A faint emerald light shone against Highfield's ebony skin as he focused on the horizon. "Contact. Inbound."

"Are you sure it is them?" Sound asked.

"It's two in the morning on a remote spur of the Southwest Corridor. We also secured this particular area twenty-four hours ago. Yes, I'm sure," he said, snapping the specs shut and slipping the device into his coat pocket. "Let's get ready."

All of them trooped out of the station onto the platform. Highfield whistled twice and at the signal the train vented jets of steam and chuffed towards them. A giant cannon emerged from the second railcar, while from the sides of the engine itself, two massive machine guns dropped into place. Wellington judged they were at least five times the size of a standard Gatling. Then buffers on the side extended out like outstretched arms ready to give someone a god-awful hug. After a long jet of steam, they angled down ninety degrees and drove themselves into the earth. Rock surrendered to the massive hydraulics that bore into the ground, securing the engine in place. These struts would deal with the recoil from such a massive cannon, otherwise the train would eject backwards in a rather embarrassing fashion.

"ISN'T THIS AMAZING?!" came one of the last voices Wellington would expect.

"You are standing next to me, Professor Axelrod. I can hear you quite adequately," Wellington said.

"Oh, yes! You must admit though. Quite the feat!"

"You want one?"

Axelrod's wide eyes were visible even with the dim light and long shadows. "Do you think the Director would commission one?"

"Afraid not, Professor," Henrietta Falcon spoke from behind them, taking a drag from her cigarillo. "First, this battle train is a prototype. One of a kind from the Ada Institute. Second, your Director mentioned you might ask me about this very matter. He is not interested."

"Damn," Axelrod cursed, scuffing his feet in the dirt.

Once the deafening cacophony subsided, a low, soft drone of remaining steam lingering around them, Chief Highfield stepped up to where the Ministry agents stood. "We've left nothing to chance."

"Of course you haven't, Chief Highfield," Henrietta said. "The Ada Institute does appreciate your willingness to have us here."

"I was unaware that the Institute worked with the Ministry on such a regular basis."

"Well," Axelrod began, "if you must know, this is really our fir—"

Henrietta struck him hard in the shoulder, silencing him as she offered, "This is our first operation with the Ministry in the United States. Utilising æthergate technology made this field test possible, so again, on behalf of the Institute, thank you."

Highfield squinted at the light still approaching them at a fast pace. He cast a quick glance to Wellington and Henrietta before he looked down to Axelrod. "Professor, are you ready?"

"Yes, rather."

"Come with me," he said.

Henrietta drew from her smoke, a slight smile crossing her face. "A rather impressive man, wouldn't you agree?"

"With all the challenges his own government and society throw at him, Highfield is an amazing gentleman. I regret not having future opportunities to work with him."

"I see." She looked at him from head to toe and smiled. "You're looking quite smart."

"I found an amazing tailor," he returned with a crooked grin.

"So I've heard." Her smile faded as she looked over to Eliza pacing by the edge of the bridge. "How is she taking all this?"

Wellington wished she wasn't so far away, but all the same he committed her to memory. "About as well as you would expect."

"Can you blame her?" she chortled, taking a drag from her cigarillo. "She loves you."

"I know." A shrill cry of a train whistle echoed in the darkness; the sound of fate perhaps. "I am concerned that I have asked too much of her at this rather critical time."

"Eliza is an amazing woman." Henrietta placed a hand on his shoulder. The scent from her smoke was sweet and strangely comforting. "She is stronger than you may think."

"I have quite the vivid imagination, Professor Falcon, or do you forget?" On the approaching train sounding its whistle once more, Wellington rolled his shoulders as much as the handcuffs allowed. "As everyone has reminded themselves tonight, we have a duty to fulfil. Let's not keep Usher waiting."

"The train's slowing down," Axelrod called out, peering across the canyon with what looked like highly-modified Starlights. "I'm not detecting any high voltage power sources, so no death rays. I do see on the spectrum heat sources characteristics with hyper-velocity weapons."

Highfield called over his shoulder, "Ready all weapons. Campbell, is your signal at the ready?"

Bruce drew a modified pistol, the barrel far larger in its bore than a usual Smith & Wesson pistol. He flipped a small switch behind the cylinder and a red light blinked on. "Flare is hot. If anything is wrong with the asset, we'll send word back here."

"Good. Get ready to escort Books."

"You alright?" Bruce asked.

"Just do your part, mate," Eliza stated as Brandon nodded to Bruce and crossed over to where she stood. "We'll do ours."

"Eliza?" Wellington said quickly. "Are you—"

"Are you really expecting me to present you to Usher like a gift on Christmas morning?"

"I was hoping—"

"If we're saying goodbye it's here, and it's now," she returned tersely.

"Then say your goodbyes," Sound insisted.

Wellington pushed down the resentment growing in his chest, but he wouldn't let it destroy this moment.

Even in the darkness of the early morning, her ice-chip blue eyes gleamed with tears and anger. Even so, they were his light. "I'm just grateful that you are here."

"And I hope you don't mind my saying, you do look quite dapper," Eliza said, pressing down his lapels, "If you are to meet the enemy at the gates, at least you should be fashionable, yes?" Her face was a pale mask, but she could no longer meet his eye. "I can't feel your arms around me. This is not right, not normal..."

"Since when has anything at the Ministry been normal, especially for us?" he said with a little laugh. "I love you, darling. This is what we agreed upon, remember?"

"I'm trusting your judgement on that."

"And I, you." He glanced to either side of him. "As I cannot take you into my arms, by all means grab a kiss from me."

Eliza rarely did as told, but Wellington was most thankful that, in this instance, she did just that and with great passion. He tasted her lips, her soft tongue, her mouth, and he tried so very hard to commit this kiss to memory. He knew what waited for him on the other side of this was nothing but uncertainty. This kiss, though—there was eternal certainty within it.

"Ready, are we?" Sound came up from behind them.

Their lips parted, and Wellington tried to drink in the last look with Eliza.

"Yes, Director," he said. Bruce and Brandon took him by the arms and led him over. "Thank you, sir."

"I'm sorry about the restraints," Sound said, with only a little bluster.

"It is best for everyone, I suppose. Everyone here and on the other side knows exactly what I am capable of." Wellington took in a deep breath. In the distance the lights of the trains illuminated the bridge ahead. It looked ever so long. His mouth was dry, but he managed to get out, "After you, gentlemen?"

Bruce fixed his grip on the Lee-Metford-Tesla rifle. "Brandon, Eliza, keep a bloody good eye our backs. Follow me, everyone."

CHAPTER TWENTY-NINE

Where the Light and the Dark Meet above the Abyss

With Bruce ahead and two agency directors on each side, Wellington walked towards the oncoming light at the other side of this bridge. It would have been a foolhardy crossing during the day, but in darkness walking across a railroad bridge at night was for someone harbouring a death wish.

In actuality there was not much chance of slipping to their end since the sleepers underfoot were closer together than usual for the United States or his own beloved England. No, the only option to plummet into the canyon underneath them would be to jump off the edge. *How far would that be?* he absently wondered.

"You all right there, Books?"

Wellington's eyes darted over to Doctor Sound. "Come again, sir?"

"You're creeping awfully close to the edge."

Wellington looked down to his feet and realised he *was* awfully close to the edge. Would he have tripped? Possibly. Would he have fallen into the dark? No. That was one thing his escort could protect him from.

"Can't have you doing anything foolish, now can we?" Sound stated.

Wellington's tolerance was crumbling away. "With all due respect sir, do you really think I would take the coward's way out?"

"Wouldn't be so cowardly, denying these Houseboys their prize, now would it?" Brandon added.

"We must remain men of our word—otherwise we are no better than the cads we do business with this morning." The train's lamplight brushed their faces. The Usher transport was drawing to a stop. "Come along, gentlemen."

With the light ahead no longer moving, wisps of smoke danced around it, revealing the silhouette of the train. Shouted commands drifted to them as soldiers disembarked. *No, not soldiers,* Wellington thought, *operatives for the House of Usher.* They were setting up their own arsenal, much like OSM had done in fortifying the position behind them.

Wellington squinted, trying to get his eyes to adjust and focus on the movement in the darkness. Four figures walked towards them. One of them was a man of average height, or at least, he would have been if he wasn't hunched over. Two others walked to the left of him; one slightly shorter, and the fourth towering over them all.

Bruce spun up the rifle's generator. "Alright then, this is it." He motioned to a small flag placed in between sleepers just ahead. "Halfway marker. Now, we wait."

Sound stepped closer to Wellington. "Books, before Usher arrives, I just wanted to thank you." He gave the others a withering look before taking his voice down to a whisper. "I know we should not be asking this of you. If there was any other way... If I could have tried..."

"Director, please, you don't need to justify what is necessary for the greater good. I understand that I am a small part of a much grander machine." He bit his bottom lip. He wanted so badly to tell Sound *exactly* what he thought. He knew Eliza would take the chance—then again, she wasn't here. "We all have a part to play, don't we?"

"Yes, quite." Sound patted him on the shoulder. "Good man."

"Very well, everyone," Highfield's gravelly voice carried over them all. "By the numbers. No heroics. We do this and we all go home."

Not all of us, Wellington thought to himself.

Chief Highfield turned to Doctor Sound and motioned for him to take a step back. The contrast of Highfield's stature, his frame and size perhaps only matched by a freight train, against Sound's rotund carriage would have been comical under any other circumstance. Wellington wanted to enjoy some humour at that moment, but he just couldn't find it in himself to smile at anything.

He wanted Eliza there. He needed her there.

If he dared a look over his shoulder, would he see her at this distance?

Their Usher counterparts emerged from the darkness, and Wellington recognised the hunched figure as Thomas Alva Edison, the famed inventor, scientist, and utter plonker. He looked frayed at the edges, but Wellington had no sympathy for this narcissist. Behind the inventor, grabbing him by the scruff of the neck to jerk him to an upright position was an Usher henchwoman, either matching or topping Beatrice Muldoon in height. Unlike the resourceful Miss Muldoon, though, this woman did not carry herself with any sense of grace. She was a tank disguised as a lady. He would prefer not to be on the receiving end of her fist-a-cuffs.

The two shorter men to one side of Edison were strangers. The taller of the two Wellington could picture at his own gentleman's club, enjoying brandy and cigars and talking politics with other men. Whoever he was, he must have been high up in the ranks of Usher to be present for the exchange. It was the other man, smiling wider at Wellington the closer he drew, that made his fists tighten. Every instinct urged him to either break free and kill this well-dressed man, or to break ranks and run back to the safety of the OSM train. Against his deathly pale skin, the man's brows and exceptionally full, manicured moustache granted his face distinction and character. The stranger's smile, though, was the smile of a predator, savouring the hunt and anticipating a glorious kill.

"Wellington Thornhill Books," the terrifying gentlemen spoke, his breath a quick puff of mist against the desert's chill. "The pleasure is all mine."

"I can assure you, yes, it is."

"I was present at your hanging," Highfield said, advancing on them.

The imposing lackey produced two pistols large enough for her huge hands. The hammers clicked back, and Chief Highfield froze in mid-step.

"Is this the part where I quote Twain to show you all how clever I am? My just standing here in front of you would be a confirmation of that." He turned his attention back to Wellington. "I'm Henry Howard Holmes, Chairman of the House of Usher."

"Good Lord," Wellington whispered.

Holmes chuckled. "Oh, tosh, Henry will do just fine."

"Mr Edison," Highfield said. The inventor twitched, casting a nervous glance over to the Amazon looming over him. "I am Chief Luther Highfield, Office of the Supernatural and Metaphysical. Are you well?"

"What do you think?" Edison barked. "For nearly three years I have been subject to all manners of madmen, and you are wondering if I am well? No, you moron, I am not well! I am a prisoner!"

Highfield nodded. "Well, that's Edison—no doubt."

The inventor leaned in, tilting his head to one side. "Hold on. I'm being traded for... him?"

Wellington did not want to deal with this man, especially right now. "Mr Edison, if you don't mind, your rather caustic disposition is merely delaying the inevitable."

Highfield motioned to Edison. "Sir, if you please, walk slowly towards us."

Sound patted Wellington on the shoulder. "Off you go—"

"Hold on a minute," Bruce called out. Rifles were shouldered, and the sounds of hammers locking into firing positions made the Australian pause in mid-step. He raised his hands and shrugged, then stood in front of Books. "You asked me to keep an eye on Eliza." He slapped his hand hard against Books' chest, pressing into him as he said, "I promise ya, mate. We'll all watch out for her. She's good value."

"That she is."

Bruce grinned as he pulled his hand away, straightening Wellington's lapels before turning around to the Usher agents. "He's all yours."

Wellington began the walk forward even though his legs weakened with each step. *No,* he chided himself, *I will not fail. This must happen.* He paused as Edison passed him on his right. The inventor did not ever spare him a glance. It should not have come as a surprise, but a twinge of disappointment rose in his chest.

The closer he drew to H H Holmes, the colder he got. It had been quite some time since he had tasted such fear. *This must happen,* he insisted.

"Good evening, Mr Books," Holmes said, his hand taking hold of Books' arm. "This gentleman is... well, he would prefer you call him by his *nome de plume* in the ranks. This is Mr Fox."

"I am," the Usher gentleman began, his eyes wide with wonder, "a great admirer of your father's work. He was quite the innovator."

"Yes, well, one man's innovator is another's heartless bastard."

"As you are an honourable sort..." Holmes said, allowing his words to trail off as he removed the handcuffs.

Rifles and pistols now trained on Wellington as Fox hissed, "What in the bloody hell..."

"Oh, would you stop?" Holmes snapped as he clapped Wellington on the shoulder. "If we are to work together, we should trust one another."

"I think it has to be earned, if you must know," Wellington returned, rubbing his wrists. At least he could get feeling back into his shoulders. Out of the corner of his eye he spotted a few of the Usher gunmen slipping their fingers across triggers.

He glanced over to Highfield, Sound, and fellow agents walking back the length of the bridge. *Phase One complete,* he thought, turning back to his captors.

Holmes looked around, nodded, and said, "Understood, but the truth remains: you are here. You could have thrown yourself off the Cliffs of Dover, gone into hiding, or put up a good fight—and yet, here you stand. Seems out of character for you, this utter lack of heroics."

"No, there are plenty of heroics in this. Edison returns to the hands of the United States, the Ministry find out who is holding the reins over Usher, and I attempt to foil you from the inside whenever and wherever I can."

Holmes nodded. "An honest man. I can respect that." He looked him over from head to toe, his smile widening. "And a man of fashion it seems."

"I am," Wellington said.

"I do approve of this cut. Savile Row?"

"Actually, no. This tailor is quite exceptional, nonetheless."

"I must have his number. I thought I understood Mr Fox's obsession with you, but you are quite a Pandora's Box, aren't you? The more we open, the more curiosities we discover."

"If you say so," Wellington said, his breath misting the light of the Usher transport looming ahead of him. "As this witty banter is growing somewhat tedious, might we—"

The air rushed out of him in a gasp as his chest took the impact. Wellington tried to catch his breath, but every muscle in his body was seizing up. He stumbled and caught a glimpse of Holmes and Fox staring at him as if he were some sort of aberration. Then he finally took in some air, and that hurt.

Then he became aware of two things at the moment. The first was the high-pitched crack of distant gunfire. The other was the warm sensation spreading across his chest.

"No!" Fox called out. "No! They're trying to—"

The second impact sent Wellington back once more, and this time he saw someone—whether it was Fox or Holmes himself, he could not be certain—reaching for him. Instead of hands stopping his fall, instead of the hard wood and iron underfoot, Wellington felt nothing. Absolutely nothing. Only a cold, biting rush of wind that stung at his cheeks.

Fortunately, that discomfort didn't last long. It was a blessed relief as the black abyss claimed him.

CHAPTER THIRTY

⋆⇒◎⇐⋆

In Which the Gates of Hell Are Opened

"How are we doing, Axelrod?" Eliza asked.

The prolonged sigh coming from him made her skin prickle. She was more than ready to give the eccentric engineer plenty of regret for his flippancy, but as she was still trying to make amends for past transgressions against R&D, Eliza needed to keep her wits about her.

"Agent Braun," he began, his tone stiff and slightly condescending, "the status has not changed in the past five minutes. They have reached the rendezvous point. Usher is in-bound. Any minute now, the exchange should happen."

She watched him fiddle with the modified Starlight Specs. The lenses clicked and hissed foreword, then back. Axelrod's posture told her nothing.

"Edison's en route," he said. "He appears to be healthy. Two legs. Two arms. We'll only know if they've got inside his head when OSM gets him back to DC Offices."

Edison? That toe-rag was the so-called asset OSM was willing to negotiate with Usher for? She understood what politicians would call "the grander scope" of this, but that did not erase the mayhem Edison unleashed in collaborating with Usher, and then with the Maestro. Edison's ledger had many deaths marked on it, but experience told her that there would be little justice for those families or loved ones left behind in the wake of the inventor's shadowy endeavours.

"You all right there, Eliza?" came a familiar, and welcome voice.

Eliza gave a derisive snort and turned to look at Henrietta who was offering her the cigarillo. "I am as well as can be expected under the circumstances," she said, accepting the smoke.

She nodded and stared off to one side. "Perhaps Wellington will do as he says and get on the inside. Perhaps he could relay to us..."

"Considering what Wellington can do, I'll be surprised if they leave him unattended in order to relieve himself."

That would be a problem as Wellington was frightfully shy, even around her.

"Anything is possible, I would imagine," Brandon offered, joining the two ladies. "Sorry, couldn't help to overhear."

Still delightfully naïve, Eliza mused. Her eyes followed the length of the rifle strapped to his back. "Is that the latest LMT there?"

"No, I brought this back with me from Whiterock. It's a Model III. Maybe not the latest model, but it will do the job."

Her heartbeat kicked up. "What is that supposed to mean?"

"You know how these exchanges can turn nasty quickly. Just want to be prepared. Ya' follow?"

Trying to calm herself, she nodded. "Wellington would appreciate that."

A whistle cut through the night. "Well now, that's pretty brave of Usher," Axelrod said, adjusting the Starlights.

Eliza waited a few moments. No reply. "What?" she asked, not caring a jot if it sounded rude or bossy—which men often seemed to fear.

"They've removed Wellington's cuffs. As this is Books that's really taking their lives into their own hands."

Eliza strained to see any movement in shadows on the bridge. In the distance, she could just make out a small lantern swaying back and forth, back and forth, as if in someone's hand. Probably Bruce's? Soon, the great Thomas Edison would return home, and Wellington...

She craned her neck as she looked at Brandon's rifle. "Is the scope fitted with Starlight filters?"

"Should be. The optics are state-of-the-art," he said, but then chuckled. "At least that is what Axelrod and Blackwell tell me."

"May I?" Eliza asked, extending her hand.

Brandon obliged and, after a final check that had its safety on, passed the weapon to her. Shouldering the modified rifle, she flipped on the scope. The shapes of several men, and one imposing figure standing tall over them all stood in a wide arc around three men. She could only assume the one rubbing his wrists, his back to them, was Wellington. If she didn't know better, the one man standing in front of him was admiring his suit.

I have to see this through, she thought to herself.

Something metallic clicked in her ear.

"Eliza," Brandon asked. She was certain he was not letting his voice carry which it could easily do around here. He was speaking only for her ears. "Did you just disengage the safety?"

Wellington shifted slightly in the rifle's scope. *Oh, Brandon, I am so sorry for this...*

In the scope, Wellington stumbled as if something hit him in the chest. Even the sensitive nature of the Starlights caught long rivulets of what she knew to be blood reaching out in all directions.

"Jesus Christ!" an OSM agent yelled out.

The spotter must have seen it too.

A heartbeat later, a single, sharp crack echoed through Eastwood Ridge. Then Bruce's flare lit the darkness.

The LMT safety re-engaged as Brandon relieved Eliza of the weapon. Her finger had remained above and away from the trigger, but that did not change what she had seen along with the spotter. *"Sniper!"* the OSM spotter called out. *"We got a goddamn sniper out there!"*

"Confirmation?" Axelrod demanded as he brought his specs to a wider field-of-view. *"Someone get me confirmation!"*

Agents from both the Ministry and OSM—all of them recognising that noise as she had—scrambled around the train, priming weapons of both short and long range. More calls rose for confirmation, but the sound could only be that of a sniper's rifle. Axelrod did not get far from her as Eliza grabbed the Starlights from his grasp. She blinked water from her eyes as she plunged her vision in the strange æther swirling within the lenses. After a moment of blindness, she could make it all out.

Wellington stumbled back, a black monster creeping from underneath his waistcoat and jacket and consuming the bright white of his shirt. He struggled to catch his breath. From the waist up, he fought to regain his balance. Then his chest exploded a second time, and without a sound he toppled backwards into the night.

A second gunshot echoed in the valley. That was an impossible shot. Even Wellington with his amazing talents could not have made that.

Then again, he didn't. He had been on the receiving end of both of them.

The specs fell and shattered against the bridge as she sprinted to the men now trying to escape to safety.

Over his echoing gunshots, Eliza breaths came short and quick. Edison, his hands still tied before him, attempted his best sprint even though his age and physique would have put such activity long in his past. His adrenaline, however, made Edison a man in his twenties again as he kept a considerable lead on Director Sound and Chief Highfield.

"Agent Braun!" Sound called out as she ran past. *"Agent Braun!"*

Another gunshot, followed by another, each gunshot preceded by the odd whir of a compressor priming to full capacity. Out of the corner of her eye, she saw Bruce aiming his LMT in the direction of Usher. After that everything was a blur of lights and the distant shadows of the Usher train.

A vice grip went around her waist and picked her up off her feet.

"Lizzie!" Bruce was struggling to keep his balance. They both toppled back against the train tracks, and the fob at her waist struck the runners and then slipped between them. She had promised Wellington she would look after that watch of his. "Lizzie, what the bloody hell do you think ya' doin'?"

"Let. Me. *Go!*"

"Lizzie, that would be a bad idea…"

They had only taken one breath, before a commotion came from both sides of the valley, but from the Usher train came a distinct order: *"Blow the bridge!"*

"But Wellington…" Eliza began.

"He's gone! Now move!" and he tugged her back to her feet, pulling her back towards the OSM battle train.

Their shadows stretched before them as underfoot wood trembled and shook. She was trying not to think of Wellington falling, not to think of the bridge around them as the explosives tore at its stability. Her feet slipped, but Bruce pulled her back up. Eliza could not—would not—stop. If she did, she would be dead—and that wouldn't do any good.

The bridge bent underneath them. What was once a flat plane started to rise and twist under them. Not a terrible incline, but the erratic swaying did not put her sense of equilibrium at any ease.

Just a few more steps…

The wood bowed and kicked them forward several feet as the bridge tore itself apart. The distorted train tracks bucked. Bruce landed next to her, but he did not stay still for long as he scrambled to his feet, picked her up, and pulled her back to solid ground. Metal rails bent and disappeared into the darkness before them while far below a dull glow of red and gold surrounded in veils of grey flickered. Piercing through the smoke, though, were the brilliant white lights of Usher's own steam train.

"They're clear!" Highfield called out. "Open fire!"

The massive cannon atop the battle train punched the air with its concussive force, its ordinance a shooting star on a trajectory for Usher. The opposite side of the canyon lit up with a bright yellow-white fire. A few of Usher's ranks fell. The train was chugging backwards, regardless of the impacts all around it. The sides of the transport lit up, and a heartbeat later came the signature report of Gatling guns. Usher had also come prepared for a potential betrayal.

Bruce covered Eliza as bullets kicked dust and dirt around them. A few hit random targets nearby, but miraculously none struck home. Their own train hummed and rumbled just before their cannon fired again.

As before, the opposite cliff exploded, dust, rock, and chunks of bridge flying in all directions, but the Usher train was now operating at full steam. It receded into the darkness, its main centre light growing smaller and smaller by the second. The dimmer its light, the more her anger grew.

"Would someone get these infernal ropes off me?!" someone shouted.

Eliza's gaze turned to see the famed inventor, the reason behind tonight's mission, standing before a small collection of OSM agents. Some agents tended to the wounded, but in that moment all eyes turned on the inventor.

"Mr Edison," Chief Highfield spoke, "On behalf of the Office of the Super—"

"Instead of formalities, son, why don't you take care of this first?" He thrust his hands out to Highfield.

The Chief stood there, licking his lips as he considered the scientist before saying, "Of course." He motioned for an agent to approach. The woman took out a small butterfly knife and expertly produced a blade from its self-parting scabbard.

As the blade worked through the hemp, Edison looked up. "Highfield?"

"Yes sir. Of the Office of the Supernatural and Metaphysical."

"So you are the incompetent agency dedicated to finding me?"

"I wouldn't have used those select words," Highfield said, clearing his throat, "but yes."

The ropes snapped free, and Edison let out a slight grunt as his bonds parted. He began to massage his wrists with his fingers as he continued. "Really? And how would you describe a rescue mission taking you close on three years to fulfil?"

"I understand, Mr Edison, that you have been through a trying time..."

"A trying time?" Edison asked, his eyebrow crooking. "*A trying time?* No, son, it wears not *a trying time*. It was three years of captivity. I was the prisoner of a complete madman. I keep this country the epicentre of innovation. I keep it lit, keep it powered, keep it from slipping back to the Stone Age, and it took you *three years* to find me." Edison stood there for a moment, keeping his eyes locked on Highfield. "Please, tell me more about how this was a trying time for me."

The tense silence had returned. Doctor Sound smoothed out the lapels of his jacket as he stepped between the two gentlemen. "On behalf of both the Office of the Supernatural and Metaphysical and the Ministry of Peculiar Occurrences, we apologise for the anguish you may have encountered."

Edison sighed. "Finally, some respect."

The cold, early morning breeze cut at her cheeks as she sprinted across to the three men. Her punch lifted Edison off his feet. He'd not even finished landing on the ground before she was on top of him, grabbing Edison by the collar with one hand in order to pull him into the punch coming from the other. Perfect strikes, each one. Her knuckles experienced no shock. A light sting, at the most, but each blow she made was effortless. Efficient. Effective.

Eliza did not know how many times she had made contact with the man's face before they pulled her away.

Words failed her. She only heard own breathing; wrecked and ragged. Eliza grew light-headed, and her footing was uncertain. When the world came back into focus, Highfield hunched over Edison. The inventor's right eye was now swollen shut, and the corner of his lip broken and bleeding. From Eliza's quick assessment, he'd lost at least one tooth—possibly two.

"That will do, Miss Braun!" Sound yelled.

No, no, it would not. "A man far better than you, far more brilliant than you, gave his life so you could return to your own creature comforts. You collaborated with Usher, *and Wellington paid for it!* Go on, give me a reason to believe his sacrifice was worth your sorry hide?"

Doctor Sound stepped between her and the downed inventor. "Stand down, Agent Braun."

"Eliza," Henrietta said to her. She was gentle, quiet. "Wellington would not have wanted this."

She spun to face her. "You barely knew him," she spat. *"You barely knew him!"*

Henrietta put her hand on Eliza's shoulder. "Director, if it is all the same to you, I think I should go on and take Agent Braun home. Any additional debriefing you need from me, I can make at Whiterock. My second from the Institute will secure the battle train and oversee its return."

His acknowledgement went almost unheard, but Sound did not question Henrietta's request. It made perfect sense to put as much distance as possible between Eliza and Edison. She still had that urge to punish the inventor for the pain and misery he brought to everyone around him, right up to this moment. He may have been a brilliant man, but that didn't make him a decent one.

Edison sat upright now, spitting blood to one side, while Highfield supported him. The inventor paid them no attention. Eliza was his main preoccupation. "I will see you *ruined*, little lady," he slurred. "I have connections. In my government. In your country's government. I will have your guts for garters."

"With all due respect, Mr Edison," Chief Highfield began, "I can with a word and a stroke of a pen turn this rescue into an apprehension."

Edison stiffened. "Come again?"

"Agent Braun here is correct. Before you were kidnapped by the Maestro and then subsequently by Dr Jekyll, you were in league with the House of Usher."

"I... I was never in *league* with Usher!" Edison stammered.

"Fine then, they contracted you to produce a weapon of incredible power. I'm sure, being the educated man that you are, you did not think what such a weapon would be used for. Excavation? Rock carving? Perhaps sculpt a few presidents into the side of a mountain face?"

"Don't be so ridiculous!"

Highfield stood up, back to his full height. He gave a quick whistle, and two OSM agents pulled themselves off the battle train. "In the time it takes these men to get here, you will reach a decision about what kind of mission this is. If you intend to press charges against Agent Braun here, then I will arrest you."

"Under what charge?"

"Oh, now let me think," he said, scratching at the white and black stubble set against his dark skin. "We have those ships, both aerial and nautical, presumed lost at sea, but which actually fell victim to that death ray of yours." Edison went to respond, but Highfield silenced him by lifting his index finger before him. "Tesla's design, but your craftsmanship. Perhaps in the future, before you start building weapons for nefarious societies, you should reconsider branding it with your company's name.

"Then there is the matter of San Francisco, a major city that nearly sank into the Pacific Ocean. The earthquake triggered by your death ray killed hundreds, injured thousands, and crippled for many months one of America's most important ports."

Doctor Sound cleared his throat. "If I may, Luther?"

"Please, Basil," he replied with a smile.

"There is also the matter of His Royal Highness, Prince Edward. Missing, presumed dead, after a calamity that you had a hand in. Mr Edison, our government and our court system would love to have a talk with you about what happened that day."

Highfield nodded towards his agents now only a few steps away. "Now you may be able to hire the best legal team to help you avoid any potential gaol time, but I have to wonder: how they will protect your reputation? People will hear what happened in North Carolina, in California, and in the AT. Are you sure your business is impregnable to the fallout?"

"This is blackmail," Edison grumbled.

"No, this was the bed you made for yourself when you agreed to the House of Usher's charge to build Tesla's Death Ray. And this morning, you learn a valuable lesson in business."

"And what lesson would that be?"

"The value of saying 'No' when ethics dictate."

Eliza smiled ever so slightly. Not that she was particularly happy, but this little slice of justice was most satisfying.

The two summoned agents stopped before the three men. Edison looked at the OSM operatives, then to Highfield. His mouth opened, but on consideration he remained quiet, hanging his head.

"Mr Edison is in quite a state. Apparently, those bastards tortured him," Highfield said as he motioned to Edison. One of the agents whispered *"Damn..."* on looking at the inventor. "Isn't that right, Mr Edison?"

His one good eye glared at Eliza for a moment, then he swallowed, spat, and slurred, "As you can see for yourselves, Usher was less than hospitable. If you would see me to a physician, I will gladly give you... fine agents of the United States intelligence community... a full account of what happened under the hands of Usher and that madman, Henry Jekyll."

Highfield gave a slow nod to Edison, then turned back to the two agents. "West, Gordon, you follow?"

"Crystal clear, sir," the shorter one replied.

"Right then. Dismissed." The agents lifted Edison to his feet and guided him further down the train. Highfield focused his gaze on Eliza, then said, "Basil, a moment of your time?"

"Of course, Luther," he replied.

The two directors walked into the darkness. At one time, Eliza would have been worried what they were talking about, and if it involved her.

Right now, she did not give a toss.

"Come on, Eliza," Henrietta spoke from beside her. "We'll take one of the ornithopters to the aeroport."

The operation continued shutting down around her. Agents were either assisting those wounded in Usher's escape, or tending to the few fatally struck by ordinance. Field operatives collapsed equipment and hustled to the cars trailing behind the battle engine. As it was with the Ministry, there would be no evidence come sunrise that OSM or any clandestine organisation had been there. There would be just the track, the desert, Eastwood Ridge, and the remains of a bridge, perhaps taken out in an act of dissonance concerning the AT.

But that was not entirely true.

Turning back, she saw the flickering glow of the bridge's remains struggling to stand in the darkness. Somewhere in that burning rubble of metal and wood was Wellington Thornhill Books. Usher didn't have him, but neither did she. She had not come to his rescue. She would take this regret to the grave.

When she finally let Henrietta guide her away, she also gave herself permission to cry.

CHAPTER THIRTY-ONE

A Letter from a Falcon

Dearest Eliza,
 With a heavy heart I write to you now, as a colleague in the field of espionage operations—something I never thought of doing—and, I hope, as a friend. As you said those many weeks ago, I knew Wellington Thornhill Books for only a short time. However, in that brief span, I quickly grew to understand how and why you feel so deeply and so strongly for him. There are few men in the world that possess his calibre and quality, and I cannot stress enough how important it is for you to hold onto that. His was a life that rarely comes along, and what you can find comfort in—at least I hope you can—is that you were not only fortunate to be a part of that life, but that you were his world. A blind man could have seen the depth of his love just in how he looked at you.

 While I consider myself most fortunate to have been in the world at the same time as Wellington Thornhill Books, I must confess to a touch of envy that he never looked at me way he looked at you. I struggle to think of any man that has ever done so. What a beautiful and rare gift to give someone, and more fortunate still for a woman such as you to receive it.

 My previous correspondences have gone unanswered, and I understand completely. Do know that in this personal darkness you are enduring, your friends are with you. They can serve as guiding stars, the points of light we all must work and struggle to reach during these times, and I sincerely hope that you consider me as such. I wish I could do something for you, but even if I had the wherewithal, the resources, and the omnipotent knowledge of the universe itself, I would step back in time to somehow prevent all this from happening. Of course, aside from the works of HG Wells, I know as a scientist that such innovations and marvels are pure fantasy. Such limitations of nature break my heart, but not as much as the loss I know you are feeling now.

I have, once again, enclosed my card with this correspondence. Please, at any time, wherever you are in the world, if you need a friend or if you need me as a faithful servant, do not hesitate to contact me. Perhaps you consider us strangers still, or perhaps you look at me just as a comrade from the field. Whatever the case, I am at your service. Now, and always.

Your humble friend and confidant,
Professor Henrietta Falcon

CHAPTER THIRTY-TWO

In Which a Case Closes

Eliza endured an onslaught of stares from the other passengers on the hypersteam she took from London to Leeds. The derision and condemnation from the surrounding poms served as motivation—despite her ennui—to upgrade her Hebden Bridge ticket from Second to First Class. Once she had a private cabin all to herself, she could be glum and moody without judgement.

She acknowledged her travelling dress was far from presentable. However, looking shabby was a conscious choice. It was not as if there were foreign dignitaries about or even the Queen herself. She was instructed to report to Whiterock. Not requested. Ordered. Doctor Sound had issued Bereavement Leave for an indefinite time. *"I will call on you when needed,"* he had said to her.

Eliza turned the æthermissive in her hands, delivered via courier and carrying the official seal of Her Majesty's government. All very formal. That being said, Sound had no control over what fashion she chose.

No one had seen Eliza at the Ministry for two months. After Eastwood Ridge, they instructed agents to give her a wide berth, issued before she and Agent Campbell had touched down in Boston. Henrietta was the only one ignoring this order. Perhaps she was not a full agent, but after her contributions to the Ministry, she was brought on as a consultant. Despite the express order of the Director, Henrietta wrote to her weekly. A true friend. It tore Eliza apart not to respond to her faithful correspondence.

She will understand eventually, Eliza assured herself.

While waiting for her connection to Hebden Bridge, Eliza had read the orders again. She would report to Whiterock for reassignment. They would assess her time in the Archives and consider her reinstatement. If she passed muster, she would be placed back into the roster. She had options. Quite a few of them, from the sound of the Director's æthermissive.

If only she cared at all about that.

Her contact picked her up from the train station. He was a young man, a stranger, so they did not share a word. She strode into Whiterock with her face a mask, and her eyes full of disinterest. None of her fellow agents greeted her or asked how she fared, and that suited her just fine. Cassandra Shillingworth's shocked expression told her how much she'd changed—and not just in her choice of fashion. With a final deep breath, Eliza tucked the æthermissive into her modest handbag and entered the Director's office.

Sound was bent over that blasted chrono-model—the source of all her pain, grief and isolation. According to the Old Man, it should now tick away merrily, showing progress towards a repaired past, present, and future. He was sure—no, *convinced*—once Wellington agreed to his plan, the device would work properly again. Even if Sound had tried so many times before and failed, this time would fix everything.

Yet, the device remained locked. The timeline still raced towards that blackout Sound had described with such urgency.

Not waiting on ceremony or invitation, Eliza crossed the office to the small table holding a collection of decanters. She didn't care what kind of whiskey it was. Eliza just wanted a drink.

"Please," Sound spoke from behind her, "help yourself."

"Think I shall," Eliza said, pouring a healthy amount of scotch.

"Although I would question your judgement in having a drink so early in the day."

Her own image reflected back at her in the window overlooking the grounds. The hollow gaze she wore enhanced her pale, sallow complexion. She looked like a ghost of her former self. After a long, slow drink from her trembling glass, she turned to Sound, who gave the slightest of flinches. She wished she could believe his concern. Maybe in this current timeline, she mattered in some universe-expanding way, and now he cared for her well-being.

"Do we really want to discuss questionable judgement?" she asked pointedly.

His concern melted away. "Do have a seat before you collapse, Agent Braun."

With a slight toast of her glass, Eliza took one of the available chairs before the grand desk. She dared not glance at the other empty one beside her. Taking another long slurp from her glass, she watched as Doctor Sound opened the dossier in front of him and reviewed its contents.

"Agent Wellington Thornhill Books, accepted the terms of the prisoner exchange between the Office of the Supernatural and Metaphysical and the House of Usher. However he plummeted to his death after receiving two gunshots to the chest, confirmed by spotters watching from the OSM side of the bridge. Explosive charges were then triggered, bringing down the bridge, but not before myself, Director Luther Highfield, and accompanying Ministry and OSM agents had successfully returned Thomas Edison to safety. There were four deaths, ten wounded." His eyes looked up to Eliza for a brief moment, and then he read, "The injuries to Thomas Edison, while alarming at first sight, were thankfully not life-threatening. He will recover from his apparent torture while in Usher captivity."

"And the world rejoices," Eliza muttered.

"On account of the damage wrought from the demolition of the bridge, neither the Ministry nor OSM operatives were able to recover the body of Agent Books. We are maintaining contact with OSM operatives in the Arizona Territories in the hopes of returning his remains to Whiterock."

"He hated this place. He wouldn't want to rest eternal here."

Sound closed the file and slid it to one side. "I read that aloud not to torture you, but so that you could hear it for yourself. There would be no wild rumour or conjecture. Agent Books, despite our best efforts, is gone."

"Thank you for the clarification, sir. Upon reflection, I should thank him for his graciousness in saving my career after my..." She gave a little chuckle. "... hysterical outburst." Even with the application of scotch, the tremble in her hand wouldn't stop. "I take it Edison received a full pardon for his involvement with the crimes against his own government and ours?"

"Considering his contributions to society, the Americans reach a compromise..."

Her gaze locked with Sound's. "Edison's building the military death rays, isn't he?"

"That part is classified, Agent Braun. Chief Highfield only offered details to me on Edison's fate on a need-to-know business."

"So, that's it, is it? Wellington offers himself as a sacrificial lamb for a man who betrayed his own country for his bank account, and what do we have to show for this effort? Wellington is dead, Edison pardoned, and your bloody device is no longer operating." Eliza barked out a dry laugh as she shook her head. "Well done."

"It should work," Sound insisted, returning his attention to the Timeline Tracker across the room. "This was the only option I had not explored, for obvious reasons."

"What a compassionate manipulator you are," Eliza said with a roll of her eyes.

When his fist struck the desk, she gave a start. Sound's pudgy face was beet red. If he had been smoking a cigar, he would have chomped through it. "This is not something I take lightly, Miss Braun. I—*was*—certain." He slumped back into his chair, the redness in his skin fading away.

Shaking her head, Eliza pulled herself upright. The world pitched to one side for a moment. *Perhaps I should take this next round a bit slower.* She returned to the decanter to refill her tumbler while pouring three fingers' worth for Doctor Sound.

Don't say it, she chided herself. *Don't say it.* "Director, you did everything you could." *You really are an idiot, Eliza D. Braun,* she thought. "In a bizarre way—and considering what we do, that is saying something—I understand your frustration."

"Oh, Agent Braun, I do hope not. The last time I struggled like this, I was trying to retrieve all twenty of the Staff to the safety of Event Control."

Eliza furrowed her brow as she offered him a glass. "Twenty? But I only saw ten."

"There *were* twenty." He gave a slight scowl as he grumbled, "Bloody Morlocks."

He took the glass from her grasp and toasted to her as she returned to her seat.

"Time travel, I thought, would be like your fanciful stories. Go back in time, point King Arthur in the direction of the sword in the stone. Travel to the future. Watch a woman become Prime Minister of New Zealand. It's far more complicated, isn't it?"

"That it is."

"So we learn. We move forward."

"Yes..." The glass paused, and his eyes glimmered. "Unless..."

A chill crept under her skin. "Doctor Sound?"

"It dawns on me," he said, a slight grin coming to his lips, "that I've been returning to the time when Wellington was first recruited for the Ministry, and I've been popping throughout the timeline just to make sure the progress was identical. His performance in the Archives. His abduction. Meeting you..."

"You were there? In Antarctica?"

"From a distance, yes." Sound chortled. "It is quite astonishing how Time adjusts when altered. Things remain the same, but end up entirely different. What I am conjecturing, is that I chose the wrong subject. Perhaps, instead of focusing on the arrival of Wellington Books, I should focus on you?"

Eliza's chill instantly became a fire. "Really? Do tell."

"As I said before, you both are the constants, and all this time, I focused on Wellington. I think, when I go back, I should spend more time focused on you. Perhaps it is a past case or an encounter with someone that is causing us to come to this—"

"An immovable point," Eliza said, on his behalf.

Sound smiled, took a deep drink of his scotch, and nodded, reaching into his coat pocket for a small journal of some description. A diary, perhaps? "Yes, exactly."

"And you are telling me all this because…?"

He waved a hand in the air as if he were shooing away a bothersome insect. "You won't exist. This *present* you, I mean. All this? Gone. Once I go back, the events and their outcome of this timeline will dissipate into the æther. None of this will have happened, you see? A new timeline will emer—"

"You. Utter. Creep."

The Director looked up from his journal, his newfound elation faltering. "I… I'm sorry?"

"Do you hear yourself? *When you go back?* Do you want Wellington to relive his optimism of meeting someone special only to discover she was an assassin? Do you want me to relive the grief when I lost Harry? Do you want me to go through the loss that I am feeling now? *Again?*"

"Oh for God's Sake, Miss Braun, this is time travel I talk of. You won't experience these emotions again. When I travel into the past, events and outcomes get altered. This current existence will have never happened."

"How do you know for certain? Are you sure that your meddling does not carry some far-reaching effect? You don't. You think that if you can give the fabric of reality just a few more cross stitches, everything will be perfect.

"But what if it isn't, Mr. H G 'I got me a bloody time machine' Wells? What if you find that it isn't Wellington joining the Ministry? Or that it isn't my own recruitment? What then? Go back to when he was born? Or perhaps when I was? Remove us from the equation completely? What then? Oh, but did you consider between serialising stories and running operations for secret agents, that if there were no Wellington Thornhill

Books or Agent Braun, there would be no one to stop the Phoenix Society? Then while the Ministry would deal with the infiltration of those wankers, San Francisco would slip into the sea carrying Prince Edward with it. And with OSM engaged, no one would know that the right hand of Her Majesty was in fact under the microscope of a madman, crafting a Diamond Jubilee that would result the death of millions." Another wave of nausea swept over her. She was drinking too fast. After a moment, she returned her gaze to the man calling himself Doctor Sound. This time for whatever queer reason—possibly on account of the drink—she needed to use his real identity. "Where and when does your playing God end, Mr Wells?"

Polishing off his own drink, Sound leaned forward in his chair and steepled his fingers before him. "Such is the science behind what I do. It never ends. It is infinite, and I am charged to fix whatever this blackout is."

"By whom? Not by me. Certainly not by God either."

"Perhaps under the influence of drink is not the right time to debate about the existence of God." He took in a deep breath. "Perhaps you do not grasp what I am doing here, but I must try again."

Eliza nodded, rising from her chair. "If, in fact, you are going off to tamper with me in the past, then I intend to take myself home and drink until I pass out. Do give me until tomorrow before going back to 1892 and fucking up my life if you please."

"Miss Braun, consider this: if I am right, and according to all imperial data I do believe I am, I will put an end to your current suffering." He extended a hand to her. "You must trust me."

"Did that already." Eliza took his hand firmly and shook it once. "My turn to play God."

Her other hand slapped around his wrist. Hard. Hard enough to make the director wince. When he looked down at Eliza's hand tightening around his, his gaze returned to hers. She saw it in his face. He was on to her.

Sound tried to wrench himself free, but Eliza kept her firm grip. He was a big man, and she was afraid the drug wouldn't take hold quick enough. The director attempted to rise from his chair, but he only made it a few inches before he slumped back into it. Maybe the three fingers' worth of scotch was helping matters along, or perhaps her tranquilizer had proven more effective than she could have asked for. He slurred out Shillingsworth's name, but the mumble would be barely noticeable through the door. He then started to lean back, lifting Eliza up and dragging her across the desk.

"Stop-stop-stop-stop!" she pleaded as she continued to slip forward, her knees threatening to reach the desk's edge.

The chair let out a sudden *twang*, and Doctor Sound stopped moving back. There was a good chance from the sound of that spring that she'd ruined his fine chair. Eliza looked down and with some relief found the chair had wheels.

"Thank you, Lord," she whispered in a quick prayer. Her eyes went to the door leading to Event Control. "That will make this next part much easier."

CHAPTER THIRTY-THREE

In Which Our Colonial Pepperpot Gets in the Last Word

Her fingers pressed into the Old Man's flesh again. His pulse was steady. A metallic bitterness welled in her mouth. If she had punched him hard in his nose, as she had wanted to, she would have earned the same result, and the bruise on his face would have been delightfully satisfactory. However, Eliza had to be sensible; that would compel him to explain to associates at Whiterock what had happened. He did possess the skills to spin some sort of yarn about walking into a door or something even more fanciful. He was HG Wells, after all, and exceedingly good at creating fantastic stories. The bumbling awkwardness he put on for people would also make whatever story to explain his broken nose all the more believable. He possessed an eccentric charm—but such as they were they no longer had a hold on her.

Eliza regretted making the promise not to harm him, especially considering his orders and the months that followed; long months of isolation, plans within plans, and copious amounts of drinking. Even for Eliza, mourning had proven a test of her stamina.

Looking down at the mug of coffee in her hands, she rolled it back and forth while considering her circumstances. This could go either way, but she had to see it to the end—but would it be worth it? Would he honour her demands, or would he attempt to undo everything?

Sobriety was working its way over her, but Eliza did not care for coffee. Unlike tea it made her jittery.

A groan. Barely audible, but there it was. His jowls trembled and his lips smacked against one another. He was thirsty. That was a side-effect of the tranquilizer.

Setting down the near-empty mug of coffee she poured him a glass of fresh water. Sound's eyes fluttered before flicking open. He let out a long, quiet breath, looked around, until his gaze rested on her. Even with the offered drink in her hand, his expression did not soften.

"You're not going to be able to reprimand me as your throat is probably dryer than an Outback desert in the summer." Eliza offered him the water once again. "Drink up, Old Man."

The skin around Sound's eyes tightened at the casual sentiment, his gaze never breaking as he took the offered drink. He took a few slurps, trying to steady the glass with each gulp.

When he drank it all, he pulled himself up from the chair, gripping the glass.

"Would you like more water?"

From the deep breath he took, Sound threatened to suck in all the air from Event Control. When he finally exhaled, his eyes aflame, he answered, "I believe you have done quite enough for one day, Miss Braun." Hearing the croak of his own voice, he held out the empty glass to her.

Eliza took it and went to the end of the terminal's long desk. The pitcher, left by one of the many polished silver automatons that occupied this place, was still cool to the touch. Was this awkward silence supposed to be where she apologised? Or was it supposed to be now as she poured? Once the water line reached close to the rim, Eliza set down the pitcher back on the desk, then walked over to Sound.

"I used enough of the sleeping potion to take down a wild boar or three," she said, placing the glass into his waiting hand. "You might be a bit groggy."

"So kind of you to care," Sound bit in reply just before taking a few more generous gulps of water.

"If I truly didn't, you wouldn't be here right now, in this place." Eliza motioned behind Sound. "With that."

Sound followed her gesture and gasped at the sight of his clockwork chrono-model. It remained frozen, just as it had been before the exchange. Not a single gear, cog, or strut had moved since the man she loved had toppled into the darkness. Even whilst the Old Man slumbered in his chair, the tracker remained silent and still.

"Are you trying to drive home a point?" he asked, getting to his feet and walking over to the time-tracking device.

"I'm trying to hold your attention."

Sound braced his rotund frame against the edge of the table, and his head sank lower, almost disappearing from view over his hunched shoulders. "As I told you in my office, I did everything I could. I returned again and again to this crossroad—to this *one point*—and according to my calculations and deductions, the chrono-model should be moving. Wellington's death should have repaired the blackout. I can't say why it didn't."

"Yes, it is quite a mystery," the voice spoke from behind Eliza. Emerging from the far end of Event Control's curved desk and the long bank of monitors was Sound's key in repairing his timeline and avoiding the blackout he had warned them all was coming. Wellington Thornhill Books stopped next to Eliza. "Perhaps we should consider another option then?"

Eliza smiled at the pure shock on Sound's face. "I saw you fall to your death," he choked out.

"Correction, you did see me fall—but not to my death."

"Good God!" he squawked, his face going a peculiar shade of puce.

"Not quite, Mr Wells," Wellington returned. "Nor divine intervention. More like advancements in quantum engineering."

The Director appeared convinced he was talking to a ghost, but on hearing those words, he deduced, "Professor Falcon?"

"After I resigned myself to my fate, Eliza did what she does best—she rescued me just like she did in Antarctica the first time." Raising her hand up he pressed his warm lips to her knuckles. A tremor of desire ran through her even as he continued. "Professor Falcon got hold of my measurements and created for me the last suit I would ever wear," he said, gesturing to the fine fashion he still had on. "I must admit, it is quite remarkable.

"This rescue suit is being designed for Navy officers and sailors in combat situations. Sewn into the waistcoat is a series of—now what did Henrietta call those again?—pressure-relief systems. On detecting a dramatic change in 'personal velocity' the suit inflates and then cocoons its occupant, protecting them from impact with the water." He cleared his throat and added, "Granted, these rescue suits hadn't been tested at such a height, but I chose to take that risk in light of the alternative."

"You. Were. Shot. *Twice.*" Sound insisted. "I saw the footage recorded from Axelrod's Starlight Goggles. Your chest exploded."

Eliza shrugged. "That was a bit of theatrics built into the suit. Falcon's own touch. She is quite the patron of the arts, it would seem."

Sound shook his head. "No, even with Starlights, no man could make that shot. In the dark. At that distance."

"You are so right, Doctor Sound," she agreed. "So I had my South Pacific big brother call in someone that could do it."

The director stared at her for a moment, and then his jaw dropped. "Ryfka Górski."

"Bruce and I came to an arrangement. Wellington took a dose of Axelrod and Blackwell's tracking isotope, which gave Ryfka a bright target."

Sound turned back to Wellington. "He slapped you in the chest. Hard."

"Ryfka would not miss." Wellington waggled his eyebrows. "I was quite relieved about that, I can assure you."

Eliza had often been on the receiving end of Sound's ire, but this time it was Wellington who received the Director's disdain. "Books, I am shocked. Shocked, I say! That you would do something so reckless!"

"Really?" Wellington asked, his eyebrow arching. "This coming from the man who has been, by his own admission, attempting to single-handedly manipulate time."

"*Repair* a timeline."

"A matter of perspective, Herbert," Wellington said with a shrug, dismissing him with a wave of his hand. "The rebel rising against an empire does not consider themselves a terrorist, now do they?"

Eliza smiled. This rather brash attitude suited him.

"You haven't even the foggiest of what you are doing by staging such a charade. With this ridiculous ballyhoo of yours, I have lost complete control of this timeline. Either the paradox cannot correct itself or we have locked the past, present, and future into a fate that we cannot avoid."

"Oh dear," Wellington said, with not a hint of concern, "whatever shall we do?"

Sound took a step back. This was not what he and Eliza had rehearsed. Even this sounded callous coming from him. Or perhaps, like herself, he had reached his fill of the Ministry Director and Renaissance man.

"Your irresponsibility, your lack of trust, and your selfishness may have doomed us all!" Sound raged. He pointed to the chrono-model, but his gaze remained locked with Wellington's. "Because of you, we may still have Operation: Ragnarök to contend with. Countless lives and cultures lost."

"It pains me to think that I have thrown a rather nasty spanner into your grand plan, but as they say—*tempus fugit.*"

"You are willing to toss the world into an apocalypse, all on account of your self-preservation?" Sound's arm lowered back to his side. He looked the archivist from the soles of his shoes to the top of his head. "Anything else clever to say for yourself, Wellington Thornhill Books, Esquire?"

"Actually, Doctor Sound... Herbert... whatever moniker you answer to... I do have one more thing to say." Wellington straightened up, tugging his waistcoat as he did so. "I quit."

Eliza jumped as a wild *clickity-clackity-tick-tick-tick* shattered the tension between archivist and director. The chrono-model had not only come back to life, it was angrily pinging and dinging as gears spun far faster than she had ever seen before. Its syncopated beats suggested it was determined to calculate whatever it had failed to do when it had been silent.

"What the—" Sound's eyes darted from one end of the device to another. Fumbling for something inside his coat, he produced his small journal. His eyes narrowed on several of the machinations as he flipped frantically through pages in the tiny book. His gaze jumped from notebook to the device. "No-no-no, this is not how it is supposed to work. I don't understand."

"Herbert, if you please," Wellington said, placing a hand on his own chest. "You claim that Eliza and I are at the root of this mysterious discrepancy in the timeline. Yet in all your attempts to repair whatever went wrong, you never did ask me what *I* wanted.

"While I remained detained here, I had time to reflect and study. The Staff here have been incredibly accommodating. I brushed up on some poetry, and there is a particular verse from Henley that struck me. Seems quite appropriate at present:

> *It matters not how strait the gate,*
> *How charged with punishments the scroll,*
> *I am the master of my fate:*
> *I am the captain of my soul.*

"I want out of this spy life. I want to live out my days far from you, from the unexplained, and from the Ministry of Peculiar Occurrences." Wellington took a place next to Eliza, looking at her with a love that thrilled her to the core. He took her hand, turned back to Sound, and smiled. "I want out."

"As do I," Eliza stated, surprised still that those words were in her mouth. "While I had planned on something more colourful in the ways of a resignation, Welly here convinced me to take a higher road."

"Just like that?" asked Sound. "You resign and move along with a life free of espionage and investigation?"

"Well," Eliza began, "not just like that. We will need new identities, case records sealed—"

"And archived properly," Wellington added.

"Of course, darling. Then, once our previous identities and exploits are catalogued and classified, we go home."

Sound's eyebrows raised. "Home? Which would be...?"

Eliza pinched the bridge of her nose and let out a long, slow breath. "Are we certain this is the same man who will write astounding classics of literature?"

"That is what Event Control claims, but that does not necessarily mean he is particularly quick."

"Evidently."

Doctor Sound's deepening blush receded as he realised what *home* meant to Eliza. "You *cannot* be serious."

"Quite, I know travel arrangements will be somewhat costly, but I have no doubt you can make certain our accommodations are the finest that White Star can provide. In fact, I am counting on it."

"Agent Braun, may I remind you, that the conditions of your expulsion from New Zealand were quite clear."

"Very clear. However, you are a persuasive sort. I'm sure you can resolve this delicate matter with great aplomb."

Sound opened his mouth, but no words came out. Not straight away. It was so strange to see her director at such a loss. Usually it was her that struggled with returns and retorts against him.

He found his voice. "Exactly how do you expect me to have your banishment lifted?"

Eliza gave Wellington's hand a light squeeze before approaching Sound. She extended her arms wide as she said, "You, Herbert George Wells, are standing in the middle of an incredible device that can take you anywhere in time and space." She rested her hands on her hips. "I am sure you can find some kind of *leverage* against Prime Minister Seddon. You know the kind I mean."

The worn notebook closed with a soft *snap* before disappearing back into his coat pocket. Sound glanced at Wellington before stepping away from Eliza and strolling over to the main interface of Event Control. The strange screens surrounding where he would sit and enter in destinations of the past and the future glowed against the stark white, featureless furniture surrounding them. Her nose crinkled a bit. *If this is the look of the future, I will stay here in the 19th century, thank you very much.*

Doctor Sound adjusted his cravat. "So because my chrono-model is working you expect me to go along with your plan?"

"That," Wellington said, "and the contingency plan in case something were to go... awry."

"Contingency plan?"

Eliza and Wellington shared a quick look. She nodded, and Wellington continued. "As Eliza pointed out, you have access to science and resources well beyond our comprehension, but you are only human. Complete with all the frailties that come with it. Your propensity for being manipulative, for instance. So, to make certain you did not do anything daring to undo our plan, I have been working with your Event Control automatons to understand how your Archives work here."

"You've been... *working*... with the Staff?" Sound stammered.

"As I said before, the Staff here have been incredibly accommodating." Wellington paused, then held up a single finger, "You are wondering how I got so close with your Staff here. Well, when we realised I would need a safe, secure place to lie low after my death, where better than here, between time and space itself?" He walked over to the balcony overlooking the rows of humming black cubes underneath them. "You see, I regarded your Event Control as an advanced archival system, but it is much more, isn't it? This is a very intricate, powerful communications device, all powered by your incredible time machine. After all, you were keeping constant connections with it from the airlock you established in the London Office. As I was here for some time, I turned to the only companions offered, and what a helpful lot they were." He turned back to Sound and Eliza, and Eliza had to stifle a laugh at the wicked smile Wellington wore. "With the Staff's assistance, I created what they refer to as a sub-routine. Any significant manipulation of our current timeline will trigger Event Control to notify the outside world of its existence."

"Notify the outside world?" the director asked. "How?"

Eliza stepped forward now. "Æthermissives, postal service, telephone calls, wireless—every conceivable device of communication short of smoke signals and semaphore, but I wouldn't rule those out either." She motioned to Wellington, adding, "That was something Welly discovered about this grand time machine of yours. To monitor the timeline and then send a signal to your chrono-model meant it connected to every form of communication through—now what was it called? *Data streams,* I think."

"The only problem with such a network, Doctor Sound," said Wellington, "is that these streams have to send as well as receive. You didn't just construct a receiver. You constructed a transmitter as well."

They stood there for a moment, the three of them, in a wide triangle. Only the low drone of Wells time machine and its Archives echoed around them.

Hooking his thumbs in his waistcoat, Sound locked his eyes with Wellington's. "You don't trust me, do you, Books?"

"Not for a bloody moment," he stated. "Eliza, on the other hand…"

She motioned around them to Event Control. "Wellington wanted to destroy this fabulous creation of yours. He believed one man wielding such a device was too dangerous. I convinced him that you should keep watch over Event Control, and over the timeline."

Sound's eyes narrowed. "Why?"

"I may not fully grasp the concepts of science such as this, but there is one thing I do know far better than you: spy craft. Secrets never stay secret."

The Director nodded. Amazing that, even at this point, they agreed on something.

"New identities. Sealed records. And we disappear," she stated.

"You are the last person I would expect to settle down for a quiet life," the old man scoffed.

"I might surprise even myself, Doctor Sound, but whether I decide to become a gun for hire or a mother of four that tends on husband and home, it really doesn't matter to you. Welly and I are, as of this moment, ghosts in the Ministry's history."

"Give me some time to make arrangements?"

Eliza slipped from inside her sash a beautiful gold pocket watch. In the corner of her eye, she caught a glint. Wellington was mirroring her, producing a fine silver pocket watch she had given him. "Do you have the time, love?"

"Back at Whiterock, it should be five minutes past the hour of five," he replied.

"Good, I show the same." Eliza slipped the fob back into her sash, "You have twenty-four hours."

Sound gasped. "Twenty-fo—"

"You've launched full operations in half that time. Some of them with me." A single nod from Wellington, and she continued. "Twenty-four hours. Not one tick more."

Shoulders dropping ever so slightly, Sound removed his spectacles and rubbed his forehead. "I suppose you have me at a complete and utter loss." He took in a long, low breath, and muttered, "Yes. Quite."

Doctor Sound leaned on his elbows, turning back to the viaduct leading to his office at Whiterock.

"Mother of four?" Wellington asked, his voice nested in its higher register.

Eliza shrugged. "Depends on what we get up to back home, now doesn't it?"

CHAPTER THIRTY-FOUR

In Which the House of Usher Looks to the Future

Wellington Thornhill Books—the product of Project Achilles—was dead, his corpse buried under the scorched remains of a bridge in the Arizona Territories.

The Ministry of Peculiar Occurrences and the local authorities had shut down the Italian workings of Operation Ragnarök.

Filippo Rossi, codename Mr Badger, had disappeared. His accounts, his dwellings in Rome, any trace of him was gone. It was as if the man had never existed.

Despite all this, Henry Howard Holmes had never been better. Today was a fresh day, and the new possibilities ahead appeared oh-so-promising.

"Well, Chairman…" Mr Tiger's tone did not sit well with Holmes. "Where to begin?"

Holmes glanced at the cuffs of his shirt, just visible under the sleeves of his jacket. He gave each of them a tug. He would not be hurried or rushed. He was the embodiment of control.

"Mr Tiger, you sound rankled by recent events." Holmes cast a glance over to Mr Fox. Under the dim light of the boardroom the poor sod looked positively ghostly. In fact, a sheen gleamed across the man's forehead. He really was a worrier. "Yes, it would be naïve of me to believe that we are not suffering from recent… misadventures."

"Misadventures?" asked Miss Bear. The diminutive Russian had been one of his most staunch supporters, especially when Holmes had defended her ability to recover so quickly from bad luck in Warsaw. Once she assumed control and restored lost resources, operations in her sector now flourished far more than they had under her predecessor. "The Ministry of Peculiar Occurrences thwarted us once again, Chairman. We have resources. We have advancements. We have upper-hand. They remain completely unaware of Ragnarök... "

"As do most of us," Mr Wolf said with a barely suppressed huff.

Miss Bear shot the American a look. She did not care for interruptions. Holmes found that trait endearing.

"This is not 'misadventure' as you say, Chairman," she stated, jabbing her finger into the table. "This? *Disaster!*"

So she was turning on him? Duly noted.

"The concern you show, regardless of motivation," Holmes began, nodding to Jeremy, "is touching. Truly, it is. And I find it refreshing that there now appears to be a camaraderie between Board Members that was notably absent before my promotion to Chairman."

"Promotion?" asked Mr Tiger. "Is that what you are calling it now? I thought what you did was more of a coup."

Holmes shrugged. "A matter of perspective." His gaze drifted over to Mr Cobra, Nahush Kari, and his cousin Makeala, known as Sister Raven. His smile was almost imperceptible, but it was there. Always there—just like his cousin. It was a strange relationship they fostered, her hand always on his shoulder, and his fingers absently tracing her fingertips. Some protested to him in private Sister Raven's presence in this higher circle within the House of Usher, but Nahush insisted. He would not leave her out of anything, like she was his good luck charm—or something else...

His own operations in India were still progressing, even as the unrest grew exponentially there; so Holmes allowed him the indulgence. Makeala would never speak, but she would whisper into his ear. Especially when Holmes addressed Nahush. Cobra was the sort of Board Member who knew more about what was truly happening between his fellow brothers and sisters, what people were planning, and who held the upper-hand. Together, he and Kari had pulled off a successful operation. Did that make him an ally? Holmes could not be sure. He could only be certain the relationship between him and his cousin was most off-centred and unsettling.

Not that any of Holmes' concerns mattered. The dissatisfied voices of the Board were not in the wrong. They should be upset, disappointed at the very least, that they had suffered this setback in Italy. What they didn't realise, and he could not fault them for their ignorance, was that this setback did nothing to impede their progress.

"I can see how you all regard our recent *misadventures*..." Holmes said again, locking eyes with Miss Bear. She was the only one who did not flinch or cower at his look. Most impressive. "... as a catastrophe of epic proportions: the loss of our breeding farm, coupled with the botched exchange at Eastwood Ridge. You must admit, though, that it shows the opposition's desperation."

"This all sounds quite wide-eyed and optimistic, and yet," Wolf grumbled, "here we are."

"You have something to add?" Holmes asked.

"You were utterly convinced by Fox here that Project Achilles would be a good fit for Ragnarök. Once again, we invested resources into finding and apprehending this archivist, Wellington Books. Once again, what do we have to show for the effort?" Wolf glanced at Scorpion and Cobra, both of whom sided with him. "Then we see the destruction of our Italian operations with Badger in the æther. With what he knows, he could turn evidence over to the Ministry and nothing would stop them in bringing the House of Usher to ruin. If I recall, you were taking Usher into a new age, where Accountability would be at its foundation, yes?"

Holmes smiled. Wolf didn't falter. The control panel activating this room's many security measures was not even an inch away from his fingertips, and Wolf openly challenged him? Incredible. "Now there's that spine you had lost for some time. You are, however, missing the lessons we have learned from all this."

Wolf chuckled, glancing to his two allies who offered wry smiles of their own. "Lessons? From this complete and utter failure?"

"If you all would indulge me?" Holmes shook his head as he rose from his chair. "Project Achilles, as Mr Fox here informed me, appeared to be an excellent fit with Ragnarök, and had we successfully obtained Mr Books, we could have added it as a new component to the operation. Alas, we did not. Has Ragnarök shut down on account of this?" He then motioned to Miss Bear and Mr Tiger. "Hardly. We are still on schedule and still progressing forward.

"And concerning the Ministry of Peculiar Occurrences, specifically Books' associate, Eliza Braun. Both agents have served as a thorn in our side. The death of Books has, apparently, dealt a blow to Braun. No one has seen the agent since the exchange over Eastwood Ridge. From where I sit, this is a matter that Usher has resolved nicely."

"I would hardly call the loss of two agents enough to take the Ministry of Peculiar Occurrences out of our concerns completely," Wolf said, clenching his hand into a fist on the table, "and considering Braun's tenacity as our intelligence has shown, what makes you believe that she will not simply reappear to settle the score?"

"Because that is not her way," a female voice spoke, her Italian accent lush, warm, and intoxicating to the ears.

The sight of Sophia del Morte entering the room caused every member of the Board, even Miss Bear, to leap from their respective seats. Usher had sanctioned a hit upon her home, so the presence of anyone from the del Morte family—especially her—entering their sanctuary was unexpected, if not feared. Only Holmes remained where he stood, calm as if a trusted bodyguard had taken a place beside him.

"She knows that Usher did not kill her beloved," Sophia continued. "Considering the crimes committed against his countrymen, it would not surprise me at all if those responsible were, in fact, from the British government."

Mr Scorpion, still gripping his chair, dared to lean closer. "Are you suggesting that the British government ordered the death of one of its own?"

"I'm suggesting that, in light of events in India, they discovered the potential danger of Wellington Thornhill Books, received word of this exchange," Sophia stated, her eyes taking in each man and woman of the Board, "and took appropriate action."

Holmes motioned to the empty chairs around the table. "Everyone, please, we're civilised creatures here, are we not?"

A few of the Board Members resumed their seats, but Fox, Scorpion, and Tiger remained rooted where they stood.

"Oh, now you're just looking foolish, gentlemen," Holmes said, shaking his head.

Fox motioned to Sophia with one hand. "Do you fail to remember, the outrages this woman has committed against the House?"

"I have taken them into account, yes, and I also I am aware of what we brought about in response to those transgressions. I extended an invitation to the delightful Miss del Morte years ago, and I am especially thankful that she realised it was a standing invitation. So you can imagine my surprise to discover I had in fact delivered it to a legacy."

"I'm sorry," Mr Tiger said, inclining his head to one side. "Did you say a *legacy?*"

Sophia lifted her right hand, and both Tiger and Scorpion gasped on seeing the signet ring of Usher. It was an older style, at least more than thirty years old, but it was unmistakable. Sophia del Morte was a blood heir to a seat on the Board.

"Before you all, I pledge my loyalty and this promise: Filippo Rossi will not live long enough to undermine the sacred foundations of the House of Usher. I will use all resources available to have Rossi answer for his cowardice."

Holmes took his seat and smiled at the new arrival. He knew the smile he gave her. It was the very one that had won him a few hearts in Chicago. "Miss del Morte, the chair is yours."

The murmur bubbled up in the room as the assassin walked the length of the table, stopping at the empty chair reserved for Mr Badger. Putting his faith in Sophia del Morte was a high stakes gamble, without question, but on hearing of her own flight from Italy, her understanding and talents, and her birth right to a seat on the Board, how could he turn her away?

Could he blame her for the rejection at London Bridge? Certainly not. It made perfect sense back then, but he admired the skills she possessed. Sophia was able to do what so many back in the America could not—she could recognise him for what he was.

Now, assuming her place in this inner circle of Usher, Sophia was no longer afraid. She respected him. She was a very different Sophia del Morte than the one he had met initially.

"My dear, why don't you explain to the Board what we have discussed."

"I did not wish to presume," she said.

"Not at all. I believe in sharing the decisions that will guide us into the future."

Sophia nodded, and she looked at the remaining board members still standing. Leaning forward, she adjusted the fine tailored suit she wore. The cut suited her. *A possible distraction,* Holmes mused.

"Gentlemen, and madam, I understand your reluctance. You know me as an unreliable asset following my involvement with abducting Wellington Books. I cannot blame you for your hesitance in welcoming me into your ranks. You would be foolish to trust me blindly.

"What I bring to you as a peace offering is inside knowledge of the Ministry's operations. They brought me into their fold. I know how they execute strategy, where they deploy their agents, and potential rendezvous points. I also offer the same concerning the del Morte family. With me taking a place on your board—"

"Why?" Wolf rapped his fingertips against the polished wood of their table. "Explain why are you here? Now? Returning to our ranks like some wounded dog searching for shelter?"

Sophia cast her gaze downward, her nod slight. "Because of the order given, Usher attacked my village, and eliminated over half of my house. You would think such an action would galvanise a family like the del Mortes, but we live—" She cleared her throat, swallowed, and after a moment found her voice once more. "My apologies—the del Morte family lives under a very different code. They will hold the daughter bringing such despair on the house responsible for her actions. I am cast out from my family and marked for death."

Holmes could hear Jeremy and Mr Scorpion gasp at this revelation. She might be a terrifying adversary, but the idea of an entire family of assassins all committed to her death was astonishing. *Quite humbling for her,* Holmes considered, finding the notion delicious.

"Before you wonder if having me as part of your organisation is an open invitation for the del Mortes to come after you, they will do so regardless. Without me in your ranks, their revenge will be swift and will be upon you before you realise."

Wolf leaned back in his chair. "So what is our proof that you were not the one responsible for Badger's disappearance?"

"You read the report. The simple truth is that if she wanted the man responsible for her predicament dead, he would be and in a most public fashion. Badger is on the run, and he's been seen."

"Wait—Rossi has been *seen?*" Wolf asked.

"There were several transactions reported in Hamburg. I have operatives investigating. In the meantime…" Holmes motioned to Sophia, giving her a pleasant nod. "We have a unique opportunity with Miss del Morte. She offers us not only her incredible skill set, but a unique insight into how the Ministry operates. We will need that insight as we move forward with the next phase of Ragnarök."

Wolf's head snapped in Holmes' direction. "The next phase? You really are mad, aren't you? Have you not forgotten that we have lost—"

Holmes held up a single finger and swivelled to Wolf. His posturing now grew tiresome. It was time to put the man back in his place. "Wolf, I am more than aware of what we have lost, but I refuse to dwell on what could have been if we had been able to continue the work of Dr Jekyll or tap into the superhuman abilities of Wellington Books. What we lost was a convenient addition to Ragnarök, not the endgame of what we have been planning since my assuming leadership of Usher."

"So, let us discuss endgame since you bring it up," Miss Bear began. "I am in need of more funds allocated to Russian operations."

"Why?" Mr Tiger asked. "You are but a secondary operation to the Asian theatre, the central operation to Ragnarök?"

"Since when?" scoffed Wolf. "Our operations, save for this Books distraction, has been on schedule as it is central to the success of—"

"Excuse me," Holmes interrupted. He kept his eyes on Wolf as he asked, "Miss Bear, how are your factories?"

"We remain on schedule, following the incidents of last year," the diminutive Russian woman said.

"Excellent. Mr Tiger, what of your shipyards?"

"Our prototype submersibles are performing above and beyond expectations," Mr Tiger, representing Pan-Pacific territories, reported, "We have tests scheduled this week for the weapons systems."

With his gaze still trained on Wolf, Holmes continued. "Mr Cobra, what of your talented engineers in India?"

Nahush leaned into the light. "We have effectively dismantled the æthergate technology that Jekyll introduced to us during the Ghost Rebellion and deduced how it works. Along with its intended use, we are currently applying this science to other weapons in development."

"As we are working in concert with Cobra," Scorpion chimed in, "we will have fully-functioning prototypes ready for testing within a matter of days." He then glanced nervously at Nahush as he added, "Which, Mr Cobra led me to believe was the intent of this operation."

With each report, heads of territories cast surprised glances to one another.

Perhaps none of the Board knew the *full* scope of Ragnarök, and that suited Holmes just fine.

"As you can see, Milford Scott Adams III," Holmes stated, enjoying the sight of Mr Wolf blanching at his real name, "Ragnarök is not one operation that your region has been charged to bring to fruition." Holmes looked to each member of the board. He could hear in his ears the gentle thudding of his heart. Yes, he was excited. It was thrilling to watch the surprise dawn over all their faces. It had been quite an effort on his part to keep everyone working on their own contribution to this event. This incredible, fantastic event. "Yes, I have led you all individually to believe that you were Ragnarök but, in reality, you were *part* of Ragnarök. Mr Wolf, we engendered high hopes for the Italian operation with Wellington Books serving as a template for future soldiers, for future citizens of this bold, new world we intend to create. Alas, it was not to be, now was it? Does that mean we shut down Ragnarök? We cannot. Not now." He looked over to Sophia and smiled. "Especially not now."

The assassin returned the smile he presented her, and his heart thrummed a bit harder in his chest. Whatever they lost with Books, they were about to gain with her.

"With Badger's betrayal, we need operations to resume in Europe, particularly with tensions in the Germanic Empire. We must now set pieces into play and do so without having any hand visible to the world. I cannot think of anyone better qualified for this challenge apart from Miss Sophia del Morte," Holmes said, motioning to the Italian, "Miss Badger."

Wolf's thick eyebrows knitted together. "Holmes, exactly what are you planning?"

"More to the point," Sister Raven spoke up, her dark eyes boring into Holmes, "what *is* Ragnarök?"

Holmes rose from his chair, and his finger hooked around a green switch set into the table. On flicking it, a low hum filled the room as the wall to his right sunk into the floor. In place of the fine art that had broken the monotony of the long, plain wall, a map of the world appeared, continents and countries all designated by recognised borders and colour-coded by empire.

When the wall completely disappeared and lights above the map flared to life, Holmes stepped free of the table and took a place in front of the once-hidden display.

"Gentleman, ladies," Holmes began, "imagine if you will a *World* War..."

CHAPTER THIRTY-FIVE

Wherein a New Adventure Begins

It was foolish, really. She was no blushing rose, no wide-eyed innocent from the country. She'd seen corners of the world both familiar and foreign. She'd toppled mad scientists and secret societies with a wide array of ordinance. She was skilled in hand-to-hand combat, demolition, infiltration and espionage. She was a progressive woman of the nineteenth century, ready to face the oncoming mysteries of the twentieth.

Yet here she was, Eliza Doolittle Braun, and her heart hammered in her chest as it had on the day they promoted her from Junior Agent to Active Field Agent status for the Ministry of Peculiar Occurrences. *Perhaps,* she considered, *it's this corset. It's so... thin.* The Ministry issue bullet-proof corset was a second skin to her, and it had been so long since she had worn a simple, *mundane* corset, that it felt wrong.

So here she stood at the head of a throng of travellers all anxious to set foot on terra firma after a very long airship voyage.

They couldn't understand what one more step would mean to her. Eliza gripped the end of the gangplank's bannister, her hold on the polished wood tightening as she took a deep breath. This was not some cruel joke, nor was it an illusion. All she had to do was let go and walk forward. A simple thing. So, very, very simple.

Opening her eyes, Eliza released the bannister and took a step onto solid ground.

She got five steps before bursting into tears. To her right a group of ten or so Māori women were dancing with their hands trembling for the benefit of the tourists. Their smiles were bright and joyous as they moved while the poi tucked into their belts swayed. That was a different dance for later she supposed. Two of the women saw Eliza, and whether it was a trick of her tear-filled eyes or their recognition of Eliza's happiness, their smiles widened before proclaiming, *"Haere mai! Haere mai!"* Come here. Welcome.

"Welcome to New Zealand, darling," a voice spoke behind her.

Eliza spun on her heels and threw her arms around Wellington, her laughter now taking the place of tears. It had been so long since she had Aotearoa underfoot, smelled the sea so strong in the air, had the warmth of the South Pacific sun on her skin, she had almost forgotten what it was like. Part of Eliza had almost believed she would never see it again.

Miss Eliza D Braun was home. At long last.

"Welcome home, my love," she managed, struggling to rebuild her composure as she released Wellington. "From the bottom of my heart."

"Your tears are nothing to be embarrassed over," he said, offering her a kerchief. "You must be slipping in your reflexes already. I completely—"

"I have a stiletto up my cuff," Eliza sniffled, "and my pounamu pistols remain holstered on either leg. Besides, I know your voice all too well."

"Ah," he said. "My apologies if I am spoiling the moment."

"Tosh, Welly," she chuckled. "You're just looking out for me, is all. Something you are very good at." A sudden meow grabbed her attention. She looked down at the pet carrier in his other hand. "And how did Archimedes take the voyage?"

"Exceedingly well. I thought he would be upset, but air travel seems to suit him."

Eliza peeked into the carrier. "It did not affect his appetite."

"Not in the least." Wellington looked up to Eliza and gave her a wry smile. "While Archimedes can still go by his given name, I am afraid your sweet pet name for me must go the way of the formidable Tyrannosaurus Rex. Extinct, remember?"

Oh, bugger all. He was right. "Remind me what it is again."

"Richard Aloysius McCaugh," he beamed. "Scholar, a learned man of science, and barkeep, at your service."

Eliza wrinkled her nose. "If we are to run a proper pub here, or in the South Island if needs be, then we do need a name more befitting. 'Richard' sound too formal…"

"And who in their right mind would wish to have 'Aloysius' serving them a pint."

"Exactly." She thought for a moment. "You could go by 'Al' which isn't... bad?"

Wellington shook his head. "No."

"Rich?"

"That fits me about as well as a top hat."

"Dick?"

"Absolutely not."

Eliza took in a long breath, suppressing a need to lash out at the man's stubbornness, but then she paused. "Richie."

Wellington held up his finger, his mouth open as if he were to disagree with her once more. No protest left his lips. In fact, he looked out over the lush vista stretching out before him, the warm South Pacific wind rippling plants and trees as if they were part of an emerald ocean.

"Richie McCaugh." Wellington smiled. "Oh that just rolls off the tongue, doesn't it? Richie McCaugh. Yes, I like that. Quite rugged if I do say so." He rubbed his palm against his cheek. "Perhaps it would be fitting if I were to let my beard grow out—let it fill in a bit more."

"Careful, Richie," Eliza wagged her finger. "I'll have you on the pitch with the lads."

He chuckled, but the laughter faded as he looked around. It struck Eliza as well and her eyes darted about until she glanced up the gangplank.

Eliza motioned to the girl. "Come along. We're here!"

Serena was a hardened child of the streets, and after some time with the Ministry, had become a valued resource for agents in the field. Eliza had seen the young girl hold her own against ruffians of all sorts, and yet in her pristine travelling dress and sweet little hat, Serena looked petite, fragile. She also looked terrified. Her eyes were wide and her skin almost as pale as the pastel colours she wore. On another enthusiastic beckoning, Serena proceeded down the long gangplank to join them on the airfield.

"Welcome to the farthest reaches of Her Majesty's Empire," Wellington said to her.

"Everything is so..." Serena looked around her, watched the dancers for a moment, then turned back to Eliza, "... different."

The honesty of children. It was truly endearing. Here, Serena could be just that. A child, wide-eyed and permitted to take in the wonder of this far-flung island paradise. "Yes, Serena. Yes, it is. You have so many things to learn. About New Zealand, about its people, about the land. School will be an exciting experience for you."

Serena wrinkled her nose. "I know plenty, Miss Brau—" and she caught herself, straightened to her full height, which was not a great deal, and said, "I know plenty, Mum, so I do not see why I need to go to school."

A tightness welled in her throat. *"Mum."* That was going to take some getting used to, but to hear it with such conviction warmed the cockles of her heart.

"Serena, no one is questioning your intelligence," Wellington said. "School is where you discover more than just mathematics and literature. You can explore science, art, music. You *refine* yourself. It won't be easy, but you do your best that will be enough."

Serena nodded. "Yes, Dad."

Wellington cleared his throat. Eliza looked to him. He looked as if he were about to succumb to vapours. "Ah, yes... we—we are..."

"They finalised the paperwork before our departure. We are a family, returning to New Zealand after a long absence." Eliza sighed, stroking the back of Serena's blonde hair. "We're thrilled you chose to join us."

"Eliza," Wellington said, "are you still upset over the others?"

"I can't say I am overly thrilled to have left the rest of the Ministry Seven behind."

"You made the offer to all of them, even Christopher. They are old enough to make decisions for themselves. They wanted to stay."

"They're also boys, Mum," Serena offered. "Not always right in the head, boys."

Wellington propped his hands on his hips. "Really? And what makes you say that?"

"Our daughter does have a point," Eliza admitted. "Remember, the last time you were in this corner of the world, it was a woman who lured you here." She looked down at Serena and then shook her head at Wellington. "No, she didn't lure you down here. She *kidnapped* you."

His gaze went from Eliza to Serena, then back to Eliza. "So this is how it will be, yes?"

"Always, my dearest Richie," Eliza said with a smile.

"Always, Dad," Serena added.

He shrugged. "Very well then. So long as I see what lies ahead of us in paradise."

"Haere mai, Eliza Braun!" a voice called out. "Haere mai!"

Eliza turned around, her fingertips tingling as the rest of her body became acutely aware of the weapons she had mentioned to Wellington earlier. That sudden surge of alertness, the rush of blood just before engaging the enemy, receded as would the ocean's touch against a shoreline. The woman approaching them could have appeared imposing with the tribal *moko kauae* etched into her skin and the traditional Māori *kahu huruhuru* rustling softly against a sharply cut suit.

The eyes and the warm smile framed by long salt-and-pepper hair that stretched beyond her shoulders brought a tightness to Eliza's throat. It had been such a delight to have her mentor at Whiterock, but seeing her here was even more special.

From the look on the wizened old woman's face, she was just as thrilled to see her charge once more on New Zealand shores.

"Aroha Murphy," Eliza said, accepting the woman's embrace gladly, her mentor's laughter in her ear the most wonderful music.

"You did it, girl," Aroha said to her. "Aotearoa welcomes you home."

Eliza gave her a gentle squeeze before parting. She touched Aroha's forehead with her own and took in a breath through her nose. This *hongi* was so new and so revitalising—even though she had done it many times before.

Aroha stood tall and cast her eyes over her shoulder. "And I see you bring newcomers to the Land of the Long White Cloud."

"Director Murphy," Wellington said, extending a hand to her. "A pleasure to see you again. I don't know if you remember—"

"Serena," Aroha said, lowering down to reach eye level with her. Wellington left his hand out for an eternal moment or two before withdrawing it. The elder woman focused on the child. "That was some impressive mischief you and your mates pulled off during the Diamond Jubilee. Well done."

"Thank you, Miss." Her big brown eyes darted up to Eliza, who nodded in approval.

"And I believe congratulations are in order?" Aroha brought herself up to her full height and looked to each of them.

That was when Eliza noticed for the first time the large envelope tucked under her arm.

"We received your status updates from Whiterock two days ago," Aroha said.

"Two days ago?" Eliza asked. "We've been in the air for close on a week!"

"Perhaps the traffic on the æthernetworks has been busier than usual?" Wellington offered. "Or secure connections tend to move a bit slower than the open channels?"

Aroha shook her head. "We should have received your legends while you were over the Atlantic, not just arriving from your trek across the Pacific. It's rather odd, don't you think?"

Eliza whipped her head around at the question. Aroha was no longer wearing a welcoming smile. She was grinning.

This was not good.

"Rather," Wellington said. His obliviousness would be charming under different circumstances. "Have your observatories noted any increase in solar weather? Sunspots have been known to play havoc with the Earth's geomagnetic activity." Eliza pursed her lips as she switched her gaze from Wellington to Aroha. Something was most assuredly afoot. "And such activity could affect æthernetworks on a global scale."

"That is exactly what Barry suggested, but recent observations from the South Island show no irregular activity, flares or otherwise." She tapped the envelope against her fingertips, trapping her bottom lip under her teeth for a moment. "We did uncover, though, the electrics in Auckland were acting irregularly. Christchurch checked in, and they are fine, but…"

"But?"

Eliza leaned forward, so Wellington couldn't see her. She noticed how he was hanging on Aroha's every word.

"But now, nothing powered by electricity works in Christchurch," Aroha said. "Lights. Devices. Motorcars. Rail. There are just… dead."

Wellington crossed his arms against his chest. "Perhaps the mecha—"

"No," Eliza stated with such finality and ferocity that Wellington, Aroha, and Serena all looked to her. "Aroha Murphy, I am on to you."

Her mentor placed her free hand on her chest, her face bewildered as she mouthed, *"Me?"*

"You're trying to entice Richie here with a bit of science, a bit of mystery, a bit of ballyhoo, and sure as Aunt Fanny's your Uncle Bob…"

"Eliza, dear," Aroha said, shaking her head ruefully, "you cut me to the quick!"

"And what do you have there?" she asked, pointing to the envelope she carried.

Aroha glanced at Serena, perhaps for help of some measure, but Eliza smiled proudly as the child had picked up her crooked eyebrow mannerism. There was no ally for her mentor there.

"I'm afraid you have me right where you want me," the Ministry director relented, holding up the envelope.

"No. *No.* And *NO.*" Eliza stepped closer to Aroha. The woman's grin never faltered, even as Eliza stated, "We are out of the game. I'm sure Doctor Sound clearly communicated that to you?"

Aroha shrugged. "That it was, but Eliza—*mate*—this is New Zealand. Out on the edge. We do things differently down here."

"I can say it for you in the Telegu dialect of India—*Kaddu*. I can say it for you in Nepalese—*Ahaa*. The Nandi dialect of Kenya? *Achicha*. A

Mandarin variation? *Bu dai.* Or would you prefer the Māori dialect? *Kao.* Pick a language that... you..." and her words trailed off.

Eliza whirled about to look at Wellington. His smile was as bright as the noonday sun overhead. "Please, keep going," he beamed. "You are doing rather well."

Her attention turned back to Aroha. "We are out. My father wanted to open a pub here in Wellington, and that is what Richie and I plan to do."

"Richie McCaugh?" Aroha asked Wellington. She smiled. "Good, rugged name."

"Ta," he replied.

Eliza did not like where this conversation was ending up. "No more chasing that which goes bump in the night. No more secret societies with diabolical plans to ruin afternoon high tea. No more mad scientists hell bent on cross breeding gerbils with dachshunds. From this day forward, it is a simple life of pulling pints, entertaining lodgers—*proper* lodgers, mind you—and maybe even putting together a rugby team for the odd Saturday afternoon!"

"Point made, Eliza, but just... hear me out."

Eliza inhaled, walked over to Serena, took her hand—not sure if it was an assurance for the child or for herself—and then turned back to Aroha.

Her mentor shrugged. "This is an old case of mine, and as much as I want to see this one through, I am too ancient to go gallivanting about the South Island."

"You have agents of your own, Director," Wellington said. "Why not turn to them?"

"They are a good lot, but this is my history. My past. I need someone I can trust." Aroha took a few steps closer to Eliza and held up the envelope. "I need you, Eliza. I need your magic."

Serena's grip tightened on her hand as Eliza considered the file between them. She owed the Empire nothing, and she'd given plenty of years to the Ministry. Doctor Sound and the House of Usher could dance on together all they liked. They were made for one another. This was to be a fresh start, not just for her but for all three of them.

Wellington's hand slipped into view as he took the envelope from Aroha. "Director, we are no longer active field agents for Her Majesty's Empire. Eliza and Serena are officially retired and as for me? Well, I am quite spry for an agent killed in action."

"You seem to be under the notion that I am here to reactive you, but that is not my intention." The corner of Aroha's mouth twitched. She cleared her throat and added, "Well, perhaps not right away. I needed a particular set of skills with this case, and you lot just happened to arrive on our shores. Honestly, it is just this one case."

Eliza took the envelope from Wellington and measured its weight. "The South Island, you say?"

"Oamaru." Aroha's hand went to the pounamu pendant of the *taniwha* suspended there. Her fingers gently traced the edges of the creature that could be both guardian and monster as she said, "Quite an adventure down there, I assure you."

Eliza handed the envelope back to Wellington. "I left that life back in Jolly Ol' England for a reason." She looked to Wellington and Serena. "We all did."

"And if you were still in England, you would be honour-bound by Queen and Country to serve." Aroha motioned around her. "But you're home, Eliza. This is how we do things down here. This is for New Zealand. The choice is yours." The old woman tipped her hat to Wellington and Serena, then shot a wink to her protégé. *"Kia ora,* Eliza."

Her mentor had not taken more than a few steps before Eliza called out, "Not for Queen and Empire. For Aotearoa? For you? My choice?"

"Your mission," Aroha said over her shoulder, "should you choose to accept it."

Aroha tipped her hat to citizens of the Empire—Eliza wagered they were vacationing Britons from their reactions—as she strolled towards the terminal. If she had other cases to tend to, other agents to debrief or assign to the field, she was in no rush to get back to the office. She was on her own time, her own schedule, and even the simplest act of walking, Aroha Murphy savoured. Eliza remembered that, yes, here in New Zealand, time did not seem so hurried. It was a very different state of mind, and yet, it was one that Eliza found she needed desperately.

Doctor Sound. The Ministry of Peculiar Occurrences. The life of a spy. It was all behind her now, behind them all. Their training would keep them vigilant, keep them alive, but they were to start new lives. Together. They were a family, joined through unexpected events and facing quieter times ahead.

"I understand," Wellington said, turning the envelope over in his hands, "the South Island is both rugged and unforgiving, and yet quite breath-taking. In fact, I read somewhere—the skies in and around Lake Taka... no, was it Tiki...?"

"Tekapo," Eliza said gently, a smile crossing her lips.

"Yes, Tekapo. The skies are simply astounding. Why you can see the arm of our own Milky Way galaxy stretch right across the sky."

It was to be a simple life for them. Eliza pulling pints of beer and cider. Wellington would lead the pub in a ding-dong at Christmastide while serving turkey and crayfish to their patrons. Serena would attend Marsden Academy, discover her potential, and go on to accomplish amazing things with her life.

Wellington's hazel eyes sparkled with anticipation. He was never one to let a mystery go, no more than she could give up black powder and dynamite.

They both looked down at Serena.

"Go on," she whispered. "Open it. You know you want to."

Eliza and Wellington shared a smile, before turning the envelope over to see what secrets it contained.

THE END

BUT THE ADVENTURES OF
THE MINISTRY OF PECULIAR OCCURRENCES
CONTINUE IN

The Curse of the Silver Pharaoh
A VERITY FITZROY AND THE MINISTRY SEVEN NOVEL

CHAPTER ONE

Truth in Distress

If Verity Fitzroy were to die unceremoniously on the dark streets of London it would be riding high speed on the back of the latest scientific innovation.

She took comfort in that thought as she tightened her grip on the magnetic clamps attaching her to the ECC Mark 11. The East End whizzed past her at a dizzying forty miles an hour, the chilled rain pelting her face and biting the exposed fingertips sticking out from her gloves. Her hair was tied back, but ash blonde strands whipped at her eyes. Through all this, her grasp on the handles was becoming increasingly tenuous.

She dared not lift herself up to the flat surface of the Mark 11's baggage compartment, lest the driver or his passenger become aware they picked up a London street urchin along the way—though she was perhaps a little old for that term to be precisely true. Still, if she'd been younger than sixteen, she would have had a far easier time of it in such an awkward position, huddled against the back of the electric motorcar.

Sure as eggs, if she let any part of her body show she would be caught. The passenger in the vehicle would undoubtedly turn around at just that moment and save her the bother of falling to her death by shooting her in the head. The thin black leather of the motorcar's roof would not deflect bullets.

Carriages, buses, and motorcars flew past Verity as the motorcar burst onto the main thoroughfare of Cheapside. She tried to conjure the image of a limpet and put herself into that mind-set. If they could bear the sea, then she could bear the wind.

Bow Bells whizzed past to her right, and Verity heard the ticking of its clock, the winches running its chimes, and the newly-constructed photovoltaic vane all starting up in her head as a grand mechanical symphony. The bizarre connection between her and technology had been happening more and more frequently in the last few months. At that particular moment it was distracting, making her somewhat discombobulated.

The Mark 11 lurched suddenly to the left, rounding a corner, but not without teetering to one side. Verity leaned to the right and the car slammed back onto all four wheels. The jostle disengaged the left clamp, and the young woman swung wildly out into the night. Her boot connected sharply with the road. When it scraped against the ground, the girl bit down on her lip or let a sharp word or two out. She might have come from a good family, but life on the streets since the age of eight taught her enough language to make her no different than one born within the sound of the church bells they'd just passed.

Verity heaved herself once more up, placed the clamp back against the car's metallic body, and primed its switch again. The clamp vibrated, and with a tug, she confirmed the magnet had taken hold.

"Watch them corners!" The passenger was just upset enough to hear over the rush of winter air and hum of the Mark 11. "You're drivin' like you done escaped from Bedlam!"

"Ah, put a sock in it, Floyd! I'm compensatin'. Car's acting like it's trapsin' through mud, she is!"

"We got a job ta' do, so don't muck it up by havin' an accident! Bloody rain ain't helpin', to be sure, but neither's your drivin'!"

"What part of puttin' a sock in it didya miss?" the driver growled.

Hearing the man in the passenger seat, Floyd White, speak summoned her courage once more. He'd been her only lead in all these months holding any connection to the man she knew as Uncle Octavius, and Verity was damned if she was going to let White get away. What started as volunteering far too many hours working at Lady Bucket's Hospital for War Veterans led to whatever caper she was involved with presently. The identity of the other man he'd met in the *White Stallion* pub remained a mystery, but he carried himself like a bruiser and definitely had a decent sized gun under his jacket.

Floyd White, ne'er-do-well and confidence trickster, had not been easy to track down, but tenacity coupled with her own unique brand of stubbornness took her to casing London's more questionable antiquities dealers. Many nights of misleading her mates on what they believed to be casing marks for a delightful score led to White as a connection to Uncle Octavius.

That was why grabbing hold of the running board on the motorcar seemed like a grand idea outside the *Stallion*. Too much invested to let him slip out of her sights tonight.

Now as Verity's muscles began to cramp and the rain showed no signs of stopping, tonight felt more and more like a fool's errand. She told none of the Ministry Seven where she was going, or what she was up to.

"Right then, Oscar, pull over. You're not blimmin' driving anymore," Floyd shouted into his colleague's face. "It's my Hummingbird and you don't even know where Miss Lobelia's house is! St Austell might as well be in hell for all you know."

Pushing aside her freezing hair, she tried to understand what a 'Lobelia' had to do with all this. It was such an out of place name, and it jammed in her head because of its oddness.

Sparing a glance to her right, she saw immediately they were passing the British Museum. It was one of those places she adored; a bastion of science and knowledge her father had contributed to many times, thanks to the archaeological digs he and Uncle Octavius went on.

"Should have grabbed him at the museum," Floyd barked. "Octavius said to nab him there to make sure he had his papers with him."

Oscar let out a dismissive snort. "Too much attention at the museum. Too much chance of not getting away at all. It's not like the professor has the Silver Pharaoh on him or anything..."

Now Verity wished she had brought the Seven with her. Two men, even if one was armed, was a not an uncommon thing for them to deal with. Emma, the second oldest girl, had once been captured by a band of thugs with plenty of evil purposes to put her to. Though they were 'only' children, the way they dealt with those men was enough to warn off any further attempts by adult gangs.

Yet that was not the case today—today there was only herself, and a belt full of her tools. Verity possessed the capacity of self-defence—she'd developed one over the many years she spent in the East End—but she was also intelligent enough to know attacking two grown men all on her own, without any preparation or devices, was bordering on suicidal.

In her mind she heard the hum of the electric motor, and felt the prickle of warm goose flesh on her skin. Then without warning, the hum stopped, and their speed began to drop. They were coasting down the wet streets, the hiss of water kicking up from their tyres the only sound.

"Right then, stop here—here—*here*!" barked Floyd.

The car rolled forward and eventually stopped in front of one of the many impressive buildings of that part of London. Carefully, Verity eased herself down off her perch. Her body ached from the ride, but she still managed to hobble over to an adjoining alleyway, her new hiding place from which to observe their plan. The men she hitched her ride with were preparing for their grab, Floyd pouring liquid over a towel while Oscar reloaded a large calibre pistol.

The fumes tickled her nose even in the alleyway. Ether.

"Just keep them eyes peeled," Oscar grumbled, snapping the hand cannon shut.

"I am!" Floyd snapped back. "Not a crusher in sight."

"It's not them I'm worried about."

Verity swallowed hard just as a thin, tall man in a top hat walked towards them from the direction of the museum. His gaze was cast on the ground, a briefcase swung leisurely from his left hand. Verity would have cried out to him, but her cry would have been for naught.

The kidnappers burst from the Mark 11 like two lions emerging from the brush towards a gazelle. Floyd clamped the towel over the man's mouth, as his colleague wrapped his gorilla arms around their prey. Verity felt her body flush with rage as she imagined her parents in place of this poor museum worker. Pushing through the soreness of her wild ride through London, she lunged forward to jab a thin knife into Oscar's calf muscle. He howled in pain, but his own scream paled in comparison to Verity's. Her bloodcurdling rage would have made any actress of the Grand Guignol green with envy.

In the East End a scream might have been a fruitless call for help, but this was the type of London neighbourhood where a bobbie could be found at the drop of a kerchief. If a policeman appeared, then maybe this poor soul would have a chance.

"Bloody hell!" Floyd stammered, the collapsed museum man threatening to topple him against the motorcar. "Where the hell did you come from?"

Oscar turned on her, his hand clasped to his leg, and Verity realized she hadn't in fact done much damage at all. She stabbed a man who must have outweighed her three times with what amounted to a vegetable peeler.

The profile of his pistol gleamed dully in the gaslight. He was armed with a standard Bulldog. She was armed with science.

Verity brought up one of the Spider's Legs and flipped the switch. The magnet hummed to life, ripped the pistol out of the bruiser's hand, and slammed hard into the device. Hard enough to knock her down.

"You little bitch," Oscar growled, bearing down on her.

The flash blinded her for a moment. When the odd grey fog in front of her eyes receded, it was to see Oscar's broad frame hit the ground, one hand grasping a small fire on his shoulder.

Another bolt struck the Mark 11 where Floyd was stuffing the professor into the back seat. "Get in the car, ya' great ox!" he yelled over his shoulder. "We got 'im. Let's go while the toff's still breathin' air!"

The bruiser's face twisted with anger as he locked eyes with Verity, but he grunted, pulled himself up to his feet and lumbered into the car.

The rapid hum resumed in her head. The Mark 11 was powering up.

Scrambling to her feet, Verity was just in time to see the car with its two men and one victim zipping down the street, threatening to disappear into the foggy night.

With the whistle of the police sounding in her ears, she pounded after the car, but then skidded to a stop as the dark figure stepped out in front of her and fired two more rounds from the Enfield-Tesla Mark III. Rain dripped from his coat as he fired a fourth time before lowering his weapon.

Verity looked up at her would be saviour...and glared angrily.

"I would have caught them at the corner, Agent Thorne, if it weren't for you!" she snapped.

"Oh really, Little Verity," Harrison Thorne, agent of the Ministry of Peculiar Occurrences, replied with a grin. "Fancy yourself a Spring Heeled Jacqueline, do you?" The bobbie's alarm echoed once more, and Harry thrust a hand to her. "Witty banter later. Running now."

With a moan of frustration, Verity took the grown-up's hand and was reluctantly tugged into the shadows of London.

photo by J.R. Blackwell

New Zealand-born fantasy writer and podcaster **Philippa (Pip) Ballantine** is the author of the *Books of the Order* and *Chronicles of Art* series, and has appeared in collections such as *Steampunk World, Steampunk Cairo,* and *Clockwork Fairy Tales.* She is also the co-author with her husband, **Tee Morris,** of *Social Media for Writers.* Tee co-authored *Podcasting for Dummies* and has contributed articles and stories for numerous anthologies including *Farscape Forever!, Tales of a Tesla Ranger, Magical Mechanications,* and *A Cosmic Christmas 2 You.*

Together, they are the creators of the Ministry of Peculiar Occurrences. Both the series and its companion podcast, *Tales from the Archives,* have won numerous awards including the 2011 Airship Award for Best in Steampunk Literature, the 2013 Parsec Award for Best Podcast Anthology, and RT Reviewers' Choice for Best Steampunk of 2014.

The two reside in Manassas, Virginia with their daughter and a mighty clowder of cats. You can find out more about them and explore more of the Ministry at **ministryofpeculiaroccurrences.com**

Printed in Poland
by Amazon Fulfillment
Poland Sp. z o.o., Wrocław